IN
BETWEEN
STORMS

By: Michael Darin

2024

ISBN: 978-1-7366975-0-4 (Ebook)
ISBN: 978-1-7366975-1-1 (Paperback)
ISBN: 978-1-7366975-2-8 (Hardcover)

Library of Congress Number: 2024924849

www.michaeldarin.com
Lee Butron - Editor

1st Edition - November 2024
2nd Edition – March 2026

No AI was used in the writing of this novel, nor do I intend on using AI for any of the writing I ever publish.

Dedication

It's said, you should pay attention to the people who stick around when your life gets hard.

Well, to these people, my friends and my family, who stood by me, when my life was falling apart. I dedicate this novel to you. Without you walking with me, it would have taken me longer to start climbing that ladder again. I will never forget that, and I love you all for it.

Dedication

It's said, you should pay attention to the people who stick around when your life gets hard.

Well, to these people, my friends and my family, who stood by me, when my life was falling apart. I dedicate this novel to you. Without you walking with me, it would have taken me longer to start climbing that ladder again. I will never forget that, and I love you all for it.

Contents

Map of Sancta

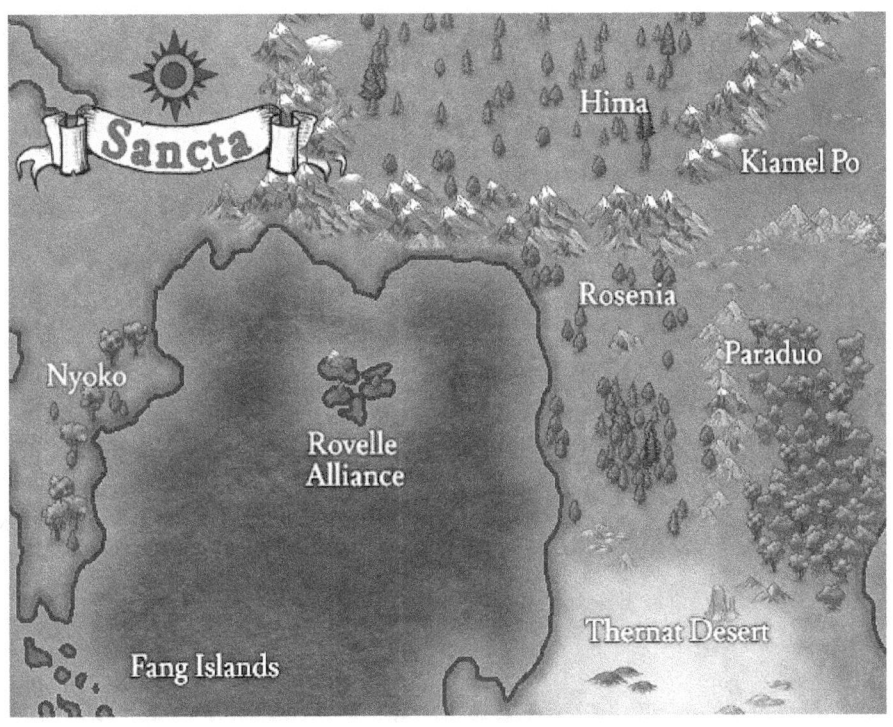

Map as referenced in book 1.

Prologue

The rough, sackcloth mattress dug into his knuckles, tearing at his skin. He gripped with all his might, fighting again the pull on his mind. Yanked away, he lost.

The sun set in the west behind the rolling hills. Dark clouds blanketed the sky and thunder echoed over the land. Lightning flashed as hundreds of hooves beat in the distance. They drummed louder and louder. A strong wind whipped the tall grass. Rain fell, slow at first like little padding footsteps, but then it poured. Riders in the distance, gray figures in the darkening evening, dancing shadows from a fog. The clink of metal rattled as plate and chainmail on horse and man clattered and clashed. A face in the clouds, an evil face of menace and hate, pouring out its wrath, ever watching.

Figures in dark-hooded cloaks moved to the road like gargoyles in the rain. The lightning flashed again, and the company drew close. Thunder shook the land. Bolts of blue and white flame shot down to the earth, leaving smoke and ruin. The hum of the gallop, the drum of thunder and the song of rain; a symphony of a storm rose.

Shadowed figures stopped moving, statues, night personified. Yellow eyes, hard and dead, crying for blood. A thrum of bolts and arrows in flight. Blood rained, forming puddles on the road. Screams rent the air, and every flash showed death. Metal clanged on metal, steel on steel, a rolling thunder, and more cloaks rose. Drowned shouts, and the sharp note of sword and spear could not outplay the storm. Dancing fire with black shadows, wisps in the dark, bursts of light extinguishing life.

Every flash summoned wraiths, escaped from their grassy tombs. Red road, gray sky, the land shook with the hammering of metal between shining stars and shadow casted shrouds. Piles of bodies mimicked rolling hills. Raining drops of blood turned red, crimson rivers of anger and hate, growing lighter to a rose pink, and last, white falling petals, floating down, covering all the land. The thunder gone, leaving only the lifeless wails of men now lost, all bloody, all covered in tender lips. The floating, white petals now bloodstained, landing softly, moved only by the wind and dying breaths. A blinding bolt of light.

He woke drenched in his own sweat. Frigid winds bit through every nook of the inn and tavern where he lodged, howling through the gutted streets of the rotting city.

The dream again, the ever-lurking dream, a nightmare mastered by the Mahr folk of the otherworld, who invade your slumber to haunt and taunt. It clawed at his mind in the day and chopped away when he slept. What could he do? A cacophony of drums in a dark cave, always beating, until his eyes went bloodshot, and his head ached.

Throwing the putrid yellow sheet off, he sat shirtless; beads of sweat gathered on his chest and ribs, racing down to his stomach. A bandage covered his tender, healing wound, also drenched in sweat. He smiled, thankful the blood had hardened, but he wished for peace and yearned to be rid of the pain.

He often kept his eyes shut for hours, squeezing them so tight his head pounded, wishing for it all to be untrue, wishing to not be there amid the storm when he looked back on his life. Sometimes he held them closed so long he fell back to sleep, right back to the beginning of the dream, to suffer through it all again. The waking hours brought the beat of guilt thrumming in him.

The dream did not come every night, though it came often enough that his sleep became precious. Certain nights, he woke up whimpering, curled so tightly his neck ached and the muscles in his back stabbed at every movement. Often someone roused him from his screaming with raps upon his door. On occasion, his own screams woke him and left his throat hoarse and sore with little pinpricks. Tonight, sweat pooled and chills gripped him to the point that his teeth chattered his jaw to aching.

Those same teeth chattered in his youth too, stricken with a constant physical illness. Bouts of cold and hot, crippled by fever, led to weeks, sometimes months of bed rest. When coin permitted, his father sent for healers. Some were mages from the guilds, others were apothecaries or herbalists, toting potions with fragrances that made his stomach lurch. He remembered one coming in a torrential downpour in the late hours to poke him with needles and drain his blood. All so they could save him from succumbing to sickness and death. Eventually they did, but now he wished for death, this nightmare was no ailment.

They could not heal him from this affliction, this curse. Who could heal someone from a dream? Who could put a magic spell on him or give him some medicinal herb that would alleviate the constant vision of blood and rain? No one, it seemed. If he even believed it could be done or someone could do it, would he dare ask for their help and give away his haunting account?

His hand hurt. In the dimness, he saw one of his fingernails missing. Looking at the sackcloth mattress, stuffed with hay, he saw his nail at the edge of a tear, where he had gripped so hard in

3

the dream it ripped off. This was not the first time. The other side of the mattress bore two tears as well.

He made a fist and punched down on the wooden frame, over and over. The thud of every hit echoed in his room, while pain shot through his hand, and all the while he smiled in its respite.

Chapter 1

The quietest places hold the most secrets.

Andross stared at a gray boulder far to the south amid the wavering emerald grass, when from behind, he heard a small harmony shatter the stillness of his mind. Had hours passed in silence? "Teslin, what are you humming?" The sound stopped for a moment before he heard a muted, wavering chant.

Three tales are told
Of giants of old
This one is of two chieftains

One ran around
With a hill for a crown
He's Athbujan the Hardy

One loved the land
And built with his hand
Strong and ever mighty

One day a competition came
They wrestled for the right

To stand alone
King for a throne
Ruling as they might

"Yes, yes," Andross cut in, spitting with every word. "We've all heard the stories of the great brutes, from every bard, in every tavern, from here to the Thernat. Of their quarrel and competition, and who among them was the greatest? How their pounding fists caused the mountains to grow twice as tall and how their wrestling created this very plain of rolling hills, where no trees grow, and we now ride. It doesn't matter."

"And yet," Teslin said, "without Ollistar the Dareian sage coming to the aid of all people by giving the two great giants one last competition, we wouldn't have these boulders scattered here. Nor the two boulders, marking the midpoint along this road. The two very boulders, where we were attacked," he said, his eyes tear-filled.

Andross bit his tongue. He should not have lashed out at the withered young man. His harsh words were wasted on him. They sat silent for a while, traveling the long road until Razelind spoke up, her voice cutting into the air.

"Who won, Teslin, between the giants? I never hear that part of the song." She smiled at Andross when he looked back at her.

He nodded at her attempt to calm the situation.

"The song says neither," Teslin said, sounding less weak. "The boulders were thrown, and they still could not decide, so they both began to fight. They were destroying the land with a furious rage, until Ollistar forced them toward a great lake. They both fell in still fighting as they sank to its depths. For weeks they fought without taking a breath. The earth quaked around them, but then winter came, and Ollistar caused the lake to freeze so deep the two giants froze underneath."

Andross remembered how in past years the withered man loved telling a good story. The memory hurt, though, as Nurame still lived in them, as Teslin's cousin, and his own closest friend.

"Some say the two giants still grapple at the bottom of some frozen lake, to the far north, waiting for the ice to thaw before they rise to continue their duel," Teslin said, looking back toward Razelind on her mount.

Andross had moved past the story by that time. In the distant sky, a single bird flew. The three galloped down the beaten road as a breeze brushed the tall grass in waves of soothing motion.

Jerked into action by his great gray warhorse, he pulled on the reins. "Cleon!" he yelled, looking over. "Teslin, keep your old gelding away." Bred on the back of many battles, Cleon did not like when others drew too nearby.

"Sorry," Teslin said, "I drew close because I think we're almost there." The young but withered man looked out in front of them and down the road that wrapped around the lower hills of the grasslands of the Helsveg region.

Behind them, Andross heard the soft chuckle of their third companion. Turning to look over at her as Teslin slowed his trot, he watched her look at the hollow man between them and roll her eyes. He pursed his lips and looked forward again to pat the muscular neck of his mount.

The great sea of grass stretched on rolling hills as far as the eye could see, except toward the north, where the great mountains of Hima rose as a wall of purple and gray. The blades stood tall enough now to reach a man's shoulders. Two months earlier that was not the case, though they had been tall enough to hide in on a stormy night. Before the season's end, they would hide a horse and its rider.

7

Teslin shouted from behind, "See there," pointing to some boulders on either side of the road, far ahead. "That's where it happened."

A pang stung Andross's heart, and he felt his throat clench. A vision of a storm flashed in his mind, and he blinked several times to clear it.

They rode on for a while longer before Teslin broke the silence again. "Yes, this is it."

Andross noticed the man's voice cracking and watched him diminish in his saddle, like the sun sapped his strength away. For a man larger than himself, Teslin looked half the size of even Razelind now.

"This is why we're here. Tell me what you remember," Andross said, as Razelind rode forward and smacked Teslin's gelding on the rump, spurring the steed back up to their pace.

"I can't. I don't want to think about it," Teslin said in a wispy voice, muffled by the horses' stamping.

"You must. For your honor, for your family's honor, and for your cousin," Andross said, wincing at the statement. What did he know of such things? Honor? Where was he when it all happened?

Teslin sat quietly. What little color had lit his face before disappeared, his eyes wide and teary. He manifested as an apparition in the daylight, until he said, "I'll never regain my honor. I am disowned, and my cousin is forever lost."

Andross grit his teeth and turned away from the others. He took a deep breath and heard Razelind: "Come now, Teslin, man up. After this retelling, there won't be anymore."

"That's not true. The questioning will never end. The stares will linger forever, and the nightmares will always crawl into my sleep," he replied, a fire brewing in his eyes.

His statement rang true, and they all knew it. A gust of wind whipped up, flicking their hair and snapping their cloaks. Razelind moved her long black bangs away from the shaved side of her head, showing the tattoo of a flying hawk, the mark of the Knights of the Hawk, the Judecai.

Andross was assigned to the same order, built on the construct that they were judges, mediators, and the eyes of the realm.

"So, you shaved your head on the side?" Teslin said, looking at her. "It seems to be the new fashion for the maiden warriors of the land."

She nodded, her sword strapped to her back and wearing dark leathers, but then she said, "When did you see the danger?" Her voice flowed softly and to Andross sounded like death in that moment. She appeared as the savage image of darkness.

Teslin shot up in his saddle for only a moment, then he withered again, and slumped worse than before. Defeated, he said, "We didn't see it until it was too late. Not until we neared the boulders you see ahead."

"Tell us, then. When was it? Stop delaying. I've traveled too long now with your whining," she said with a snap.

"Come now, Raze," Andross said, flicking a bug off the hilt of his sword hanging from his saddle, "let him be. I don't want him frazzled when he tells us. I want him calm, and I want his mind free."

"It's not going to help, Sir Andross," Raze said. "The man, the boy, whatever he is, is broken. Maybe he was once a good knight, but this tragedy, this thing, eats at him."

Teslin only sat bouncing in his saddle. He said nothing, acting as if he had not heard her.

9

The truth hurt to think about. Teslin was broken, withered as a wild-faced, gaunt man resembling a hermit. Months earlier, he had stood a bounding youth, only just knighted, his face then aglow. Andross remembered the ceremony.

What the young knight witnessed and lived through broke him. Could Andross blame him? He had almost broken, and he had not been there. Then again, that was the problem weighing so heavily on him. The shame and guilt stemmed from the same place as Teslin's but manifested in a different way.

How was Teslin living with himself, and how could he expect to do the same?

"Fine, I won't say anything else to him, but I'll say this to you. He's fruitless now, and this trip will be too. We should be heading north to Kiamel Po to investigate, not trying to get him to recall the events." Razelind almost sounded as if she were pleading to him.

If Andross were honest with himself, he did not think much would come of this. Maybe it would have been better to have journeyed alone and investigate without distractions. With these two in tow, it felt like having young siblings along for the ride.

"You know, Raze, you have no idea," a small voice mumbled.

"What, Teslin? Did you say something to me?" the woman snapped, her braided hair swinging around, her dark eyes penetrating.

Teslin shot up on his horse for a moment. "You don't know what happened. You have no clue what I saw. The destruction of our comrades, the death in the storm. Don't, don't you…" Teslin's voice wavered at the grave face of Razelind. He then shrank in his saddle again.

Andross saw her face like fire, and then it calmed, and she said, "You're right. I wasn't here."

10

"That's why we've come," Andross added. "We need you to tell us. We need you to bring us as close to the actual event as you possibly can. The Judecai need understanding. So does the royal house, your family, they need to know. The kingdom needs to know," Andross said. He breathed deeply. "I must know."

The nagging in his mind and heart never stopped. It pulled him here, to travel the long road and see for himself.

He dreamed of the Sea of Winds, its tall grasses, hues of green and yellow, of the miles and leagues of mostly uninhabited land. It whispered to him to come find the truth. It got so bad; he went to the Dreamers' Guild for answers but found none. Over time it grew more crazed, more about his vengeance, but always returned to his guilt.

They rode on and grew closer to the great boulders. The sun lingered far to the west.

Andross looked out over the surrounding fields with their scarce but scattered boulders. The breeze bent the grass to its will, and a large bird still flew above. He rubbed his gloved hand on the top of his head, feeling his short, dirty blond hair.

"They were there," Teslin's voice echoed in his mind, breaking his lonely journey. "Behind those two great boulders. See how they're on either side of the road," Teslin said, pointing ahead.

"These boulders mark the midpoint of the Palm Road," Andross said. It bothered him that the smallfolk were calling it King's End. "They lay between the city of Dawn, the high seat of the Graymorns, and Thumbs Tip, the high seat of the Egans. Now tell me what happened." The two gray and green masses stood ominous on either side, looming three times their height and just as wide.

11

"They stepped out. It was raining. Only light at first, but the closer we drew, the harder it poured. We were heading east, just as we are now, toward Geowm. My cousin intended on meeting a delegation from Paraduo, about the border defense against Kiamel Po."

Andross nodded. "Yes, I remember. The warlords of the Kiamel Posians continued to cross ours and the Paraduan borders to raid and pillage. The meeting was to discuss how to deal with the threat. Nurame mentioned it before sending me south to Blood Harbor." It bothered him that the last conversation between him and his friend had concerned trade in the realm. How could he ever have expected such a tragedy?

"How many were in the escort?" Razelind asked, looking up toward the top of one of the massive boulders, where the large black bird now sat perched, watching them.

"There were one hundred in the entourage. Mostly Knights of the Thorn," Teslin said. "It was supposed to be a simple escort mission, there and back in a matter of days. All taking place within the confines of our protected borders."

"There were ninety-five Knights of the Thorn," Andross said, trying to remember the many he had chosen for the mounted guard. "All great knights, including you, Teslin. Then there was Lord John Redpool, whose brother I traveled to see, as well as Lord Ovid Tierney, and two others. I can't remember the other two."

Teslin's soft voice cut through the air. "The two boys."

Andross had not remembered—or had not wanted to remember. "Yes, the two young boys, Joseph Donlevy and Philip Hames, both heirs to their houses. Nurame brought them everywhere."

Razelind spoke in a harsh tone. "Boys, yes, slain just like the others. Joseph was twelve and the son of Lord Jacob. Philip Hames was fourteen, nephew to his uncle, Lord Amory, who can't bear children. The king took them as wards and squires."

"Yes, I remember. Good lads the both, kindhearted, much the same temperament as Nurame. He constantly played tricks on them. Sent them for lemon cakes in the west wing kitchens once. There are no kitchens there, so when they returned with the cakes anyway, he questioned them. They melted under his commanding gaze, and confessed sneaking into the city to buy them. Nurame only laughed and let them eat the cakes themselves," Andross said, going silent for a moment. Then looked back toward Teslin: "Then what?"

Teslin focused back on the boulders, "We were riding hard. We were running late, and the storm was coming. The forward scouts pulled in close as the rain fell. I rode in the rearguard," he said, looking back and past Razelind. "We rode three to a row except for the forward scouts and the rearguard. We were wearing our black surcoats with the white thorns surrounding a white sword. You know the one, the formal armor. My cousin wanted us to be presentable when we arrived to meet the Paraduan council. He alone wore plate mail, the rest of us were in chain…" his voice faded.

Andross shook his head, believing in safety over presentation. "How did it begin?" He wanted understanding of the situation, not a description of gear.

"We were riding hard, traveling quickly in the darkening day, when the hooded shadows came out from the rocks. Within seconds, the front guard lay lifeless on the road, pierced by bolts and arrows. It didn't make sense; they cut through our chainmail

13

with ease. Then things grew worse. More shadows rose from the surrounding grass, all firing bows and crossbows. And if not that, fire and lightning spells flashed among us." Teslin's voice grew shallow; he seemed to be looking past the boulders, back to the event itself.

Andross smiled at Razelind, nodding to her as he motioned his eyes toward the withered man.

Teslin continued looking from side to side; his eyes glazed over. "They were toppling the horses. Those were the first targets, and before we knew it, most of the mounts at the front were down or wounded. Some even fell on top of their riders."

"Who was in charge?" Andross said, dismounting Cleon.

"Sir Derek Alwin still stood as captain of the guard. He ordered those close enough to form up around the king and then sent a charge of maybe ten or twelve to break through the line of shadows. It failed," Teslin said, unblinking as he gazed down the open road.

Andross stood next to him and his mount now. Razelind pulled up close behind, her face blank, and he tried his best to mimic it, but he was having a hard time. "Why didn't they break through the line? It's what I would've attempted to do. It makes the most sense," he said, almost a whisper. "How many were on the road, blocking the way? How many were there?" He wanted answers. These same questions had been asked before, but now here, facing the very place of the attack, he hoped it would jog some memory in Teslin's mind, some answer to point them in the direction of justice—or was it vengeance he wanted for his lost friend?

A fire grew within him. He had just left Blood Harbor when news came to him that Nurame had been killed. He had charged toward the capital but returned to Nowann too late. The great city cried in mourning, as the news still spread across the kingdom.

14

Razelind spoke up: "Answer us, Teslin. How many?"

"On the road in front, I don't think that many. Not enough to stop a charge, but they were ready. They hid tripwires on the road and in the grass. As well as the several hundred shadows rising from their hiding places all around. It was a flurry of arrows and bolts. I would say three hundred, maybe even five hundred, and the bolts just pierced everything they hit. Every knight who stood their ground with their shield was torched alive by flame and lightning, burned where they stood." Teslin's face hung pale; he looked sick.

Andross helped him down off his horse, and the frail man immediately sat cross-legged on the trodden, dusty road. Razelind dismounted and took Teslin's reins and led her mount and his to graze nearby.

"So, you're sure there were mages?" Andross said, standing above him. "You did mention a storm. Could it have been the weather?"

"The weather was bad, unnatural in its fury. The wind almost pulled most of us down, and yet their shots always found the weak spots in our defenses." Teslin sat shaking his head. "Lightning kept flashing above and the thunder echoed across the hills. I remember the thunder well, every blast a respite from the screaming of the horses and from us." He trailed off for a moment. "There were mages though."

"Then what?" Andross said; his heart pounded in his chest. With every moment Teslin looked sicker, he felt more anxious and angrier. He knew bringing the broken man would not be good for his sanity, but he needed some clue to help unravel the mystery. *Who are the dark cloaked figures, and why did they assassinate my friend?*

15

Razelind drew near, listening just as intently as he did. She adjusted a dagger at her hip, the sword of the Hawk on her back, its crest of a bird of prey standing atop a bed of thorns. The road lay empty except for them, and quiet save for Teslin and their questions.

The withered knight looked up, his eyes red and teary, but his voice leveled out. "A bolt hit high on my gorget, breaking through like thin wood. It sliced the side of my neck, and I guess when I recoiled, I fell and hit my head."

"You were knocked unconscious," Razelind said, more a statement than a question. She stood like a shadow above him.

"Yes, but only for a few moments, I think." With pleading eyes, he focused on Andross.

"Go on, you must," Andross said, reaching out to reassure him.

Teslin pointed to a spot. "I was there in the grass when I woke. I looked up and we had dwindled. We killed some of them, but our numbers were no match, along with their surprise and coordination. It was a constant barrage, men falling, horses tripping and stumbling. What could we do?"

Andross wanted to hit the man and scream. *There had to be something!* He knew deep inside that Teslin was right. The attack seemed too perfect. Everything had fallen into place. A delay leaving Dawn, night falling, a storm, the foolish anticipation of an easy mission. He could not fault anyone; he believed the same thing. Who would attack an escort of knights so large in their own peaceful kingdom?

"Sir Derek fell when a bolt pierced the back of his knee, and then one followed through his visor. Regaining myself, I saw it," Teslin said, his voice beginning to waver as tears poured down his face.

Andross fought back his emotions of anger and pain. He wanted to shake Teslin, to yell at him; he wanted him to rise with the same anger he carried and help him. He just wanted the withered man's aid to find the truth, but he was staring into the face of a sobbing child.

Before he knew it, Razelind was tearing at his wrists, twisting them off and pushing him away. Teslin gasped for air. He had been choking him; his hands were clasped around his throat. He fell back when he realized what he had done, and stumbled to the dirt, dust flicking up into his face. He heard Teslin still gasping behind him, Razelind trying to console him.

"Here, drink this," she said, handing him a waterskin.

"No," Teslin lashed out. "You see, I'm nothing now. I have nothing to give. If this burden doesn't kill me, then someone else will, one of you even. I'm disowned by my father. He forbade anyone from my family to speak to me, even my mother. The Knights of the Thorn resigned me to steward's work, cleaning quarters and archiving the histories of the knighthood. Even that's too much for me to bear."

Andross pushed up in pain, "No, I'm sorry, Teslin. I know you're not to blame. This was only your first assignment out of the city. There were only two things you could do. Die, or survive to tell us what happened."

"I should have died," Teslin said in anger. "I should have died with my cousin, even my father wishes it. He stood not far from me. I could see his armor through the rain. Armored in plate, adorned in gold and silver, shining in the storm, the rose of my house crowned and bloody. He stood over the fallen bodies of the boys. The poor lads only wore leather, lifeless in the grass. They

17

were pincushions, pierced so many times." With every word Teslin spat, he grew more enraged, and yet the tears still streamed.

Andross looked at him now, and a small glint of young Teslin's former strength seemed to have come back to him.

"Four men and a Goblin rushed my cousin, and he slew all five."

"There was a Goblin?" Razelind said.

"There were several. I saw them. Many hoods were torn off by the wind. That, or their confidence had grown. I saw some of their yellow eyes. A bolt struck Nurame at the shin and almost passed completely through. He stumbled but still slew another attacker and rose again. The rain poured down. I remember wiping it away from my eyes, trying to see through it and my dizziness. I could still make him out, as the last one standing, defiance emblazoned on his face. When the enemy saw it, they laughed. I tried to get up, but my ankle seared with pressure. They were now drawn up between us, closing in around him, not aware of my presence behind them." Teslin looked out into the tall grass, focused on the area he pointed to before.

Andross stared at him, seeing the horror on the man's face begin to take him. He could not judge him for his injury, but at the same time he hated the man, and hated himself. He closed his eyes.

"A large man with an axe came up behind my cousin, and with a swing—sheared off his head. When it hit the ground, his eyes were looking at me, staring at me. I screamed, shock, pain, anger, all of it rose out of me. I screamed without any control, and their eyes turned on me. I pushed up on one leg ready to die standing, but a horse jerked next to me. Reeling in pain, I mounted it with bolts whistling by. I fled as fast as I could. I didn't stop, not even to relieve myself. I rode the poor beast to exhaustion," Teslin said, shaking his head.

Andross pounded the ground, the pain in his fist was a relief from the internal struggle that now raged. He now felt his own eyes water; a tear fell and hit his glove.

"You asked about the mages earlier. They were there in the darkness. I felt a blast of fire explode behind me; its heat singed my hair. I saw its orange light and heard the rain sizzle in its flame." Teslin shrank away from the sun as he said it. "In that moment, its heat became a momentary respite from the cold rain, from the malevolent night. I'll never forget that moment of peace, before the blood and screaming flooded back into my mind. It never goes away now."

A deep silence fell over them. Teslin fell flat to the ground. He whimpered as he lay. Andross sat, staring at the broken man, and Razelind stood above them, her face still and emotionless.

It was she who broke the silence: "Did they try to chase you?"

"I don't know. I don't think so. I truly don't remember much after that. People told me I made it to Dawn, was cared for and escorted by the Graymorns onto Nowann, when I could travel again. I don't really recall. Besides sending me on, they sent a company here, commanded by Lord Gregory himself," Teslin said, dirt forming dry creek beds on his cheeks.

"Yes, I rode with them," Razelind said. "I was in Dawn on a mission when you arrived. Lord Gregory mounted almost immediately. He brought a band of five hundred knights and mounted soldiers. He also sent messengers to all surrounding lands, as well as called to arms most of his men. He worried that war was coming."

19

"I know you've told me before, but what did you find when you arrived?" Andross said, standing to his feet. Like Teslin, he had regained some of himself.

"It took Teslin almost three days to ride to Dawn, and even in great haste it took us over two to get back here. What we found is still unpleasant to think about. The bodies of our comrades littered this area, but there were no clues about the attackers. While many of us gathered bodies, the rest searched and found no evidence of the enemy. It was ominous, unreal, like they never existed," Razelind said, her eyebrows furrowed.

"They were real, I swear it," Teslin shouted from his prone position.

"No one is refuting that," Andross said, in a soothing voice. It seemed to help the young man relax where he lay. "We're here for proof, evidence of these assassins. We aren't saying that you all fought each other down to the last man, but we need something to point our way. Other than the single bolt found on the dying horse of Sir Adhem Nightstead, the only other survivor, there was nothing."

"And even that," Razelind said, "is somewhat fruitless in some people's eyes, a bolt of Kiamel Posian make."

"That includes my eyes," Andross added.

"You can't be serious. They were on the way to meet about the raids of the Kiamel Posians. Where else would such a bolt come from. One with the power to break through armor as easily as theirs do?" she said, beginning to pace.

"I thought the same, Raze, and I spoke it as well, in the meeting of the high council and with the high lords and the grand knights, but Sir Minton Dubary in his wise old age, and in his calm demeanor stood up without a word and left. It caused quite a

20

commotion. Twenty minutes later, as we called for war with the tribes of Kiamel Po, the short, stubby knight walked back in, unannounced, and threw a hundred Kiamel Posian bolts on the floor. He said he went to our own grand market and bought them there, where there were many more to be purchased."

"It doesn't mean it wasn't them," Raze shot back.

"I completely agree, but until I'm given leave to take a group of Knights of the Hawk across the border to investigate, it's been declared there isn't enough proof of their involvement, and an infraction with them could cost us the unstable peace we have." Andross said it with full conviction, but deep inside he knew if it took too long for him to be granted permission to investigate, then he would go in secrecy, even if only to further boost the truth.

Teslin whispered, from the ground, "What more of Sir Adhem? I've only heard bits and pieces."

"There isn't much to tell. Sir Adhem escaped as well, but toward the east, where they probably tried to break through. Apparently, he blacked out also, but his horse dragged him in its flight away. The attackers tried to stop the horse, but believing Sir Adhem was dead, they only shot a few bolts and arrows at it. One hit its mark, and the horse died when reaching the gates of Geowm. Dule soldiers found the horse collapsed and a rambling Sir Adhem, bloody and dying, still hanging from it."

Just in that short exchange, he and Raze could hear a rhythmic breathing coming from Teslin. "I think he fell asleep," Raze said.

"Leave him for now, we can wake him if we see travelers on the road," he said. He whistled for Cleon and the horse trotted nearby. "We'll camp here tonight. The sun's already setting." The sky began to fade, and a small pink and orange hue spread across it.

"Poor Sir Adhem," Razelind said, "He was engaged to be married to Marilynn Dehring. I saw them courting once at a ball in Nowann. They seemed jubilant about the arrangement."

He only slightly listened to Razelind. She did not ever seem one to notice those sorts of things, and it confused him for a second.

"I was kind of jealous. I did always think Sir Adhem a handsome man," she added.

He laughed. "Oh, now it makes sense. You had me stumped on that one. I didn't think you were much for marrying."

"Oh no, you're right about that. I'm more like you, Andross, a loner, but that doesn't mean I don't think about a good bedding now and then," she said with a laugh.

It made him smile to hear any levity at this point, to have laughed himself. Amid all this sadness, despair, and death, life still lingered. His life was shifting, he knew. No longer yearning to be the greatest knight in the land, now he wanted justice or vengeance; it did not matter which, just whatever presented itself first. He was searching his saddlebag when he heard Razelind again.

"Did we learn anything of value from Sir Adhem?"

"No, nothing really. Nothing that made sense. A fever took him. Pierced by an arrow, it punctured a bone, and the bleeding caused an infection in his marrow. Something like that, the healers said. He lived for two more days, rambling about incoherent things mostly. Scribes were able to write down some of his words, but there was little to make of it. Every woman who came near, he called Marilynn. Sometimes he would just scream out, sometimes cry. When questions were asked, he would babble on about death and blood, lights in the dark, and shadowed cloaks dancing in fire."

Just then, Teslin shot up with a scream, and Andross rushed over. "Teslin, are you alright? It was only a dream."

22

The hollowed face of the young man, pale and sweating, looked through him and he said, "Not a dream, it's only ever a nightmare," before lying back down and going back to sleep.

Andross looked up at Razelind. She looked concerned. He shook his head. "We'll move him in a bit. I'm trying not to be hard on him. He's been through so much. He has no one now."

"No one and no purpose," she said. "His life as a knight is pretty much over. I'm not sure how you recover from that. How do you pull yourself back to a place of focus and purpose once you've given yourself to this kind of despair?"

He only shrugged. The answer for himself, and one Razelind would not understand, was a focal change in his life. If he had to burn Sancta to the ground to find the truth, he would.

*****

Later that night, while staring up to the stars, he thought about his lost friend, his only true friend. In the darkness of a stormy night, assassins came and killed Nurame Lintrel, first of his name, King of Rosenia, the man he swore to protect in duty and in friendship.

By coming to this place, would he find the truth he searched for? Would he find forgiveness in their blood?

It was not his dream that woke him, but a commotion. He grabbed for his sword as he rose. Cleon usually warned him of danger, but the horse only stood calm nearby.

Movement to his left made him turn. "Andross," Razelind's voice shot out through the darkness, as a silhouette in the swaying grass.

"What is it, what's going on?" he said, calming his stance.

23

"It's Teslin. During his turn for watch, he stole off into the night."

"Fool. Why?" he said, leaning down to pick up his things.

"I don't know, but he has a good distance head start. I'll catch up to him and make sure he gets back to Nowann. You stay and continue your mission. Find the truth," she said.

"Are you sure this is what you want?" he said, looking out across the shadowed landscape.

"Not really, but he's not in his right mind, and I think he fled south. I'll chase after him, and when I catch him, I'll escort him back. He needs help. You don't. Keep going. It's the whole purpose for this trip."

He nodded, unsure she could see him, so he said, "Fine. But Raze, be safe. Be careful with him too. I don't know what kind of mindset he's in if he feels the need to leave us unprotected in the night." Clearly a piece of the young knight had really shattered the night of the storm.

Razelind mounted. "I always am," she said, then turned her horse and galloped through the darkness and into the rolling grasslands.

Chapter 2

Drums beat as the sun began to set. The darkness drew in early, deep in the mountains, where the peaks of the mighty stone giants loomed high.

Keeping an eye out on the surrounding heights, from the shade of an overhanging rock, Dreyandol rubbed his cheek. His hand felt warm in the cool of the pass. Using the same hand, he signaled for his three companions to drink at a small stream. It would not be long before the night fell thick upon them, and they might not get another chance. Mountain streams were plentiful, but many were inaccessible in the deep fissures.

The two newly graduated casters out of the academy lapped up the water as fast as they could, and louder than they should. His long-time friend, Zenthis, with his red-pupiled eyes and top-knotted hair, moved close to them, and without hearing the conversation, Dreyandol knew he condemned them for their ignorance.

Zenthis reached down as both pairs of inexperienced eyes focused in, and scooped water with a cupped hand while keeping an eye on his surroundings. Before long, his friend climbed toward the overhang, while the other two disappeared into the brush. "They send us out to meet with our contact and give us two graduates who slurp down water like they're piss drunk in a tavern."

"I'm glad you set them straight, but it's not entirely their fault," Dreyandol said in a hushed voice, shifting his position to check their flank. "The academy focuses on combat and spell usage. They sometimes forget to teach common practices."

"Still, this is an odd time to be sending two fresh faces with us," Zenthis said, shaking his head.

"It's about the experience. We're struggling to maintain our ranks. We've been holding the gap against the Predan for too long. The militia receives too few reinforcements, and the Crimson Order continues to put out new casters all the time. If they can't find a master, why not send them here for experience?"

"You say that, and here we are trekking into the midst of the Predan territory with these two who make too much noise. I'd sooner leave them behind." Zenthis signaled to the two to keep their eyes open, with what seemed like agitated movements. "What about you?"

"What?" Dreyandol said, looking to his friend.

"You'll have to head back to the city soon so you can finish the testing for your rank, then pick a recruit for yourself. I bet you can't wait for that. No doubt your father will be ecstatic as well."

"Please don't bring him up. His desire for my life is like a millstone grinding my eyes. Constantly, he sends letters to the militia leaders and the Crimson Order demanding my return to the city. He doesn't know I choose to stay. We need to move out."

"Of all things, my friend," Zenthis said, giving more hand signals to the others, "you love the dreary life of skirmishes in the passes and fighting among the rocks, when you could be warm and comfortable with a woman on your arm in the streets of Ajencain."

Dreyandol nodded at the thought. "I love the idea of not being tied down, not tending to my father's political aspirations and his dealings with the king. Freedom, adventure, I want to see the world and taste its flavors. You know politics doesn't suit me." He thought about the light, gray walls of the city and its sky-piercing spires and shook his head. "Once I reach the rank of combat master and become a warmagi, I'll find an apprentice and ask to be stationed away from Rovelle. Maybe Nyoko, where the stories are of color and mystery, or Rosenia, where its expanse and grandeur alone is enough to make any traveler stand in wonder."

"You sound moronic," Zenthis laughed, as he moved around some short trees. "With Rosenia, you'll have better luck. Apparently, there's a shortage of masters and teachers there. They don't have enough trainers for the waves of new recruits who are joining and graduating."

Dreyandol signaled to move on. With light steps the four moved north along a tree line, using it as cover. After some time, only a small glow of the remaining sun could be seen on the outer edges of the peaks. He knew down in the great Dareian city of Ajencain they had another two or three hours of sunlight. Ladies were donning their fine gowns for balls and parties, adventurers gathered in the safety of warm-lit taverns, and his father paced in his study, planning the next way to get him reassigned.

The darkness plunged deep tonight; only vapors of light from the moon were present. The brilliance of stars above only fostered his urge to be free. His eyes reached out, parting the blackness in a way some races would have difficulty.

Stopping at a dip in the pass, he reached for his sword hilt and rested his palm on it. He listened; they all listened, but nothing caught his ear. The cold, crisp air bit at their cheeks. He put up his hand and motioned them on.

One of the new casters, Hesadin, with his clean red doublet, which he wiped with his hand at every stop, took the initiative and darted across. After his signal, the other young lad, Fedoris, followed. His eyes, dark red, showed his Dareian youthfulness. They were children, but not much younger than himself. Not even

27

enough years separated them to be worth mentioning, and yet he felt old.

Months of warring with the Predan and leading deep scouting missions took its toll. Some days his body ached. He rested when time permitted, often thinking about if there was a better way to fight this war.

The Predan people claimed ownership of the Rotsinora, also called the Roost Mountains, and its surrounding foothills. The rising peaks hid their villages and homes. It made sense, but the foothills did not. They never came out to the roots of the mountains, until after word reached them that a Dareian city had been settled. Almost a hundred years passed before they knew and reacted.

"Do you hear that?" Zenthis said, on whispered breath, moving next to him.

At first Dreyandol stood motionless, his ears reaching out for a sound. "Maybe a small hum?"

Zenthis shrugged. "I don't know. I feel like I hear something."

They moved on, clambering up a rocky slope to a cliffside. Reaching for each handhold with calculated motion, he climbed. Several times he looked at the others to check their progress. The cliff face rose only a little way above, but he did not know everyone's climbing skills.

"You hear it now?" Zenthis said, as they lingered on a hold for a moment.

In the darkness of the night and looking over at his friend, Dreyandol nodded. "I hear it. It's beginning to sound like drums in the distance."

"That doesn't bode well," Zenthis said, reaching up to another handhold, his fair skin dimmed in the night. "Something must be going on. Do you think they're mobilizing a large force?"

"I'm not sure," Dreyandol said, getting his own foothold, "but the sound isn't far off, and Carrun's home isn't far down the other side, once we reach the top. Whatever's happening, we'll be able to see then."

Reaching the top of the cliff, they slid behind the cover of some boulders. Bits of snow caused small crunches with every step as they crossed toward the far side in silence. Without delay, Dreyandol signaled for them to stoop down and into the shadows. A red glow stretched out over the edge of the far ridge. An image rose before them that stole their hearts.

"Time to be hidden from sight," he said, looking at the others, mainly the two, new casters. "Hesadin and Fedoris, concentrate, focus on the spell and nothing else."

Whispers and hand gestures from all four followed. All at the same time, they performed a spell, and even in the darkness of night their images blinked out. For the two new casters, their presence wavered faintly in the deeper shadows of the brighter ridge. For Zenthis and himself, it could have been the light of day, and they would be hidden from eyesight.

"Stay low and move silently. There may be scouts nearby. The Predan don't have the best hearing or vision at night, but they're always vigilant."

The red glow of an illuminated night sky was pause enough for the four, but what was causing it? At a swift crawl, they moved low, only using their hands to balance out their movement. A short distance brought them to the far ridgeline, where they could look over and down, but when they reached it all their breath caught in their throats.

A lake of fire extended through the small valley below. Burning torches and braziers covered the landscape. Thousands of bird-like people, beaked and feathered, stood in groups and within rows, stretching out across the distance. The ones grouped nearest them were adorned in pieces of brass or bone armor, but they wore no clothing, only allowing their feathers to cover them. Thousands of blood red flames licked the night, ominous and unnatural. The darkness seemed to press in harder where their light did not reach, pulsing like a living thing.

"It feels wrong," Zenthis said, "I feel like I might be sick. What magic is this?"

"I don't know, but I feel the same mad nausea over me. I've never wished to have a normal flame in hand so much in my life," Dreyandol said, glancing over to see the ghostly visages of the two new companions.

Drums boomed out, echoing off the mountain walls and through the cold, dark night. Even now the frigid temperature seemed to be biting Dreyandol through his clothes and light armor. A dark chill stabbed at his neck with his hair rising in an unnatural way, like a manifestation of menace pressing down on him.

The fires threw wavering spirits all around, in a sickening manner. Each Predan face bore an ominous look, long shadowed curves and hollowed eyes, deathly in design, and no one stirred.

"What the...?" Zenthis trailed in. "What are they doing?"

"I have no clue. I've never heard of such a thing," Dreyandol responded. He glanced toward the other two and watched as they shrank down even closer to ground to hide themselves.

"Look there, they seem to be facing that area," Zenthis said. No doubt he pointed, but Dreyandol could not see him, so scanning across the reddening lake, he followed the gaze of those in attendance.

It led to an area not far from them. "That's right next to Carrun's village and his home. Do you think this concerns him?"

"I don't know, since I don't even know what this is. Some ceremony, some dark ritual?" Zenthis began to move to the right. The two heard him and moved back to give him space, and though Dreyandol had the strong urge to not move, he forced himself out of cover to follow.

Moving along the ridge drew them closer to the gathering, and even closer to Carrun's home. For a moment, as the two acolytes followed, Dreyandol's heart jumped. In the light of the fires, their images were mostly dimmed, but their breath hung visibly, reflecting the valley of fire. "All of us must cover our mouths." He pulled up some cloth hanging around his neck and tied it behind him. The others did the same.

Looking back down in the valley, the closest Predans were only about a hundred yards away. Tall warriors armored and brandishing cudgels and spears, they were vicious fighters, unable to take flight but able to leap long distances. Adept at stone masonry, their clubs and rods were well made, and deathly. Where they caught the inexperienced warrior off guard was with their powerful legs. The thought of taking a kick from one made him wince in pain. Many died, crushed from the impact.

A further hundred yards past the rows and rows of warriors, past the smaller groupings of female Predans with their longer beaks, and the small children, stood what seemed to be an altar. Braziers of red flame leapt up on it. Surrounding it, Predans of notability were gathered, visible by their armor and jewelry, one even wearing the skulls of fallen Darei. "Look, Zenthis, chieftains, sorcerers, shamans… this is something very big."

31

"This is sickening, I feel sick. Some power lies here and is putting some hold on me," Zenthis said, in a muted tone.

"I feel it too, as if I wanted to just give up and lie down. I don't know what's going on here and waiting to find out may not be a good idea. We'll need to head back soon and warn the commander," Dreyandol said, his hand on his hilt. "I don't want to get caught before we can warn people of this."

"Yes," Zenthis said, swallowing deep and inching back, "I don't think anyone who sees this and isn't Predan is going to be treated very well."

Just then a line of warriors strode to the altar. With them they carried a large carven cross. They stood a saltire up and then positioned themselves in front of it. A Predan sorcerer moved toward them. He handed them what looked like a cup, and as they took it, they each drank.

Dreyandol had never witnessed what happened next, but more than enough times had dealt with the result. A craze came over their eyes: anger, madness. They drank what the militia forces called Death Spirit, a potion they made from the roots of a mountain weed. It made them angry and aided in suppressing pain. They screamed as it took hold, their faces frozen in anger and hate.

The sorcerer, adorned in bone armor, a feathered headpiece upon his head, drew a dagger from his side and stabbed each warrior, one by one. They toppled to the ground, but only then did Dreyandol notice they had been standing in a shallow trench. Lifeless, their blood streamed down the trench and toward the end of the altar, where it narrowed to a point and another sorcerer stood with a large cup, filling it.

"It's some sort of sacrificial ceremony. I've never heard of it before," Zenthis said. "I don't understand though, the Predans aren't known to be very ritualistic, especially in harming their own. They killed the warriors in front of the cross, but who are they chaining to it?"

"I don't know," Dreyandol said, but just then he saw their contact detained and supported by two Predan warriors, slumped down as if not awake. "Look there by the corner of the altar, closest to us. They have Carrun. They're bringing him to the saltire."

The first of several sorcerers looked over and signaled. His outstretched arm cast a long, flickering shadow as he pointed to the prisoner. The two large Predans dragged him forward. The drums beat faster and louder. Every blast shook in his ears.

"Don't," Zenthis said.

"I must..." Dreyandol loosened his sword in its sheath.

"Why, Drey?" Zenthis said with strain in his voice. "I understand he's an ally, but how do you expect to not get caught with those thousands of Predans? Not to sound terrible, but what makes his life so valuable?"

"I don't know but send Hesadin back to the pass now. He's the fastest of the two and tell him not to stop for anything. They must prepare messengers for Ajencain. I believe the final attack is on its way. Then wait for me to signal you."

"How are you going to signal me? I can't see you," Zenthis said, looking in Dreyandol's direction but looking right through him.

"I'm going to make my way to that right side over there. See how the log for the brazier isn't fully in the fire. When you see I've pushed it in, then I'm ready. Just make sure to cause a large distraction and then run," he said, sharp with finality, knowing his friend must accept the command.

"Respectfully, this is idiotic. You still haven't given me a good reason why this is necessary. I'm not one to scoff at life here, but we're talking Carrun's life, or both of your lives."

The drum beat on, almost drowning out Zenthis' trepidations.

"Carrun saved me once. Hid me from a patrol. I owe him at least an attempt. Besides me, the lives of so many of us have been saved by his information." Dreyandol started away from his friend, then turned. "Be careful."

"You too, damned fool," Zenthis replied, tightening his lips and filling his lungs.

Dreyandol moved to Fedoris as Zenthis spoke with Hesadin. "You're staying with Zenthis. After I give him the signal, you both will cause a distraction and then make a run back to the pass to warn the others. If you get separated, just keep going. This is bigger than each other's individual lives. Try not to kill anyone down there. Maybe they won't pursue as hard if you haven't."

"Yes, sir," Fedoris said, nodding at every word. "How though?"

"I don't know. Break something, knock something over, if you can from this distance. If not, shout at the top of your lungs and draw their attention."

"I can probably send a good gust of wind," Fedoris said, glancing back to the valley.

"Good, try that."

"Sir?" the young lad said, his face showing fear.

"Yes?"

"Hesadin and I could hear just about everything you and Master Zenthis were saying about us."

Dreyandol looked at his transparent face. "I know. Make sure you learn from it." He turned and stole off into the glowing night.

34

As he moved further down the slope, silent like a shadowed cat, the Predans were cleaning off the altar's surface. Red fire flicked all around, and the feeling suppressing his decision to move forward weighed on him. A dark magic oppressed his will for action.

Coming upon the first group of Predans, he began to focus only on not being found. If caught, it would give less time for his companions to escape. At this point, a plan for escape had yet to form. Pushing all thoughts out of his mind, he moved on. Finding a narrow opening in the rows of onlookers, he shot through, trusting in his hidden form. He scrambled toward a rock and clay-built hovel, one of their many kinds of homes. Using it as a barrier, he skirted around it and split between two rows of warriors, who did not notice his movement. The drums boomed loudly but were not as loud as from their vantage point above. Diving over a stone wall and through the walkway between some homes, he came to the back side of the altar.

When his eyes fixed on it, his rage grew. Standing in the place of the five warriors were five Predan children, adorned in bronze, their eyes empty with Death Spirit. A small amount caused the rage and painless savagery; too much caused a trance. They had been given too much, and one by one they were felled by a stab to their sides. Their eyes vacant of life. He winced at the sight, then anger took him, and he wanted to jump out and slay the sorcerer.

Reaching for the log, he pushed it into the fire, trying not to give himself away. The drums still beat with the darkness all around. At the same time the large cup with the children's blood came to the altar, held next to a sorcerer with the warrior's blood.

Dreyandol waited for the distraction, hoping they would hurry. His fingers were numb, and his toes hurt. He stood only feet away and noticed the trance on Carrun as they poured some of the blood across his face and forced the rest down his throat. A feeling of disgust and sickness overtook him. The second sorcerer moved to pour the children's blood on the bound Predan, when a strong gust of wind blew across the altar, knocking the sorcerer and himself over. Rising to his feet, he heard a commotion from the ridge as Fedoris and Zenthis stood, yelling with all their might. The young lad danced lit in red.

The Predans did not react immediately to their enemy. The lead sorcerer, wearing a silver bird mask that reflected the light of the red fires, shrieked. First, he focused on the altar, then looked at the cup and cried out. The goblet that held the blood of the children had fallen and spilled.

With screams, the Predans' squawking chatter commenced and Dreyandol recognized their meaning as the main sorcerer called out, "*Shineek, shineek.*" *Kill, kill.* Dreyandol poised himself to make a move, but the warriors were not looking to chase his companions, they were looking at the lifeless, entranced body of Carrun.

The second sorcerer drew a dagger and four Predan warriors with spears leapt to the altar. Dreyandol, in a blink, moved between them, his form still not visible in the firelight, and with his first attack he sliced at the second sorcerer and sent him screaming. The physical attack drew him from his hidden state, breaking the spell.

The drums beat on; he hoped his companions were already running. The first sorcerer screamed, "*Shineek, shineek!*" The crowds began to scramble in every direction; the chieftains yelled for guards, and from his right, hooded figures chanted, but their chanting seemed to waver.

The four warriors pressed forward on him, intent on death, and for an instant he thought. *Now what?* Then he felt a powerful blow to his back. It sent him flying over the warriors to hit the ground. The world spun around him; he saw light flicker in and out of his mind. Blackness stormed in and then pushed back; pain burst through him, and his back ached. He tried to rise, but for a moment could not, staggering only to fall to cold stone. Expecting death and unable to defend himself, he waited, but it did not come. A moment went by and his head slowed its swimming. His ears began to hear again. The drums were gone, but the screams were still there.

Turning over, he looked toward the altar. Predan warriors with spears were on it, now crowding around. He watched one charge forward, then saw the head snap to the right. The body gave way and crumbled.

Confusion rang the bell of his mind again. The world swirled. Who was fighting? *Did Zenthis come down to help? How foolish.* He looked again to see blood gush from a wing being torn out of its socket. An ear-shattering scream tore through the air and made his already ringing head pound. He grabbed at his ears and looked up again.

More warriors rushed forward, some leaping high, weapons drawn. They were thrown in multiple directions. None of them even noticed him. The sorcerer still screamed the kill order, but also yelling things Dreyandol did not understand. He pushed to his feet. More Predans rushed in, a craze in their eyes, brandishing spears and great axes.

What was happening? He saw a glimpse of Carrun's face. Distorted, covered in the filth of blood, a crazed rage flamed in his eyes too, bulging red, reflecting the light of the fires. Dreyandol stood for a moment and felt himself draw his sword. Predan

37

warriors, fighters of great prowess, were falling before him to one of their brothers.

Carrun, who had helped him so many times, who had aided in the protection of Ajencain soldiers, who believed in the peace between their people, now raged out of control on an altar before him, slaughtering his own people, with a wild, sickening, bloodlust.

Suddenly, a figure appeared next to him. Startled, he jumped back, sword in hand. Standing before him adorned in his silver mask, glowing in the night, the head sorcerer said, "Help. Help us kill the beast."

Dreyandol looked at him for a moment, seeing fear in the eyes of the creature that stood a foot and a half above him. He felt the confusion rise in his face. He shot a glance back at the fighting but quickly returned to the sorcerer. "Please help," the sorcerer said again, his screeching voice piercing through the terror.

In that very moment, the sorcerer floated up. Dreyandol saw terror on his face of the Predan as the silver mask fell. The Darei, confused in the moment, then saw blood squirt from the sorcerer's eyes, and his body fall limp. He no longer stood alone amid a torrent of Predans. The beast stood before him. Warriors hit him with clubs and stabbed at his back, and it glared at him.

Dreyandol dove away. The beast slammed down where he had been standing. Flying to the left with great speed, he thrust out his sword but only seemed to hit stone. He dodged another attack by only a hair.

Chieftains who were the great warriors of many of the Predan tribes, stormed forward barking orders. He tried to dodge as a warrior's body flew at him, but a leg clipped him, and he went down. Leaping back up, he rose and began to run; he needed to keep moving. More warriors charged, red fire in their eyes, but others began to fall back, the fear taking hold.

He saw a tall chieftain wearing a dark wooden mask. He ran to them. "Can you understand my words?" For a moment the chief looked at him but then nodded. "I will help you. Will fire work?"

The chieftain shook its head. "We must break the body," a sharp voice came back.

"Your spears and clubs are doing nothing," Dreyandol answered. His lungs were heavy, but the oppression of the dark ritual felt lighter. "Can we crush it?"

"Yes, we must, that is best," the chieftain answered.

"There. Those rocks, can your warriors climb and make them fall?" Dreyandol said, pointing up a cliff face.

The Predan nodded and ran off. Dreyandol searched through the crowd for the beast, but it was not necessary. The beast was pushing toward him. He slid past another attack and moved around. He needed time for the orders to be relayed. More warriors stepped forward to attack, but their attempt was futile. Spears pierced but did not seem to dig deep into the beast; clubs and cudgels only bounced off. Even the kicks from the great warriors only served to shove the beast. It even sent a kick back, and snapped an arm and shoulder clean off a large brute.

Its focus turned back on him, and so he climbed. He jumped on a house, standing above the beast. It turned, Carrun in form, but rage fumed from its eyes, bent on death, and it leapt up as well. With a jump Dreyandol flew to the next roof. Landing, he fell through, slamming hard on the ground. He scrambled out the door as the beast crashed down behind him. Warriors met him outside and tried to attack the beast, but it pushed through them, snapping limbs and spears. Dreyandol tripped in the throng. Near him, he saw the bone dagger of the head sorcerer and grabbed at it, his sword having dislodged from his hand.

After retrieving it, he glanced to the rocks and saw several warriors in place. The beast came on, fixed on him above all else. He could hear its steps behind him. Even with his speed and the attacks of the Predans, he heard it gaining. He ran and slid under the crossing beams of the altar's saltire. The beast broke right through. It came on harder, and so he ran harder, his breath heavy on him.

The night burned; red fire spilled into the night as the fighting toppled braziers, catching houses aflame. He heard the squawks and screams of the Predans. He turned. The beast stood before him, dripping blood and sweat. He stepped back, hitting the rock wall. A shriek from the beast rang out, and for the first time he perceived that it really was once Carrun.

Its long, whipping tongue hung to the ground, where it twisted and slithered as if in agonizing pain. A broken beak told him someone had landed a good blow. Patches where feathers once sat showed the unbroken skin below. In one shoulder, a spear tip lodged in place, broken at the haft. Still, it focused on him and his death, in that moment he realized his circumstance. His plan and life hinged on those who were his enemy. Was his trust in the Predan chief in vain?

A pain struck him next, powerful and wet, piercing his shoulder. His ears rang from the explosion of the boulder that slammed down. It not only crushed the beast but cracked the ground below, a shockwave battering him back. He shook his head. The dark magic still held so strong, both hands of the beast writhed around, fighting for destruction, though the entire upper torso and head were crushed.

From the relief came the pain. The sharpness he first felt came from the thrust of the beak of the beast, having shot at him from the force of the impact. It hit his shoulder and ripped through his doublet. Blood dripped from his face, with the beast's flesh covering his armor.

He slumped down the rock, breathing hard. Exhaustion took him, the oppressive power of the dark ritual, the exertion, and injuries, coming together to make him swoon. The sudden change, where once screams and shouts echoed, to the silence of a cold night, tore through his mind. He sat and looked up at the darkened sky, the stars exhibiting their beauty. A spear tip grazed his throat and brought him back to the faces of his enemies.

*****

When they ungagged him and took off his blindfold a day later, he felt the warmth of the sun on his face. He stood in the valley before the Ajencain pass, right outside the battlements, where he had fought many times before.

Pain racked his body, shearing through his back with every step, but his shoulder was bandaged and dressed. Standing across from him was the chieftain he had worked with. He remembered the wooden mask. Their feathers were orange-brown, and they held the serpentine bone dagger clasped in their winged hand. Behind them were another two warriors, decked out in armor and masked in bronze, each holding an ornately carved spear.

"Take this as a gift. You are free to go," the chieftain said in a harsh voice, handing the bone dagger to him.

He looked over to the defenses and saw a small band of soldiers filtering through the gate but coming no closer than several

41

hundred yards. The green and yellow flags of Ajencain flew high, and every defensive post was manned by Dareian soldiers and Crimson Casters.

He reached out and grasped the bone hilt of the serpentine dagger. "What was that?" Dreyandol said in a strained voice that led to coughing.

"A foolish decision," the Predan answered.

"Why, though?"

"Why fight this war? Why call forth our warriors, why raise your banners and defend this pass? These lands we believe ours, you believe yours. Pushed to the brink, even the smallest bird might peck an eye. We wanted an advantage, and foolishness followed."

"Releasing a dark beast? What advantage is there in an uncontrolled monster?"

"One might find the distraction of such a creature useful in the time of war, but no, the beast only came at your disturbance. Carrun was to be our next Akuman, our great chieftain. He would unite our people against you," the Predan said, standing tall before him.

"My disturbance? I came to rescue him. It looked like a sacrifice," Dreyandol said, shifting to alleviate some of his pain.

"You spilled the blood of the innocents. Their blood was meant to balance the rage, but the cup spilt at your wind and the blood rage came. Only three times in our history have we called forth Akuman, and until now only once had the dangerous ritual gone wrong. For your aid, you are free to return to your people, and long will it be before battle comes to this pass. You have done a great service for us, and for it you are gifted your life."

"For helping you destroy that monstrosity?" He rubbed his cheek, trying to contemplate the statement.

"Yes, when last the beast raged, we lost many times more and called for the aid of others to help us destroy it. We should not have tried again," the Predan said, beginning to turn.

"Your cause to you is so great? Why not come to Rovelle and take your place on the council? Treat for your lands?"

"Oh, red-eyed one, it is difficult to plead for a thing you already believe is yours." The chieftain nodded and turned to leave.

Dreyandol watched for a moment and then spoke again, letting his voice carry further to them. "I am Dreyandol of the House Gilthoni. What are you called?"

The Predan stopped, as he watched in wonder. They reached up and removed their wooden mask. As they turned toward him, he saw the face of a female, with the wider but longer beak, large dark eyes, and lighter brown feathers.

She stood silent for a moment and then said, "I am called Kaerluftala, by my people. I am chief of the Qiracorgle."

Chapter 3

As the final light of the sun diminished over the bay, Aija drew back and fired a fake arrow at the half-moon hanging above. She laughed at herself, moving from one shadow to another. She bowed and blew a kiss to the building she left behind. "To you, good sir, you served me well."

People still meandered in the streets of the great city of Robo, but most headed indoors before the night set in. No one saw her. No one noticed her. A small voice in her mind chimed in. *Darkness is a companion, sometimes embraced, sometimes kissed, other times waved to, but never forgotten.*

A dog barked in the blackness of the streets as she scrambled behind a stone wall. Pretending to be tired, she took deep breaths and then wiped her forehead. A wain rattled by. She glanced at it but stood like a statue in the dark. A group of men accompanied it. *Workers no doubt.* All of them were covered in rock and dirt. One even looked towards her in the alley but did not seem to notice her. She rolled her eyes, before bounding up the wall to the top of the nearest building.

A woman giggled, her laugh echoing down the cobbled road. Early night stretched out her shadowy arms, birds halted their chattering, and the night creatures began to stir. Families broke bread for the last meal of the day, city guards changed shifts and merchants now locked their doors. Like any great city, a new world arose at sunset.

The smell of the sea flooded her nostrils as she jumped from dark corner to dark corner, a shadow in the night. From her new vantage point, she could see out into Gilded Bay. Black now, except for the traces of moonlight that kissed the far-off waves at the edge of her sight, small islands jutted out like specters against a darkening horizon. Each one was speckled against the blackness with fires from ports, storerooms, and homes. She loitered in one of the many residential districts of Robo, tapping her finger against her lips.

Lepfor Bulsei worked as a dock warden in the commuter district. His blue-tinted skin announced him as Fissionari, the original settlers of Robo, the golden city to the sea, as it was called. Five nights a week, before heading home to his wife and six children, Lepfor came here to the arms of Delia Primm, the unfaithful wife of the dock warden who relieved him for the late shift.

Aija sat on the roof in the council of shadow and found him guilty of hypocrisy. *The damned wribit*, she thought.

She looked down one avenue, only catching a glimpse of a boy turning on a side street. She looked back toward Delia's house. *By the order of Klor Dem, the Black Needle assassins, Lepfor, as warden of the commuter docks, respected Roboan, and family man, must die in humiliation*, she stated in her head.

In years past when tasked with her first mark, she remembered being told by her master, "To the customer, our duty is but one: to kill. They should never feel like we care about anything else. However, we don't remain a powerful assassin's guild because we're just killers. If given enough time, investigate, find the reason, find the end goal. Knowledge is a great asset to the shadow."

Through some investigation, she unfurled the truth, or at least a credible motive for murder. Known as a hard warden, Lepfor commanded his shift as a taskmaster, allowing no exceptions, giving no slack to his workers or the ship captains who docked with him. He did not take bribes or tinker with the books; he followed the law. Many around the city knew him for the outward love he bore his family. Like the sun, they shined at many events, his wife always draped on his arm, his children spoiled with the nicest things.

So why put a hit out on him? Delia's husband did not have a clue to her nightly cavorting. What, then? Through her investigation, she discovered Lepfor was the means to an end for her current customer. Not being a prominent enough figure in the upper echelon of the city, his own death carried very little weight, but as nephew of Forpod Bulsei, the marshal of the docks who sat on the high council for the city, he could be a tool.

Forpod controlled all goods and people that entered Gilded Bay, the main entrance to northern Rosenia that led downriver several days to the capital, Nowann.

Klor Dem's customer tried to pay the two off. They wanted them to turn their heads from the slave smuggling trade through the docks. Rosenia stood proudly as a slave-free kingdom. Forpod's hesitation about the matter and Lepfor's outright disgust due to his principles were in the way. Finishing the mission would scare the marshal into compliance and get rid of his cousin all in one turn.

Documents and letters found in Forpod's office seemed to back up the idea. She smiled at her fun when pretending to be a Roboan guard, after stealing the uniform from a drunk she found in the street. *Or did I get him drunk?*

She now sat atop a roof just across the street from Delia's house. She smiled again and wiggled her head back and forth in glee. Tonight was the last night she needed to watch this farce of a good man. For two weeks she had stalked him as he paraded around the city, the prince of principles. His upturned nose and pompous smile ate at her. She laughed at the thought.

Delia, however, ate at her even more. She lived in a two-story home, built in a style for Humans, with large windows facing the sea and a flat roof to spend nights looking out over the city and bay. A wonderful place to live out her days.

She spied him coming down the street, his bodyguard walking two steps behind. *Right on schedule.* He never deviated. From her stalking him, she found every morning he went to work and administered his duties. Day after day, ships docked, were inspected, unloaded, loaded back up, and headed back out. Use of the commuter district meant they carried mostly passengers, traveling from all over the Crescent Sea, as far west as Nyoko and as far south as the Fang Islands, and further to places she knew nothing about. Lepfor only handled the few problems that came about. In those mornings, she spent her time looking for answers regarding her mark. She traveled all over the city, sneaking around, reading ledgers and listening to conversations, all to piece together the most sensible conclusion.

When noontime came every day, Lepfor ate lunch, and this was the only part of his life that seemed to be inconsistent. Some days, he would go home, where his loving family awaited him with sweet kisses and adoration. It almost made her sick to think about. *Disgusting trickster.*

Aija reached over and adjusted her black boot, eyeing a passerby on the street below. The man turned the corner and kept going.

Some days, Lepfor stayed at his office by the docks for lunch, too busy to eat or having brought his own, usually some sort of fish pie. On rare days, he visited one of the eateries or nearby taverns.

He met friends or important officials in the city but never met Delia. She existed as a secret, hidden in a dark cavernous hole, far from any eyes.

Wherever he went, his bodyguard traveled at his side. The silent protector came across like a living statue. They shared no friendship. The employer only ever spoke to his employee when necessary. Aija did not know his name and did not care to find out. However, she knew him just as well as Lepfor and Delia, and he was the only one who knew of their affair.

The man stood a hand's width taller than Lepfor, making him about a foot taller than herself, middle-aged, and having already lost much of his wiry, black hair. At the thought, she ran her hands through her own and took a deep breath.

The guard's deep-set, dark eyes could be considered menacing, but she liked his full beard. He wore a long-leathered coat that hung to his knees, where he hid a dirk, a club, and a crossbow. His movement told her that he knew his business. Very different from her usual quarry. Too many in his same profession, or even soldiers, did not seem to know the business of killing. If there was anything she knew, she could hunt, and she could kill.

She made a face at the thought and shrugged. As proud and happy as it made her at finding someone who could be a minor challenge in a fight, he would be oblivious to her presence, never knowing the truth.

Only a few minutes earlier, she had paid a young boy to run with word to the authorities to tell them of Lepfor's murder. She stood up knowing she had better get started, though. They would be there within the hour.

Looking out toward the Primm household, she breathed in deep one last time, mentally preparing herself. Delia and Lepfor were probably just getting started in their lust. The upper window was closed now, but sometimes she could see the lovemaking between the two. It made no difference; she knew the house well.

It was part of the stalking. She had slunk inside one day and studied it, while also studying Lady Primm. She spent all day in the house moving from room to room while Delia did her daily duties, which Aija found, consisting of drinking too much and yelling at her maidservant. An unkind woman, she exuded a heartless and cold manner toward everyone except Lepfor.

Robust, though not fat, Delia's large curves and light brown hair made her desirable, she supposed. Frivolous in her expensive tastes, she ate and drank more than her poor husband could afford. Worst of all, Delia hated the poor man, while he seemed to care for her very much, doting on her every want and need.

She'll be dealt with soon. She pulled on her black gloves.

Aija loosened her dagger in its sheath and then pulled a leather-bound booklet off her belt. She opened it with the slowest and most tender touches, then pushed a locket of hair behind her ear. Down the middle of the fold lay a black, thin blowpipe. To either side were black needles, each with small, colored feathers for fletching at the ends. Some were dark green, some light green, some were red, some blue, but most were black. She took out a blue-feathered needle along with the pipe and loaded it. Taking out a second needle, she slid it into a fold on her black leathers. She put the booklet back on her hip and the tube longways in her mouth. Last, she pulled her dark leather hood up, covering her deep black hair, and then pulled a cloth from around her neck up over her nose. The only things exposed to the outside world were her dark shining eyes and bits of her fair skin. She flitted, no more than a shadow, in a darkening night.

She took a deep breath, and in a bound jumped off the roof. An imperceptible puff of dirt crunched when she landed below. Next, she darted through the shadows to cross the open street. Deep breaths filled her lungs, building her excitement. Like a cat, she climbed the side of the house toward the second floor, using windowsills and anything else she could grab onto, every move as silent as a whisper in a deaf man's ear, a wisp of air in the stillness.

She noticed the sky, clear and bright, as she looked up. Star upon twinkling star, like small bastions of strength, shone beautifully. It drew her to a better place for a moment. She loved the night and its celestial canopy. The constellation Phyros, a red-starred phoenix, flew like a flame. She loved the stars and their lofty freedom. They were a constant reminder of light in the darkness. Her other great love, the thrill of the game, devoured her in a black void. She loved the planning and hiding, the sneaking about, and even the spying. Often, the killing itself proved disagreeable, and at best she held pride in her skill. She knew all darkness held some light and wondered what her light might be.

As she grew closer to the window, she could hear Lepfor and Delia in the throes of their lovemaking. She peeked through a crack and saw them. A candle danced in the room and their shadows flickered on the wall. She knew she was never obvious enough to be a flicker, only a wisp of breath. Delia moved on top of Lepfor, proving lucky for Aija, as she made sense as the first target. They were so drawn into their passion; Aija could have fallen through the roof and not disturbed them.

She pushed the window open so slowly. Her breathing made more noise. They seemed to be at the height of their ecstasy when she made enough room to climb through. She wanted to chuckle. She took in some air through her nose and let a quick puff back out.

A blue-feathered needle stuck in the back of Delia's neck. She did not notice, but before another moment slipped away, a second needle stuck in Lepfor's neck. Delia noticed it, but by that time she began to slump over.

With lightning speed, Aija crossed the room, catching the curvy woman so she did not fall on the floor. She retrieved the two needles and slid them back into the booklet. Her orders were to not leave any evidence of her work, not even their black burn mark on the wall, the resemblance of a needle. The request did cost extra though. She giggled at a thought. If the people of Rosenia knew how many murders Klor Dem took part in, they would rise up and hunt them down.

Taking her arm, Aija moved the paralyzed woman down next to her lover on the bed. Delia's eyes darted around in their sockets and then fixed on her. She could see the fear grow and she felt her heartbeat faster. She smiled at the fear. She moved Lepfor over, making room so the two would be lying next to each other, in the same positions.

"Calm yourselves," she said, like a soothing mother. "You're stunned at the moment. Your bodies are paralyzed, and you can't make any noise." She moved the blanket over the two of them, tired of their nakedness. Lepfor was not fat, but she held no attraction for his blue, tinted skin on a wiry frame, and she certainly did not like women that way. Unless the job called for it. *Anything for the job*, she thought, wiggling her head back and forth.

"Right now, the authorities are on their way here," she said, moving toward the door to listen. "By order of Klor Dem, you've been sentenced to death, and I'm here to be your executioner. I'm sorry, Lepfor, you've been a rock in the community and a lying snake to your family. I know you love them. I've been watching

51

you, but how foolish you've been." She looked toward Delia: "Does it bother you to know that? Does it bother you to know you're only for pleasure and he loves his family? Oh, I'm sure it doesn't matter, not with your heartless soul. Your husband works at the docks to support your unreasonable life while you're here, badmouthing him and taking advantage of his kindness. It's sick, and you're really sick. I mean, I've met a lot of people and you're up there. Maybe not a murderer or slaver, but really, woman?"

Aija knew how evil she was being. She knew they understood every word she said, and they could do nothing about it. Their eyes were probably drying out right now while saliva collected in their throats. She knew from experience, and the thought almost planted a seed of pity in her mind.

Difficulty came with joining the Order. To become a member of Klor Dem, she must succumb to some of the needles they used, by either feeling their effect or by living through them. She remembered how awful the pooling of the spit felt in the back of her throat, while her eyes dried out, but even that thought did not sway her from the job at hand.

She remembered the paralyzing power of the popsi plant as a test too. Child's play compared to some of the other tests she endured to receive her first mark. Besides the fact, she must be proficient in a variety of different weapons and skills. They were one of the most powerful and well-known murder-for-hire guilds in all of Sancta, for anyone who knew to seek out their services.

"Delia, my disgusting heifer," Aija said, still smiling, "the contract called for me to end the life of Lepfor, and in doing so, to humiliate him. You, however, are not on it." She moved closer to the woman lying motionless on the bed. "If you'd been a better wife, a loving wife, and maybe kept your legs closed, you wouldn't be in this situation." At that, she punched Delia in the face. The woman's nose began to trickle blood, running over her lips and down her cheek. A tear also fell from her eye. "Oops, I better finish. Your popsi is wearing off."

In control again, she looked them over. She hated people who took advantage of others. It drove her mad as one of her pet peeves. She would have killed anyone like Delia for free. She would never tell her order, though.

She uncorked the top of a small, black, glass vial she took from a pouch on her hip. Filled with a clear liquid, it had no smell. "This is Jesap. It's a poison from Kiamel Po. They take it from the eggs of an eel found in underground streams. There's no antidote, and it only takes a few seconds to do the job. I want you to know, Delia, that after you kill Lepfor, you... kill yourself."

Aija had planned this out from the beginning. A small knife for emergency purposes hung on Lepfor's belt. She chuckled: *a useless tool*. She took the knife in a flash from where it lay on the floor, put it in Delia's hand, and used her hand to stab down into Lepfor's heart inch by inch. Lucky for him, the popsi dulled the nerves, which annoyed her, wishing Delia had felt her punch more.

Lepfor's dark blue blood began to soak the sheet covering his naked body; his large black pupil eyes closed. Just to be sure that he died, she took the small vial from her belt and let a single drop fall on his lips. It was overkill; if even a smidge of the drop entered his body, he would be dead. A whole drop could kill a family of six. She knew because another member of Klor Dem had used a drop to do just that.

Checking his heartbeat, Aija nodded. "He's done. Now for you, Delia. I have to be quick. The authorities will be here soon. I figured I'd hear them coming by this point." She looked at the prostrate woman with an evil smile and shrugged.

"I really don't have to kill you. They'll find you soon enough, see you killed Lepfor, arrest you, and sentence you to death. However, I don't like you, and I don't like how you treat your husband, or even your maid for that matter. See, I'm going to free your husband from having to worry about you until you're executed, which he will, because he loves you. He won't have to stand by your side at the trial, or defend you, or even support you. He'll be free to start a new life," Aija said the last part with anger in her voice. She pulled out her booklet again and took out a needle with an orange feather on it. She then pricked Delia's ear with it, then she put a clear vial on the stand next to the bed.

"When they get here, they'll think you murdered him and then drank poison to kill yourself. It will most certainly be poison that gets you, just not from that vial. This needle will start soon; it'll cause a pain so horrible you'll feel like you're on fire from the inside, like molten rock is flowing through your veins. The worst part isn't that it will kill you in about five minutes. The worst part is you're paralyzed and can't reach the water I just put on the stand to pour on your ear. Just this little bit is enough to neutralize the toxin. This poison overwrites the popsi's pain neutralizer too. It's an evil thing that some sadistic villain concocted, and they had the audacity to call it Fire Lick. I love the name, but the burn should be starting... now."

The popsi had worn off enough that Delia's eyes widened ever so slightly from the pain. The room now sat empty and silent. The candle flickered on the wall, a dog barked in the street, blood soaked the bed and caked her face, but no one saw the tears run down Delia's rose-red cheeks.

Aija sat on the roof, back across the street, with her legs hanging over the side. She smiled a little as she watched the scene unfold. Kicking her legs with a mixture of glee and disgust, she hummed an old tavern song called the *Revenge of a Forlorn Row Man*. Roboan soldiers, with their conical gold-plated steel helms and their sea green and blue doublets banged on the front door, lanterns and torches in one hand, spears in the other. Short swords hung at their sides. The captain on duty, astride his brown destrier, shouted for the door to be opened. Lights in some of the houses were being lit, more with every bang. People were coming out of their homes to see the commotion, just like the followers loved to do.

They ended up breaking down the door, and not too long after they pulled a bound, balding man from the house. "What's going on?" he screamed, his voice echoing in the night. "My master is Lepfor Bulsei. Unhand me."

She watched the torchlight move to the second floor and enter the bedroom. Shouts of murder rang down, and the bodyguard started to deny anything had happened. She knew two things could happen to him. They could believe the poor wretch and let him go or not believe him and try him for murder. She thought it doubtful they would do that though. She had left more than enough evidence to support Delia's murder suicide. Barring the judges having a bloodlust or being apathetic, they would release the guard.

After all, this is Rosenia, she thought. *Justice is law, and honor and principle are its guiding hands*. She laughed, and for a moment in the commotion a guard reacted to her laugh, but he immediately turned back, not finding its source in the dim of night.

She pulled her hood and mask down again. She took her black, leather gloves off and ran her hands through her dark chin-length

55

hair. A cool breeze whipped from Gilded Bay, carrying a small chill. Her hands felt warm as she rubbed her face and she raised her eyebrows, delighted with her work.

In the morning, the news would travel all over the city and trickle into the countryside, as it so often did. Her one act of simple murder would spark a chain reaction that would be felt by many in the kingdom. Klor Dem would receive their payment, she would get her share, and except for a handful, no one would be the wiser.

Forpod might bend his knee to the slavers and smugglers. Maybe they would get some of their slaves through the inspectors, maybe it would go on amiss, but Aija loved to see the ripples she and the order created. It might take some time.

A thought jumped into her mind. She remembered another task she wanted to complete before the morning wrapped back around.

Over the rooftops, through the darkened streets of Robo, over the fire-lit homes of the unknowing, past the business and market districts busy with their money changing, past the garrison, and through much of the docks, she made her way like a bird in flight. She trained herself to run for miles without stopping and to not make a noise while doing it.

The great port city always bustled, even in the heart of slumber. Ships entered the bay at all hours of the day or night, and countless sailors were in port at any given time. Still, with all the people out in the dark of night, she made her way across the gold city without a single person noticing her.

She passed a man being robbed outside a tavern, and heard him repeat, "I don't have any coin," even as they began to beat him. She saw two Roboan soldiers fighting for a laugh—ironic, because they were around the corner from the man who needed their help. She saw more than enough sailors taking runs at the local whores in dark alleys. Nightlife could be a dangerous life, but more than fun to see. As the richest city in the kingdom, and not by just standards of wealth, the mixed cultures made for a wide array of living. People of all races and kingdoms found their way here, the gateway into the growing, grand kingdom of Rosenia, the pinnacle and power of central Sancta, where society reached new heights and justice and honor reigned supreme.

When she entered the commuter district, only one ship sat docked, unloading her passengers. Embroidered on the sail: a picture of a swirling red whirlpool. If her memory served her right, the coat of arms belonged to the House of Redpool. They were a rich shipping family from the south, along the coast in the Caihn region. The ship's hull was stained a dark brown wood, trimmed with red. The chatter of exiting passengers and the shouts of dockhands echoed through the night. Not there to watch the interaction of what she considered the sheepish life of the grazers, those who never seemed to truly live, she continued.

She found Justin Primm where she usually found Lepfor in the mornings. He worked in the same office, using the same desk. Primm was younger by a few years than his now-deceased wife. His light brown hair grew to his shoulders; his gray eyes searched a parchment. He always seemed to have a layer of scruff on his chin. He worked hard too, but unlike Lepfor, many of the dockworkers and sailors got along well with him. He sat at the desk, a smile on his face, writing something in the candlelight.

Aija slipped around to get a closer look. From the window behind him, she could make out a letter to Delia. It seemed a love letter, and his grin sat heavy on his face. He began to whistle a well-known love song about a sailor and his new wife. She smiled, recognizing the tune as the same she had just been humming.

This poor fool, she thought. She made sure they were alone, masked herself again, and used what little magic she knew to cause the candles in the office to go out. In an instant, she entered the room, her dagger at his throat.

"Don't struggle," she said, right into his ear, "I might accidentally cut you, and that's not my intent. I'm not here to hurt you, I'm here to pass on a message." His hair tickled what little part of her cheek sat exposed.

"What do you want?" he asked with a quiver in his voice. "You can have my coin if you like."

"Don't talk. All I want you to do is listen." His scent was intoxicating to her; it caused her to squeeze even closer, to the point that she felt the heat from his cheek, and her lips grazed his ear. With a whisper, she said, "I've watched you, and you're a good man, at least one who loves his wife." She paused for a moment. "Tonight, I freed you of that bond. You'll learn the truth but use your love on someone who deserves it. Love should never be wasted. There's so little in the world. When you go to her tonight, she won't speak to you anymore, but she'll reveal her story to you. Don't let it harden your heart. Let it grow, let it start anew."

Aija pushed the back of Justin's knee in and let him fall to the wooden floor.

He stood quickly, moving back against a wall. He shook with fear; his eyes were beginning to adjust to the moonlight coming through the window. They darted around in confusion, looking for a person in the room, looking for danger. He lit a candle and realized the room lay empty. *Delia*, he thought in panic, and glanced at the desk, where it now sat empty.

Chapter 4

Afternoon set in after a long day in the Sea of Wind. Andross gazed into the distance, toward a small village nestled between two hills. At their foot, branches of streams flowed toward the great Andar River.

The relief of a long day's ride through the warmer breezes of Helsveg's heat flooded him and the urge for even this small village's hospitality lifted his spirits. Not since the glowing morning when the breezes of the plain cooled him and the grassland's seeds danced all around, had he felt any relief.

He smiled and patted Cleon on the neck. "We'll get some rest here."

Descending from another rolling hill, he thought about Razelind and hoped she found the broken man. In the distance, small lights caught his eye from inside the hovels, built from bog mud and topped with green, living sod. Every structure was constructed in the same manner and rose like small hills themselves. Even the walls used to pen in their livestock of donkeys, cows, and pigs, were formed from the dark nutrient-rich peat of the bogs. Every roof, layered in green, growing grass, looked vibrant and alive.

Still, some way from the village, an overgrown road cut across his path. He turned Cleon onto it, suspecting it led directly into the center of the village. Along the way, a broken sign rose where the arch had rotted away but still read "Tall Sod." He squinted, trying to make out the symbol below, and if not for the fish he would not have recognized the house sigil of the Dules, a leaping bass and a bison on checkered blue and green.

He shook his head. "Broken sigil. Broken house."

On the outskirts, the signs became more apparent. The living hovels were more like burial mounds, overgrown and unkempt. He waved at a child who peeked for a moment from the tall sod on a roof before the youth lowered back into it. What seemed like a picturesque, warm village from a distance now portrayed crumbling chimneys, muddied streets, and a pungent smell that made him breathe less deeply.

Passing two older women holding brooms along the road, he nodded and they only stared back. They watched as he drew closer to the heart of the village. He was used to this sort of treatment, as a knight, and always stayed wary. Sometimes he felt safer on the front lines of battle than in some of the older, untraveled villages he visited. More than enough times, as a representative of the kingdom, he found himself unwelcome by those not used to being checked on. The only officials the people ever saw were tax collectors from their liege lord.

Closer to the village center, he found children who stopped their playing, and women watched from windows. The men with their farming tools, pitchforks, and hoes, moved to cut off his progress.

The tallest and most imposing man of a group of seven stepped forward. Young with dark, sunned skin and reddish-brown hair, he scowled. "Sir knight, what can Tall Sod do for you? We don't much like for strangers."

"Do you have an inn in this village? I only need a place to stay and some food," Andross said, looking down on the big man with the pitchfork.

"We got no inn here, knight. We're just a poor sod village, as the name says. Truth be told, we'd rather you not stay here. Don't knows we can trust you," the man said, pointing the fork at him.

"Fear not, good sir, I'm Andross Delaqeen, Knight of the Dove, a knight of the king. I'm not here to cause problems for you and your village." He tensed for an attack. It would not be the first time a small out-of-the-way village tried to drive him out.

"Well, I be Tobel, the mayor of this village, and your name don't mean nothing to me," the tall man said, looking around at the other towering men and laughing, his reddish-brown hair jostling with every shake.

"Mayor Tobel, you seem young to lead these people," Andross said, looking around at the crowd that had gathered.

"Not too young. I be old enough to kill the last mayor for trying to work us to death in the bogs. I'm the strongest in the village," Tobel said, as some sort of explanation.

Andross saw a young woman begin to cry and run off from the crowd, and then said, "Well, you do look the strongest. The strong must lead." Looking away, he rolled his eyes. In many villages and tribes, authority fell to the mightiest, not always the best suited. "I'm here by order of King Coram, to search for clues in the murder of his brother Nurame."

In a flash of anger that surprised the knight, Tobel shouted, "We don't know nothing about that. Nothing you can find out here, and no one's going to talk to you about it. Just leave, sir knight. If you don't, we'll run you out."

Sometimes the declaration of the king's orders worked, but for some villages, having never witnessed the authority of their own lord, the king's word meant little. Forced to return to the most consistent method of gaining their trust, Andross spoke again, "I have gold liefs. If you let me stay the night and search out some clues, I'll share some with you." He patted a sack of gold on his hip. The jingle of coins cut through the silence.

The young mayor's eyes grew large. He licked his lips and said, "There's a barn. You can stay there tonight. I'll have one of the womenfolk bring you a plate, and you can ask questions to those willing to answer but trust me when I say no one will speak to you." Tobel's tight, unblinking eyes looked around at the grumbling villagers.

The knight could see that the young mayor thought himself clever. No one would speak to him. He could see their fear and distrust. He nodded and said, "Your hospitality to a knight of Rosenia is greatly appreciated," and threw him one of the leaf-shaped golden coins. "I'll pay more in the morning when I continue on my way."

The barn, though roofed in sod, comprised more wood than mud. It seemed older than the sod buildings around it. He settled Cleon and moved back into the village. The night approached, and though he expected little, he wanted to see who would talk to him.

He found little luck, even with the enticement of coin, moving from villager to villager. He saw fear mixed with hatred; many did not acknowledge him. Any man he approached told him to be on his way. Asking about King Nurame's murder led to angry looks and cursed words. The children of the village stared but then ran as he made his way toward them. A group of old crones washing clothes would not even look at him as they wrung out shirts and trousers.

The village sat away from any well-traveled roads. Guests were unusual and unwanted. A large, old building stood near the center of the village, probably their town hall, its roof black, burnt, and caved in from a fire. It, too, seemed to be made more of wood than of mud. He puzzled at it for a moment, when he heard someone calling from a side alley.

Peeking from behind a corner, hid the young woman who had fled from the crowd earlier. She waved him over. Cautious, he looked around and then moved toward her. "Yes, Miss?" he said.

"Have you gotten anyone to speak with you?" she said, her eyes darting around and past him.

"No one, except you now."

"They're afraid, I'm afraid. Tobel is a vicious man. Plus, we don't trust strangers much."

Closer to her now and looking through the dirt, she seemed older than he originally thought. "Why so much mistrust? I mean you no ill will."

"I asked my father once. He told me his grandfather told him that centuries ago we weren't like this. Apparently, the Lord Dule at the time went to visit the vile House of Lairhety and died at the dinner table. Poison, it's said."

"Yes, I've heard this same story as to why the Dule family doesn't like the Graymorns. Who's to say what's the truth?" Andross raised his eyebrows.

"Don't matter—vile Lairhetys, proud Graymorns—either way we don't trust no one, and we don't trust you," she said, her eyes locked on him.

He knew more of the truth. The people of the Dules' lands were once owned as slaves, but he knew it would do no good to bring it up. "Why talk to me then? Why be so hidden?"

She looked over his shoulder again. "Sometimes necessity calls for it. Tobel is ruthless, and the others as well. They'll snitch me out for a carrot."

"And yet they won't take my coin. What's he done?"

"I can tell you more later. I'm going to visit you in the barn after nightfall." She brushed her red hair away from her mouth.

"Why not now?" he said, furrowing his brow.

"Too many eyes, they're watching."

"What is it they're afraid of? What are you afraid of?"

"Not now. Later, sir knight. Be safe and watch yourself. I'll come later. I think someone is coming." She darted away, and he stood for a moment, and when he turned around, back toward the square, two tall men with narrow eyes and blond hair were staring at him.

He smiled at them as he drew close and they moved to cut him off, one going to speak, but he barreled on, cutting between them and almost knocking one over. He grabbed the falling man and said, "Pardon me, I didn't see you. I'm so lost in thought." Truthfully more annoyed at the lack of answers over his friend's death. He had known it would not be easy to find evidence of the assassination, but the apathy of his subjects who benefitted from him, or would have if he still lived, ate at Andross.

Before either man could answer, he added, "Night approaches, gentle sirs. I'll head to my shelter." He turned and strolled on, listening for any following movement. On his way back, the idea of the village's mistrust and unpleasant demeanor bounced in his head.

Nurame loved to speak on the behavior of his people and how it trickled down from above, how he had to stay exalted and above reproach and let it be an example to them. Clearly, the ideals of a noble man only stretched so far.

The Dules themselves squandered resources, wealth, prestige, and in current times lived more akin to ruffians and the harbingers of miscreants. Their control over their own land waned, and the time soon approached for either a neighboring lord to take leadership or for some power within to assume control. The skies only knew why it had not happened yet. The city of Geowm, their house seat, harbored a den of rascals, gamblers, and whores. After their herds were mishandled and lost in raids to Kiamel Po, and the overfishing of Lake Troylus, gambling and whores were how they stayed relevant and in power, but only by small threads.

When night fell, and the sky darkened but for the brilliance of the stars, he laid down his bedroll on a pile of dead grass stored in the barn. He undid his sword belt as the door opened behind him. In a flash, he unsheathed it and faced the intruder.

He recognized the young woman holding a small candle. Her red hair framed her fair-skinned and lightly freckled face. Hidden behind dirt and mud, and the remnants of streamed tears, it was hard to tell what she looked like. She smelled like old clothes and sweat.

"Sir Andross, I'm sorry for bothering you after nightfall. I shouldn't be here, but it is safer. I know something that happened around the time of the king's assassination," she said, her eyes brightening in the torchlight.

He felt his heart leap and drew close to her. "Tell me please. Your people were less than helpful, so any information would be great." He was skeptical at the young woman's appearance while containing his own excitement. "There's a lot I need to know."

She breathed heavily and began to pace back and forth. "My father, Jormund was the mayor before Tobel." Her voice wavered. "Tobel killed him not long ago. He's vicious and ruthless as I mentioned before. He wants none of us to speak to you." She lowered her face. "He said if any of us spoke to you about anything, he'd kill us." She moved forward; every step seemed painful, but as she did, she whispered even lower. "He has killed several times already."

65

"I'm sorry about your father," Andross said, his eyes examining her face. Young and scared, he did not see any deception in her appearance, but he gripped caution tightly, like he gripped his sword.

"I'm not," she replied, with a snap. "He too had a cruel heart, bent on only himself. He beat me all the time and treated the village terribly."

He squinted his eyes, looking at her. He could not trust her. After all, how could she prove any of it? "Tell me what you know," he said, still holding his sword, with one edge polished to a mirrored sheen and the other edge black in the firelight.

"I will, I promise, but you must promise to take me away from this place first." Her eyes were wide with pleading, but as much as he wanted the information, leaving with her seemed more a risk than a reward. She could be using him to get away from here, only to tell him later of her deception. Adjusting the grip on his sword, he tried to read her face. At the least she seemed to be fearful of being rejected on her proposal.

Movement outside stirred them: doors closing, the shuffling of footsteps, and men's voices. "They're coming for me, we must leave," she said, looking over her shoulder and turning away from the door. She moved to his side. "They know I'm trying to tell you what I know and mean to stop me. They'll kill me."

He feigned a smile and hoped the value of her secret was worth her death to them. A terrible thought, he knew, but with the tenuous situation for himself, it needed to be worth his life.

He tried to avoid interfering in the lives of Rosenia's people. A rule he loved to stick to, but not as easy as he would like, so he did not follow it often. After all, as a Knight of the Dove, his job mandated he insert himself where needed.

"It seems to me you're in more of a dire situation than myself," he said, his voice stern and strong. "I want proof you know something, before I put myself into danger."

Her hazel eyes grew wide, as the group gathered outside the barn door. She looked around and then back at him, silent for a moment. "A few months ago, two men came into the village with a Goblin. They stayed with my father. They knew each other. I don't know how, but they did. He wouldn't let me hear much of their conversations, but I snuck out of my bed as they drank and talked. I heard one say, a huge oaf of a man, had finished trimming the rose, whatever that might mean. My father asked if he died crying like a woman, but the large one answered, 'He died fighting.' A few days later, a traveling hawker brought word of the king's death, only just south of the here."

Andross had heard enough. Maybe it was a lie and maybe not, but the story she told intrigued him enough to want to hear more. "All right, I'll take you, but I want to hear more of this tale. As soon as we're far enough away, you're going to tell me everything. If you're lying, I'll bring you back here and let them have at you. I'm not one for causing discord among the king's people. I'm supposed to keep the peace."

At that moment, the group started yelling from the door. The girl ran over and slammed the crossbar down, bracing it. "Well, Sir Andross, I'll tell you the whole truthful tale, but you're caught up with me now. They know a lot about the night the king fell, at least many of the men do. If they find me with you, they'll kill us both." She looked at Cleon. "They're already trying to figure out how to get your gold. I heard them talking."

"You seem to hear a lot you're not supposed to. I guess I can't be mad about that."

67

"I'm a curious person, it can't be helped, but it's not just my curious nature they mean to kill me for. They mean to sacrifice me to the fire. It's reaping time, when we pray for next year's harvest, and I have little worth to the village," she said, panting.

He rolled his eyes as the banging at the door began. Under the grime, she looked attractive enough. She could make a suitable wife or lover to a man in the village, and that seemed reason enough to let her live for men such as they seemed.

A voice rang through from the outside: "Sir Andross we're looking for the girl Mahley, daughter of the late Jormund. Is she with you?"

She looked at him, her hands together, her face pleading. He walked over and pulled his crossbow from the saddle and loaded a bolt. Whispering, he asked, "Can you saddle a horse?" She nodded. "Saddle mine and get my things up."

He walked over to the door and yelling through it said, "Did she run away? Is there some way I can help find her?"

"No need to help, My Lord," Tobel's voice boomed, "she's an adulteress and must be punished. We plan on giving her to the fire."

Andross wanted to be sure of the situation before he committed to it, so he said through the door again. "She's here with me and she's told me everything from the nights around the king's murder." If the young mayor seemed clueless, the girl might be lying. If a different reaction played out, then they were both in trouble. He heard the villagers gathering more, and the chatter grew.

Tobel was smarter than Andross gave him credit for; he almost played it off perfectly. "I'm not sure what you're referring to, sir knight, but if she's with you, we wants her sent out." Almost a perfect answer to disprove the girl, but scurrying footsteps moving

68

to all sides of the barn gave them away. Why surround them if they only wanted the girl to be handed over?

He looked back at Mahley as she packed the last of his things. He motioned for her to mount, and though she looked at the great warhorse with apprehension, she put her foot in the stirrup and vaulted up. Cleon gave a huff in disapproval but calmed at his look.

"Send her out, sir knight, and we'll leave you be. It's getting late and we need to punish the whore who shamed our village."

Andross thought he could fight his way out, but he could hear more people gathering outside.

"We's impatient, sir knight. Send her out. If you take any longer, we'll just punish her while she's in there with you and burn the barn down." Tobel laughed. The others laughed with him.

A slow chant began to rise and then turned to a song the knight did not recognize. He looked at the door, then at her on the horse.

"They're going to sacrifice us in here," she said, now trying to yell over the song.

Negotiating now with the fever of a mob would be fruitless. To get out, he would have to fight. He heard Tobel yell again, "Do it," and the crowd cheered. Orange light began to flicker through the seams of the wooden planks behind them.

Years earlier, Andross took a crossbow off the lifeless body of a Horak chieftain he slew. A magnificent prize plundered from a long-forgotten treasure hoard. He kept it for its beauty, intricate gold filigree placed down the body, made of bull horn and red wood. He showed it to a Dwaling crafter once. After studying it, she told him its crafting came from the old days, made by the great father crafters of her race.

He had used it a few times since, but on nothing more than practice. So, when he pointed it at the barn door and pulled its

69

trigger, it surprised him when the bolt shot clean through and hit something with a thud outside. He had only wanted it to go through and scare some of the crowd, but a scream went up, and the feet of scattering steps sounded.

More screams echoed through the street and the trample of more feet could be heard all around as he fired again. He looked at Mahley. She sat astride Cleon, waiting, her eyes wide with fear. Now with the firelight, she carried an illuminating beauty to her. With the commotion, he flung the crossbar up and ran to mount. With her holding on to him, he made her string her arms through his shield, so it covered her back. With a snap, he charged Cleon through the barn door. The great warhorse needed little persuasion as the fire leapt and danced behind them.

Several men were dragging a bleeding Tobel away, making a split in the remaining crowd. Others fled, not wanting to be shot by the crossbow. Andross directed the warhorse right up the gap, trampling the dying man. The men scattered, and he glanced back at the mangled body of the young mayor. Cleon knew exactly where to step.

He sent a shot out to an archer who had positioned himself up on a roof and watched him grab his stomach and fall back. Experienced with crowds, the charger flew through. Cleon snapped at those standing in his way, as Andross leveled a few men who tried to grab or stab them with their pitchforks.

Having gotten through most of the crowd, a small group of men blocked the road with their farming tools. They were the only ones left before they were free. He knew better than to charge through; the forks would skewer Cleon. He could not turn around, as the crowd was charging after them. He heard them screaming for blood and sacrifice by fire. The girl whimpered at his back, her arms squeezing his torso.

With some luck, he grabbed a torch from a woman who came out of her house to watch the commotion and charged headlong at the men. He looked for the man who showed no fear and went straight at him. Right before he got to them, he lifted the torch and threw it straight at the brute. The man turned to flinch from the flame, knocking another man over and causing a commotion with the others. It made enough of a gap for Cleon to fly through without being pricked. He felt a stab at his leg. *Thank goodness for armored leggings.*

They raced into the night as fast as the muscular Cleon could carry the two of them. He trusted in the strength of his four-legged companion but carrying them both would be tiring. They needed to put some distance between them and the villagers.

On their way over a stone bridge that crossed a dark stream, he spied a large bonfire out in a field. Likely the fire they meant to throw Mahley into. The flames leapt high into the dark night. He could see images dancing around it, black shadows. A thought flashed in his mind, *Fire-dancing shadows.* For a moment, it pulled him back to the words of Adhem Nightstead and a sick taste rose in his throat. Two arms squeezed at his torso again and he came back to the present. He caught a glimpse of the girl looking out into the darkness at what was to be her end, and he felt her bury her face in his back.

Riding through most of the night, they fled as far as they could over grassy hills, and west along the stream with its black flowing waters from the mountains. The high peaks loomed to his right; some of the hills were spotted with clumps of trees, lit by the moon, but they galloped on, the young woman holding tight.

When daybreak approached, he felt the thin arms of Mahley slacken around him. He did not think about how hard a ride like this would be for her. He stopped and dismounted, helping the weak woman off. Cleon's deep breaths echoed in the night. The great beast traveled far and hard and again proved invaluable to him.

He held the young woman in his arms and tried to shake her awake. He worried about her health and the secrets she held. Her dim face was covered in dirt and utter delight, a weightlessness not seen before. Unexpectedly, she reached out with soft lips and kissed him. He pushed back, but when she came in for a second try, he did not reject it. He only accepted the warm, sensuous kiss.

Chapter 5

Dreyandol stood on the deck of a speeding frigate; the creak of wood and splashing water filled his ears. His short, silver hair ruffled by the wind and his red eyes pierced the farthest reaches of the vast sea. He pulled on his red, curve-brimmed hat. He smiled as white foam broke away from the ship and the dark blue Crescent Sea rose in high peaks all around. The deep intake of air filled his lungs with the salty taste of an expansive, flowing world.

He turned away from the white caps toward the catlike face of his new, short-furred Malkienon apprentice. She smiled, her silence befitting the moment, her large, burgundy eyes wide from taking in all she could. With the lightest of steps, she moved closer to his side. "Master, I'm happy here."

"I am too. If we weren't being sent to Rosenia on this mission, I'd just as soon stay on these ships and travel the seas. Take up with the captain and just sail. There's a freedom here on the water."

She looked back over the waves, a tuft of burgundy fur atop her head bent in the wind. She took in a deep breath as her orange and brown-hued tail flicked.

"Was this what you hoped for when you joined the Crimson Order?" Dreyandol said, looking back over the water.

She stood silent at first. She often stayed silent. He loved it about her, because he also disliked unnecessary chatter. "In small ways, yes." She did not continue, and he meant to leave it that way, but then she added, "I wanted freedom, adventure. I wanted to see new places, learn as much as I could. Did I know I would be here on my way to a new kingdom? No, but I hoped. If anything, I thought about eventually heading toward Paraduo or the Fang

Islands to the south. Stories say they're still on the edges of the untamed wilderness."

"It's why I chose you. I mean you were skilled with your blade and fast enough to keep up with me, should the need arise. Even my favorite quality about you, which is a love of silence, was not the final stamp." He nodded and looked down at a white bird gliding nearby. "You looked bored—maybe that's the wrong word. You looked ready for more. Ready to stretch your legs and find a new challenge."

"You could've been wrong," she laughed.

"Maybe, but something about the way you completed some of your drills grabbed my attention. You didn't seem to want to be a perfectionist, you looked like you wanted to understand. Always asking your instructor questions and for tips, and one time I saw you in line waiting for your turn, asking a Dareian woman all about where she grew up. I hadn't heard you really speak and carry a conversation before. You came off so genuine and curious."

"I was. There's too much out there, to trap myself into living a certain way," she said, leaning against the rail.

"I know, I've told my father the same on many occasions," he said, shaking his head.

"You didn't at least once think about following in his footsteps? Being an important advisor to the royal family?"

"Once I did," Dreyandol said, gripping the railing in front of him. "I was a young boy, but one day I thought I caught my father looking out the window over the land and smiling. In that instant, I believed, truly believed, my father wanted more. From there the thought ingrained in my mind to reach beyond what I knew. When I asked about it, he only answered about duty. To me, so young, the thought of duty getting in the way of joy made me sick."

"You're here though. Duty now calls you across the sea. Toward a kingdom overrun with new recruits where you're needed and with the hope of adventure and finding a second apprentice," she said, glancing toward her Dareian teacher.

He furrowed his brow and shook his head again. "It's not the same. I find joy in the different tasks and missions the Order has for me. Every day something new, something different. With him cooped up in the palace, dealing with the same complaints and issues every day… it sounds horrible."

The Malkienon, in her red apprentice doublet, nodded. The wind whipped up and the ship creaked around them. The shouts of the crew echoed across the deck.

Dreyandol closed his eyes for a moment, living in the moment, when a thought popped into his head. "Neesa."

"Yes, Master?"

"You know this mission to find a second apprentice involves you as well?"

Her small fur-covered nose tightened. "What do you mean?"

"What I mean is that I didn't spend so much time searching for the perfect apprentice, completing my mage's test, to have the opportunity to find a second apprentice, all to mess it up by choosing someone who doesn't fit our little group."

She looked at him and cocked her head.

"What I'm trying to say, Neesa, is I want your input with who our new companion will be. I of course will have the final say, but your comfort with the next person will be as important as mine."

She nodded at him with a smile. "I'll make sure to tell you if I find them obnoxious, or too loud."

"We both know it's more than that. If we get someone who doesn't work well with our skills, or we can't trust to help in bad situations, then it might cost us our lives."

"I knew what you meant," she said, with a small laugh.

She always seemed to know what he meant. Within weeks of accepting his proposal to be his apprentice, they had created a bond that seemed to transcend having to say everything. She understood what he wanted without him having to say it. Often in combat they were so in sync they never said anything. Sometimes it became as simple as a gesture of the hand or even a glance.

They stood quiet again on the deck, breathing in the salt sea air. The sun moved past midday, when she spoke up: "How much training will I need before you think I can take the arcane exam?"

"It depends. I spent years training. Magic never came easy to me. You've had less experience with it, but it may come easy for you. If you're half as quick learning magic as you are at how fast you learn combat skills, you could probably take it in two years' time. Longer depending on your ability to grasp it."

"I'll try for two years, then," she said, standing up taller.

"In the meantime, you have your combat exam to work on," he said, raising his eyebrows.

"I'm ready for it," she said, popping up to look at him.

"I've no doubt you can pass the exam, but we won't have time to get you scheduled to take it. As soon as we can have it done, we will. At which point you can choose to take on your own apprentice or stay mine until you finish your arcane exam," he reached up and wiped saltwater from his cheek.

"Can't I just pass the combat exam, take on my own apprentice, and stay with you also to keep learning?"

Dreyandol laughed. "I honestly don't know. I've never heard of anyone doing that."

A Bronling, about two-thirds the height of the shorter Neesa, walked up. The crown of his head was made into a top knot, while the sides of his head were shaved. A tattoo of a sea filled with whales covered the open area. "Captain wants to see you, sir Darei."

Dreyandol nodded. "You'll be okay here, Neesa?"

Saying nothing, she looked at him and then ever so slowly she nodded and turned back to the sea. He only chuckled at himself, as he walked away.

"So, Raendel, what do the tattoos mean?" The Bronling was second mate with his twin brother Raemon. They were both a lively group, them and the other Bronlings. In the late evenings they danced and sang at dinner. Last night Neesa joined them, and they were amazed at how well she learned the dance.

"They're the marks of our tribes and family. My tribe in the common tongue is that of the current, so I'm marked with the waves. Among my tribe, my family is that of the whale, close-knit and ever traveling."

"Are you all marked in a similar fashion?" Dreyandol said, examining the tattoos more as they walked.

"In all, there are seven tribes, and hundreds of families within each tribe. Each tribe once held a different part of the Fang Islands when we lived there," he said. "But yes, most of us are marked. It's an easy way to distinguish us from each other and from our Linga cousins, the Dwaling."

"Why did your people leave the Fangs?"

Raendel halted at the question, and Dreyandol stopped and turned back toward him. In an unwavering tone he said, "We don't speak of it, but from what I understand, we could return. Few have, but I don't think we'll ever settle the islands again." He then started walking again.

"I'm sorry if I asked something I shouldn't," Dreyandol said, puzzling in his mind what could have caused them to leave their home and be a people known for starting new colonies and settlements across the Crescent Sea and along many of its outer shores.

"No, it's not that at all. I don't know the truth. There are stories, old wives' tales and such, but the older generations aren't willing to pass the information on. Some of the younger of my race were only taught to say that we don't speak of it. So, when someone from the outside like yourself asks, it catches us off guard and we think to ourselves: Why don't I know?"

A sea bird screamed in its search for food and Dreyandol broke his thoughts to listen. The ship they hired passage on was named *Dead Coral*. Not exactly the most uplifting name, but Captain Phinias swore he named the ship after his dead wife. It broke through waves with swift ease, to the joy of Dreyandol, who worried the advice of many in Septimar might be wrong, that it may be a slow, arduous voyage.

Phinias steered the wheel of his pride and joy. He stood as a stout, dark-skinned man, with hazel eyes and a short graying beard. He wore a curving black hat, and a thick brown jacket that protected him from the ocean spray.

"Ah yes, my good Darei. We aren't but two days out from Robo, should the winds hold," Phinias said. "Are you and your apprentice still holding up?"

"Yes, Captain, we're well. I was just discussing with her that if we didn't have duties to attend, we would very much love to take up with you for some time and sail the seas. Learn the ways of the sailor and just work here."

"You'd be welcome. I've got a lively crew, a loyal crew, but there's always room for a few more. Both of you have taken up chores and helped without need, like decent folk. There's always room for a mage and strong fighters. Your order is well known for its strength."

"We like to learn. This is Neesa's second voyage, as she came from the lands of Delcom, but this is my first, so getting to learn from you and your crew has been a pleasure." Dreyandol looked across the deck at the crew. The first mate, Roger, with his one-eye, barked orders, while Raendel moved below deck.

The ship rose on a wave and Dreyandol looked back at the captain. "So, Captain, do you only ferry passengers in the Crescent Sea?"

"No, no. We do it often and usually with more passengers, but on occasion we carry goods. As this is my ship, we aren't really tied to a specific job or a company. Where the work calls, we go."

With a laugh Dreyandol asked, "Do any unsavory work?"

The twinkling eyes of the normally jovial captain shot across at him, and for a moment he thought he had made a mistake by asking.

A smile rose on the captain's face and he said, "Sometimes, when the need calls, there's good coin in having a ship that's as quick and agile as mine. I'll just leave that to your imagination."

Dreyandol thought on it a moment, and not wanting to give the captain any satisfaction on being mysterious, he added, "Still wouldn't change my mind about joining you, if life ever allowed."

Phinias nodded and scratched his neck. "What about you, sir of the Crimson Order." His tone sounded like a soft jab, but the smile on his face said otherwise. "You ever do anything that might be deemed unsavory?"

"I'm here, aren't I?" Dreyandol said, pursing his lips. "My father's a great and noble man in Ajencain. He'd like me to follow suit. Maybe not the worst of offenses, but strangely the one that creeps into my mind most."

"Sometimes a man has to make his own way. That's what the sea's for. You only feel bad because your father doesn't wish it on you for his own gain, but for your betterment. Just means you love him as much as he loves you." Phinias glanced to the left and whistled an order to Roger.

"Do you have any children, Captain?"

"Other than this band of loyal seadogs, no. Coral and I talked about it once, but it was before she grew ill. We both knew it would mean me staying on land more. She thought I wouldn't have any of it, but truth be told, I'd gladly have it now."

Dreyandol could not tell if the captain's eyes looked wet from the stinging wind or from something else, but he changed the subject. "What's Robo like?"

A smile returned to his face. "Oh, just the biggest port city in Sancta. Ships come from all over the Crescent Sea and further to make port there. The wealth that moves through it could make an emperor of a beggar. You'll see before too long, but it's filled with life and power, overflowing with inhabitants coming to and fro."

Dreyandol felt his heart race. "Anything Neesa and I should know?"

"No, for its size there isn't much to worry about. The city has its hoodlums, but the city guard does well to deal with them. Rosenia boasts of safety for its people, even more than your Rovelle does. Skies forbid, crime overflows in the city and causes the amount of coin to drop. That would be more dangerous than any foolish criminal that tries to cause any problems. See, the Gold City also leads to the capital, Nowann. While Robo carries the glint of gold to the common eye, Nowann almost causes a man to want to bow on one knee. I saw it once, didn't much like it for its distance from the sea, but I traveled from Robo down the Andar River, and when I looked on it, it took my breath away and then choked me with a rope."

Just then a shout rang down from the crow's nest. "Ship to the port! Ship to the portside!"

Phinias reached for a looking glass in his coat, and holding the wheel, turned to look behind. Dreyandol saw his face grow stern.

"What is it, Captain?" he asked, turning to let Roger by as he joined them.

"Seems to be a ship, my good Darei. Not unusual in these shipping lanes." A quick, nervous glance flitted over to the first mate and Dreyandol caught it.

"Something's wrong?" Dreyandol saw anxiety on the two men's faces. At that same moment, he caught Neesa's odor behind him. She moved *too* quietly for his liking sometimes.

"Now, I'll be perfectly honest with you, lad. From what I've seen through this looking glass, the colors it waves may be pirate," he said, with a sullen look about him. "Twon't know until we get closer. Raendel!" he screamed, and the second mate came running up the steps.

The captain gazed through his eyepiece when he said, "Go unlock the weapons chest and then rouse the crew below. Tell them a storm may be approaching. Don't tell them of pirates just yet. I don't want to excite anyone too soon." Raendel nodded and took off back down the steps two at a time, leaps for such small legs.

81

Dreyandol knew what the captain surmised. Hundreds of ships a day traveled along this route. Just because you did not recognize the colors of one ship did not mean they were pirates, but then again, who in their right mind took chances?

Legends of the exploits of the Rosenian naval fleet, the Sea Wolves, were heard in every tavern. They did their best to protect the trade routes, but it was an almost impossible task to stop all piracy. Hundreds of cargo and passenger ships meant hundreds of pirate ships, and the pirate guilds grew smarter with each attack. They learned to lure Rosenian naval ships away, allowing lone ships to slip through and attack.

A light sprinkle of rain began to fall, and in the distance with his Dareian eyes the other ship began to grow larger. It looked like any other ship he had seen, but it sailed on a course to cut them off.

The sea rocked, and the crew from below began to come on deck. They were not stupid; they all looked out to the ship in the distance. Dreyandol looked over at Neesa, and she nodded and ran off. Seconds later, she came back on deck with her bow and quiver in hand, and Dreyandol's longsword in the other. When the crew saw this, they started to scamper back down below.

"Captain, can't we outrun them?" Dreyandol said, belting on his sword.

"In a straight line we could, but before long we're going to have to change course. They know that and mean to cut us off. The *Dead Coral* is a fast ship, but some of these interceptor ships are faster. They have to be, to sneak in through the naval blockades."

He had not been sure, but feeling the anxiety of the captain, Dreyandol wanted to be prepared. He saw Neesa using a spell to dry her bowstring and then another to keep it dry from the rain and waves. That's when the captain spoke: "All hands on deck, Rog," his voice flowed as a menacing calm. "Pirates off the port bow."

Roger amplified his words with a booming voice.

Not long after, as the two ships grew closer together, Dreyandol caught sight of the ship's flag. "Captain Phinias, I see its colors now," he stated, pulling his curved, brimmed hat down more to shield his eyes. "An orange crab holding a skull in each pincer."

"Hmmm, I've heard tales recently of this lot. This be a new pirate's guild, the 'Crawler's Crabs,' been hitting small frigates on this route. Not too much into the killing of crews, unless need be, but sure do make spectacles of guests and captains, and I'm not one much for that part of the tale."

"Nor I, Captain. Why avoid killing the crew though?" Dreyandol asked, as Neesa nocked an arrow. She focused on the other ship and her fur pricked up like it did before fights.

"They swear by the pirate's code of Fino Trotellu, who believed every seaman stood just one step from choosing piracy. Give them a chance and they're the new recruits replacing lost crew. Plus, he believed, if you kill all those akin to ship and sail, you've no one to pirate against." Captain Phinias yelled a command to his crew and went on. He always went on; he enjoyed talking and storytelling more than most. "'Course this is opposite the pirate's code of Asani Bornhold, or as most know him, 'Captain Red River.' His code: kill or be killed."

Dreyandol had heard the stories of Captain Red River before. After taking a ship, he would hang all the crew members, dragging them through the water to leave a small wake of blood behind his vessel, *Mother Shark*, aptly named for the parade of sharks that followed in its wake.

The other ship grew closer with every passing moment. Larger than the *Dead Coral*, it looked like a crew of more than fifty. Fighting that many would not be easy. Looking over at Neesa, he spoke to her with no words and she understood. She flew up to the prow and got ready to let loose her bow. He knew if they boarded, many members of the *Dead Coral* would die, if not all of them. He wanted to try and scare the other ship off.

Flames began to sprout on the deck of the other ship. He saw them lighting their arrows. With the falling mist, and him there to put out the flames, he was not concerned with the ship but with the sail on the main mast. "Captain Phinias, they're lighting arrows. I know we're trying to outrun them, but if they get in range, they could shoot the sails and make us an island."

Years of sailing and fighting pirates made the captain a wise man and a man of the sea. The possibility already crossed his mind, so he nodded, and with disgust on his face, began to spout out orders to pull the sail down. "Get it down, boys."

At the same time, Dreyandol heard a whistle as Neesa let an arrow fly, hitting a man on the other ship. With her Malkienon bow, she could shoot a couple more before they could retaliate. Expert craftsmanship, and made from wood not easily found, there were not many bows that could match it. The Haldarei, cousins to his people the Somdarei, were known to wield great bows, but never having met one of his cousins, he could not compare.

The *Dead Coral* lurched to a snail's crawl as the crew grew ready. Some were on deck with swords, bows, and cudgels in hand, while others dragged up buckets from the sea and wet down the deck. You could never be too safe from fire.

"Neesa," Dreyandol yelled, "hit their sail with fire. If we aren't going to have one, then they shouldn't either." A flame sprouted from her hand and lit her arrow. It glowed rose pink; Ever Flame, magic fire that water did not easily quench. Risk ran high while using it, but the situation called for it. Regular fire would have been easier, and the arcane flame spent much more of her strength, but it would do a better job.

He watched it cross the now much smaller expanse and hit the sail. The other downside about Ever Flame, it burned much slower than a normal flame. The other ship still grew closer. A volley of lit arrows flew and landed in the water next to the deck. Not much longer and they would be in range.

Dreyandol saw the crew on the ship's deck. Some men, some Goblins, and even some Bronlings, ran about ready to attack. They held all manner of weapons, and those without bows formed lines. They were hard looking, but clearly a well-kept crew. A gray sail pulled the ship, and its prow boasted an evil sea serpent. The crab flag whipped in the wind, and a large bald man stood near the wheel, his long blond whiskers halfway down his neck, and a scar ran along the top of his head. He wore a long, open coat, with a tattoo of a crab on his chest to match that of the flag.

An arrow whistled by Dreyandol's head. Neesa's arrows rang out as consistently as noontime bells, hitting their marks with every shot. The other archers on the *Dead Coral* were firing also, with much less accuracy, but they were still occasionally hitting an enemy. He used magic to move the air in great gusts just off the ship to disrupt their enemies' arrows. It frustrated the pirates as their ship began to slow, and pink flames began to spread across the ship's sail, climbing their way up.

Dreyandol smiled, as one by one, crew members on the pirate deck were either being killed or running for cover into the lower decks. His hope changed when oars began to come out and row the large ship toward them.

The two ships' momentums still carried them toward each other, but would it take enough time to thin out the other crew? With the oars, they would be boarding the ship even sooner. Neesa still fired, but the crew of the *Dead Coral* began to prepare for the collision and attack.

An arrow from the other ship flew near Neesa and she dodged it without issue. Firing back, Dreyandol saw her attacker fall with an arrow through the neck, blood spurting. That's when the grappling hooks began to be tossed over to reel the ships side by side. Captain Phinias shouted for Raendel and Raemon to cut them, but Dreyandol leapt forward, cutting them in one slice of his sword. Both ships rocked with a jolt, sending sailors everywhere. The collision sent out the snap of cracking wood and the screams of both crews.

Shouts rang out as pirates swung across, only to hit a wall of air so hard, it felt like hitting the stone face of a cliff. It dropped the first few who attempted boarding unconscious into the sea. Dreyandol would not be able to perform the spell again, as the other crew had seen him and were focusing their attentions on disrupting his casting.

The ships' wooden sides grinded on each other, as the first enemy jumped across. To the man's ignorance, he died before his feet touched the *Dead Coral*'s deck, Dreyandol's gleaming longsword in his chest. Blood splashed back onto his crimson jacket as he withdrew the blade to dodge a Goblin's swinging axe. An arrow pierced the Goblin's eye and he dropped. Dreyandol noticed a quick smile on Neesa's fur-covered face, before she nocked another arrow with lightning speed and let it loose.

Captain Phinias shouted orders and morale boosts like, "Kill those dogs, they aren't but rats preying on true men of the sea!"

Dreyandol fought and killed two men with cudgels, as Roger stabbed another Goblin in the heart. Both crews were in the full heat of battle now, as he used magic to unbalance an enemy Bronling from off a rail.

The crew of the *Dead Coral* held their own. He glanced up toward the prow to check on Neesa and did not see her. "She always does this, runs off and makes me search for her."

A short half spear stabbed at him and he dodged it. The man who thrust it laughed in a low rolling voice. "Lucky for you, you're so quick, Elf. Otherwise, you'd be an ornament on my stick." The attacker grinned, showing a lack of teeth, surrounded by a face camouflaged in what seemed every kind of dirt imaginable. The man wore a row of ringlet earrings down one whole ear, and three rings in his nose. A tattoo of a bleeding heart showed on his neck, and so it became the target for Dreyandol's attack.

He parried the second spear thrust and watched as the tattoo bled real blood. He heard the man gurgle as he fell.

Moving toward the captain, he yelled, "Are you wounded at all, Captain?" The captain shook his head but pointed over at Roger, who was bleeding from a large gash in his leg. Dreyandol nodded and answered: "Watch my back, if you would for a moment, Captain." Summoning up his concentration through all the chaos, "*Antulli hansra atuca Henrumai*," he shouted. A bright, white light glowed from his hands; the same white light could be seen on Roger's wound.

The first mate's eyes grew bright, and the pale color in his face dissipated. "The pain is gone, and the wound is closed," he said in amazement as he stood up.

87

"Yes, the wound is closed, and the pain is gone, but it's not fully healed. It'll take a bit of time," Dreyandol answered, as he flew back down to the main deck, engaging another man. This one moved with great speed and cunning. He could tell from the way the attacker carried himself, and his dual daggers, that he knew how to fight. With his Dareian speed, Dreyandol jabbed with his sword and shot left, avoiding a strike, and stuck the man in his leg. As the man recoiled from the pain, Dreyandol flew at him again and stabbed him in the side, killing him.

The battle went on like that for a while longer. Dreyandol would fight and then heal when he could. Due to the crew of the *Dead Coral* being more adept at fighting than he gave them credit for, the outcome turned out better than he had guessed. The crew fought together as a whole, watching each other's backs, like fighters who fought together often. While Dreyandol killed many, the crew killed their share too, and though suffering injuries, only lost four men. The lookout from the crow's nest fell, slain by a Bronling's sling; two other men died by arrows, and another by the dual-dagger wielder.

His eyes were drawn away when he noticed the crew's attention focused on the other ship. When he looked, he saw Neesa with her curved katana drawn, facing the bald man with the crab tattoo on his chest. In one of his hands, he held a long, thin bladed sword, like a rapier, and in his other a hammer.

"So that's where she disappeared to," he said to himself, "Always wanting to hunt out the source of the problem."

As a tactical thinker and ambitious in her own right, Neesa's move did not surprise him. She believed the only way to get better was to test herself, and to do so she always tried to find the hardest fight. In a case like this, it meant the captain of the pirate ship who held the most prowess. Most used fear and intimidation to control their crews.

The bald man chuckled; all the crew of the *Dead Coral* watched. Dreyandol moved closer. If Neesa became outmatched, he wanted to be in a position to help her. She had proved a great warrior in many of their sparring sessions, but he believed anything could happen to alter a fight. He wanted to be close, just in case.

The man lunged at her with his rapier, and at the same instant swung his hammer in a sweeping downward strike. With a calm expression, Neesa deflected the sword and eluded the hammer. The man came on hard, spouting vulgarities about females and the Malkienons. She eluded and defended the attacks with almost blurring speed. For a couple minutes, she made no attacks of her own. She studied the man's every move, to some extent playing with him. Dreyandol did not like how she played sometimes, but since he knew she also learned from it and he trusted her skill, he never reproached her.

He watched as she began to get bored. Then her face changed; she bent her knees to get into the pounce mode of the Malkienons. Dreyandol knew the end drew near.

In a flash, she dodged the man's hammer swing, and playing off his momentum, jumped toward him and kicked him in the throat. He dropped his hammer to the deck, and as he stumbled, she crouched down and elbowed the back of his knee, collapsing him, hitting him in the back of the head so hard she probably knocked him out. He fell forward, and with blazing speed the men of the *Dead Coral* could not see, she pulled her dagger and put it in front of the man's falling body, having him land on top of the blade. He did not die right away, but Neesa waited there next to him until he did. Her large, burgundy eyes were focused and strong.

It felt a bit cruel, Dreyandol thought, as he watched the game she played with the man. Not giving him a quick death came across as apathetic, but if Neesa carried a flaw, she was quick to anger when someone insulted her femininity, and she was unforgiving in her response.

The Malkienons were a matriarchal society, where females held the strength and renown. Dreyandol knew she would not let that part of her ever falter.

Chapter 6

Eight times this week, Andross stood in front of the tapestry at the top of the grand stairs that led to the throne room. He pursed his lips and shook his head.

He wished to be the great Dareian knight depicted on the intricate tapestry, armored in shining sky-blue armor, wielding a long lance and fending off the great sea serpent. He fit that life much better. He wished all the more now that his friend no longer ruled. The younger brother of the two now relied on him for duties he felt others were much better for.

"Eight times," he whispered to himself. He glanced down the stairs to where there stood two Knights of the Thorn in black surcoats emblazoned with a white downward-pointing sword surrounded by white thorns. They each held an ornate halberd, and a short sword hung at their waists.

A door opened and another two Knights of the Thorn approached him. It was the same every time. With the raising of his chin, he saluted the two and they responded with the slight lowering of their own. "Sir Andross, have you left your longsword with the quartermaster?"

"Yes, yes," he said, rolling his eyes. "Again, I've left my sword with him, and my horse with the stablemaster. And my pride with the livery maids, and my time with the watchmaker."

"By decree of the king, only short blades are permitted in his presence, though to pull it without cause means execution," the knight went on.

Andross only nodded and began to stroll past, his boots echoing. One reached out his hand to slow him, but he slapped it away and continued. He heard the warnings every visit and they were getting old. He felt a little bad. The fault did not lie with them, and as a knight himself, he expected them to do their duty.

They followed behind as he passed another two knights at the great gray doors. These two were not in full chainmail. They wore white, velvet doublets with silver filigree and the emblem of the Thorn at their chest. At their sides they only wore short swords, as they were the door wardens.

Through the doors, he entered a smaller throne room, where another two knights in full chainmail stood at attention, while eight more were scattered around. This chamber was intended for small audiences. Another sat on the first floor, used for larger events.

A robed figure in purple and gold wrinkled his hooked nose at him and gave a hateful stare as they passed. He laughed loud enough for it to echo through the chamber. He heard the figure shift behind him, but he continued to walk on and laugh. The boom of the trumpeter broke his chuckle, and he heard the herald: "The pardon of the king's advisor Azziza Zattu of the House Nadal. Welcoming Sir Andross, High Knight of Rosenia, Knight of the Dove, of the House Delaqeen."

Closer to the dais stood a knight decked in platemail watching his every step. Even in the discomfort of the room, the standing knight wore an intricate helm with white-gold filigree and a white plume atop: the station of the royal sentinel, confined to the king's palace and the king, honor bound to join him wherever he went.

In the earlier years of his knighthood, Andross held the post for his friend, but briefly. It lasted until Nurame appointed him one of the high knights of Rosenia, a Knight of the Dove. Though weeks like this made him regret the move.

His boots echoed on the marble floor. Reaching the dais, Andross bowed low. "Your Majesty."

The king stared with a hard face. His Majesty Coram Lintrel was younger than him by two years. A twenty-year-old king, wise already, much like his brother. Andross looked at a face framed in long, dark-brown hair, dark eyes, a squared chin, and with a smile more smirk than jovial. The king leaned on the armrest of the throne made of red marble, with cushions of gold velvet. A blooming rose carved from a white crystal decorated the top of the backrest.

"There's much to discuss," Coram said, focusing on the knight. The sentinel stood like a statue, except for the eyes that watched Andross' every move. When he bowed again, they followed.

"It's my pleasure to serve you, Your Majesty," he replied, rising. Standing straight, he pressed down on his surcoat of a white dove on a green field, the mark of his station and symbol of peace. The sigil of the minor House of Delaqeen appeared as a blue and gold lobster in a net.

"You know what," the king said, with a smile, "let's not talk here. Let's move to my private chambers. It's more comfortable." Coram rose, and in all white finery, except for gold lace at the cuffs of his wrists, ankles, and neck, walked toward the back of the hall. Every step echoed like an execution drum.

The sentinel followed close, adorned in his black surcoat and steel armor. The door wardens pushed on a great white marble door, carved with roses, while another four guards with swords and spears followed them to the entrance of the chamber. There, only the king, Andross, and the sentinel went inside. "Please sit. It's easier to discuss things here, the need for formality isn't nearly as stringent."

"Yes, My King," he said, sitting in a large, light green chair softer than his bed. Not that he liked a soft bed; he preferred to sleep on the floor.

"As we've already discussed several times this week, strange things are happening in Rosenia and in its neighboring kingdoms," Coram said, removing the heavily jeweled crown from his head and placing it on a dark mahogany desk, littered with parchment.

"You wore the full crown today?" Andross said, with a smile.

"I did, I had to. It intimidates Azziza. Sometimes the only way to deal with his pushiness is to be pushy myself."

"Is it really being pushy if you're the king?"

"I don't know. That man confounds the mind. I'd be through with him, but he gets things done and seems to have a grasp on where to focus."

Looking at the great crown, Andross remembered Nurame's coronation. The kingdom celebrated for twelve days. The same could not be said when Coram became king. The loss still weighed heavily on him and the people.

"Moving past the dealings of my advisor… to the east, Paraduo still deals with Horak and Mongrel raids in the jungles. History tells us destroying the Horak and Mongrel tribes is a painful task. They breed like roaches, and finding their dens is almost impossible. I feel we should do something to help. We signed that damned alliance between our two kingdoms after the war, and peace between us is still rocky. You saw Azziza on the way out."

"Yes, Your Majesty," Andross said, smiling. "Maybe we could ask if they would like aid in the way of Horak hunters. It could help them with their problem and strengthen goodwill between us. Maybe a job for the Crimson Casters to do. They have more than enough members. Oh, and Azziza looked to be in *great* spirits." He rolled his eyes.

"Ha, that fool of a man makes me want to throw the crown at him sometimes, but all the same it's my fault," Coram said, standing and beginning to pace. "I appointed the over-ambitious, over-important fool. I told him to come up with some way to better strengthen the alliance between us and Paraduo. Your idea is a start, but things like a marriage are out of the question, unless we betroth my future heir. I don't think it's a necessary step just yet."

Coram stopped for a moment, while Andross sat watching, "Azziza thinks we should break the alliance and crush Paraduo. A ridiculous idea as well. His prejudices are unwarranted. Both sides know the skirmishes only began because of miscommunication. The House of Greenfall will never live that down. Plus, Aranean only stepped into the fray because the route through the mountains became the battlefield."

Andross nodded, remembering the stories about how Nurame's and Coram's great grandmother, Queen Thesia, sent out troops to settle a boundary issue and put the wrong general in command. General Cardin Greenfall, from several meetings with the enemy, took their taunts of cowardice as more than just them being Paraduan. A characteristic of their people, something in their blood, the idea of bravery and courage stood above all else. Their greatest possession, but also their way at jest between comrades.

When they spoke with the general in peace talks, instead of taking their pokes as fun prodding, he mistook it as a slight on his honor and the honor of Rosenia. The next morning, in his misguided fury and to prove his bravery, he rode his cavalry into the midst of the unhorsed soldiers of Paraduo. The Paraduan captain, Gomor Belshezy, rallied his troops and slew General

Cardin and his men, and then charged the remaining Rosenian soldiers' encampment and slew them as well. Thus, the War of Men began, and minor battles and skirmishes occurred for almost a hundred years, until Nurame made a peace treaty with them to foster an alliance.

"Azziza is not mad about having to bolster our friendship with Paraduo though. He's mad because I'm appointing you to my council," Coram said, smiling. Or was he smirking?

Caught off guard for a moment, Andross blanched. He did not want to be on it, no matter the honor. *Why me?* He often found himself asking the same question when he visited the king. He rubbed his hand through his short hair and then the end of his chin. "Your Majesty, what can I add to the council? I'm a man of war. I've been tutored in diplomacy and finance but never interested in them, and honestly never suited for it."

"Isn't it obvious? You're an honorable man, and loyal to my house. I dare say Azziza isn't untrustworthy, but one can never be too sure. With all the high lords of the kingdom on the council, sometimes it's good to have someone who isn't invested in making a better name for themselves. I need you to be an honest member whose best interests are in the well-being of the land, its people. Do you accept this office, or will you make your king a court fool?"

"I dare not deny it, but what of my other duties? I'm a high knight of the kingdom; it's my responsibility to travel the land and make sure your kingdom is being run according to your will. I'm appointed to keep my ear open for everyone, from the peasants to the great lords, from the paupers to the rich." Andross was confused about what being on the council would entail and how it would change his freedom to travel. He stared down toward the desk, but his eyes were focused far beyond it. He shifted in his seat, rocking the muscles in his back side to side.

"For a man known for his bravery, you scare easily. That's one of the reasons I need you on the council. As it is, the duty of a high knight is to maintain my peace in all the land. I know you keep your eyes open. You'll speak for those who need to be heard and watch out for those who need to be seen. You won't be needed here all the time, but when you're in the city, you'll be expected in council. You'll bring attention to those who forget to look around. Remind them there's more than their wallets, their bloodlines, and their lands at stake. Is this something you're willing to take on?" Coram asked, again looking straight at him, the smile gone.

"Yes, My King, I accept," he said, with a pinch of worry in his chest. He rose and bowed.

"Good, you're now appointed Sir Andross of the House of Delaqeen, Grand Knight of Rosenia, Knight of the Dove, and Warden of the Kingdom." Coram nodded. "Good, now that's settled, there are other issues that need attending to."

Andross nodded again but still pondered what good he could do on the council. He did not care about the pushing and pulling of lords to win favor; the game annoyed him. What difference did it make telling the king directly of the issues he witnessed, versus telling the king and council? He could not reject this appointment and incur the wrath of Coram, but he wanted to.

"Back to the issue with Paraduo. One thing I thought about, to bolster our ties with them and with other kingdoms, is to have a ball. A grand ball, with dancing and celebration, something beyond the norm. At the same time, I want the common people to rejoice in the streets in their own festivities of friendship. I want this to be an event held in all the kingdom, every year, something the people can find joy in," Coram said, smiling, his eyes open and bright.

"Invitations have already been sent out and preparations begun. Messengers were dispatched weeks ago, to all corners and to other kingdoms to spread the word. The great lords will be in attendance, along with the king of Paraduo and his court, as well as those of Aranean, and even diplomats of Rovelle. Furthermore, you are to attend. As the newest member of the council and warden of Rosenia, I want you there, not just for your new station in the realm, but to keep a keen eye. You've always been good at keeping a close watch, reading people. Keep an open ear to any news and an eye on any feelings that may be passed around. I think the council is withholding problems from me. There's a quiet murmur that drifts through the chambers, as if they're trying to keep an issue away from me. You'll be one of my agents to discover the truths of the realm and you'll start at the ball. One can learn much from these sorts of events."

"Yes, My King, of course. However, I have an eye better suited for the intents of a warrior and less so on the intents of people's games," he said, trying to smile.

"Maybe so, but remember Andross, some of these men who play these games are also warriors. See if you can read those intents in their eyes as you mingle. Large problems cannot be hidden from me, but small things can be, and if unchecked they can grow large. Anyway, good, I love these meetings with you. There's no arguing, very little discussion, things get done. Makes me almost feel kingly, which is different than the constant arguments I have with Azziza and the council. Few understand, as king, I can't always just wave my hand and have everyone do as I bid." Coram frowned, waving his hand.

"The next issue you need to hear about are rumors coming down from the lords to the north," Coram said, then drank from a golden chalice in front of him. "There are more and more raids from the Norte tribes. The great barbarians are getting bolder. I sent Sir Daven, in his older age, to assess the situation with the tribes. Something will need to be done, but I have others looking into possible answers."

Andross wondered what his fellow high knight, Sir Daven Elenbrant, would find. The Norte tribes were being forced south by the Nordarei of Hima, who no longer had patience dealing with the raids. That meant the raids were becoming more common on Rosenian lands. It could be more than just a tribal issue with the different Norte tribes, but also a political issue with the Nordarei city-states.

King Coram stared at him for a moment. Andross sat quietly. It almost caused him to adjust in his soft chair, but then the king said, "Do you still investigate my brother's murder?"

"Yes, My King, I won't stop until I find answers." He breathed out softly. "I've discovered a clue from a young woman I saved from a village in northern Helsveg." Andross noticed the king looked anxious.

"Good, don't tell me anymore right now," the king said, looking down, his face sullen, almost broken. "Keep all information of it to yourself. That duty I leave on you. Unless I say otherwise, I want you to never stop searching for answers. My brother's loss to the realm will echo in the minds of its people and its enemies for a thousand years. They believe in our vulnerability now. We can be touched within our own borders. My brother was the more experienced warrior, more dangerous to our enemies. Until some justice can be done, that can't be rectified. Only when you find the culprits in this matter or if you deem something necessary, should you come to me about it. Is that understood, sir knight?" the king said with force.

Andross leaned forward in his chair. "My King, is it now possible for myself and a few others to enter Kiamel Po under secrecy to try and obtain some information on the matter? I still believe this pursuit would answer many questions. Even if to fully discount their involvement."

Coram stared down at his desk. "Not yet. I can't under these circumstances let you do it. The talks between myself and several of the warlords are still ongoing. I mean to make peace with as many realms as I can, to protect Rosenia. Since we still don't know what really happened, I don't want to falsely accuse anyone of anything, let alone have people secretly enter that savage land to find out." Coram turned and looked at a map on the wall.

"Whoever did this is immensely powerful, much more than I think we first realized. With the recounting of the event by the survivors, it can only mean they used great mages. This is why I've made it so important to employ the services of the Crimson Order. Maybe if we'd used them from the beginning, my brother would have been protected from magic users. This kingdom won't make that mistake ever again," Coram said, his voice now raised.

"I understand," Andross said, giving a slight nod, though unhappy with the cautious measures of the king. What good came from having the most powerful army in Sancta if others dictated your movements?

He changed the subject for his own good. "My King, how is the queen?" Andross asked. As of late, he had heard very little of Queen Sehra's wellbeing.

"She's doing well from the messages that I've received, getting some much-needed rest. These have been difficult times for her. She seems to thrive in that bitter cold land, with her family there it's good for her. I told Sir Daven while he passed through, to check on her at Garian's Den. It's a beautiful place, but too cold for me to want to spend much time there," Coram said with a chuckle.

Andross knew it well; he had traveled there with Nurame several times. Garian's Den housed the high seat of the Vulfreund, the queen's family.

"If it's not beyond my place to ask, My King, how are you?" Andross immediately second-guessed the wisdom of being so bold.

"As Warden of Rosenia, it is beyond your place to ask my well-being," Coram said, with a hint of aggravation. "But, as a friend, I'm doing all right. Being king as an apathetic ruler is an easy job, left to those who would destroy a kingdom for their own pleasure. For a king who cares, it's tedious. Not only to make sure things are being carried out to my standards and instruction, but to also keep the lords in line with their dealings. You'll understand this more now that I've given you this new appointment, but at the same time, I hope your appointment will alleviate my need to be as vigilant."

"I'll do what I can, My King, always," he said, with another slight nod.

Coram chuckled, his voice echoing in the chamber. "I know, that's why I knew this would be better for me than it would be for you."

Andross looked toward the sentinel in the room, still standing motionless, his gauntleted hand on the hilt of his sword. His armored visor up, but his eyes still staring.

He remembered for a moment only a few years earlier when he would stand like a statue in the presence of Nurame and some lord

101

or other royal, or even the queen. It hurt to think about. If not promoted to a high knight, if he still held his post as a sentinel of the Knights of the Thorn, would his friend still be alive? Could he have done anything at the ambush to save his friend?

The interruption of his self-questioning came from Coram: "You and I will have many more conversations in this room. You'd better go before you begin to hate it as much as I do."

"Of course, and thank you, My King. I haven't taken the time to express my appreciation for this honorable appointment," Andross said, rising and bowing again.

"Don't thank me yet. You haven't dealt with the council. Farewell," Coram said, half laughing.

Andross took three steps back, still bowing his head, turned and exited the chamber. The door wardens saluted with a nod as he passed, and again his black leather boots echoed through the great hall. Gray and white marble pillars rose to windows, letting in daylight on the painted, arched ceiling, that hung sky blue. If someone looked at it right, it seemed to rise into the heavens like being outside.

When he reached the courtyard and the fresh air of the day entered his lungs, he felt better. The idea of being on the council still seemed odd. In his youth, he only wished to be a Knight of the Thorn. He remembered this change in mind came a few years before returning to his family's holdings in Caihn. Still in the Knights' Academy, he wanted to live near the sea, but friendship and the grandeur of Nowann changed him. Sometimes small pains of regret took him, but then he would wave it away.

His family's holdings were meager compared to other great houses, but the life of being a minor lord excited him in his youth. His late father had been a good nobleman, but he never knew his mother. He tried not to think about his life by the sea. It distracted him from his duties.

Already saddled Cleon whinnied, as Andross took his sword from a knight. Holding the grip on it reminded him of his decision. He chose this life, a knight, a warrior, a life in service to the crown. He would not let this new appointment change him.

Riding out of the palace grounds and down the King's Pinnacle toward the fourth tier of Nowann, he thought of his new guest, Mahley. The clue she gave him did not point many directions. She told him the two men and the Goblin who showed up in Tall Sod were traveling north. She did not see them and did not know them. What it did affirm was that Kiamel Posian raiders did not attack the king, and nor did unorganized highwaymen. The whole thing was orchestrated by tactical minds.

He wished her father Jormund still lived. He could answer many questions, even if Andross needed to force it out of him. She told him the visitors claimed they were the lucky ones, and the only ones left.

Her village's secret of sacrifice by fire came across as something they hid from outsiders, and as the only outsider to ever see it he began to understand. There was more to his kingdom than chasing criminals and saving damsels. Some secret lay there, hidden in the flame or in the shadow, maybe both, but what did it mean?

Chapter 7

Gnik Goglok woke with a jump. Sweat ran down his chest as he sat up. His head swam with pain. Blinking, he tried to clear his eyes.

It was the dream again, the cursed nightmare, controlled by the spirits of the otherworld, the Mahr. Would one ever show itself? Evil in their designs, they loved to play in people's nightmares. They were jailed in Parallin, the other realm. Forever haunting sleep unless the dreamer denies their challenges.

He stood up and went to the dirty basin, almost stumbling over a half-broken mirror. He had dropped it earlier in the night, when the whore he paid for would not stay to talk. He had wanted someone to talk to, to keep himself awake. *Why would she?* He did not pay her for talking, though he should have. She had not been impressive; he should not have paid her anything. Much too large for his desires, and she smelled of dirt and sweat. Worst of all, she had no personality.

He pulled on filthy, withered trousers with a grimace. They were starting to wear in spots; one hole had worn through on his right hip. He pulled on his nice, yellow silken doublet; it matched his yellow Goblin eyes—eyes he could not look at in the mirror any longer. He double-checked to make sure his stash of gold still lay hidden away and then shook his small purse to hear the jingle. Why he checked, he did not know. He always had enough lately.

Weapons were not allowed downstairs in the tavern, so he hid a knife down his boot. He went back to the mirror and ran some water through his dark hair. It had been long and wavy only a few months earlier, but now it thinned out at an unnatural rate. His short-fanged teeth were not in the best shape, chipped and yellowed, but no Goblin's were. He stepped into the hall, locking the door, the wood creaking beneath his feet and the sound of commotion echoing down the stairs.

The Wilting Oak Inn sat off one of the side streets in Geowm, the northern haven for criminals and ruffians who did not want to head south to the mage's city. Filled with gambling, brothels, thieves, and smugglers, it sat cradled as the last major city before heading either north or east into Kiamel Po or south into Paraduo.

Coming down the steps, he spied out the night's crowd. Standing behind the bar, the Kiamel Posian immigrant who ran the tavern, Toantoan Li was a wisp of a man, with a temper so anger-filled that one of his own employees had tried to bash him over the head with a mug the night before. They missed by the good grace of his larger cousin.

Gnik went and sat at the bar. The almond-red-skin man with his squinted eyes looked at him. "You look sick. Want a drink?"

"I wouldn't sit here if I didn't want a drink," Gnik said, looking down the bar toward the door.

Toan laughed and moved to grab a mug. "You never know, some people like to talk to the barkeep. I hate those people. That's why I like you so much. You hate to talk."

"I just hate talking to you," Gnik said. "Your moustache and long black whiskers that hang past your chin. Looks like a cat's rotting tail. And to look at you, well, I guess I do feel sick." He looked at the man, who stared back.

Toantoan began to laugh so loudly the whole bar took note. Gnik joined in but not as enthusiastically. "You're a funny Gob, aren't you?"

He shrugged his shoulders. "I wouldn't know. You're the only one who laughs."

"There's your answer, then. If I laugh…" He cut off, his attention pulled away. Yelling across the room, he said, "Stop that right now. You're spilling the ale. I didn't hire you to dance. Pour it and move on."

A bar wench with dark brown hair tore away from an old drunk man who had accosted her with pinches. Toantoan Li did not care for his staff, only the ale. The barkeep left the bar; his yelling at the woman echoed across the room. It reminded Gnik of one of the plays held in Nowann. Entertainment like this drew a crowd.

The patrons of the bar erupted in laughter. Many came only to see these tirades. Having stayed in the tavern for several months, Gnik could not tell if these tirades were true madness or Toan knew exactly what brought people in.

The door opened and another Goblin came in and sat at the far end of the bar. He stared at him, trying to decide whether to find another tavern to drink at. He was not in the mood to swap tales with one of his own kind. Lucky for him, the Goblin seemed to be in the same spirits. He glanced at him and then looked away.

"Well, yellow eyes," stated Toantoan Li. He puckered his lips and gave Gnik a disapproving look. "So, you're here every night. Want a job? I don't think I can trust my fat, lazy cousin to work anymore."

Gnik glanced at the door, where the reddish-brown face of a large man stared back, shaking his head. "I think he heard you."

"No matter, he knows he's fat. Stupid cousin."

A shout from the door rang out: "Shut up, Toan."

"No, you shut up, Dedo you fat pig. I pay you every night and you let a woman in here who tried to hit me with one of my own mugs," Toan shouted back.

"You hired her," Dedo said, in a lower tone.

"See, yellow eyes, I need someone to keep peace. You're here, I'll pay."

"How much?" Gnik said, shaking his head to Dedo.

"Discount on room."

"Nah, I like my job," he said, before Toan could say more. He did not want to work for the crazy man. He held a good job with a gang of local thugs, swindling coin off travelers. He sold fake maps and gave them fake information about roads into Kiamel Po or Paraduo, where one could easily lose their way, or so they told them. The rumor started years earlier, and now every unsuspecting traveler heard the same.

"Stupid Gob. You're missing out," Toan said, pouring drinks and putting them on a tray.

"You know, I don't think I am," Gnik laughed. He did not mean to; it just came out. He expected Toan to erupt again, but he did not. He joined in the laughing.

Gnik liked the owner well enough, but working for such a nasty man would be a mistake. A glass of apple ale slid across the bar before he could ask for it. Around him, the tavern sang with life. Dark-haired bar wenches served the customers. Most were related to Toantoan in some way, whether a niece or sister, or even daughter. He did not seem to care much about them either, even when it came to the way the patrons treated them. Grabbing and groping seemed to be all right with him. However, breaking a glass brought on his rage. Once he forced his large cousin to break a man's arms for dropping a mug on the floor and not having the coin to pay for it.

Not the kind of day Gnik felt like dealing with. He distributed the maps and lies about the routes. Other members of the gang did the waylaying on the road. He pick-pocketed and stole a few things as well, but that was for his own gain. Just about everyone in the city did it.

Toan walked away again, and Gnik drank on. He glanced around again to see who the patrons were. The usual familiar faces, some travelers toward the front; he thought he overheard one speak of a contract. He saw a group of Rosenian soldiers in a dark corner and watched them for a moment, cautious as to their intent. None of them seemed to be paying him any mind, dressed in their shining chainmail and dark blue surcoats, the white rose sigil of the crown emblazoned on their chests. They were focused on a woman they had brought in from the street. To his left near the door, a group of men huddled in bright robes so white they seemed illuminated. They were members of Lights Touch; a guild focused on learning light magic and healing. They were always noticeable, as their robes never looked sullied by dirt or dust.

The only other caster in the tavern was a Shadow Mage. He sat four seats down at the bar, sipping on some black wine. He wore his guild's gray hooded cloak, with a circle on his back made of half black and half white. It represented a balance between light and dark magic. They were also known for their combat skills.

He shook with the cold. A brazier kept the tavern warm, but a bite of the chill still hung on him and would not let go. He found it too cool this far north, even in the warm months, and it annoyed him more the longer he stayed. Besides the ever-lingering cold to persuade his departure from the area, a price hung on his head. His act of murder stabbed at him, and his fear led to the paranoia that he might be discovered.

This far north, he served in Hornwild, the keep of the Blake House. He was stealing deerskins from their tanner and making a good profit, until the apprentice boy, Toby Guilhide, caught him. He liked the boy, but Toby threatened to tell the master tanner, so Gnik, in a flash of lightning and blood, threw him into a pot of boiling oil. He did not want to. It just happened, and so he fled. He wandered for a few weeks until he ended up here, in the Wilting Oak tavern.

He rubbed his eyes at the thought and took another deep swallow of ale.

He did not want to go south though. There were smaller prices on his head for pettier crimes, but there were more of them. Rumors of Goblins leaving Rosenia intrigued him, but at the same time he did not enjoy being among his own people.

"You know, Goblin, I like you. You pay for drinks, and don't keep a tab. I like that," Toan said, with a squint-eyed smile, having come back.

"The last thing I need is another person looking for me because I owe them coin," he said. He did not blame himself for all his crimes, he held himself as a decent person, until that night and the dream, until it entered his mind and began to make it rot like a worm-infested pumpkin.

He put his mug to his lips and chugged without stopping. It tasted like cinnamon spice. When he finished, Toan put another full mug on the bar. It became a regular thing. He watched lustily as a curvy serving girl with dark slanted eyes and dark hair balanced a tray of mugs on her head. Several of the patrons clapped their hands, while one clapped her on her rump and she almost dropped the tray.

A group of five dirt-covered men sat in a corner. They were from the iron mines and played a game with a hooded snake. The point of the game was for everyone to buy in with a certain amount of coin and put it in the middle near the snake. Then without getting struck, they began to pull out the coins one by one as fast as they could. If you pulled out more than you put in, then you were a winner. He thought you were a winner if you survived. He had played once, and when the snake struck at his hand, he barely pulled it away, so the venomous fangs went one on either side of one of his fingers, leaving scratches on the wooden table.

A few hours went by in the tavern, patrons came and went, then in came a stranger, a Black Paladin. He wore full black plate armor, except for his head. Young in the face, with blond hair and light green eyes, he drew the attention of everyone. Tuom, Toantoan's giant of a nephew, especially for Kiamel Posian standards, stopped the Black Paladin at the door and asked him to remove the war pick at his side. With Dedo, he handled bouncing duties. Gnik heard the knight tell someone in the street to watch the horses, after throwing the weapon to them.

The whole tavern stopped to watch and small whispers began to flutter around. Not often did one see a Black Paladin, especially in their customary full black plate armor. It seemed to be crafted so anywhere it could, it came to a sharp point.

With a large, boyish smile, the Paladin sat next to Gnik. "How do you do?" Gnik only nodded back, but that seemed enough for the man in black. "I've been traveling for days, and I've had a thirst for some good mead. I hope this is a good place for that. I came from the coast, having sailed from Nyoko, far to the west across the Crescent Sea."

Gnik did not care about the knight's travels or to even talk to him. Still, he listened or pretended to listen, knowing it would not be good to make a man of this status mad. He almost forced himself to smile.

The Black Paladins were rumored to be a dangerous group of mercenaries or adventurers. They could use bits of dark magic and at the same time hack you to pieces with their scythes or great two-handed axes. A small group settled in Rosenia, but not many. Rumors claimed there were many in the islands of Rovelle and further to the west across the Crescent Sea.

That must be the Nyoko place he referred to.

"One of my brothers and I are headed to Paraduo. We seek the famous Galvorn smiths." The man talked too openly for Gnik. Speaking of your destination could get you killed, especially in Geowm. The next thing you knew, you could be ambushed in the streets by thugs and recognize them as the men you had broken bread and wine with. Then again, who would be stupid enough to attack Black Paladins?

Apparently, himself, as he began to wonder if he could snatch the paladin's coin purse. It must have been the ale thinking.

"We're going to see if we can have some things made by them, as it's the only place in the world that can forge Galvorn."

"Galvorn, that's a pricey metal. Is that what your armor is made of?" Gnik said, eyeing it, but straining his face to not give away how he coveted it.

"No, no, too expensive to have a full set of Galvorn armor. At least it's too much for me. I'll be having a new war pick made.

111

Here, look at this knife. Be careful of the blade though, it's black Ashnon," the young paladin said, pulling it out.

"Black Ashnon?"

"Sorry, yes, I don't know why I said that. Galvorn is black Ashnon."

Toantoan eyed the knife but said nothing. Gnik took the beautiful shining, black-bladed, black-hilted knife off the bartop. He noticed how light and balanced it felt. Pushing on the blade, it flexed, and when he dropped it to the top to see if it would stick, he jumped when it pushed into the bar a full two inches toward his legs.

"Gnik, you ruin my bar," Toantoan said, when he saw it. "No weapons."

"Sorry, Toan, here. I didn't know that would happen," Gnik said, throwing a silver petal to the small man, who still looked angry, but said no more as he put the coin in his pocket.

"It's rare," the Black Paladin said. "One of the strongest metals in Sancta. Ashnon to most, Adamant to the Dwaling. Ashnon can be forged in several colors, but most have to be inlaid or enameled."

Gnik still stared at the knife in the bar, listening but not.

"Black is only forged in Paraduo. Just as strong, but lighter than all other Ashnon. More valuable, rarer, a secret the Paraduans will not part with. The Bohatilinga and the Darei long ago tried to pay for the secret, but the Paraduans would not share it. Now it's an expensive treasure."

"Bohatilinga?"

"You don't know the Bohatilinga? They're the rich sect of the Dwaling, who try to control much of the mining and metals," the young knight said.

"It is beautiful," Gnik said, still staring at the blade. "You mean to get more?"

"Yes, just my war pick. I've saved a lot for it. My companion and I will make our way to Kageria, the Paraduan capital, and barter with the smiths."

The Goblin nodded for a moment as a man and several of his drunken companions entered the tavern. He looked at them in horror, and so did anyone who lived in the city, as they were well-known bullies.

Large, and leading the group, stood Brock Ersman, who liked to frequent the taverns of the city looking for fights. He towered over Gnik. If someone told him Brock Ersman had some troll blood, he would have believed it. The man's face did not seem normal. His hair shaved closely, except for a short spot of beard growing on his chin. His eyes were set so deep in his skull they seemed to be black and hollow. It was one of two reasons he carried the nickname: Black Eyes Brock. The other reason was he liked to give people black eyes, along with broken noses, crushed skulls, and shattered ribs. Some survived and some did not.

For weeks, Gnik had avoided any confrontation with the man, crossing streets when he could. Until now, the man never came to this tavern. Even the large Tuom and Dedo feared him.

Brock killed men in fights and several others just because he wanted to. The rule in Geowm was, if you were willing to get in a fight, you were willing to die in it. This and apathy kept the Rosenian soldiers from arresting him. It always seemed to be the other guy who started the fight, or so said Brock's companions when asked.

"I'm going on break," Tuom said, getting up and heading out, not waiting for an answer. Gnik saw the Rosenian soldiers get up

113

and make their way out as well, their eyes never leaving the large brute. Were they calling for help or running in fear? He worried tonight might be his night. He tried not to make eye contact, but he could hear heavy footsteps coming his way, mixed with the loud laughter and scoffing of the companions.

A deep booming voice sounded right behind his shoulder. He reached down toward his boot for his knife, trying to act as if he did not hear. He would kill this man before giving him a chance if he must. Unsure how many of the companions he would be able to take out, he would make a go at it and die fighting.

"I heard there was a..." *Here it comes*, Gnik thought. What luck at being a Goblin. "A Black Paladin in the Oak tonight," Brock finished.

Gnik almost fell off his stool in relief, except for the flash of lightning and spike of momentary disgust. He really did not mind slitting this man's throat, but he liked to do it when nobody watched so he did not catch the blame.

"I ain't never fought a Black Paladin before. Seems now's as good a time as any to test my strength."

The young man did not seem to be listening. Smaller than Brock by a lot, and almost smaller than Gnik, he did not budge. Toantoan looked at the Black Paladin, shaking his head, no doubt fearing for his bar.

Brock began to roar. "What's wrong with you, black fool? Have you no tongue? I'm Brock Black Eyes and I'm talking to you. Are you craven?"

Others from the tavern began to get up and move to the door, while the curious stood to give room and watch.

"I have nothing to say to you, sir," the young knight replied, still not turning around to look at Brock. It was probably a good thing too, as the brute stood about a shoulder and head higher than him.

"So, he does speak, good. I hoped that the only noise I heard from you wouldn't be your screams. Maybe you're too afraid to talk to your betters. Well, I've plenty to say to you. We're going to fight for any reason I can think of. I can use the 'You're sitting in my stool, or you smell, or your mother's a whore,' reasons, but we'll still end up fighting."

The companions, like so many bullies' companions, just stood and laughed. More and more people exited the tavern, even the Lights Touch mages were gone now.

The young knight put down a few copper petals and thanked Toantoan for the drinks. He tried to get up but then Brock picked him up, armor and all, and tossed him toward the front door, onto a table, breaking it into hundreds of splintered pieces. As the knight got up with a calm demeanor, Brock picked him up again and threw him right out the door.

When any fight or brawl occurred, Gnik felt inclined to go watch. Maybe he could swipe a few purses while people focused on it.

Out on the dark street, a small crowd formed, most of which were drunkards and whores, but there were members of various guilds, and the Black Paladin's companion. The young knight stood, and Gnik saw him waving off his friend and the weapon he tried to hand him. Brock stood in front of him with his fists up. Silence stretched across the onlookers.

The longer they waited, the more people began to murmur. One of the horses whickered and Gnik saw the other Black Paladin standing near the horses. He noticed black platemail tied to one of the mounts.

Brock then charged. The young knight dodged to the side and punched the brute in the face, but Brock did not react except for the small stream of blood that started to come down his nose. Broken but unbothered, the monstrous man yelled in rage. He charged again; his roar filled the busy street, and the knight kicked him in the stomach and then tripped him. With a great thud, Brock hit the packed ground and yelled in anger. Some of the crowd stepped back.

This went on for another minute, a pause, a charge, and every time Brock got bloodier and bloodier. His anger now overflowed to the point where he picked up a random woman from the crowd and threw her screaming at the paladin. Using some sort of dark magic spell that amazed the crowd, the Black Paladin slowed her flight, caught her and helped her to her feet. The paladin's act shamed the giant in front of the huddled onlookers. The brute charged again, but this time the smaller man sidestepped and kicked the big man as hard as he could in the side of the knee.

Brock stumbled, angry and limping. He reached in his coat and drew a dirk. If the authorities were coming, they were taking their time. Brock took out his dirk and so did his companions. Gnik had seen it a few times before.

The other Black Paladin came up and handed the first his war pick. Two on five, not exactly fair numbers. Gnik was not sure how strong they really were. The first held his own, but they were outnumbered. The second only wore traveling clothes.

As the fight began, flashes of light struck in his mind, disgust and anger flowed through him. He walked straight up to the bully closest to him, took his boot knife out, and slit the man's throat. Blood spurted, and the bully grabbed at his neck. It pooled on the street; lightning flashed in Gnik's eyes, and he heard screaming and horses; blood rained. It flashed again, and he stood back in the street.

One of Brock's minions flew at the first Black Paladin. His dirk grazed off the armor and the young knight laughed. Using the flat side of the war pick, he hit the bully on the head and dropped him to the ground, crumpling like a ragdoll. The second Black Paladin wielded a club with metal spikes.

Around the other two of Brock's bullies grew a bright green light. It illuminated the street and the audience, watching in wonder. Dread covered the attackers' faces; their movements grew slow. When one tried to swing his dirk, the second Black Paladin simply took a calm step back to avoid it, but then in a flash jumped forward and hit the two men, knocking them unconscious. The gathered crowd began to laugh. Brock and the first knight stood facing each other.

The second Black Paladin made his way toward Gnik, a smile on his face. The crowd edged back even further than when he had just opened the bully's throat. This paladin looked as young as the other, except short brown hair sprouted from his head. He wore a brown leather jerkin with a gray wool jacket over it, black riding pants and riding boots. With a strange rolling accent Gnik did not recognize, he said, "Thank you, my good sir, you have our appreciation. I wasn't exactly sure what to do about him. It is difficult holding even two with my spell. They really fought to get out of it, and probably would have, given more time."

Gnik just smiled and nodded. He did not speak much, especially compared to non-Goblin folk. The most he spoke lately to a Human, or anyone, were the conversations with the innkeeper, because he kept getting drunk at the bar.

117

When Gnik looked over at the two, fear sat in Brock's shadowed, dark eyes. The Black Paladin knew it, the crowd knew it, and Brock himself knew it. He was not the smartest of Goblins, but he knew who not to pick a fight with. He looked at the man he had sliced lying dead in the street. It looked like he had drowned in a black pool.

As the crowd began to laugh at Brock's fear, it stoked his anger even more. The beast of a man knew he was outmatched, but either the embarrassment or the drunkenness forced him to charge.

He swung his dirk at the young knight several times, and the small man dodged it, but then Brock did something the knight did not expect. He went to his knee and threw dirt into the knight's eyes. Blinking and reeling back, Brock tackled the Black Paladin. The huge man seemed to swallow him with his girth, even in his armor. Gnik watched as the brute took small cuts from the sharp points of the black plate. It did not stop him. The young paladin took a hit in the face and dropped his war pick. Brock reached one hand around his neck and began to squeeze, lifting his dirk for the stab.

That was when the second Black Paladin headed over to help, but before he got there Gnik noticed the first's eyes stared with fear but also seemed calm. The paladin hit the palm of his gauntlet on the ground and four spike-like protrusions shot out around the knuckles. With his last bit of consciousness, the Black Paladin swung his fist and plunged the four spikes deep into Brock's face.

They were not long spikes, but the giant screamed in pain, blood pouring from the holes. He dropped his dirk, reeling from the agony. In one swift movement, the second knight kicked the war pick toward his comrade. The hold around his neck loosened, he gasped, grabbed it, swung it around, and embedded it deep in Brock's temple.

It took the help of the second Paladin to get the dead weight off his companion. Black Eyes Brock would no longer bother anyone. Gnik almost felt bad... almost. The brute had made a terrible mistake forcing this fight. Numbers were not everything, he supposed. It was a lesson he would not forget anytime soon—but then again, he never really forgot anything.

The crowd had already dispersed, save for the few sneaks who were picking Brock's pockets. Some even kicked the dead man.

The two men came over to Gnik, sweating and breathing hard. "Ah yes, the Goblin from the bar. Thank you for your assistance. I hope this doesn't put you in harm's way. I'm Liam, and this, my friend, is Dylan."

Gnik nodded to Dylan again. "No problem at all," Gnik said, lying in that he only really cared about them bothering him. "Their ruffian antics grew tiresome. They've been bothering people around the tavern district for some time."

"Well, if there's anything we can do for you, let us know," Dylan said, rubbing some dirt off his jacket. "We're in your debt."

At first, Gnik thought of gold as payment, but then something else came to mind. Maybe his time here had reached its end. "Which way are you dark fellows headed again?"

Chapter 8

Andross lay blindfolded, his hands bound behind his back, until two gripping arms forced him up and out of the carriage. He stumbled onto a cobblestone street. The cloth tied around his eyes and head was so tight it made it hard to hear anything.

He had been ambushed while putting Cleon up in the stable near his home above the baker's shop. He had thought something amiss when the usual pock-faced stable boy did not run out to meet him. Instead of waiting, though, he had decided to put his friend up himself.

He had closed the stall door and rubbed the warhorse's neck when it gave a start. He turned just as three large men hidden in the dark jumped him. One grabbed at each of his arms, and the third went straight for his sword. Caught unaware with his guard down, he barely struggled. He was right across from his home, Mahley, and in the stable he frequented almost every day. He scolded himself for his foolishness.

The two attackers who had grabbed at his arms had forced him down to the ground and bound his hands with rope. He had fought and shouted; the rope had chewed at his wrists. He had wanted one of the stable hands or anyone near to hear him, but one of the men kept saying, "Calm yourself, My Lord, we don't mean to harm you. It will go easier for us all if you relax."

The next thing he knew, a piece of cloth had pulled tightly around his eyes, and a gag forced him to stop yelling. He felt himself hoisted up and thrust into a carriage. The ride in complete silence seemed several hours long. He had tried to worm his way toward his dagger, but a deep voice had said, "None of that, My

Lord, it won't be necessary." He tried to ask questions through the gag, but it did no good. Though the ride seemed long, he knew they were still in the city; he could make out the sound of cobblestones as they rode.

Now out of the carriage, they hoisted him up some steps and pulled him through a doorway, having shifted his angle to get through. Once through, his steps echoed down a long hallway. His wrists ached and his legs felt numb.

"Stand here and wait, please," the deep voice said again. The only thing stopping him from trying to run or fight was the idea that if they wanted him dead, they would have done it in the barn.

He could hear them moving around him. He heard what sounded like his sword being put down on a wooden table.

Coming back to him, the deep voice said, "My Lord, I'm going to remove your blindfold first, then your gag. Please don't fight or scream. You'll know soon enough why you're here."

He blinked as light flooded his eyes. The gag came off next, and as it did his eyes began to clear, showing him the room. In front of him stood a dark doorway leading down a staircase. There were two lit lamps next to the opening that hung from sculpted walls. He turned and saw he stood in a large circular room, with more lamps and doorways. It felt like a grand foyer to a great building. A rug lay on the floor; its intricate designs seemed to be of Nyokian artistry. Orange, blue, and vibrant green created a symmetrical and circular design.

He noticed his sword behind him on a large table. Two large, masked men stood guarding it and the doorway that he assumed led back out. Neither looked at him, but both wore armored hauberks and carried swords at their hips.

121

Turning to the man who had taken off his gag, he saw another masked brute in the same steel hauberk and white breeches. He did not wear a weapon. "Don't ask any questions. I can't answer them. Walk through the doorway, down the steps. When you reach the bottom, another one of my brothers will be there and he'll explain everything to you. Have faith, sir knight."

Facing the long dark, he hesitated. Whatever mystery lay before him, he was not the type to want to be a part of it. He thought about trying to make a fight of it, but with his hands still bound he knew it would be futile. *What do they want?* Other than the kidnapping and bonds, they had not harmed him. No beating, no punches to the gut, not even a cruel word; it made the feeling of threat subside a little. He knew it could still turn sour, preserved for a worse torture to come. However, his options were limited.

The man near him undid his sword belt and took his dagger. He also checked his boots for a weapon and found a knife he kept hidden there. Andross watched him put it on the table with his sword. "You may head down, My Lord. Your things will be well taken care of."

He gave a stern look, but the man did not seem to notice. He stood tall and strong; his chest filled, and his muscles tensed. The three other men in the room were near giants to him, much like the warriors of the northern Norte Tribe. He shook his head, releasing his will to fight, and headed through the dark doorway.

With the first few steps, cool air hit his face. When his eyes readjusted, he could see the steps and walls of stone, and a light at the bottom. On the way down, he kept trying to think of where he might be and how to get himself out of it. His heart pounded; every step seemed to be burying him, taking him deeper into the earth.

"Hello, My Lord," a jovial voice said when Andross reached the light at the bottom. He turned and saw a smaller man in the same hauberk, white breeches and black boots as the three up the stairs. The man's face looked thin, with a sharp chin and clean-shaven. He smiled, taking him by the arm, and led him down a curving hallway.

"I am Xavi, Lord Andross. I'll be explaining your presence in a moment, but first let me say, you've been exceedingly easy to deal with. Often, we have difficulty bringing people here. It is the price that comes with trying to kidnap someone." The man chuckled.

Andross nodded, looking him over. "Why am I here? Where is here?"

"Soon enough, My Lord, soon enough," Xavi said, pushing his black hair to the side. "And let me say you have a most exquisite sword. That legendary blade is a piece of craftsmanship Sancta may never see again. Don't worry, it won't be harmed." He held his finger up, his grin glowing through in the dim light.

"Good, it's important to me," Andross answered, looking the smaller man over. "I have three swords, it's easily the most valuable and most battle sturdy."

"Yes, I know. Forged by the greatest Dwaling smith, Ambra, and his closest friend, the greatest Dareian smith, Nenoli, from a piece of ore that fell from the heavens, the color of red flowing blood—or so the myth says," Xavi added with a wink.

"The sword is real enough," Andross said, and then asked, "What is your intent here, is it to kill me?"

"Oh, My Lord, please." Xavi laughed and then said, "That all depends on you. As for it being me to do it, very unlikely."

The threat in Andross' mind rose again, but as it did, they reached the end of the curved hallway and walked into another large, circular room, even larger than the first. He blinked again. Many lamps and torches hung along its walls, where they rose to what seemed three stories above.

One story up from the floor where they were now standing, held open arches encircling the room. Standing and watching were over thirty figures, all in light gray robes with silver and white trim, like fog tied in silver string. They were only separated by pillars and three statues of warriors holding different swords: a great sword, a scimitar, and a serpentine. He guessed they might be from the Healer's Guild or Lights Touch, or even mages from the White Paladins, but they were all masked with a silver, shining mask in the face of a fox. All eyes watched him.

Xavi pulled a knife and Andross stepped back, raising his hands in defense. "Not to worry, My Lord—only to cut your bonds."

"What's going on? Who are these people?" he said, looking for a way out. The only escape he could see was the doorway he and Xavi had entered through, and a stairway descending from the second floor, where all the figures stood motionless, their mirrored faces reflecting the torchlight in an orange haze.

"Good. The questions can now be answered," the small man said with a laugh and a dance. "My Lord Andross, welcome."

In a singular echoing voice, the rest of the masked figures shouted, "Welcome."

"My Lord, you've been summoned here to the house of the Gray Foxes to be tested as a swordmaster."

"The Gray Foxes, who are they? And tested how as a swordmaster?" Andross said, backing up again and looking at the masks around him. He balled his hands into fists. "I don't understand. This flair for the dramatic is long past my patience."

"Simply put," Xavi said, smiling, as if it were a game, "we're a secret guild made up of many of the greatest sword fighters in Rosenia—and some neighboring lands. As a well-known warrior and hero, mentioned for your prowess with a blade, and being the bearer of the great Ambra Nenoli, you've been chosen for a trial by combat to see if you're worthy to be one of us."

"What if I don't want to be one of you? What if I don't like this whole situation?" Andross said in a harsh tone. He grew angrier at the idea he was there to prove himself in a sword fight. In his mind, competitions of might were not how a man proved himself. He loved to fight, he loved competition, but for him it was about two things: surviving and training to survive better.

Xavi went silent for a moment. "My Lord, please be patient with us. This is a secret brotherhood of noblemen, sworn to the sword. You may ask to leave if you want, but if you do, we will kill you."

Andross stared at the small man, sizing him up. "You'll kill me?" He nodded and pursed his lips. "I'm ready, then."

"Come now. As I said, this is a secret order. The knowledge of us may never be known, our whereabouts never found," Xavi said, still smiling as if he had not just threatened Andross' life.

"So, I'm here against my will? I'll be made to fight and prove my skill, because if I choose not to fight, you'll kill me? That sounds more than reasonable," Andross said, shaking his head and rolling his eyes.

"Listen first," Xavi said, sighing, the smile gone.

"Wait, what if I don't prove my skill?" he replied, his eyes focusing on the smaller man.

"If you fail, you'll die," Xavi answered, mirth returning to his face.

"So, against my will, I must fight to survive?"

"Yes, but isn't a fight for survival always against your will? Please listen first, My Lord."

It rang more a question than a demand, so he lowered his fists and stood straight.

Xavi continued: "Under painstaking study we watched you and learned of your great skill. This kidnapping is only by a long process of choosing. If you live up to your standards, then you'll be a member, one of our brothers. If by all accounts your stories are fabricated, or what we've seen in you is misplaced and you lose the fight, then you'll die. We'll mourn another mistaken loss but killing you after you lose is for our protection. Should you have children, a family, they would be taken care of by a secret benefactor," Xavi said, without remorse and in the straightest of tones.

"This is ridiculous. You kidnap people, force them to fight, force them to win or die, but you're telling me if they fail you regret their loss?" Andross began pacing, his eyes flicking to the figures in gray standing above.

"Part of being a great sword fighter is understanding your opponent," Xavi said, with a sense of seriousness. The only time he sounded serious so far. "Finding the right candidates is a tool that must be sharpened. We aren't perfect, but we're getting better at finding those we deem right for our cause."

Andross stopped pacing and looked around, and then yelling up to the figures said, "Fine, I'll play this mock game. Let no one say I wasn't willing to fight for my life."

Xavi looked at the figures too and then said, "Good. Three swords will be brought to you. You may choose any of the three.

You cannot use your own. Fear not, your opponent will not be using his own sword either."

He heard movement in the hallway they had entered through. "You'll also be allowed to choose from three of our members. You cannot see them, but you can ask a few simple questions about them. Your choice will help us determine your quality," Xavi continued.

"What must I do to win?" Andross said, looking straight in the eyes of the smaller man.

"What did you have to do to win before?" Xavi answered.

Andross nodded, his face contorted in anger. He wondered how many of these people he could cut through once they gave him a sword. If they were all swordmasters, then it would probably not be many, if any at all.

Three men came in from the hall, each carrying a sword. The men were all dressed in gray with their silver masks, but each sword was different. The first sword's blade curved, a saber with a guarded hilt, plain in design.

"You may pick them up and feel them, My Lord," Xavi said, standing to the side and watching. "You may also ask questions about your possible three opponents."

"Who are these three people?" Andross asked, looking at the second sword, a rapier with a long thrusting blade. Lighter than the saber, he preferred something with a little more slashing power.

"I can't tell you who they are, but I can tell you one is a lord, one is a knight, and one is a farmer," Xavi said, counting on his fingers each time. "I can tell you one of them has a family that depends on him, one has only a wife, and one lives alone."

"Can you tell me who belongs to which?" Andross said, picking up the third sword. A bastard sword, hand and a half, double-edged, and steel forged, very similar to his own. He knew a strong sword when he saw it, but it was nothing compared to Ambra Nenoli.

Luckily, the reason he kept the other two swords, one passed down through his family and one bestowed on him as a Knight of the Hawk, was to practice with the different weights. No intelligent fighter would let himself get used to such a light sword as Ambra Nenoli. The change in weight could alter the fight enough for him to lose his life.

"Good choice, My Lord, and no, I can't tell you who belongs to whom," Xavi said, as the three figures walked away.

"What sword does each man wield?" Andross asked. The sword a man wielded said a lot about him and about his fighting style. He eyed each one, contemplating every movement, every lean, how they carried their weight.

"The knight uses a sword like your own. The lord uses an epee, and the farmer uses a short sword." Xavi said.

Andross spent most of his time practicing against other knights. The epee was a faster blade, used for thrusting, but he could overpower it. As for the short sword, he would have a reach advantage on it. However, if the other was a master, as they all were supposed to be, then the farmer could maneuver his attacks inside, and he could lose due to the farmer's mobility.

"Have you made a decision, My Lord?" Xavi said, beginning to move away from him.

"One more question: who is the best of the three?" Andross asked.

"My Lord, I'm not at liberty to say. I haven't fought any of them, not truly. We spar sometimes, but never a real fight amongst ourselves. There is the trial, or the alternative way into the brotherhood. I found myself in a random duel with another master and killed him. That is as fair at it gets," Xavi said, standing a little straighter.

"That's possible to do? Couldn't that let in those who may spread the word of your order?"

"Sometimes we don't invite them in. That way we don't have an issue with the more unsavory types." Xavi scratched his chin and smiled. "So, do you choose the lord, the knight, or the farmer?"

Andross shook his head again and waved the sword around, loosening up his arm. Thinking the farmer had a family, the lord might be married with a family as well, and the knight might or might not have a family, he said. "I choose the man with no family."

Xavi's eyes widened. "So be it."

Movement from the second floor echoed and his eyes focused on a robed figure who started down the stairs. Once at the bottom, Xavi helped them both disrobe, but the mask stayed on. He watched as a longsword hung at the hip of the armored figure.

Xavi moved up the steps to the top and pulled a mask over his face. The knight loosened his arm and body, then stepped forward and said, "You honor me, Lord Andross. You may begin when ready."

"It doesn't seem fair that you know me, and I don't know you," Andross said, regretting the situation and wishing to be home with Mahley. He might kill this man, but then this man, a swordmaster, might very well kill him. He knew his abilities were strong with a blade but fighting in battles with many foes changed the tactics drastically from a one-on-one fight.

"You'll know my name when you win… if you win," said the masked man, still shaking his body to wake his muscles.

Not knowing how to take his opponent's words, he bowed his head. His heart pounded in his chest and sweat pooled on his brow.

129

Cool air drafted in the dark circular room, but he burned up. He looked at the sword, turning it in his hand, and began to strafe in a circle. His opponent mimicked the movement. "Begin," he said.

Wanting to test the knight, he came on quickly. Their swords clanged on each other, sending an echo through the open room. He noticed the knight used the hedgehog defense, keeping him back with small jabs and parries. So, he mimicked it, hoping to draw the man in.

"Ah, copying my hedgehog, interesting. Then I'll come at you with viper style," said the man, coming in hard. However, the man did not go viper. Expecting two attacks at his mid, Andross parried the first and spun out to attack the man where the second should be. However, the second mid attack did not come, and he narrowly blocked an attack from above.

"You should never listen to your opponent. They may try to trick you," the other man said.

With an arcing blow, Andross put the man off balance and then came underneath. The man sent out a kick that pushed him back and into a defensive form. The knight came on. Too often he fought one on one for sparring. He needed to change his mentality; he needed to kill the man.

He parried a thrust and made an attack at the man's right side. When the other man pushed it away, he moved in close and sent out his fist, punching the man in the stomach. The man jolted back from the hit but did not seem stunned for long.

A flurry of attacks came on and Andross defended against them. He countered an attack with a slice at the shoulder of the man, the blade only cutting across the man's armored arm.

"Very nice, My Lord, but a touch for a touch," said the man, coming on again but breathing hard and sending a graze across

Andross' chainmailed knee. "You must be faster to best me, My Lord."

At that, Andross began to move faster, spurred on with the challenge. Taught by his father, and many of the great tutors at Knights' Keep as a boy, his mind let go of the hundreds of lessons; he needed his experience to be in control. He also needed speed; it could neutralize any situation if one had enough of it. He moved like a blur. He loved being quick.

Turning his body into a wavering tree in the wind, he sent out swift attacks to every area of the other man. He moved fast enough to attack and then move away before dealing with a counter. He did this for several repetitions, nicking at the man's armor. When he thought the man caught on, he faked, causing the knight to lunge at him and go off balance. Andross shot his body into him, knocking him over.

In a flash, Andross' sword came down and bounced off the dirt floor, where the man fell. He rolled out of the way, and attacking from the ground sent a stab up, but Andross moved and knocked the thrust away.

In a string of careful attacks, he came on the knight again, not letting him up. Before long, he knocked the man's sword from his hand with a strong hit at his wrist that even with armor would send a wave of pain. The sword landed on the ground and Andross kicked it away. The man lunged at him to try and knock him away, but he expected the movement and knocked him back down. He put his sword to the man's throat, readying for the finishing blow. Soon this farce would be over; he only needed to thrust.

"I'll have your name now," Andross said, breathing hard. His heart burned in him. The man had proved very skilled. He had never sparred in such a flurry, with a change of so many styles back and forth.

The man reached up and pulled his mask away, breathing hard. "You already know me, My Lord."

Andross stared at a very familiar face and immediately pulled his sword back. "Prince Owen. You're not just some knight," he said, looking into the fair-skinned face of the man. His dark brown hair matched his thin moustache and beard; his eyes were a light brown almost red. "Xavi said I chose the knight, but you're a lord."

"We lied. Life is unpredictable, my friend," the prince said, smiling.

Andross stepped back. "I can't kill you. I won't. The queen, if she ever found out, she'd have me flayed—worse even, fed to the rats under the city after being flayed."

"She'd do worse, but you don't have to kill me. I yield, unless you don't want to be a swordmaster and you yield," the man said, now chuckling. Echoes shot through the chamber as all the robed figures laughed.

"I can't yield. Xavi told me I would be killed to keep your secret," Andross said, the sword still pointing at the man but wavering in his confusion.

"That, too, is a lie. We only say it to make sure to get a real fight from you. As you've won, you now have a choice to be one of us in our noble cause or to reject us and walk away, though sworn to secrecy. Here, help me up," the prince said, reaching out his hand as Xavi came down the steps.

"It's all true, Lord Andross," Xavi said, "we're not a brotherhood of killers and kidnappers, but a brotherhood of fighters whose goal it is to keep Rosenia strong. We mentioned swordmasters to keep you interested."

Andross lowered his sword and reached out. "I can't say I wouldn't have killed you, but I'm happy I don't have to. I'm very confused though. Lies and kidnapping." Angered, he held it in. "This isn't a pleasant experience."

The surrounding figures laughed. "In its way, it's not meant to be. To put someone on edge, push them to the limit with fear of certain death, and then see how they react to it. What choices will they make? We're looking for those who would make the right decisions."

"Please forgive me. If I knew, I never would have fought you," Andross pleaded, his stomach in knots at having almost killed Prince Owen, brother to Queen Sehra, brother-in-law to the king.

"Come now, Andross, we're long past that. You didn't have a choice," Prince Owen said. "It's the reason for the masks. Don't worry. Though possible, it would've been rare for this to have ended in death," said Owen, hitting him on the shoulder. "Now, you've not answered us. Will you join our Order and help us in our fight to keep our realm strong, brave, and courageous?"

"You make it sound so heroic, though I'm still not sure of your true purpose," Andross answered, closing his eyes for a moment and taking in a deep breath.

"As one of us, a Gray Fox, we take it upon ourselves to keep Rosenia and our allies strong," said Xavi, taking his sword. "We task ourselves with teaching others to be good fighters and warriors, not with just weapons, though they are a focus. We train those we can, and test those who train. In a time of great prosperity and little war, people can grow weak and lazy, content with harmonious living. We keep our eyes open to the things that might endanger the realm. We try to stop the atrophy that can bring great kingdoms to their knees by teaching people to be strong. It's happened in the past. This is something you do already, Sir Andross. You know a kingdom's greatest threat is itself."

Andross pondered the situation. He paced again, feeling Xavi's and Prince Owen's eyes on him. "It's true this is something I worry about. After my friend's death, I worry for the kingdom's safety. Sancta is growing every day, its prosperity overflowing." The realization that this secret order did not represent some bloodthirsty death sport gave him a new perspective on it. He found their tactics in recruitment barbaric, and overly dramatic, but their purpose held sound for him. Knowing a current member made it easier for him to answer.

"I accept. I'll help." While looking at the approving smiles of the two, he wondered what would be asked of him. For now, he would keep his wall of skepticism up.

At his acceptance, the other figures removed their masks and gathered around him. In unison a chant went up, filling the room with echoes, "Gray Fox, Gray Fox, Gray Fox…"

Chapter 9

The streetlamps glowed as the sun set over the high sharp spires of the city of Faor, the towers of a peaceful city, a haven for many of the rich. Soldiers marched in unison, their shields bearing a golden city amidst an azure lake. People crowded the streets, though shop owners and merchants closed, and children scurried home, their faces covered in dirt and smelling like sweat. They laughed and played with joy, jumping and screaming.

Aija watched a small group as they fought with sticks like swords. They laughed as one child fell to his knees, feigning death. She tightened her lips, wanting it to be humorous. If only death were so clean.

She took out her own fake sword and pretended to stab out at the world. She laughed and then waited for the soldiers to be well out of sight before she exited the shadows and walked to a building, illuminated from its windows by firelight. As she reached the door, the hair on her neck stood. She felt someone stride up next to her and her hand moved to where she hid a dagger in the folds of her sunflower-yellow dress.

"Lady Anya, you're back from your trip. How was it?" said a smiling, clean-shaven Edwin. He had deep creases in his face that exaggerated his cheeks. He stood taller, puffing out his chest, when she looked toward him. His light brown hair combed over to one side, neat and proper, he feigned confidence.

"Oh, Edwin, you startled me," Aija said, moving her hand to her chest, pretending to catch her breath. She truly had been startled. For a split second, her street name, Anya, had caught her off guard.

"I'm sorry, M'Lady, I saw you cross the street and didn't want to yell for you," Edwin said.

Aija knew he lied. It was not near as much happenstance as the young man made it out to be. Every time she returned from one of her uncle's trips, he hid waiting. She could only blame herself.

Years earlier, she had bloodied another young man or boy senseless for trying to steal from an old lady. Edwin watched the scuffle and from that point became enamored with her. He had failed to help the old lady when she had succeeded.

"Are you busy, Anya? I'm glad you're back. Can we speak?" he said, his face flushing as he tried to straighten his long brown coat.

"I'm only just back now. I'm sorry, but at the moment I'm a bit busy. I'll call on you if I get any time to myself before I'm off again. You know my uncle's business is a busy one." She smiled, looking into his eyes, eyes that in no way stirred the fires within her. He was a nice boy, kind and chivalrous, but his gaunt face and lanky body did little for her. Nor did she really have time for his adolescent infatuation—she did not have time for anything other than her duties.

"And, Edwin, please, you must stop sneaking up on me. It's quite disheartening," Aija said, trying to come off startled.

"Well, then as always, Lady Anya, I'll wait for you and do my best to make my presence known." Edwin nodded his head in respect, a look of defeat on his face, but still determined. He turned and walked away.

Aija waited for his footfalls to be out of earshot before she knocked on the door. She felt sorry for him. It would never be. The poor lad had just chosen badly.

Before the second knock landed, the door flung open, spilling light into the street. She lifted the hem of her dress and stepped inside the storefront of the tailor shop. Cloth reams of hundreds of colors and designs were piled around the room. A thick, luxurious rug covered the floor, just as colorful as the fabric. Mannequins wearing some of the kingdom's current fashions were on display.

In the middle of the store, an old man who wore thick glasses, his skin worn and wrinkled, sewed at a large table. He did not look up but only kept sewing. She smiled at the smell of the place and at seeing him.

The door shut behind her, and as she turned, she heard someone speak next to her: "So again, he waits for you. He waits every day. Seems he has little to do but wait for you. I worry that if he watches this place too much, he'll begin to suspect it's more than a tailor's shop." The voice flowed smoothly and silkily; every word made the fine hair on her neck stand again, but different from minutes earlier. "He's a danger. Maybe I should talk to him."

She turned and looked at Arnus. With his chin pulled in tight and leaning against the wall, his light blond hair hung, framing his smooth face. His deep blue eyes were penetrating, making her uneasy. Taking a deep breath and with a straight face she said, "That won't be necessary. Edwin is just a simple boy, with simple fancies. He has no clue that this place is anything more than it is. Don't be foolish and draw attention."

"Maybe so, but he also annoys me to my core," Arnus spat back, turning and walking toward the old man at the table. "He's like a buzzing fly, and I love killing flies."

Aija stood still for a moment, waiting for the old man, her supposed uncle, to say something. "Lock the door, young one," said the old man, his voice hollow, flowing out in complete calmness. "This day's work is over."

She turned the bolt until it clicked and then went to close the shutters. She heard Arnus say, "Maybe she's right. Since the boy seems to be a halfwit, he couldn't possibly figure out what goes on here." He chuckled.

The old man stood like a slow-rising sun and put some needles away very gingerly in an ornate blue box. Without looking he said, "Leave us, Arnus, I must speak to Aija."

The young man nodded and disappeared to the back of the store. She only caught a glimpse as his golden hair rounded the corner. The hairs on her neck were still standing, and she breathed in deep with a quiver.

"He likes you, you know," the old man said, raising his eyes up to her. His thick glasses made him almost look bug-eyed.

"I'm sorry, Master. I never should have beaten the boy in the street. I drew attention to us that the Order can't afford to have." Aija bowed her head, averting her eyes. One of the sacred rules of Klor Dem: never draw attention. Its secrecy was paramount.

"No, not the poor boy from the street, child. I meant young Arnus," the old man said, taking her hand and shaking his head. "He's drawn to you, and why shouldn't he be?"

"What? No, he's always annoying me, mocking me when he can," Aija said, pushing her hair behind her ear and looking back at the old man.

"He does it because he likes you. He doesn't know how to express himself properly. As much as we teach you, and as much as this order knows, only a few of us ever learn to conduct ourselves in..." He hesitated: "...a normal fashion. The boy is talented in handling his missions, but he doesn't know how to tell you he likes you."

"Why doesn't he just say it?" Aija sat straight and looked the old man in the face.

"Fear. The boy can handle nearly a dozen soldiers without a problem, but he's afraid to speak his mind, especially to you. Do you like him?" the old man asked, moving around the table, closer to her.

"I don't know. I thought he hated me, so I never considered it," she said, her heart thumping in her chest and her throat tight.

"Well, child, consider it now. In all my long years as the head of this order, I've never had a child born into it. It would be a strange thing to have two members train their very own child from birth to be an assassin. You and Arnus are two of the brightest students I've ever taught." The old man smiled and embraced her. His head only reached her shoulder, and she leaned her head on him in comfort. The old man was the closest thing to a father she could think of, but an emptiness rose in her. "Come, the others will want to see you."

She followed him to the back of the store. She sighed, then smiled.

"Did you do what needed to be done?" he said, with his back to her.

"You know I did. I mean… yes, Master. I was successful."

"Good girl. And the necessity of the collateral?"

She stopped, wondering how he knew. Somehow, he always knew. "Not necessary but deserved."

He laughed and carried on toward a door. A flight of wooden steps rose to the left, reaching into the upper living quarters. Straight on sat a door that led to a storage area, which held more reams of cloth and other supplies for making and mending clothes. To the right stood a door the old man unlocked with a key. Beyond, a lit stairwell descended to a cellar. The air grew colder the lower they went.

"How did you know, Master?" she decided to ask.

He laughed softly and labored. "I just do. I have my ways."

"Will you ever pass your ways on to me? I would like to know as much as I can. I assume you have spies all over," she said, her steps in unison with the old man.

"A lesson for a different day, young one."

In the bottom room were stored casks and food cabinets. The old man went to one cabinet and opened it. Hanging inside were radishes and potatoes, sacks of flour laid on the floor. He reached up and pushed some hanging herbs out of the way; their smell hit her nose, fresh and strong. Behind them was hidden a small hole in the wood. In a movement barely perceptible to her, the old man flicked out a golden needle and pushed it into the hole. She heard a click, then the whole back panel of the cabinet moved away.

She shuddered at his speed. No one knew his real age. Even the oldest of the Order remembered him being an old man, training them and teaching them. Following him, she stepped into a passage behind the cabinet. It ran narrowly but tall, made for only one person to walk through at a time. As cold as the cellar had been, it became much warmer when they rounded a corner into a well-lit area.

Walled in stone stood a large room with three wooden doors. In front of them, one led out into the sewers under the city. Used as a second entrance or an escape route. She never used it, but others did, sneaking in and out at all hours.

To the left, another door led into another storage area for food, weapons, and other supplies, acting as the true vault of the Order's hideout.

Lastly, to the right a door led into the sleeping quarters for the Order, where there were shared beds and storage trunks for visitors.

In the center of the large room stood a circular table with no middle. It came in four pieces so it could be pushed against the walls to make a training room. In the walls were cut-away sections for fire, where the smoke flowed into the chimney of the tailor shop above. It still smelled like smoke, and she found it unpleasant most of the time. On the wall was a burn mark in the shape of a sewing needle. She reached over and touched it as she entered. She never felt truly home until she did.

Sitting at the table were four others, but there were seats for thirteen. The most seats she had ever seen filled were nine. Two people from the training farm came to visit and brought two young trainees that day. Today, six of the seats were filled.

A member of Klor Dem for three years, she still had not met all her comrades. Two of them she had only heard stories about. She did not know where they lived and only knew their names as Keane and Daidri. Once, the master explained that they were always on their mission and only received new orders in the field because their identities must never be revealed. She always wondered who they were and what their missions were.

Taking her place at the table, as the old man, their master, took his, Arnus sat across from her. His penetrating eyes watched her until she showed that she noticed him and then he looked away. To Arnus' right sat the master, short and thin, and to his right sat a squint-eyed man with a duck face named Begla.

141

Begla looked like a man mixed with a variety of animals: lips like a duck and forehead like a monkey. She could not help but giggle every time she saw him. It also did not help how idiotic he could be. He bragged about how he made his marks die with a comedic edge. He called it his own special art form.

He claimed to have caused a man to slip off his tower on an ice patch and fall to his death on a salt cart. She could hear his squeaky voice add, "A shame he didn't lay that salt on his tower."

In another story, he pretended to be a governess, dressed up in women's clothing, and pierced the ears of his victim for earrings. With his slow-working, poisoned needles, the three-year-old little girl became sick and died days later. Of course, the new governess disappeared, never to be seen again.

She squeezed her face at the thought. Why anyone would hire them to kill a little girl seemed beyond her, but the story always made Begla howl in a fit of laughter. Always adding to the story about how good he looked in a corset.

The master looked over to a woman in black robes and nodded. Her wispy red-brown hair hid most of her menacing face. She stood and said in a loud voice that echoed in the chamber: "In the night, the moon raven scavenges, and in the day the rats run to find the mark that never survives us. Shadow of shadows, needles in the haystack of Sancta, we are Klor Dem. We do not fail."

In one loud voice, including her own, the room said, "Aye."

Sani stood rigid in her late thirties and held two roles in the Order. First, she maintained the tailor's shop, the farm, and the missions for each assassin. The other was as unofficial second leader after the master. She organized the Order. Stern and grim-faced, no one crossed her. In the early years, she made it her business to punish Aija and test her with some of the hardest missions available. It only made Aija hate her all the more.

Four years training at the farm and another two as an apprentice, doing missions without the aid of the needles, was hard enough. With Sani there to sadistically torture her, life became almost unbearable.

If a trainee survived it all, they were inducted as a full-fledged member of the Order and given their needles. Now a full member, Aija only disliked the woman, but the fear still lingered, always tapping at her mind, when Sani drew close. Sometimes called the *coordinator*, she taught her the importance of hardships. Her skills and understanding made her into the young woman she was today: a killer.

"Please, welcome back Aija from her mission," the master said; a smile widened across his face. Arnus looked over at her, his face emotionless, or did she notice a glint in his eye?

The room nodded to her, and she nodded back to them, sitting up in her chair proudly. The firelight in the stone room showed wavering shadows on the wall, symbolic of what they were: just shadows, appearing and disappearing on command. Begla smiled, Sani sat as an emotionless statue, and Arnus just stared with his hollow eyes.

"Sani has the next marks for a few of you," the master said, looking around. "Even in a kingdom built on the morals and strengths of this one, there's much work to be done. We are doing well, maybe as well as it has since the early years, when every lord in the kingdom scrambled for power, and we were the nightmarish story on every mother's warning lips."

Begla laughed with a chill, and even Sani seemed to smile. Aija never really had a mother. She only knew scary stories were not worse than the torture of her training.

"The farm is still training the two recruits. Both are showing great progress. They will be fine additions to our family when they are ready. Does anyone have anything to add?" the master asked.

The new recruits: always one boy and one girl at the farm. Constant hardship and pain were the only ways to describe what happened there. Strengthening the body, while keeping it nimble and quiet, became a tool most would never need, and fewer would be able to accomplish. That was unless they were broken down to nothing more than a blank slate, like herself. Learning to fight, groomed to kill, ending life—the ultimate skill.

She loved to learn how to watch and stalk—reading a person for what they were, understanding their weaknesses, understanding their lives. Naturally swift and graceful, she had acquired a talent with daggers and the needles, but her true skill came in the form of perception. It awakened her when she figured someone out.

She stirred from her thought, blinking her eyes and stretching her chin, when a large, ebon-skinned man with a shaved head and corded muscles that pressed on his black leathered clothes, rose from his seat. "I'm not able to make my way here often from my station in Paraduo, but for those who don't remember me, I'm Iknon Gemanti." He smiled so largely, Aija almost thought for a moment he might really be happy.

"The master asked me to stay here for a while to train and teach anyone who would like to know more of the customs of Paraduo and of poisons that are not administered by our needles. The master believes before long we'll have to do more work in the daylight, and more work in public situations. Understanding the importance of applying poison to our more combat-based weapons could be vital. Some of our lower rivals already use this technique." The large man nodded with a twist of his head and sat back down without even a noise from the chair. She pondered what she might learn from him if she decided to ask about poisoning her daggers.

The meeting concluded with a small footnote from the master: "Be wary of our rivals. The other assassins' guilds will feel our effects. As we grow stronger, they will grow weaker. To compensate, they will begin to interfere with our work. Be vigilant. Keep your eyes open."

She loved the way he never stopped teaching them. A true leader to the end. She wanted his knowledge and experience one day. As master, he never took on contracts, but his wisdom was invaluable.

The advice was sound as well. Being a cutthroat often seemed like a cutthroat business to her. Rival guilds caused problems for many in her order, but not for her. She knew the day would come. What bothered her more than that thought proved to be the multiple times she caught glances from Arnus. They never lasted long, but they were there.

They became siblings, brother and sister, in those early years, the product of being trained together from their youth. He grew to be the happier of the two at first, but then his mood changed to sullen over time. She never thought about him liking her as more than a friend. He never said anything. What did the master see that she did not?

Handsome, with his sharp chin, muscled body, and blond flowing hair, every time she looked at him, a hollow feeling came over her and the hairs on her neck stood. Who was she fooling? Maybe they were signs she felt something for him as well.

But if she did not have time for the adolescent infatuations of the homely Edwin, then she did not have time for Arnus' either. At least not right now.

After the meeting, when more cordial greetings were exchanged, Aija heard Sani call to her: "Child, I must speak with you. Your next assignment needs haste."

She cocked her head and pursed her lips. As much as she loved the hunt and being out on her own, she felt as if she needed some time in the tailor shop. She had not been able to work on her studies into magic with the master like she wanted. She wanted to learn how to alter light and shadows more to aid her missions.

Her face gave her feelings away when she found Sani, because the woman said, "As heartless as I am child, I know. You've been away from here more often than most. Three marks back-to-back-to-back, and yet I have one more. The master wants you on this specifically and promised when you return from it that you'll be able to stay here for a while."

Aija did not like being read, nor the awkward concern from the woman, so she lifted her chin, smiled and said, "I'm fine. What fun situation am I needed for now?"

"This is no game, foolish girl," Sani reprimanded.

The change in Sani's demeanor put her on edge. She kept back from the woman and on the balls of her feet, her muscles tensed. For as long as she had been in the presence of the Order and this woman, she never saw any form of care from her. Then to switch back so suddenly disheartened her.

Sani smiled with an air of menace in her eyes. "Foolish again, child. If I meant to lure you in so I could strike at you, I wouldn't wait until after the meeting. I would have killed you during it."

She believed the older woman; her stance loosened. It would not have been the first time a member was marked by the Order. She remembered, as a child trainee, sitting in on a meeting when a young woman about her age now fell face forward on the table. Blood splattered from her nose as it broke in the collision. A needle protruded from her neck and the master said, "This is what happens when you fail your mark." Then in the rhythm of the chant: "We do not fail."

She never failed, but Sani was acting strangely. She relaxed a little more before the woman began again. "The master demands you leave immediately and travel south in great haste, to the region of Caihn. There you will kill a lord and his firstborn son of eighteen. The lord is a younger cousin of Lord Nikolis Dorian. His name is Rupert Dorian, but he lives in the keep in Sarn Peligmo, with Lord Hadire. Be discreet, but if you cause a scene, make sure it causes discord among the noble houses of the region. We've been paid handsomely for this mark."

Aija nodded and turned to leave, not even two hours after she had arrived. She wanted to say goodbye to the master but saw him speaking with Arnus. The young man looked excited. He looked up at her, and she gave him a small wave. She saw a glint in his eye and the corner of his mouth turned up ever so slightly.

Chapter 10

Andross lay in his bed, a thin sheet covering him as the light from the morning came through the slats in the window. He stared at the ceiling wondering what he should do with Mahley.

She lay next to him asleep, her red fiery hair in messy curls around her fair-skinned face, her naked back exposed to her waist where the thin sheet showed her sensual curves. This strange turn kept him wondering. Never had he considered himself a one-woman man, nor did he now, though he was playing one. She was staying with him since he rescued her and brought her to the capital.

Having always been a man of the sword, he never thought it proper or right to settle with only one woman and did what he could to keep them at a distance. How awful were the nights for a woman who loved a man who never came home, always away, and in his case always in danger? That burden on someone could be devastating, let alone thinking of having a family and children, and placing the same burden on them.

In his early teens, a few girls caught his eye, girls around his family's lands, even one of the Redpool daughters, but none were worth giving up the sword for. When it came time to squire and time to be a knight, he put all his focus on it, working every day to be the greatest he could be, especially coming from such a minor house. The real shame in his unwillingness to father a true heir came from being the last of his name. The Delaqeen House would disappear if he did not marry and have a child.

His mother died in his youth, and his father died after he graduated from the Knights' Academy. His father had no brothers or sisters, and his mother's family were common folk of the area.

They sent letters for him to come home and visit, but the memories were hard to face. *A life of love and loss, is it any different now?*

Mahley moved in the bed, mumbling something inaudible. Since he rescued her, she had lived with him in the small quarters above a baker's shop in Nowann. It worked well, and in a way still did. She stayed there taking care of the place, cleaning and cooking, and she sometimes helped the baker, making a little money for herself.

How would this end? Andross thought, getting up to get ready. He heard her stir but did not turn to face her at first.

"You best get nice and neat," she said, blinking her large hazel eyes.

Andross turned to her and she stared at him, smiling wryly. "You sent my fine clothes to be cleaned?" he said.

"Of course I did. You asked me to do it and I did. I still think you should've bought some new finery. It's not like you don't have the gold for it. You're a knight of the crown, and now warden of Rosenia."

Whatever that means, he thought. Pulling on some black trousers, he said, "I don't like to spend coin if I don't have to. Maybe it's the part of me I hold on to from my youth. We may have been a noble house, but we had little extra. Crabbing isn't as lucrative as many might think. My father Lord Mander always taught me to be frugal with my coin."

"Now where's the fun in that? Tonight, you'll be talking with the great lords of the land, you'll be feasting with the kings of three nations. It isn't enough to look nice. You're representing your king. I'm just of common birth and even I know it's important to look respectable," she said, kicking one of his boots over with a look of disgust.

149

He laughed thinking about when they first met and how mud and dirt had covered her face. "It has nothing to do with social standing. You know that because it's instinctual in you as a woman," Andross said, with a chuckle. "Plus, there's nothing wrong with what I'm wearing. It's fine, and I only wore it to Nurame's and Coram's coronation."

"Several years have now passed since Nurame's coronation," she said.

His heart dropped at the thought for a moment, and he closed his eyes to the glimpse of the city that filled the streets in joy.

"Coram's was only several months ago. He'll remember it, and so will the others of the court. You'll look like you didn't care enough to be presentable for a major event held by your king," she said, standing up and walking towards him.

She was still naked, so he watched her every step.

"First of all, he's your king as well. Second, I do care. So, what should I do?" he said, grabbing her and kissing her warm lips, his hands caressing her skin.

"I'll get dressed and call for a tailor," she said, a smile forming on her face with a look of victory. "You won't need something made exactly for you, that would take too long since the ball is tonight. You just need something that fits, something green. The work will come with the embroidery of a dove on your new doublet." She jumped away with delight.

He watched her dress, yearning to make love again and not worry of clothing, but only said, "Embroidering a dove on me will also take hours. It'll be impossible."

"Usually yes, but…" she said, picking up the doublet he wanted to wear, brown with a white and silver dove on it. She tightened her nose at it and shook her head. She then tore at the dove. "If we just use this dove, then the tailor can sew it on."

"Why did you do that? Do you know how much it cost me?" he said, rubbing his hand on his forehead.

"Not exactly, but I'm sure it's more than I've ever seen," she said, tearing at it more, until she pulled one of his daggers from his belt and began to cut it away.

So, this is what it's like to have a woman around. He could not handle much more of this. He did not care how he presented himself. Maybe if he showed up a little unpresentable, the king would not want him to attend future functions. He would have preferred to be in the jungles of Paraduo fighting Horak or Mongrel tribes, where the king sent Sir Jarret Sabin, another high knight with a retinue of a hundred mounted Knights of the Wolf and some Crimson Casters.

When Adento the tailor arrived, all short, wispy, unkempt one hundred pounds of him, he took his measurements for his upper body. Adento needed a stool to reach high enough on him. "Ah, My Lord, I have just the thing for you," he said, with too much enthusiasm. "It will cost you a bit of coin though as it is very fine, but it will fit and be magnificent."

Andross shook his head in disbelief, and then said, "It's Sir Andross, not *My Lord*."

"My humble apologies. I was told this is for the new Warden of Rosenia," Adento said, bowing from the stool.

"I am that man, but I prefer to be known as a knight and not a lord." He saw Mahley's disapproving face.

"Of course, My L—sir knight. Now, Sir Andross, what of the lady? Will she be attending the ball with you?" Adento said, looking over at her.

"Don't think I didn't see you roll your eyes just now. Some men are meant for finery. I'm not one of them. Give me a sword and armor, let me fight." Andross' voice boomed in the room.

"Yes, we get it, but not tonight," Mahley said, rolling her eyes, easily noticeable to him. "You're big and tough and scared to go."

Adento let out a small laugh, until Andross sent a murderous look at the man.

"I'm not afraid of these events. I'm uncomfortable. That's different. It's not something I know," the knight said, pulling his lips tight.

"Still, sir knight, what of the lady?" Adento asked again.

"Oh no, I'm too lowborn for such an event—I'll be staying here," Mahley said, with a smile. This smile almost reminded him of the wryer one she gave him earlier in the morning.

"Even still, My Lady, there will be a great celebration in the streets. You should be dressed accordingly," the tailor said with a flourish of his hand.

Andross heard the chiming of coins in his head, but before anyone could say anything else, he said, "Fine, get her something nice, and I mean nice for a common lady, not nice for a noble woman. Go with the tailor. The last thing I need is you here nagging at me while I try to shave and clean myself."

She ran over and hugged him, then kissed him sensually—so sensually the poor tailor felt uncomfortable and turned away. The next thing the knight knew, the door closed, and he sat alone.

What was this? he thought. So, he rescued this woman of twenty, and now she lived with him, taking care of his house and himself, sharing his bed, nagging him, and now he bought things for her. This is what he had wanted to avoid…

*****

The crowded city streets, with the night's celebrations of dancing and feasting, were more appealing to him than where he stood now. The smells of roasting pig and goose, and the echoes of laughter, were winning out over the formality of the guests around him.

He stood in a velvet, emerald doublet with a white and silver dove on his upper left chest. He breathed in deeply and smoothed his hair over. He wore black breeches and black, shiny leather boots. Over the doublet he wore a long fine black coat with silver trim on the collar and seams. He had shaved his face clean, with his hair cut short, but he could not help running his hands through it.

Waiting at the entrance to the great hall, there were people everywhere, dressed in their finest. A line of luxuriously dressed lords and ladies stood waiting to be announced by the herald. He also noticed more Knights of the Thorn, wearing their black surcoats with the white thorns, and saluted several he passed with an upward nod.

A trumpet blasted with every name. "Presenting Lord Ashton Ramherst, who is escorting Lady Danelle, his wife, Lord Peter Ajax, and Lady Senise." The announcements went on and on. He wished he could just find another door and enter there. He hated pomp and ceremony, and with it the attention.

Behind him, coming through the palace doors, he saw the Paraduan royal house. King Muradim and his retinue were escorted by a small guard wearing white-leathered armor. At the bottom of their armor skirting sat the sigil of an eye from a peacock feather in green, purple, and black. He only ever saw a peacock once before when a traveling caravan of performers came through, carting many rare creatures. Paraduo held the bird in highest regard, much like the House of Lintrel did the rose.

He saw King Muradim with his dark, ebon skin, a head taller than the rest of his group, and even then, the Paraduans were large in stature. He wore a cloak made of dark, scaled leather, his doublet threaded black and gold, and his trousers matched the cloak. On his head he wore a circlet of gold feathers, each with an emerald gemstone.

After examining those around him, he found himself at the main entrance to the hall. "Your name, My Lord?" asked the herald.

"Andross of the House Delaqeen," he said. Then the herald made a bow.

The herald's voice boomed: "Announcing Lord Andross of the House Delaqeen, Grand Knight of the Knights of Rosenia, First Knight of the Dove, Member of the Royal Council, and the new Warden of Rosenia, by royal decree of His Majesty King Coram of the Royal House of Lintrel…"

The trumpets blew, and Andross felt awkward as so many turned from their conversations in the hall, to look at him. For a moment, he felt as if maybe his new doublet did not do the ball justice but then realized his title had been grander than most who had arrived before him.

He walked forward as if the eyes of the many were not boring through him. At one point he smiled wide and saluted two soldiers with a nod. He thought he saw one smirk. He paid no one else any attention until deep into the ballroom.

Inside the great hall, he made his way to King Coram, though crowds were lined up to speak with his majesty. As usual, a royal sentinel stood next to him, and strangely a second on the other side, where Andross saw Queen Sehra. He had not seen her for many

154

months, having missed Nurame's funeral; he had seen her for a brief moment at Coram's coronation.

Her dark brown hair was swept up in a bun with an ivory circlet inlaid with rose gold filigree. Adorned on it were gems of blue and white, diamonds and sapphires. Her gown of dark blue silk hugged her body. She nodded greetings to anyone who came her way, with a welcoming smile—though not the same smile he remembered from their youth. It used to be filled with joy and laughter, now worn with duty and honor. Had his smile changed also since Nurame's death?

Reaching the king, Coram only gave him a nod, less than a greeting and more a command to mingle. Though Andross felt uncomfortable, the king's examination of his appearance looked approving. He would have to thank Mahley later for her help, though he did not cherish the thought of her gloating.

He wondered for a moment what she was doing just then.

Examining the great hall, he spied out how people were forming together. He watched as the high lords were all speaking to each other, their wives doing the same. In smaller groups hovering together were the lesser lords. They also seemed to be speaking with those of their own neighboring lands. The lords of Caihn were talking together, lords of the Helsveg or the Hand the same. Inexperienced with balls, he wondered how they went. Maybe as the night settled more mingling would occur.

With well over two hundred people in the hall, more in the gardens and the dining room, not including the Knights of the Thorn along the walls, at the doors, and at every pillar, he could not hide. Not that he intended on hiding, but he hoped if he found himself in an empty void, he might just stay in it.

Making his way to one of the corners of the hall, he found a large table of food. This was something he could handle. As a lover of good food and drink, he could walk from station to station. This would give him the opportunity to try the delicate foods provided for the celebration but also keep his mouth full and avoid speaking to others.

He grew annoyed when it did not work like he hoped. After drinking down a glass of one of the finest wines from the vineyards of the House of Percy, he found himself face to face with an old man with a long, gray beard. "Good evening to you, good sir knight," the old man said. "I am Lord Ethan Edwyre. I wanted to speak with you."

He bowed his head in respect. "How may I be of service, My Lord?"

"No, My Lord. I must bow my head to you. The title of warden of Rosenia outranks my station," the old man said, bowing. "I know you don't have the power to grant me an audience with the king, but I do hope you could put his ear to some counsel."

Furrowing his brow, Andross looked at the man, waiting.

"I've tried to warn many, sent letters and even traveled to speak to others, but no one will listen." The old man stopped and began looking around, acting as if he did not want anyone to overhear.

At that moment, Andross remembered who this man was. Lord Ethan of the House of Edwyre was once a very respected man. His knowledge and love of the kingdom and its workings were of great importance. Known as a historian, he had archived many of the events of the last several decades. Rumor had it he was respected within the realm of the Ulmindarei, a sub-race of the Darei who were rarely seen but known as the keepers of knowledge across the lands.

The old lord recorded the histories of the times and held the archives in an extensive library in his holdfast. He employed scribes to copy those books, as he believed it important to spread the word.

As of late, however, his history and knowledge had turned to the ravings of a madman. Even his close friends within the historian's guild were talking of the outlandish ideas he swore the Ulmindarei passed on to him. His credibility and respect were faltering with his sanity.

"Sir Andross, it has come to my attention," he started, his eyes flicking around the room and running his hand through his beard, "that the Goblins in the land have grown restless. As the second largest race in Rosenia, they're a force to be reckoned with."

The nonsense of the statement forced Andross to tune the man out a little. In all his travels, he had found little issue with the Goblins. In all of Sancta, Rosenia was the most racially diverse. There were always exceptions, but most Goblin people were hard-working, in their own right. He only kept nodding at the old man's rant. *This would happen to me of course*, he thought. By avoiding normal conversations with the more level-headed guests, the ranting of a well-known fool had landed in his lap.

The old man looked scared. "More importantly, Sir Andross, I've heard rumors that a warlord or several warlords in Kiamel Po are giving asylum to the Goblins and there is talk of them building a great city for themselves. The first of its kind in thousands of years."

"How is it you know all of this, Lord Edwyre?" he said, putting his hand on the old lord's shoulder.

"Simple. The Ulmindarei told me."

157

"And their word is good enough to believe? The keepers of knowledge in Sancta, hoarding away their knowledge from others, came to you instead of someone else, and said Goblins are building a great city with the Kiamel Po...?"

Andross knew his fears were unfounded. Even if the Goblin race, harsh and tough, now grew restless and were leaving to make a great city among the vicious warlords of Kiamel Po, it meant nothing to the safety of Rosenia. More so it was well known that if the Goblins, who were once known for their warlike ways, were to rise up, they could not stand against the power of the Rosenian army and the three orders of the royal knights. Not to mention the armies kept on hand by many of the great lords.

"An alliance with the great warlords gave them the land to build such a place. Have you not seen it? Fewer and fewer of our Goblin companions in the streets?" Lord Ethan stood unblinking; his eyes affixed on Andross.

"Thank you, Lord Ethan, I'll keep this in mind and bring it to the attention of the king next time I speak to him," he said, bowing his head and walking away. As he left the lord's presence, it seemed Lord Ethan had more to say, but he would not give him the chance to continue. There were more dire issues at hand, and no proof of such a claim.

After wandering around as the night passed by, he spoke with many of the visitors. Some of the lords of the north, Belanov and Malikova, were less congenial, but they were always that way. The same could be said of the House of Nadal in the far south. As Nadal was the house of the advisor Azziza Zattu, none of his family carried much love for him either.

At one point, Lord Winston Jayne asked if he would squire his son, but he respectfully declined, using the excuse that he had no time in his traveling to squire the boy; it would be unfair to him. He was not willing to invest himself in someone who could be hurt if something happened to him.

In truth, though he did not want to admit, he feared losing someone again. To be hurt by their loss was difficult to grasp. Too many were lost, in far too short a time, who were dear to him.

Several times he passed King Coram, who only nodded, and then erupted in great laughter with whoever he conversed with. It seemed a hard thing to be such a young king with so many more experienced rulers around vying for attention. Having to understand their games became important to keeping one's head above water, but he did not know how to feign interest and mingle. He said what he meant and took people at their word. He shook his head and tried to seem busy.

Reaching for a crab cake from a servant's platter, he felt a soft touch on his shoulder and turned to face a beautiful young woman with light brown hair. She wore a flowing yellow dress and her hair curled into a bun. She bowed her head and said, "My Lord Andross, I've been watching, and your longtime friends of Paraduo have been keeping a close eye on you."

The woman looked stunning, and her innocent demeanor was alluring. He answered, "Yes, My Lady, they have indeed been watching me. As a matter of fact, they've been watching me since I entered the grounds."

The woman smiled and said, "It seems your heroics in the War of Men have left you a target of distaste among their people. Maybe you should go over and say hello," she said, with a teasing smile.

He chuckled. "I should go over and take you with me. Maybe your beauty will calm their jaded hearts, though I think you'll only serve to stir them." He was not a man to play politics the way the lords did, but he knew how to intimidate people, and he saw nothing wrong with infuriating those he had fought against not so many years earlier. "The truth, though, is I'd rather say hello to you, My Lady, and not bother with them," he said, taking her hand and kissing it.

The young woman blushed only a little and did a small curtsy. "My Lord, you are a wicked man, but please."

He shifted his head. "Is that truly what the ladies of the court know me for?" Did his unwillingness to marry or settle make him a womanizer? Surely not his intent, but then again, if the ladies thought of him that way, they would expect nothing more from him. Of course, it did not help him with his situation with Mahley.

"Please call me Sir Andross. The title of *lord* is tiresome, and says nothing of who I am. And, My Lady, whose name I have yet to hear, would you like to dance?" He reached out his arm for her to take.

The woman nodded in agreement, and he led her to the dance floor. "I'm Lady Winnifred of the House Noye. You may call me Winny."

The music played softly and slowly, and they moved in unison with the other couples dancing on the floor. He found her smile intoxicating. Was he doing something wrong though? Were he and Mahley anything more? *No.* The answer came almost at once. Lady Winny was a beauty, and his first respite of the night. "Would you like to leave and walk the gardens?"

"If by walk you mean something more strenuous, My Lord," she said with a roguish smile, "then no, I cannot. You're an interesting man, but I'm only here on the request of my lady to see if you truly were the man whispers claimed you to be. It seems you are."

Annoyance flooded his mind. She had played him. *Of course, I'm in a game.* In a ball, as the Warden of Rosenia, with the high lords of the land. The whole event played as a game. Why would this young woman be any different? He shook his head, not sure if he felt angrier about forgetting those facts, or angrier that he had been played.

"Please forgive me, Sir Andross. My lady only wished me to come over here and see how you conducted yourself before asking you to see her." Winny still smiled, but more evil than before, a hint of innocence, but evil, nonetheless.

He did not like the game, so in his brazenness he pulled her close, their bodies touching with him still leading her around the dance floor, and whispered in her ear, "Well, My Lady, it's truly the shame of the century, then, isn't it?" When he looked back at her face, her cheeks reddened, and he laughed at the effect. "Who's this lady who sent you to tease me?"

Winny stopped dancing and curtsied low to him, her face serious and harsh. "My lady is Queen Sehra, My Lord, and she wishes to speak with you." She turned without hesitation and left him.

His face grew hard and his ears flushed. He gazed around the room looking for the queen, unsure of what she wanted. Had he done something? They had not spoken for some time. His worry subsided when he saw Queen Sehra, with her ladies, laughing as proper ladies of the court do, with as little movement as they could muster.

As he approached, he smiled and bowed. "Your Highness."

"Oh, Andross," Queen Sehra said, watching Lady Winnifred walk behind her to the other ladies, "you're still the man ladies think you are."

161

"And to you, My Queen? Am I that man to you?" Andross asked. Too much time had passed since their last conversation, when he had given her a quivering, weakened apology for Nurame's death. Not even at her second wedding, when King Coram took her to wife in order to keep her honor, had they spoken.

"No, Andross," she said, her brown-red eyes looking hard at him, "I know you too well. You were a ladies' man with my late husband, but you didn't play, you only spoke. Even now I know you're only committed to one thing, and that is this kingdom."

"Thank you, My Queen," he answered, with a slight bow of his head.

"My brother says he saw you in passing recently. He said you seemed as stoic as ever," she said with a chuckle.

"I've always liked your brother, but he's worrisome and bad for my health." Andross took a deep breath. "But is there really any other way for me to be?" he said, causing the queen to laugh.

"Do you remember when we got lost in the Rose Wood years ago?" she said, looking out toward the gardens.

"Yes, My Queen. Coram and Teslin left for the keep earlier, and in our wild adventures, you, me, and Nurame continued deeper into the wood. If I recall, we were searching out a pink rose, when we got lost."

"You helped me calm down and not be afraid. I'll never forget that about you, Andross," she said, her face soft and emotionless. "You were always the rock, Nurame the sail."

"A very long time ago, My Queen, before the world seemed so serious," he said, looking at a pink rose on a bush through the great open archway. It hurt to think back to better times when games were played for joy and not power.

"In those woods, Nurame was heir to the throne. I floated in my joy as his betrothed. Coram stood as the second rose prince. And you were just you, the same Andross, brave and wild, unwilling to give up, and loyal to us all. I remember when you found out that Nurame and I were engaged. You in your innocent youth got down on one knee and proclaimed you would protect me at all costs, as the future queen of Rosenia." She smiled now, the one he remembered from their youth.

"I meant it, My Queen," he said, his voice lost in the noise of the ball. She knew what he said and grinned, as if being pulled back to a better time.

"I know, and that's why I need you to keep searching." Her face grew serious again. "I'm worried. I need you to keep looking for my late husband's killers. I need answers, Andross. Without motivation or reasoning I have no place to lay the worries for my coming child and for myself." She breathed deep. "I must know what happened to my..."

"A child, My Queen? What wonderful news," he said. A strange feeling filled him, and he only later realized it was the feeling of despair in that the child would have been Nurame's and not Coram's.

Her face lit up with joy and then went firm quickly. "Please don't speak of it to anyone, just yet," she said.

He nodded. She did not mention any worry about Coram. He knew their marriage was one of convenience and strength, stronger with a child on the way. The House of Vulfreund, a strong noble house of great lineage, and Sehra, the prize of the land. The people loved her, just as they had Nurame. They were not married long before his murder, and she had not yet borne a child. So, in his love

163

for the realm, Coram took her to wife in order to keep the perception of power and to uplift the people.

Sehra refocused on him and she continued in a low voice, "Bring what information you find to me. All of it. Leave no details out. There are things here that don't feel right."

He hesitated to answer at first, but the look in her eyes seemed familiar to him. Determined and filled with loss, they were like his own. "I will, My Queen," he said, worried of how the king would feel. *Where does my true loyalty lie?*

"Good, and thank you, my old friend. Be careful in this endeavor. This assassination makes me and my family uneasy. That's why I'm in the north so often. I feel safer there." Sehra smiled and waved to a passing couple.

"Yes, My Queen," he said, with a feigned chuckle and a bow, while stepping back to leave her. The relief he felt made the entire event worth his presence. He had forgotten there were people besides himself still feeling the loss of his king. People who still loved him.

"Oh, and Andross…"

He looked at her, the queen that the kingdom had showered with a million pink roses at her first wedding. "Yes, Your Highness?"

"Don't break too many hearts," she said, smiling in jest, back to the face of duty.

Chapter 11

Andross pretended to be shopping for some yellow apples at a stand. As always, the great market of Nowann bustled with vendors and hawkers and those wanting to buy their goods. Servants shopped for their masters' favorites: oranges from Rovelle, breads and cakes from the bakers, and meats from butchers. Others bought potions, knickknacks, and crafts of all sorts.

He searched for a scarf. His green cloak, bearing a white dove, hung behind him matching a surcoat of the same symbol. He wore it when he went deep into the city, to remind the people of the Knights of the Dove. There were five knights who had earned their right to travel under no command but the king's. He earned his right in the War of Men, fighting along Nurame and his host. With his new station as Warden of Rosenia, the eye of the king was always on him.

With a long moustache and a thin face, a vendor tried his best to make a sale: "These here, My Lord, are apples grown in the groves of Faor. Yellow they are because of the strange soil there. Some say this be magic apples which help a man to heal from injury."

Andross only half paid attention. He knew the stories the small folk passed around. Healthy *yes*, but red apples did not heal illness, green apples did not keep you young, and yellow certainly did not help heal wounds. Still, it might be best to buy one; they looked fresh today and he needed to look busy in the market. The copper petal he used ended up buying three apples; he ate one and gave the other two to some young boys begging for coin.

The prosperity of the kingdom flourished. Rosenia held great wealth for centuries, but after the War of Men it thrived even more and sat as the center of trade in Sancta. Even with its greatness, not everyone was fortunate enough to have a meal every day. As a place of wealth, it attracted those in need from all the corners of Sancta, and all its races. Most were harmless, but there were more than enough willing to cause a problem to get their share.

He walked over to a fountain where some other children splashed in the water and enjoyed the beauty of the day. The sun hung high in the sky and the heat burned dry like dragon's breath. One of the children, in her revelry, splashed him the moment a troop of Knights of the Thorn marched by.

"Oy, you kids get out of that fountain. It's no place to play," yelled the captain of the group, his face hard. Young and proud, he wore his silver cape with distinction.

Andross put up a hand, staying the young captain. "Leave them be, *Captain...*" he said, emphasizing the question of the young man's name.

"Captain Willam Lawlurd, son of Richard Lawlurd." The man stood even straighter, until he realized he forgot to salute, and his head bent down until his chin touched his chest.

Andross saluted back by raising his head in return. He knew the Lawlurds, lords in the southeast region of the kingdom, known as Caihn. They were under the High Lord Archum of the House Hadire, who reigned in the region.

The Lawlurds held themselves in high regard for decades, believing they played a major role in the defense of the south from the raiders of the Thernat Desert. Under the command of Lord Dimas the First of the House Nadal, the forces of Nadal, Lawlurd,

Hadire, Quinlin, and Rodrig, hunted down many of the raiding tribes.

Well-known by historians and anyone of decent knowledge, the Houses of Nadal and Hadire did most of the fighting. The Lawlurd forces took the tribes near the coast, not only getting lost, but they only found one tribe there and many of Lord Ambel Lawlurd's men died fighting them. The rest of the tribes on the coast had fled south or into the Crescent Sea.

"Ah yes, Captain Willam, I've heard good things about you." Andross watched the boy puff up and look over his shoulder to his men.

"Thank you." Willam smiled, his eyebrows raised. "I've done what I can at this station. Maybe soon I'll be moved to one of greater prestige," he said, looking at Andross as if hinting at something.

It did not move him. "Good, good. The protection of the king and his people is paramount," he said, looking over the other knights. He was not in the market to do a surprise inspection, but as he held more rank than all leading knights of the three orders, the Wolf, the Hawk, and the Thorn, and more rank than most of the generals of the armies, he did not find anything wrong with taking a second to do his duty.

Willam followed Andross in his inspection of the men. "My men should be in perfect condition. I inspect them every day before we head out on patrol. Every inch of armor polished and cleaned, with every thread in place."

"I can see you keep your men in prime order. Good work, Captain," Andross said, looking back at him and nodding.

"Thank you, Sir Andross," Willam beamed, "it's a great honor to hear those words from you."

In a quieter tone and away from the other knights, Andross said, "As for the children, let them play. They're causing no harm. Children should be children. Remember, you're a representative of the king. It's best to show the people the kinder side of his majesty, through your kindness," he said, with as little rebuke as he could. He did not want to offend the young officer, though truly he had heard nothing of value concerning the captain. He came off too regimented on his men and the common people; the only thing that seemed to matter was the presentation of his squad.

He felt lucky to rebuke the captain. The young lad could learn from it or continue his harsh ways. Did he think it would help? No. But he smiled anyway.

Young Willam nodded in agreement, though his face stayed firm as he turned and ordered his men to march on. Wearing white doublets with the thorns and sword in black embroidered on their chests, they needed to remember they served the king and protected his people.

He wondered what about certain people let power go to their heads. In a place of great authority, he never tried to throw his weight around unless he thought it truly necessary. With too much of it going on in the kingdom for his liking, he did not want to contribute to it. Most people lived hard lives already. The last thing they needed was another person coming along to make them feel worse.

A woman dropped a bucket of dirty water only a few feet away, when he saw the sign. A yellow scarf hung on someone's hip. He could not see who at first but moved to catch up. He forced his way through a crowd of women, who called for him as he passed: "My Lord, My Lord, have you a wife?" he heard them say and then laugh to themselves.

Trying to avoid the crowds, he moved down one side alley and then down another. At the end of it, a man with a yellow scarf hanging from his right hip gave him a quiet nod from the shadows. Average height, with black boots to his knees and a bandana around his head, he waved.

Andross only waited a moment, then the man began to make hand gestures: pointing at himself, he made a gesture of climbing and then pointed up to a rooftop. He then pointed back and gestured for him to go around the front of the building and climb the steps to get to the roof. He nodded and turned around. He knew the building. He was not sure how he would gain access to the roof, but he would find a way.

A bell chimed as he entered the front door, and the smell caught his nose first and then his eyes caught the many colors. Unless they were picked in the wild, flowers were a rich man's luxury. Sweet smelling and bright, this shop was much different from the rest of the market, which sometimes smelled like rotting meat or fish, depending on how late in the afternoon one shopped. This shop, "Princess Present," smelled like a beautiful spring morning mixed with the scents of fresh berry pies and lemon cakes. The owner, a wrinkled old lady with a dress a noblewoman normally wore to court, stood behind a counter while her younger daughter fixed an arrangement next to her of white and purple tulips.

"Oh! My Lord, I'm honored to see you in my establishment. How may I or my daughter, Flor, help you?" the older lady said, with a sharp bird-like voice. She shoved her daughter at him, hard enough the girl almost bumped into him. Her lips were the color of a pink rose; she had doe eyes, curled brown hair, and a slim curving body, but he was not there for her.

The girl smiled with an air of seduction on her face. *Oh, she is a temptress*, he thought; the way she flicked her eyes at him proved it. Young, she already understood the mind of a man, and the ways to manipulate it. She posed a danger and he wanted nothing to do with her.

While her mother's voice chirped like a twittering bird, Flor's voice soothed like a songbird. It flowed out in a harmony, but he could not get over her superior nature: "My Lord, is there a specific flower you're looking for? Maybe one for a special lady? I hope she's worth it."

"No, I'm sorry, I'm not here for personal matters," he answered in haste, noticing both women's congeniality fade, though only a little as they spoke to a member of the royal council. "I thought I saw someone up on your roof."

"Oh dear," the old woman exclaimed, throwing her hands up. "What's someone doing up there, My Lord? Should I call the guard?"

"No, no, madam, I'll check it for you. Most likely just my imagination. All I need is for you to point the way." He smiled and bowed his head.

"Oh, through the door, My Lord, up the steps, and there's a ladder at the very top. Please, My Lord, pay no mind to the mess up there, we hosted company last night. Oh, Flor, go with him, show him the way." The older lady's voice wavered as she seemed to hesitate.

He put up a hand. "Not necessary, I'm sure I can find the way. I don't want your lovely daughter in harm's way should there be some rascal on your roof."

Flor smiled; she must have enjoyed being called lovely.

He went through the door and climbed the stairs. The upper level of the store housed their living quarters. What he found on his way up made him sick.

The little old lady and her daughter, who owned a very quaint but popular store among many of the rich in Nowann, lived like pigs. The store was staged so clean and neat, but their home was as vile as a beggar's alley—worse even.

All over the stairs, clothes were strewn in heaps that needed cleaning. When he glanced into the rooms, he saw dirty plates with old rotting food. The smell permeated death, almost worse than what he smelled days after a battle, when men still littered the blood-soaked field, bloating in the sun while carrion birds pecked at them. This did not happen in a single night. Some of the food left out must have been sitting there for days. He could only think of one thing as he climbed out onto the roof: taking in as much fresh air as his lungs would allow. Some people could be so beautiful on the outside, but downright horrid on the inside.

The man sat waiting in the shadowed alley—not Human at all, but a Goblin. The Goblin stood up with a smile, his small fangs shining in the sun, his large, hooked nose and the yellow eyes of his race visible. Someone new from the Guild of the Rusted Dirk met him every time.

"And what's your name?" Andross called out.

"My master said you could call me Crabapple," the Goblin said.

Every meeting was the same; the messengers were like their master, named after some fruit, found across Sancta.

Years earlier, he caught the leader of the gang with a cart of medicinal herbs, stolen from a local apothecary. As a promise to let the thief go, Master Lemon would become the eyes and ears for him in the city and in the kingdom. Once a week, when in the city, he would go to one of the four established locations and watch for someone in a yellow scarf. The first week of the month, the market marked the rendezvous.

The whole exchange made Andross uncomfortable, but he benefitted from it, and though unknowingly, so did the kingdom. At first, it took him a while to trust the messages from the master thief. Trusting a street lord was like trusting a starving dog, not to eat a freshly killed rabbit lying in front of him. Master Lemon had explained to him the honor among successful thieves, and how by making the deal they forged an oath and bond between them. It took evidence to prove the master true. Of the several years they worked together, there had not been one false piece of information. At least not one he could prove. He was not so naïve to believe everything straight out, even after so much proof.

"Master Lemon bids you good day." The Goblin bent his neck, his voice scratchy and his smile unnerving, like most smiles of his race. Fang-like teeth filled many of their mouths, put there by their own choice. An unsettling tradition to Andross, which many still partook in.

"Good day to your master, and to you, Crabapple," he said back. "Why do many of your people sharpen their teeth?"

The Goblin looked at him for a moment and licked his lips. "To remember, sir knight. Through our history we fought. We fought for food, for land, we fought the Darei, we fought even you Humans. We cannot forget how even today we fight."

The explanation was filled with conviction, but Andross had a hard time believing some of the things Goblins said. Of all the races in Sancta, they were the second most prevalent. Most were productive members of the growing society, farmers and dock hands, soldiers in the army, yet they viewed life in a different way than other races, having different priorities.

Clearly, through history, Goblins had lived harder than most, broken physically and mentally in war—hardships tearing a once noble people apart, splitting them into a diverse race who often seemed lost in life. Only within the last several hundred years had they begun to settle into society. Some flourished to great heights, but many still clung to the harsher ways, apathetic to the plight of others, sometimes angry, sometimes detached from the rules. For those detached, they found work in criminal organizations, workers, laborers, soldiers in a war for the underbelly of Sancta.

They were not alone. The diversity of Rosenia was great, and all races took part in acts of criminality. While the different groups of the Linga, be it Dwaling or Bronling, or even Humans or Darei, many chose to be ruthless. Most Goblins who chose that life, only ever found it the easiest or most enjoyable path.

"What do you fight for?" Andross asked, curious.

The Goblin only looked around. He rubbed his large nose. "Master Lemon said to tell you he heard rumors of one of the minor gangs wanting to rob one of the warehouses at the docks on the Andar this week. Just in case you wanted to send an extra troop of soldiers down there."

Andross realized the Goblin did not know what he fought for. He nodded to the news though. The Andar ran as a wide river that flowed out to the Crescent Sea. Trade boats and barges came from Robo to help supply the royal city. There were hundreds of storehouses along the docks. "I'll send a patrol and put spies to watch for unusual movement."

"The Guild of the Rusted Dirk played no part with the iron ore that went missing from the Anvil Guild's storehouse the other day,"

173

the Goblin continued, "nor for the murder of the butcher down on Green Stem Road. However, Master Lemon did steal two young colts from the Healer's Guild stables last night." The Goblin smiled, his short fangs sat atop of his lower lip, as if Master Lemon had been very proud of this acquisition, and the messenger played a role in it.

Andross frowned and calmly said, "Tell your master... secrets stay secrets. This is his one secret for the week."

The Goblin went wide-eyed and began to fidget from leg to leg. "I'll tell my master right away. I'm sure he'll be very grateful." His eyes began to dodge around in fear. "Master Lemon also instructed me to tell you word traveled from some of the river runners at the docks. Lord Danon Cortney confiscated bits of the supplies coming into the city and taxed the runners more than he's supposed to."

"How do you know this?" Andross said, furrowing his brow. "This is quite an allegation."

"I don't, sir knight, except what the master passes on."

This needed investigating, and then to be brought up in council. The punishment for this thievery would be strong, as this was the second time Lord Danon had skimmed on the river route. The shrewd man attained wealth beyond most of the houses of Rosenia, and he never seemed to have enough. To him, gold and power were in short supply.

His lands sat west of the capital, running along the Andar River in the Golden Grove region, aptly named because it was the wealthiest region in the kingdom. Robo sat within its borders and the Andar flowed the goods in. As the High House of the Golden Grove, the Cortneys benefited greatly. They were a strong family and loyal to the crown but known for underhanded dealings.

During the War of Men, many weapon supplies disappeared. It always happened to the lord camped nearest the Cortneys. None of this could be proven because the weapons were never found, but Andross carried strong suspicions of their guilt.

"Tell your master that if this information is proven true, a great favor will be due him."

Crabapple nodded with a smile. "Word from the north is the House of Belanov is pushing for war. They're restless with the House of Ash and Blake controlling trade routes."

Glancing off over the city roofs, Andross said, "I'll pass this on to the council as well. The kingdom doesn't need any war within its borders right now."

"I don't know, My Lord Knight, with war comes the opportunity to make gold and lots of it. I'm sure you could do with some," the Goblin said, dancing up on his tiptoes.

"What am I going to do with gold? I'm a servant to the kingdom. A war may be fine for a thieve's guild, but for myself, who's trying to keep the peace, I don't want it. Now, how did your master come by this tidbit?"

"I'm not at liberty to say, but Master Lemon keeps eyes and ears everywhere he can plant them. He's a man of many talents, as you already know," the Goblin said, with a look of apathy on his face.

Andross nodded. "I'll send word north soon." Sir Davin should be there. He could send news back. The long rivalry between the northern houses has now become more than cumbersome for the crown. "War is not the message we wish to convey to the realm right now."

"Also, My Lord… my master looked further into your inquiry and found nothing, though he continues to search." The Goblin seemed confused by this part.

The lack of clues surrounding Nurame's assassination bothered him. He breathed deep and looked out to the open sky, shaking his head. Asking Master Lemon to investigate missing gold stolen from a local merchant or to gather information on a mother and her two children murdered in the guild quarter proved beneficial. It was different to ask him to try and find clues about the attack and murder of Nurame.

"My Lord, is there anything else my master can help you with?" The messenger smiled again and Andross wanted nothing more than to punch that smile off his face. Rage boiled in his mind, his hands clenched. He always got heated when he thought of the death of his friend. But today's messenger could not be faulted.

He smiled back at the Goblin and shook his head.

"Good, then I shall depart." The Goblin walked over to the wall and began to climb back down into the alley.

Maybe next month, Andross thought—another meeting, a different "fruit or vegetable" messenger. The guild leader probably employed over a hundred members in his thieve's guild. Next month he might send a Dwaling or a Human, or maybe even a woman. They would have more news for him of thefts or murders, of uprisings in the east, or pirate attacks in the Crescent Sea, but would the same fruitless news be true? Would there ever be any news of the ambush at King's End?

Exiting the small shop, the two women accosted him again. "No one there, ladies. I do apologize for the inconvenience. You have nothing to worry about."

"My Lord Andross, please, you did not answer me on the issue of my beautiful daughter," the mother said, pushing her daughter forward again.

He shook his head in annoyance. "Sweet lady, I've no time for a romance with your daughter. Maybe it would be best that instead of cleaning her up so much to gain the attention of a man, you put her to work upstairs cleaning your quarters."

The faces of the women went pale. "Well, I never. We held a party last night, that's why it's so messy," the mother said again.

"Doubtful. The only things willing to spend time in that mess are pigs." He felt bad for being so rude, but he had enough of the woman's pushiness. It did not help that the daughter was still giving him a wanton eye, trying her best to lure him into her trap. Nor did it help that he had gathered no new information on his friend. If he did not find some answers soon, his obsession would drive him to insanity.

"Please leave, Lord Andross," the mother said, pointing at the door. "I will not be insulted in my own shop."

In his shortness, he snapped back. "I would have been gone already if you did not stop me. Good day, and it's *Sir* Andross." He turned and stepped out into the mixed smells of the market, happy to be away from the two women.

As he walked toward the western side of the great city, he thought about his next mission from the king. He would travel for a second time to Rovelle, to attend the Mages Congregate, the great gathering of magic guilds. Maybe the trip and the time away would be a good respite from his duties in Rosenia. His only task on the trip was to be a direct representative of the king, to listen and see how the mages' guilds progressed in their knowledge of the magical arts.

177

A pang of annoyance struck as he thought about more time wasted not hunting for his friend's killers.

Chapter 12

Dreyandol stood on the parapets of the Crimson Order's training grounds, not far from the city of Cliffwater, in the lands of the Anderoys. He stood intent, assessing the many recruits. A breeze flowed off the sea from the west, and the smell of a fresh salty day filled his nose. Neesa stood next to him, the early morning sun shining on her orange and tan hair, her long tail flicking behind her. There were others of the Order there too, soldiers, mages, warmagi, and magelocks. There were grand masters, masters, and apprentices all standing and watching, their deep red attire juxtaposed against the day's blue sky. He had been doing this for weeks now.

His main mission for the Order was to search for his next apprentice, to take on a new student. *One master, two apprentices.* The secondary mission was to help in teaching the many new faces. The large influx of recruits here and the large number of masters in Rovelle called for a change of scenery. Now he and Neesa traveled in a new land, eyes open to possibilities.

For months he scouted and studied all the trainees to see who would fit well in their duo. He only rested when he and Neesa helped train some in combat, or when they took small trips around the area to explore, or when they went to the library.

The cliffs near Cliffwater were a beautiful sight to behold, gray walls topped with green grass; it became their favorite place to visit and look out over the azure expanse of the Crescent Sea. Some days they stood in silence and gazed out.

Rubbing her forehead with the fur-covered back of her hand, Neesa said, "I still think young Roran of the Bronlings would be good. He's fast and soft-footed like us, so he can keep up. At the same time, he's magic-oriented and could make a good balance to our trio."

"And again, you're right," Dreyandol answered, shielding his eyes from the sun. "But he's being eyed by some of the higher masters, and because he's so magic-oriented, I think it would be too short of a time before he's unhappy with how little I can help him grow. He'll one day make an exceptionally good magelock."

She nodded, though her face twisted in disappointment.

A small group was trying to learn to disappear or almost disappear—one of the great spells of the Crimson Order, which helped them blend into the environment, making it almost impossible for them to be seen. Very few tools were better to aid them in scout missions, which the crown now paid them for.

"We could complement our speed with the strength and intimidation of one of the larger recruits?" she suggested, turning toward a group of larger brawlers. "There are a number of them from the Passing Mountains, and one ebon-skinned man from Paraduo. I saw him throw one of the training stones clear across the fountain."

"Yes, we could, but would you be willing to deal with a slower companion who would call attention to us because their intimidating presence?" Dreyandol asked, looking over his shoulder at her.

She looked at him; her nose twisted with a definite look of rejection. She sighed, and then he sighed. The search had been fruitless. No one seemed to stick out as a good match. "You know, Neesa, it was different with you. I knew the moment I saw you. No one here is like that. Maybe you set the bar too high?"

"I did," she said, a smile creeping to the ends of her mouth.

He shot a look at her and then chuckled. "It really isn't fair. We're holding all the recruits to your criteria, and none are meeting the challenge. There are several I really like, but they just aren't the ones."

"Truth be told," she said, smoothing the fur around her face, "you're looking for someone as quiet as me. Everyone out here talks too much for your liking."

He closed his eyes. "I don't mind so much someone who talks, so long as what they say is worth me listening to."

"Can you imagine having a Bronling around?"

He chuckled. "They'd talk our ears off. One problem with Roran is he talks too much. He's very nice, and very talented, if not a little clumsy, but he talks and talks. It's good Master Edonde has his eyes on him. He'll fit there."

The sun blazed high in the sky, not a cloud in sight, and the breeze from the Crescent Sea still brought in cool air. They both stood for a while longer watching, more than anything just enjoying the day. He thought about how much time he and Neesa spent just enjoying life.

When they trained, they took it seriously, but it felt fun at the same time. When they went on trips, they rode their horses or walked in silence, sometimes talking about their races' cultures or their families' characteristics, but it stayed calm and easy between them.

They both wanted someone with an easy demeanor, but also someone who took life to the fullest and loved every minute of it. They needed a kindred spirit, not someone who fit their sparring sessions, or who made good soup.

As of late, besides their normal training of combat and magic, they were learning to cook in the academy's kitchens. They cooked everything from fruitcakes, vegetable soups, and meat pies to scrambled eggs and roasted chicken. They did not mind helping anywhere they could.

Dreyandol, like many Darei, understood plants, and thus cultivated a great understanding of herbs and spices. It appealed to Neesa, being of the Malkienons, who loved burning spices. She kept a bottle of them in her things. In return for letting the two of them in the kitchens though, they also helped and taught those around them.

"Want to try some of my spices today?" she would ask with a grin.

Dreyandol always answered, "My heart desires to feel the fire burst forth within me, but not using those." One of many inside jokes.

They spent much of their time, as did many of the masters, in the library. Both believed much could be learned from the books of old, especially about magic. A new form of learning magic had reasserted itself in Sancta due to the great wizard Tratton's studies. It was climbing new heights, and some of the old ancient tomes spoke of small groups of mages from days long passed who claimed to be able to do things no one in the present could, like making a castle wall crumble or taking control of a person's body and mind or even changing the weather.

The Orbel of Rovelle were known to be some of the oldest magic users in Sancta, but they were primitive in their lifestyles before the Nordarei and Aknon shipwrecked on the island. They were a quiet race and their history and secrets were seldom shared. Some swore they held the power of resurrection, able to bring back someone who had recently died, an ability Dreyandol could hardly fathom.

He often got into debates with some of the higher masters on the potential of magic. What were its limits? What could be achieved? The resurgence broke new ground, changing the way people viewed it.

The other big debate was the true purpose of the Order. Neesa believed it was to bring balance to a world on the cusp of magical learning. Dreyandol thought otherwise, believing they were there to protect how far it could be pushed.

"Let's go," he said to her, motioning his head toward the entrance of the tower that led down to the grounds.

He turned and began walking, habitually glancing back to see if she followed. He could not hear her steps most of the time; she moved like a ghost. She was there, as always, right behind him. They descended down the spiraling stairs to the main floor.

"Where are we going?" Neesa said, jumping the last three steps without making a sound.

"To the grounds and then the library," he said, in a dull voice.

"Good, my favorite place, the quiet library," she said, smiling wide. If he let her, she would stay there morning, noon, and night. He knew she liked it there more than he did. It helped that she read so much faster than him and was not pulled into debates.

"First the training grounds."

Out on the training field, he took a closer look at some of the recruits. It was dangerous to do, he knew. Being up on the walls watching made them nervous enough but having someone shadow their every move really pressured them.

"I remember the masters in Rovelle, down on the grounds watching. I always felt a desire to do more, and when I did, I did worse," he said, watching the trainers in their tests.

"So, you aren't good under pressure? Is that what you're saying?" Neesa said, her tail flicking.

"I don't think it's that," he said, looking over his shoulder at her. "I've been in worse situations and come out unscathed. Just something about being watched. I don't like attention so much."

"I get that. I learned to sneak well so people didn't see me. If they can't see you, then you don't get attention. The worse part about parading myself in training was I had to get their attention."

They stood and watched a group fight with gusts of wind, trying to push each other off tree stumps. Both sent powerful blasts, but the female combatant conjured better. He watched her leap high with an air spell to dodge an air attack and send one back at her opponent. He nodded at them and moved on. "What's her name?" he asked Neesa as they passed.

"Jolie. She's experienced with magic, especially with air. She may work better as an elementalist trainee though. She does have a harder time with fire because she can't conjure the flame." Neesa conjured a small flame that blinked out as fast as it ignited.

"You may be right. They're looking for new trainees to train in that specialty, especially those who seem to have an easier time with elements already at their disposal. The truth is we may want to take some time and look into it ourselves," he said, heading over to a group shooting targets with bows.

"I've already started reading about it and taking a few small lessons from the trainer here."

He stopped and turned to face her: "Where did you find time for that? You're always with me."

"Oh, I do it when you have your meetings with the other masters. I figured I can stand around waiting or getting rest like the other apprentices, or I can go learn more."

She smiled and continued past him.

Stern faced, he said, "That's what I like about you, Nees', always willing to learn." He turned back toward the archers. "Well, that means you can show me some, then."

"Yes, Master, of course. It's my goal in life to become your master one day," she said with a laugh.

When they reached the archers, they were met by one of the trainers, Master Leyton Lairhety, a cousin to Lord Gaelin Lairhety. "Ah, my friends, how are you two today?" Leyton was a tall, thin man, with a bald head, and could shoot a bow with accuracy in his sleep.

"Morning, Leyton, how are today's archers?" Dreyandol said, eyeing the group and watching as one shot wide of the target. He winced a little at the sight.

The tall man rubbed his naked head and said, "Well, they're not too much different than they were the last couple of times you watched this group. Most can hit their target when they need to, but if they're not standing directly in front of them, they've a bit harder time."

Dreyandol nodded and looked over at Neesa, thankful he was a very good shot with a bow, and she was even better. Why could they not find a match, an apprentice to join them? He wanted to start training someone and he wanted the three of them to go on missions for the Order. There were a lot of things the Order could do and needed done. He would show his worth. He needed to.

"This is frustrating," he said. "Maybe, we should travel to the recruitment stations and see if there's someone we can train ourselves."

Since they were not tied to an army, they were more like an adventurer's guild that roamed the lands. Most adventuring guilds looked to do good in hopes of getting some reward for it, but there were a few who were troublesome too. The Crimson Order was more organized than a regular adventure guild. They were loved by the Rosenian king and were often asked to help with important missions.

In his homeland, the Order was more established but less leaned on for things. They were freer to do as they wished, but either way there were benefits. He found it more convenient in Rosenia to stay in one place and help train if one wished. This could and would establish a strong base for recruits and a growing order.

In Ajencain, at the high headquarters of the Crimson Order, they required one to move around and accomplish great deeds to show himself worthy. This could be a blessing and a curse, forced to take what jobs were available. Some could be more embarrassing than fruitful.

"We were right, you know?" he said.

"What's that?" she said.

"This kingdom, Rosenia," he said, his face tense, "it removes the pressure Rovelle so often magnifies with its attempt to force members into a role. We have more liberty here. If you and I were just lying around all day here, how long before a higher-ranked caster came around to rebuke us?"

"I want to say never, but truth be told, maybe a year or two."

"And how long under the masters in Ajencain?" He focused on another shot; this one missed the target as well. He saw Leyton shake his head and move toward the recruit.

"They don't let you lie around. Whether there's too much to do, or they find things for people to do, there's always someone on your heels, pushing you further," Neesa said, combing her cheek with her hand.

He breathed in deeply. "There's freedom here." In Rovelle, his name held power, but here his worth gave him respect. Not because he constantly did something, but because what he did created value.

"I've had enough," he said, shaking his head. "Let's head to the library."

"Yes," Neesa said, under her breath. "What to learn today?"

"Maybe see if there's a way to conjure a spell to find the best option for our team."

"There isn't," she said.

He looked at her with a puzzled face.

"I already looked," she said, with a wink.

It smelled musty and cool as they entered, just as they expected. "I love this smell."

Neesa did not respond, but he heard her take several deep breaths.

The smell of old paper flooded their noses. It was darker than some of the great libraries Dreyandol had been in, but much grander than the ones Neesa visited. Still, it offered countless shelves of books, parchments, and scrolls to study.

The House of Anderoy, as large supporters of the king and the Crimson Casters, gave over the old unused castle as a place to train and teach many of the recruits. In return, the Casters would do favors for them if need should call. With the keep came a large kitchen, an extensive library, and many rooms, but it still took a lot of work for the Order to make it habitable. A village of workers sprouted outside the walls. Casters and recruits brought their families as well as their professions from before joining.

They named the new village Crimson Cliffs. Many of the trainees and unchosen apprentices lived there, with many of the teachers and masters living in the rooms of the keep itself. Its organizing was different from Rovelle, where the Order's infrastructure was more rigorous and more focused, more like a military academy. Families were not allowed to be a distraction. Only when you were an apprentice could they join you. Here they helped cultivate a working village, farmed, and worked many jobs.

The only real rules in Crimson Cliffs were you must be associated or related to an actual member, and one must always contribute, which meant no leeching off the community.

In the library, Dreyandol looked up at the walls covered in books. There were benches and tables set up at random, some with members of the Order stationed at them murmuring away in debate or reading to themselves. Light from great windows, as well as some magic-induced candles, lit the room.

They planned to start on opposite sides of the door and make their way around the room, looking for any books that might be interesting. When they discovered something, they either let each other know or passed along the title of the book so the other could look at it when the chance arose. It was hard work, as almost everything they picked up interested them.

In the accounts of an old book called *Of the Ancient Ones*, it listed the major races that came to be at the start of the Second Age. There were four races, two of which were gone or changed, one only within the last hundred years. The first race, the Gillari, were the fair ancestors of the Goblins, and the other, a line of the Diversi, fathers of the Drogan the dragon herders and Humans. The Drogan were the more recent to disappear into oblivion. The Gillari disappeared during the Great Drought, marking the end of the Second Age.

The thing that interested Dreyandol the most, of which he knew a little already, was the account of his people, the Darei. Three great sects were formed over hundreds of years, the Haldarei, the Ulmindarei, and the Somdarei. The Somdarei who were now more notably known as Nordarei.

The book spoke of the time before the Great Drought, when they were the tenders of plants, mostly flowers. Another book stated they were no larger than the flowers themselves when they first came to be. This would have been strange to read, except many of the stories told to young Darei spoke of them being small. Over time, for some unknown reason, they grew to a much larger size, the size they were now. Then again, stories were stories, and it was not often one could find the truth they were derived from. It fascinated him to read the tales of old.

He saw a book called *Clouds on the Horizon* and wondered what information could be held within its bindings. Maybe it spoke about the hardships of life and how to get through them, or a fictitious story of great evil. As he opened it to find out, someone called him, and when he saw who, he put the book back.

"Dreyandol…" said Master Edonde in a hushed voice.

"Yes, Master," he said, walking over to the man sitting at a table with what seemed to be a game in front of him.

"You know how to play this?" Edonde asked, pointing to a rectangular brown and blue board.

"No, I'm not even sure what it is," Dreyandol said, taking a seat across from the master with his slender face and long black hair.

"Really? How strange. I figured Neesa would have told you about Meonia—or Fish Tail in Malkienon," Edonde said.

"Well, if you tell me about it, I'll play with you," Dreyandol said, eager to learn something new.

"Ha, I got this game on my trip to Nyoko, and it took me three months to even understand the concepts," Edonde said, rolling his eyes and moving one of the flat number tiles to the edge of the board. "Bring Neesa over here and I'll play her again, though she'll beat me like always."

Dreyandol called her over, and she shook her head and rolled her burgundy eyes. "Master Edonde," she said, smiling and sitting down at the wooden table next to Dreyandol. "I know you want to get better but playing me won't help you. This is a game Malkienons are taught in their youth and play their whole lives. For you to have picked up the concept on your own in three months is amazing. You need someone better fitted to your skill level to learn with. How about this? You and I can play while I explain the rules to my master so maybe you two can play against each other in the future. The terrible thing is, I'm not even good at this game. At least not compared to my mother."

Edonde nodded and said, "Fine, explain to him as we go. It's so addicting and yet so frustrating. There are days I feel like quitting the Order for the sole purpose of learning its many secrets."

"Please understand, it's just as important to know your abilities in the game as it is to know your opponent's," she said, her tail flicking.

"Master," Dreyandol said, interrupting.

"Yes?" Edonde replied.

"As a grand master, can you give me some advice on finding my next apprentice? I mean, I was sent here to search out and train a recruit, but I'm unable to come to terms with any of them," Dreyandol said, looking down at a wood knot on the table.

"Listen, Drey, I think you're putting too much into this. You told me before when you found Neesa that it was obvious. It's clear to all of us: the two of you are a perfect fit as master and apprentice.

You're practically the same people. However, you're over-concerned with your next choice."

Dreyandol watched him set up his portion of the board—or were they already playing?

"You were sent here by the Order to train people," Edonde said, moving more tiles. "Already you're doing this with Neesa and the classes you both help in. There's no time schedule for a second apprentice. When the right one comes, you'll know it. It'll hit you like almost anything important does and it'll feel right. Stop stressing and listen to the instructions your apprentice is about to explain."

"Thank you," Dreyandol said, meeting eyes with Neesa and raising his eyebrows in satisfaction, "that not only makes me feel better, but helps me understand my purpose a little more."

"Oh, really quick, before we get started, a mission came in from Nowann." Edonde stared hard at the board. "The king is looking for a few Crimson Casters to escort some dignitaries north to a city called Targon Vale, the house seat of the Belanovs. They need help in settling some disputes up there, maybe act as mediators. Master Jensing asked if anyone would like to accompany him. Would you and Neesa be interested? You mentioned wanting to see more of the kingdom if the chance presented itself." Edonde looked up at him with a questioning look.

Dreyandol glanced at Neesa, who was already looking at him and nodding in excitement. "We would love to, Master Edonde," he chuckled.

"Good, you and the one who beats me too easily at this ridiculous game can leave in a few days to Nowann and meet Master Jensing," Edonde said, smiling jovially at Neesa.

"If you'd like, I could let you beat me, Master Edonde." Neesa said. "Then again, I do like telling everyone I'm better at this than you. Well, you and my master." Her cat-like face and large eyes beamed at them.

"Well, as I know nothing of the game that seems so important to your own people, I guess I'm at an unfair disadvantage," Dreyandol said, but he thought about the new adventure they would get to go on. It could be he would find his apprentice along the way.

"I promise to teach you as much of this game as you have taught me of combat," she said, laughing so hard she almost fell from the bench.

"I'll make sure you learn more than you bargain for," he said, squinting at her.

She sat up straight, the laughter gone. "Of course, sir."

"Oh, don't even. Just play your silly game," he said with a smile.

"See, Drey," Edonde said, fixated on the board, "this is what I meant about the perfect relationship you two have as master and apprentice. The friendship and trust between the two of you is what binds you together. Be patient, both of you. You'll find another apprentice, I promise."

Chapter 13

Weeks after Aija left the tailor's shop in Faor, she still missed it. It was the only place other than the training farm she called home. As instructed, she left that very night, within minutes of receiving her new assignment. She gathered supplies, restocked what she had used on the last mission, and left on her horse. She did not see Arnus, nor her master, after leaving the main chamber of the basement, and it bothered her that she did not say farewell.

After days of traveling west and then south, she now knelt on her hands and knees, scrubbing the wooden floor of the high seat of Hadire in the great southern city of Sarn Peligmo. High Lord Archum was marshal of the entire southwest region, which ran west to the sea and south to the desert lands of Thernat.

Her arms and hands hurt from cleaning the floors and washing pots; her back always felt stiff after a long day in the palace, where the other maids now knew her as Anya. She wore the rough-spun brown dress of a servant, with a strip of cloth wrapped around her head to keep her hair out of her eyes. She wrapped cloth around her knees to keep them from getting too sore and bruised. What the other servants, soldiers, and lords who marched by did not know was that she hid two small daggers in her sleeves, and a small leather-wrapped pouch of needles strapped to her thigh. Not the full assortment of killing needles, but enough for the job.

One must make do with what can be hidden. For this mission, she decided to take a more upfront approach and carry it out in the daytime, to raise suspicions among the lords. She needed to keep her tools hidden and herself visible.

Her first goal was to infiltrate the palace. It stood as a sand-colored tower in the middle of the city, and garnered heavy protection. She had pulled some strings to gain access. Sometimes she threatened people or disguised a payment or offered a bribe; other times she pretended to be someone else. This time she had disguised herself as an older gentleman looking for work for his half-witted, partially deaf daughter.

She now worked in the palace, no less in the private chambers for Lord Hadire's retinue. Often, the lower lords, Jason Lawlurd, Matteo Nadal, and Devom Alwin were in the city, as they were close to the high lord. Last, and always tagging along, the round-faced, large-nosed Rupert Dorian, and his taller handsome son, Gerhart Dorian.

She scooted further down the hall, still scrubbing. The water wrinkled her fingertips and parts of her dress were soaked. She scratched her ear and looked around. Soldiers often patrolled the halls, and more often than not came and went as they pleased.

Thinking back to what she had already discovered, she smiled at how much could be learned pretending to be a deaf woman in the kitchens. Rupert's more feared cousin, the high lord of the House of Dorian, Nikolis, was said to be a worthy man. Rupert, however, was an overambitious, overlooked cousin, who served his family by maintaining their lands in the War of Men while the rest were away fighting battles, fortifying locations, or guarding trade routes for cattle herding.

His son was not much like him in looks, but very much like him in personality. Several times she had smiled at the strapping Gerhart to see if she could get his attention, but it seemed in vain, as he focused more on the ladies of the court. As an unnecessary ruse, her plan had little to do with the attention of the lord's son. Still, it added some fun to her game.

She dunked her brush in the dirty pail and scrubbed a little more of the floor. As soon as she finished with this hallway, she would remove the dirty water, clean herself, and it would be time for her to bring a breakfast of two boiled eggs, sautéed eel with lemon peppers, spiced beans, and rice to the chambers of the lords of the House of Dorian.

As a master of disguise, she blended in wherever she went. The necessity of infiltrating certain jobs was branded a chore by many in her guild. To her, being able to experience different jobs, different lives than just the assassin, added spice, flavoring.

She threw the wet cloth in the air, letting droplets of dirty water fling around the hall, smiling from ear to ear. This was another life lived.

*****

In the early morning, the platters she carried smelled delicious as she walked from the kitchens to the upper floors. Tempted to try some, she breathed in another deep breath. There were always two platters, one for the father and one for the son. Passing one of the guards of Dorian, in an armored doublet with a sword on his hip, she giggled and gave him an alluring smile when he tried to pinch her rump in passing. She turned and blew a quick kiss; he did not have time to react before she was gone again, giggling down the hall. She heard him call for her as she rounded the corner: "Wait, wait."

Another guard opened the door for her, and she entered the lavish quarters. She listened for the door to shut before continuing deeper into the chamber.

The sun broke over the dry, plain land outside. She could see it through the open curtains. As far as the eye could see, Caihn lay flat as an expanse of fields and high yellow grasses. It made its wealth from the herds of different cattle. It was lucrative, and most of its people played a vital role in its economy, tending crops and raising cows for milk and meat, bison, donkey, and some horses. It rained enough to maintain the grasslands, but not enough for forests or greenery. The region's rockier south held ore mines that were also prosperous. Beyond that were the dry deserts of Thernat.

The Dorian chambers were dim, with only lines of sun coming in through the curtained balcony, framed by sand-shaded pillars. Sheer white and sky-blue curtains draped the edges. A blue couch sat in the middle of the room, with tables along the edges holding ornate sculptures of horses, bulls, and bison. One tapestry on the wall showed a white bison, its massive head and shoulders ramming a knight on horseback. The knight's lance plunged into the bison's hide. She wondered for a moment who had won the battle. Bison were mighty beasts, and the knight in the picture looked frightened.

On the balcony stood the plump Lord Rupert Dorian reading a large parchment. Aija recognized him from his armor. Usually he wore his fine clothes; he must have things to do today, falconry or hunting, or was he going somewhere? If he left, then she would have to start again. She breathed a sigh of relief.

She moved across the chamber, not seeing Gerhart. He usually slept in, as he stayed out late with the other young lords for tavern hopping and cavorting with young ladies. She had followed him one night and admired how the ladies swooned over him. They flocked to him everywhere he went; every phrase from his mouth was followed by a chortle of pathetic laughter. She became even more annoyed when she realized how much she had been paying attention to his looks and how she could not seem to help it.

Rupert walked over and sat down on the couch as she put the tray on the table. He did not so much as notice her; he kept reading the parchment. She did not need to be too discreet about the killing blow, so she pulled a dagger from under her dress—not one of her weapons, one stolen from the Alwin chambers, with the mark of a black bull head on a yellow field, adorned on its hilt. The idea was to cause more grief between the houses, and what better way than to leave some damning evidence?

She stacked plates from the night before, twirling the knife in her hand the whole time. He sat, so enthralled by the parchment, he did not realize she had lifted her dress up to reach the blade, showing her undergarments and trim legs for a moment.

She stood right over him and gave a small laugh to pull him from his reading. When he looked up in surprise, she slid the dagger deep into his throat. Other than his face, his neck was the only part of him unarmored. She thrust the dagger so hard, she pinned him to the couch. *No chance of survival.* A small bit of blood shot out on her, and much more poured down, mixing with the blue couch and turning parts of it dark purple in the dimly lit room. She watched as part pooled in a beam of light and dark red blood drip to the floor.

"My Lord," Aija said and bowed. She still held the dagger in, as the last push of his weakened hand had tried to grab at it. He made a small gurgle as he gasped for air. His eyes looked at her with fear, and a second later, when his hand fell palm up in lament, they did not see her anymore.

She knew it was not the cleanest kill, nor the most humane, if any murder could be humane. What little she had discovered about Rupert and his son from this mission was minimal, especially with all the maid's work she had been forced to do to keep up appearances. For the most part, her information came from the other servants in the palace. They always gossiped about the lords. She felt bad about how little they spoke of their own lives, but she did not speak of hers ever.

Lord Rupert was known as an irritating man, and only respected and feared because of his cousin, Nikolis. Rupert often forced his nose into things he should not. A minor lord, with only small holdings in the Dorian lands, he saw himself as much richer, more influential, and tried to interject himself as someone in a place of power. Many used the ploy to great success, but the lords surrounding Lord Hadire were far more intelligent than Lord Rupert. All of this was revealed in a single night at a feast, when she had listened to the conversations while she served.

Someone hired Klor Dem to put him away, having become very tired of his antics and uneasy demeanor. Most recently, the other servants gossiped that he had called Lord Jason Lawlurd and his father, the High Lord Mason Lawlurd, buffoons for thinking they could start a trade route with some of the more civilized tribes of Thernat.

She, however, knew from the servants and some of her own reading of the parchments in the Dorian quarters, that Rupert in his brazenness had already made a trade route for cattle with the tribes using his lord cousin's cows. Secretly, though, he took a larger portion than he should from the earnings, stealing from the generosity of his own family. Besides that, he did not get along well with Devom Alwin, who held the respect and ear of many of the lords. Many factors presented themselves as reasons to kill him.

She frowned at the thought. The one thing that might have protected him more from the other lords was the approval of Nikolis. If he had been sent as a representative of his cousin, then a protective hand would be on him. However, he had stayed in Sarn Peligmo for his own gains, trying to strengthen his own holdings, all the while causing his powerful cousin to lose face among his lordly peers.

She guessed Nikolis did not hire her, as it was still a terrible thing to kill a family member. Those who were caught conspiring against family lost much. She guessed it was one of the other lords, who had grown tired of his antics.

She used the couch to wipe some of the blood off her hand; it too seeped into the cloth. She looked at the parchment, hoping it held important information, but it only read about the cattle movement through the region. She pondered more about who had really called for the hit. Sometimes, her curiosity over who had hired her was stronger than she liked to admit.

She shrugged and put a piece of eel in her mouth. She smoothed out her dress and stepped over the blood.

Now for the handsome son. It would be a shame to end such a specimen of a man—at least for a minute or two. Picking up the second platter, she walked over to a wooden door. As she moved into the more shaded room, where the thick curtains were drawn, she shut the door behind her and was surprised by a shirtless Gerhart standing in front of her.

"I'm sorry, did I startle you?" The man was a foot taller than her. He stood almost a giant, powerful and radiant, looking down on her with penetrating amber eyes.

"Yes, My Lord," she lied, in a humble tone. Startled was too strong a word. Normally he stayed in his bed as she left his breakfast. People were getting too close to her as of late; she would have to be more vigilant.

"Please forgive me, I didn't mean to put you at unease." He stepped closer to her, only the platter she held between them.

Her initial plan to slit his throat while he slept might not work. She would have to think of something else. These turns in a plan always made things more interesting, so using the platter she pushed by him and headed over to the nightstand, where she usually left it, to set it down.

"What's the hurry?" Gerhart said, following her and cornering her again. "Do you have some other duties? Surely the other lords can wait a bit longer for their food?" What little she could see of his eyes penetrated deep into her.

"Yes, My Lord, I'm needed in the kitchens to wash out the morning's pots," Aija said, stepping back, as if frightened by him.

"I saw you smile at me a few times. Have you been trying to gain my attention?" Gerhart said, as he seemed to flex his muscles. The movement caused her to tense her own.

"A lady does not say, My Lord. The other maids do talk of your... umm, handsomeness." Her heart raced, and her cheeks felt hot.

"What do you think of my looks? Do you like them? Is that why you smile? That's why so many girls like you smile. I have that effect." Aija saw his eyes become more menacing as he drew closer.

"I… I cannot say, My Lord. A lady does not speak of such things," she said again, pulling back, her hands up to ward him off. She blushed, her cheeks red flame now. Was she pretending to blush? Could she pretend to blush?

"You're no lady, you're just a scullery maid. I've heard maids say things that would turn a whore's mind to mush, vile thoughts no true lady would ever comprehend. And I know you like me, that's why you smile. Have you ever been with a lord before? I mean, lain with one?" Gerhart took another step forward, the little bit of light in the room framing his muscular physique.

She admired him, his handsome chiseled jaw, toned body. Even his smile would make a normal girl quiver. Still, she was no ordinary girl, let alone a scullery maid. She tired of his arrogant attitude because she liked a humbler man, like Justin Primm, whose letter she read almost every night.

"Yes, My Lord, I've been with one, but he wasn't near as good looking as you," she said, now smiling at him, with an air of innocence.

"I bet not. Did he force himself on you?" Gerhart asked, reaching out with his hand to grab at her.

She stepped back and said, "No, My Lord... I took him."

"Really?" Gerhart said, in surprise. "You maids are a naughty sort. Who was the poor bastard, overpowered by you, little maid?"

"Your father, My Lord," she said, and in a heartbeat, a small knife shot out from her sleeve. In one movement, she sliced at his throat and inner thigh. She did not know if the surprise on his face was from the shock of her answer or his blood spilling all over the floor. She shrugged at him.

Caught off guard, watching the blood drip down to his chiseled abs, he threw her onto the bed as he fell and she tumbled off the other side, immediately rolling back onto her feet, ready to pounce.

A sharp but brief pain shot up her elbow from the landing. She jumped up and went to see if he lived. She did not find a heartbeat, and she had not been able to bring the death vial in her dress. She pulled the curtain and let the light in. The half-naked man lay on the floor, and then, moving to the fireplace, she stepped past a mirror. In it she saw her bloodied dress and blood-covered face. She was pleased the curtains had been drawn; she had small bits of blood on her from Rupert that Gerhart might have seen. Those spots were dry in the mirror; Gerhart's blood still held a wetter look to it. A lock of her black hair hung down, and she breathed deeply.

She stripped off her clothes, the cloth around her head, her dress, even her undergarments. Standing naked, she threw them all in the fire and went to a washbasin to wipe the blood droplets off her face and neck, as well as the blood covering her hands. When she finished, she checked the fire to make sure it consumed what she had thrown in and then poured the bloody basin in the fire. It sent a wave of smoke up the chimney and almost doused the flames.

Under a dresser, she pulled out the bundle of folded clothes she had tied underneath days earlier. She unfolded the clothes and began pulling them on. She put her daggers on, hidden in her sleeves, and hid her needles in a pouch, sewn inside the waistline. She tied her bobbed hair up into a ponytail. Last, she unwrapped a handkerchief she had stowed with the bundle. Inside lay a delicate strip of hair matching her dark hair. Picking it up, she pushed it against her top lip, smoothing it all the way across. There was a small bit of honey glue she had made on the other side. Licking her thumb, she smoothed it all down.

She went to the mirror again to make sure she looked right and shook her head with disagreement. The moustache looked passable but seeing herself as a man did not appeal to her. Picking up the twine that tied the bundle, she put it in her pocket and walked to the balcony. From behind a curtain, she watched the guard on the wall make his turn. Once he was gone, she leapt the edge to land on another balcony.

The balcony belonged to the Alwins, but they were always going to the bathhouse early. Timing the guard's turn again, she jumped down and landed on the ground, rolling into a shadow. She took a deep breath, listening for any sound of alarm.

She picked up some dirt from the ground, rubbed it in her hands, and then rubbed it on her face at her jaw line. She stood and walked around the corner into a building.

Being in disguise was something she always found enjoyable but knew she needed to work on. Some of the other assassins of her guild were experts at being someone else. Some only ever made their kills while in disguise, especially Begla. The master once told her, "If you're always in disguise, how will anyone ever be able to expose you?" Klor Dem, the Black Needle, were not real; they were nothing but a figment, a shadow in the corner of people's minds.

As a point well taken, she believed this and practiced it. She always felt better about a kill if she was herself. She felt dishonorable when hiding behind someone else's face.

Inside the building, it smelled like horses and hay. A man was cleaning out a stall, just as he did every day. She tapped him on the shoulder, and when he turned, a look of surprise and fear fell over him, until she pricked him with one of her needles and he went limp and fell into her arms, unconscious. Looking at his face, she thought, *Close enough. The moustache is perfect though.* She smoothed it down.

She pulled him into an empty stall and covered him in some hay. He would wake in a few hours and not know how he got there, but his stalls would all be cleaned, and he would be none the wiser for it.

As Aija waited a few minutes for the stable master to come in, she thought about Arnus. Like Gerhart, he was muscular and handsome, but also like Gerhart, Arnus gave her an uneasy feeling in the pit of her stomach. Was it just a loss of control for her feelings, an attraction she could not wrestle with? Was she giving into a more primal instinct? She laughed aloud, spooking a horse in their stall. How ridiculous for her to be dressed like a man, shoveling horse dung and contemplating whether she should be with Arnus. In a feigned deep voice, she said, "I'm a grown man, I do what I want."

The door to the barn opened and a bearded pock-faced man poked his head in. "Time to take the lord's horse out for grazing."

Without turning and continuing to clean, in her best deep, mimicking voice, she grumbled, "Sure, sure. Be right out." She put the pitchfork down and tied a rope around Lord Archum Hadire's prized gray stallion. She walked the beast out of the barn, past other stable hands, who paid her little mind, out a side gate of the palace grounds, and into a large, open, grazing plain, with short and tall golden grass reaching into the far distance.

She let the horse free, a massive muscular beast, to do as it wanted. It never went far, as it was the only horse allowed to graze there, and there was plenty of grass for it.

Aija looked back at the palace, and at the guards along the wall. The banner of a gray horse in front of a yellow rising sun flapped in the light breeze. She thought about her two dead marks, and the horse wandering around. She thought about Arnus and Justin Primm, and her life as a member of the Black Needle. Then she smiled, turned to face the wall of yellow grass taller than herself, lining the outskirts of the palace and the boundaries of Sarn Peligmo, and like a shadow, disappeared into their tangled blades.

Chapter 14

Liam and Dylan sat around the campfire while Gnik laid out a sleeping mat on the hard ground. They had discovered a small glade next to the road at the border crossing into Paraduo and decided to use it to rest.

Paraduo was mostly a hard, hot jungle land of treacherous roads and dangerous creatures. It would still be weeks before they reached its capital, Kageria. Liam and Dylan had let Gnik join them on their journey south, but he had started to second-guess his decision. The warmer temperature would be good, but traveling with them for the past few days had become cumbersome.

"Gnik, good fellow, you think any more on our proposition?" Dylan asked, pushing his short, dark hair back on his head. The light from the fire reflected his staring eyes.

"No, not really," Gnik said, sitting down on the mat and turning toward the warmth of the flames.

"Listen, I think it would be in your best interest to join us. The Order of the Black Paladins is an order of honorable men—well, and women. It's a place for outcasts who have no one. Not to say you don't..." Liam said, taking a bite of the rabbit they were cooking over the spit.

The smell of the rabbit enticed him, and using the knife from his boot, he cut a piece off. When he took a bite, Gnik wondered if he had cleaned his blade enough after cutting the thug's throat a few nights before. Just as fast as he thought it, he did not care anymore and took a bite. The meat tasted good, succulent even. Dripping hot juices spilled from the corners of his mouth with every bite.

"You're handy with a blade," Dylan said. "We can attest to that. You probably also have other skills. Maybe not such savory ones, but skills nonetheless, which can be used to help our Order."

Gnik nodded. "Could you use someone good at sneaking?" He said it in jest, but they took it as a serious question.

"We aren't a guild of thieves or assassins, but being quiet and hidden is always a good trait to have," Liam said, stretching out his legs and rubbing his chin. "Think of it like this, Gnik. Guilds aren't like the knights of Rosenia, who are regimented. Or noble houses, even. You don't have to be born with good blood into a prominent family to join one. The guilds will take anyone just about, and where one doesn't, another will. The Black Paladins don't care about blood or race or riches. They're looking for those individuals who can strengthen its ranks."

Gnik thought about his father. They shared no blood, as his father was Human. Still, he missed him and felt guilty for not having gone to see him. Was he heading to Paraduo or running from his father? Why would he not visit the man who raised him, maybe the only person who cared for him?

"You would be one of the few Goblins in the Order," Dylan said, nodding his head as he spoke. "It would give you some status among us. There are nearly four hundred members, most in the islands of Rovelle. Some are in Delcom, and a few in the Fang Isles."

At the thought of four hundred, lightning flashed in Gnik's head—blood and rain—then he was back, and Dylan still rambled on about what they do as a guild. "Wait, say that again. I lost myself for a moment."

"Well, for the most part we help protect some of the wild lands in Rovelle from the different Predan, Horak, and Terap tribes. In

Nyoko we're an established Order, and participate in their coliseum events, as well as their dealings with their enemies. Still, we don't just do that, we have been known to go on missions, escort important items, and people, even search for lost treasures," Dylan said, excited to be sharing the information.

"So, in some regards you're mercenaries, and in others you're hired guards?" Gnik said, looking for more meat from the rabbit. "You get paid much?"

"Enough that we're currently on our way to Kageria to purchase a Galvorn war pick."

The word, treasure, caught Gnik's attention. He loved the idea of treasure and treasure hunting. He had heard more than enough stories of the lost treasures of the older races and civilizations to envy anyone who went searching for them.

"Wait, why do you fight these tribes?"

"As you stated, we're mercenaries. We receive payment for handling some of these situations. When we don't get paid though, sometimes it's still worth fighting the tribes. Many of them hold treasure and trinkets of value we can sell. At the same time, we help protect the people and the land, which is of course our way of rationalizing the killing," Liam said, with a chuckle. "That sounds crass I know, but we do add a service necessary to Rovelle's survival. It's a more savage place than Rosenia."

"I guess what I mean is… why are the tribes fighting?"

"Some are fighting for what they believe is their land. Horaks fight because it's what they do," Liam said.

"We aren't trying to pressure you, by any means," Dylan added. Though to Gnik, it felt like they were. "We just think it would be a good fit for you. In these days of traveling with you, we've learned a little about you, and it makes sense."

Gnik thought about all the lies he had told them, and all the truths he had not. He would never tell them about the dream, about his father, and not about the murders and thieving. It was lucky these two were young and naïve. Someone a little older might have seen through his ruse. They might have seen the Goblin running to escape something. Then again, maybe they did see and did not care.

"What does it take to join?" Gnik asked, reaching for another piece of the rabbit, not really concerned with the answer.

"Well, there's a lot of training—it's hard work. The idea is to train powerful warriors with the abilities to fight hand to hand and use destructive magic to defeat their enemies. This training could take several years depending on your willingness to learn and the abilities you may already have. For you, the length of time would be with learning magic," Liam said, and then took a drink from his water pouch to wash down the rabbit.

The night grew cooler, and even though Gnik sat close to the fire, he pulled up a thick blanket and wrapped it around himself. Magic seemed worth learning but taking a couple years to do it was out of the question. He did not like hard work. He did the bare minimum to get by and was beginning to regret leaving his gang in Geowm, because of the ease of earning coin. He knew if he wanted, he could go back, but that would be dangerous with the amount of people looking for him. All he ever did now was run.

The best thing for him was to keep moving. If it meant traveling with the pushy Black Paladins, who continued to try to get him to join their little guild, or it meant going somewhere else, he would stay with them, hiding from those who sought justice.

"Thank you for catching the rabbit, Gnik. It tasted mighty delicious," Dylan said, leaning back against a fallen trunk to relax. He put his arms behind his head and smiled in comfort.

"Not a problem. Thank you both for letting me join you on this journey. I needed to get away from that whole area. It brings bad things around."

He thought of the authorities… and the constant dream.

He rubbed his yellow eyes; the night drew in. They had traveled a long way in a day with the three riding horses and the two pack horses. His rump and legs were sore. He always found it strange how riding a horse was almost as tiring as making the trek on foot. Then again, the horse did travel further.

"I feel sore," he said, rubbing the back of his left thigh.

"You know," Dylan said, still with his eyes closed, "in Rovelle we have horses, but we also have two-legged reptile creatures called Lazens. They can't carry as much supplies, but they can run further and faster."

Gnik began to understand his partial annoyance with the two, came from the idea that young Dylan was a wealth of useless information. What good was knowing about Rovelle if he never intended to go there? His fake interest in joining the guild served a purpose though, a ruse to stay traveling with them and make them comfortable with his presence.

Liam looked at Gnik and said, "In Nyoko, some people ride great gray beasts with long noses or trunks. They're called elephants, and others ride large, ferocious cats. They all seem to have different benefits."

He nodded, trying to give the impression he cared, thankful the night drew in and he could stop talking to them soon. Though worse might arise. The dream might come tonight. Even if it did not, he would be awake so long trying to hold off sleep that he would be exhausted anyway. The same happened every night. The constant battle to stay awake to avoid the dream, until sleep took him— even harder now because he did not have a constant flow of ale to help him relax, or sometimes black out.

"I'll take first watch," said Dylan, leaning back into a comfortable position.

"Good, then I'll take second," Liam said, trying to fix his bedding.

That meant Gnik would be third. He might not get any sleep tonight. If he stayed awake on his mat long enough, it would be his turn. "Night," he said, lying down and looking up into the open expanse of the darkened sky. The constellation Henathi, the Dareain Queen, loomed above him. The stars shone like precious gems in her crown. He filled his lungs with cool air and wished he could get a decent night's rest, but deep inside he knew he would not.

Would his life be different if the dream did not hound him? He was not so much a brigand before. His father was not the greatest of men, but he taught him the skill of being a conman. Relieving someone of their gold, especially those who owned too much, proved profitable, but what was Gnik now?

A murderer, and a downright thief—going so low as to steal from a poor woman trying to take care of her three children…

He turned over and closed his eyes. His thoughts wandered to his father and his health. Then they went to the boy Toby he killed, wishing he had not pushed him into the boiling oil. He had only wanted the gold from the furs. Some of the coin remained, but he was hard-pressed to let it go. It seemed to mean something to him.

As he lay thinking about the same things he thought of every night, his mind went to the dream. He tried to push it away, but it could not be helped. He tried to distract his mind with other things: women, piles of gold hidden in forgotten caves, and a shimmering lake that reflected the moon off its waters that he did not recognize, even being drunk. None of it helped. It was a curse, some awful curse that gripped him, never loosening its hold, an eternal prison sentence for the wrong he committed. The thought broke when he heard Dylan and Liam begin to talk.

In a whisper, he heard Liam say, "You think he's asleep?" They did not seem to know much about Goblins and their abilities. There were not many in Rovelle and Nyoko. Most Goblins could hear better than most of the other races. Not as good as the disgusting Darei or beasts of the forest, but good enough to hear the two men.

"Yes, the poor man," he heard Dylan say. "He's clearly torn about something. It's a shame we can't help him with it. If he joined the Order, we might be able to talk to the master about his dreams and nightmares."

They were quiet for a moment, when Gnik heard, "Did you hear why the master is well versed in those things?" Liam said.

"No, why?" Dylan whispered back.

"You may not have heard of this, but Master Rizan's father was friends with the first Black Paladin, before the creation of the Order. Apparently, at someone's wedding, a Dareian adventurer was murdered and raised back to life by the Orbel. He traveled to Parallin or Darowak, as the Orbel call it, the hidden world, but when revived and brought back to Sancta, another being entered his body at the same time, and they struggled for dominance."

Gnik still listened to the idiotic story because he hoped they would go back to the part about the dreams.

"Oh, I know who you're talking about," Dylan said, sounding excited. "You're talking about the Dark Paladin who rode around Rovelle in the dark days, causing havoc among the Alliance and the tribes."

"Yes, exactly. The Dark Paladin saw things. Once the two parts of him were separated, he knew things about Parallin and dreams. He understood they're in the same world but two different places at the same time, woven in and out of each other."

Gnik gritted his teeth in annoyance. No one died, went to Parallin, and came back. What a ridiculous concept. Now he knew the Black Paladins were filled with idiots. He wanted to jump up and laugh at the two, but figured he would keep pretending to sleep.

"Well, the master might be able to help, if we can ever get Gnik to join us," Dylan said, with a sigh.

"What's the next mission, once we finish retrieving the Galvorn?"

Back to reveling in his own demented mind, Gnik thought they were not talking about anything worth listening to; he only wanted to hear about dreams. Maybe one day he could find someone to help him with his.

Tired, he felt himself dozing off as the two still spoke in hushed voices. He was surprised; it might be the earliest he fell asleep in a long time. Then he heard Dylan say, "The master wants us to try and look for some clues on Nurame's murder while we're here."

Fully awake again, Gnik focused his ear on them. His heart thumped in his chest, and he worried they could hear it.

"Apparently the master met the dead king years ago, when they were younger. The king, though a prince at the time, traveled to Rovelle for a meeting with the Alliance. Besides being smart and kind, Master Rizan found him generous, as he paid close attention to the poor in the streets. He says since no one can find out what really happened, he figured you and I could dig around a bit."

Gnik no longer lay in the dark listening. Rain and lightning took him. The thump of hooves and rolling thunder echoed. Dark gray

213

skies blanketed the land, and a strong wind blew a sea of grass. There were screams and shouts, flashes of fire. It rained blood that fed the earth. Sometimes they would turn to falling petals, pure white petals floating down, then tainted by the red. The red flowing blood, the streams of lost life, thick and warm.

Then he came back, back to the campsite, the warmth of the fire behind him and on his hands. Warm hands... warm hands brought him to focus; the horses were whinnying, and he saw it. He was holding a knife, the hilt protruding from Liam's chest; warm red blood covered it. He jumped back startled, almost falling into the fire. What did he do? What happened?

The vacant eyes of the young knight looked at him, or were they? His mouth hung open like he had tried to say something, but he did not move. Gnik went to scream and then remembered Dylan. Looking around, he saw him lying motionless, asleep away from the fire. Was he asleep though? He went to him and pushed him over.

Vacant eyes stared again, and a slash opened at his throat.

Now he screamed in horror, falling back. *What have I done*? He did not remember doing it, but the two were murdered before him, his hands were covered in their blood. The dream, the dream did it. It must be the dream. Cursed, his senses were leaving him; his mind must have been faltering. He could think of no other explanation, and no reason to kill them.

Wait... he remembered them bringing up their next mission, searching for clues about the murder of Nurame, and the dream happened. It happened while he was awake; it held power over him even in his waking hours.

He picked up the water sack and rinsed off his hands as fast as he could. The horses were still uneasy from the smell of blood. He searched around the camp and started picking up the valuables. He could not stay here. He doubted anyone would find them anytime soon, but he could not be around more death. A flash of lightning again… and raining blood.

He packed as much as he could on one of the horses and readied another to ride. He grabbed all the food packs, the water skins, and rummaged through their pockets looking for coin. When he gathered it all, the amount surprised him. The Galvorn pieces were going to be expensive, because he carried enough coin for him to live off sparingly for the rest of his life. There was so much that he forgot for a moment that he needed to get away from the slain.

Coming back to his senses, he took everything else, including Dylan and Liam, and piled it up. Then, taking a piece of still burning wood from the fire, he lit it up and let it burn. Just before he did though, he remembered something else. The dagger, he wanted the Galvorn dagger, so light and so sharp.

Several times while traveling with them, he thought about whether he could steal it or not but knew it would be impossible. Now he must have it. He shifted the two dead men around and found the black blade on Liam's hip, still in its sheath. He undid the belt as the fire grew, consuming the pile. He yanked it away.

Looking at it in the orange glow, his yellow eyes grew large. It shone, a beautiful thing of black metal, reflecting every wave of firelight. He put it in a pack on the horse, turned and began to light the pieces of cloth that would catch on the heap. He untied the other horses, and they ran off in the night. They would be good money to sell, but too many questions would follow, wondering where he got them.

Trotting away on Dylan's brown gelding and pulling the horse he bought for the trip as his pack animal, he traveled on. He wondered where to go. With the fortune he carried now he could go anywhere. He would probably head south to warmer temperatures, away from the chilling bite of the north, but not into Paraduo. Maybe he would travel to see his father, maybe as far south as Telaporawein, the city of the mages, where anyone could hide, but he knew he would never come north again.

He focused on what happened. Already it ate at him. What had he done to overpower Dylan on watch? Took him by surprise, no doubt. How much had the dream been in control? He remembered nothing. Then to kill Liam in his sleep. He was cursed, some abomination born into a more peaceful world. The dream raged as more than a nightmare. Could guilt be so strong? It must be one of the Mahrfolk, an evil spirit haunting his sleeping and waking worlds. It would follow him to the furthest reaches. The curse posed a danger, making him dangerous so long as it held him.

Chapter 15

After nine days of rocking and salt sea spray, the small frigate, *Wave Jumper*, with its red hull trimmed in gold paint, came in sight of Septimar, the capital of the Rovelle States.

"Feeling all right, Sir Andross?" Captain Howe said, standing above him at the tiller, his slicked long silver hair moving in the breeze. He wore a long brown coat and brown leather boots, with a rapier at his side.

"Aye, Captain, for now. Of all the evil in Sancta, sailing is the one I fear most," he said, with a laugh.

"It's that bad for you, is it?" the captain said.

"If not for the mages on the boat, who continue to do things to help me feel better, I wouldn't be well enough to have this conversation with you or stand here and admire the grandeur of the bay."

"So, you like what you see? It's a magnificent sight, the island city rising high with its large bridges, when you come on it at this time of day," the captain said, looking out over the water as well.

"I don't know how it was done, but it's a sight to behold," Andross said, as his stomach bubbled. "Do you know much about how it was constructed?"

"Not much, just that the Darei, Aknon, and Humans worked on it together, and incorporated the help of many mages to complete it. See there, that's the central tower..." The captain pointed at a large island with a rising tower. "Where your Mages Congregate will take place. You'll find it to be the neutral grounds of the Rovelle Alliance."

Andross shook his head at the sight, as it rose high in the sky, a couple miles wide. "Yes, I do believe I recall that." He remembered now how the eight islands, connected by many bridges, rose by roads and stairs through each tier of each island.

"So... I don't know much about this meeting of mages. What's its purpose?" the captain said, squinting.

"Every four years, the many mages' guilds and academies, or any one of interest, meets here in a gathering. They discuss what they've learned, what they're trying to create, and what they've discovered from the older tomes. Rules are made as well to keep things in check."

"Sounds unpleasant. I'm a man who works with his hands. I imagine you're the same?"

"To an extent," Andross said, looking at his hands and then back out over the waters that reflected a setting sun. "There's usefulness in honing one's arcane abilities. I've been shown a few things. At the same time, this whole thing is to make sure magic doesn't get out of hand."

"Sounds dull."

"I can take a day of it, but in the second day it does start to drain on me. However, it's one of my duties. I'm only a liaison for King Coram and the Rosenian Council, here to be the eyes of the kingdom."

"Well, that's a good thing," the captain said, shifting the ship's direction. "Better to have the eyes of a loyal subject whose every moment isn't built on more magical powers. We'll be escorted into the port soon and dock in maybe an hour. I hope you'll get some rest after how sick you've been."

"Thank you, Captain. If nothing else, I hope I won't be vomiting for a few days."

"I am contracted to take you back at the end of the Mages Congregate. I'll see if there's anything I can do to make the return voyage smoother. The weather did not cooperate for a few days."

"I'll be better. Maybe I'll get some sleeping potions and sleep my way through most of the return trip." Andross laughed.

The captain joined in. "Well, good sir knight, I would hate to have to tell all my friends how I met you and found that while you're born on the stories of many a bard's tongue, that the one foe who defeated you was the sea." The captain laughed and so did his first mate.

"Nor would I want to tell my friends how a captain I once knew disappeared into that sea," Andross said, looking back at the captain. They all began to laugh. He liked the captain. He was an honorable man, strict with his crew, but still a man with a jolly sense of humor. It also helped in their friendship that Captain Howe had once been a Knight of the Wolf, specifically a Sea Wolf. They were knights assigned to the Rosenian Naval Fleet.

Unlike some of the other passengers who traveled on the ship, with war stories to swap, Andross and the captain got to know each other quite well as they dined. Other than the crew, there were fifteen others, all of which were mages. For Andross, as mages went, he did not get along well with many. On this voyage, he spent a lot of time talking to Athiny of the Crimson Order, who also joined him and the captain at dinner. He was not stuffy like so many other mages.

As they drew closer to the city, they could hear the echo of horns coming across the water. "What's going on, Captain? Is this normal? Surely, they don't blow horns for every ship coming into port. They would be blowing all day." There were ships all over the docks, and many boats and barges in the surrounding waters.

219

He ran his hand through his dirty blond hair as the door to the lower decks came open. There, wrapped in a white sheet, and carried by six naked Bronlings, all part of the crew, lay the body of an old man who died on the journey. He passed away in his sleep the night they entered the Dalari Pass, which led between two of the great islands of Rovelle, Darehalyn, and Laridona.

Jordan Lafont was a wrinkled old man, and though part of the crew, Andross never saw the man do any work. What he did see was an overwhelming amount of respect given the elderly man from the crew and even more from every Bronling crew member.

"It's not normal as far as I know. Some of the crew mentioned there would be a ceremony for the old man. He did not do much on the ship, but joined with a few Bronlings some months back, and they said they'd pay his way. I liked the man. He kept to himself, except when a good story seemed necessary. Boy, did he have some crazy ones," the captain said.

The six naked Bronlings, with the tattoos of their tribes on their heads, were followed by another Bronling dressed all in white. It looked to Andross as if they had taken white sheets from a cot and wrapped the old man in it as well. His face sat solemn, and in his hands, he carried a knife. It seemed no different than any other knife with a wooden handle that you could find in the ship's kitchen, and yet it was held across his palms with great reverence, almost as much as the body itself.

Everyone parted for them as they made their way to the port side of the deck. Then, one by one, the Bronling in white began to make a small slice on the pointer finger of each of the bearers. They held their finger up to the air while still holding the body, almost like they were checking the wind, and then wiped the blood in one long sweep across their foreheads and along their tattoos.

Athiny moved next to him, an older mage, wearing his crimson robe. His lips were pushed out, his eyes staring in contemplation. "I've heard of this before, but never thought I'd see it," he said.

"What are they doing?" the knight said, staring in wonder as the seven Bronlings looked silently out over the water as the horns continued to echo over the afternoon's ripples.

"This is called the Rite of the Sea, the funeral ceremony of the Bronlings. Strange, it's only accorded to those of great renown among their own race. And stranger still, that old man, Jordan as he liked to be called, was Human." Athiny still held a puzzled look on his face, his curly gray hair disheveled from the wind. "The only thing I can think of is maybe some of the crazy stories he told the first night were true."

"You mean the stories of the great Bronling exodus from the Fang Islands? About being in Robo the day the first Bronling ship made port. That's ridiculous. That happened over two hundred years ago. He told us he was a boy of fifteen when it happened. He would be about 220 years old. There must be something else. I won't say he hasn't won some great honor from them, but being over two hundred years old..."

"It's not unheard of, Sir Andross, for someone to live that long. The Darei do it all the time," said Athiny with a nod.

"True as that might be," Andross protested, "they're Darei, Elves. That's how long they live, some of them even longer."

"I've heard tell there's a woman in the great library of Nowann, King Nurame's library, who can tell you when they built the second wing, and how there used to be a stairway that led down underneath the library. If you listen closely, there are stories all over about those who live longer than normal," Athiny said, looking at him with raised eyebrows. "The true mystery isn't how anyone could

221

believe such nonsense. The true mystery is why would these stories exist? Isn't it at all possible to believe some of them are telling the truth?"

"Well, maybe so, but it still doesn't explain this," Andross said, motioning to the ceremony.

They pulled alongside the docks. After he went below deck and retrieved his things, he noticed a line of soldiers waiting, and another line near the warehouses and buildings at the end of the dock. The horns were much louder now and seemed to be sounding all over the city.

"Look there, Sir Andross…" Athiny pointed, as the gangplank was set and the ship tied off. "Look at the crowd in the streets. Those guards are lined up holding them back."

Several hundred yards down the docks, up in the main streets of the Septimar ports, he could see hundreds, if not thousands, lined up in the streets. He was not sure why at first, and many looked like children. After a closer look, he realized the streets were filled with Bronlings.

Just then a large soldier stepped across onto the plank. "Captain, I am Commander Astibo Gilga of the Septimar Guard. May I board?" As one of the Aknon race, the soldier stood large, with broad shoulders. At near eight feet with thick arms, a light layer of brown fur, black eyes, and a black tail, the soldier towered over them. Andross had seen Aknon before here in Rovelle, but they were still a daunting sight. They were the size of Ogres or bears, almost giants.

Like all the other soldiers, the commander wore light-blue plate armor trimmed in silver, the six-pointed star of the Alliance on his breastplate, and on his helm the same star, but in the middle sat the symbol of a double-peaked mountain. This was the symbol of the

Aknon race, who were descendants of the Yheta, who had been chased by a large group of Somdarei out of Hima, the mountainous region north of Rosenia, and were followed across the sea.

He remembered the story. Both were shipwrecked, and both were forced into an alliance to survive on the islands against the local inhabitants. The alliance became the start of the Rovelle States.

"Thank you, Captain." The commander nodded and then said in a deep vibrating voice: "I have been ordered to inform you that the Bronling embassy has requested you allow for one Jordan Lafont to be carried off the ship before allowing the rest of your passengers to depart. Once they are off, you may allow the rest, but none may pass the bearers until the procession is through the city and has arrived at its destination."

"Of course," Captain Howe said, "we will respect the wishes of the guard. Not to sound disrespectful, Commander, as Jordan has been a friend and crew member of my ship, but what is this for?"

"I'm not completely sure, Captain. I was hoping you knew," Andross heard the commander say in almost a whisper. "All I know is General Voldair, on the command of the chancellor, ordered me to make sure this happened, and to not allow anyone to hinder it."

Andross watched as the six Bronlings carried the body across the plank, followed by the one in white. Once they reached the dock, the other mages, including Athiny, began to exit the *Wave Jumper*.

He heard many of the mages begin to complain even through the blowing of the horns as they drew near the crowd. They could see that none of the baggage carts that were supposed to meet them were there waiting. He was amazed sometimes at how much mages

223

complained. When it came to doing anything physical, most wanted nothing to do with it.

Pulled from the thought, he gaped at how many people were there, and how the majority were Bronlings. They stood stoic and tattooed, the men with their topknots or shaved heads, and the women's hair braided up in their fashion of sailor's knots. They crowded the streets in thousands. One of the main bridges was filled with them trying to enter the main city. Following at a slow marching pace, he listened as they all cried in great despair. Some of the women were hysterical, falling or fainting to the cobblestone street. Children stood red-eyed and whimpering. Bronling men, short in stature, stood tall like worn, weathered statues.

As the body reached the outer ramp that led into the main body of one of the easternmost city towers and out of the port district, the horns stopped and bells began to chime. Their echoing reverberated through the streets and over the surrounding waters. The crowd filed around the procession, marching up into the next level.

At the Merchant's Tier, the city became more crowded, and the city guard was out in force, lining the streets and holding everyone back from the procession. In the commotion, Andross heard someone yelling his name.

"Sir Andross. Master Athiny, over here. This is them, Captain, the ones I'm waiting for," yelled the gaunt figure of a young man with thin black hair and a pockmarked face. The line of guards parted, and he and Athiny moved out of the street, the line closing behind them as the procession moved on.

"Hello, hello, good sirs. I'm Apprentice Baylan, sent here by Master Edonde to be your guide through the city. He wanted me to meet you at the docks to help with your things, but the guards wouldn't let me through, so I had to meet you here and beg the pardon of the captain to let you out of the throng. I want to take you up the stairway to the next tier. That way we can bypass the procession. Apparently, they will be marching through Merchant Tier, and then back onto the ramp, through Quarters Row, where we are all staying, through the residential area, and then ending at the house of the Bronling ambassador here in the city. However, Master Edonde figured you wouldn't want to wait through the long march. Can I carry anything?"

This all came out of the young man in a single breath.

Andross glanced at the older Athiny where the mage just shrugged. He was happy to skip the march, and shook his head no, as the young man took a bag from the Crimson Caster.

"Do either of you know what's going on?" Baylan went on without taking a breath. "I only heard something about a great Bronling hero died and they're giving him some ceremony. I never heard of anything like that from their race. I always thought they gave their people back to the sea, as they all seem to think that is where they came from. Mother Sea, they call it. I think it is *Wapa Ma*, in their tongue, but don't tell anyone I know that. You know how the Bronlings are about their language. They don't share their tongue often…"

The young man continued, and Athiny leaned over and said, "Talkative young lad, isn't he? He's being trained by the great Master Edonde. He must have great skill." He rolled his eyes. "Still, it's odd, the boy brought up a strange point. They don't share their tongue with anyone, and yet I thought I heard old man Jordan mumbling to one of the Bronling crew in their language. I dismissed it as me hearing things. More mystery for your puzzle."

Andross shook his head but had let the thought drift out of his mind. Too many mysteries burdened him now to take on another. King Coram had sent him to be his ears for the congregate, not to worry about an old man.

He found it sad that the king felt it necessary to send him to watch the proceedings when his top advisor and a partial mage, Azziza Zattu Nadal, also attended at the king's command.

As they entered the next tier, Baylan chattered away about the flowers on the garden island. Andross would be happy to be done with him. They headed down the main street. Inns lined each side. At the end of the street stood the barracks of the Septimar Guard, walled off on its own, a fortress inside a city; there were more on every island tower.

He remembered being given a tour before. It was well fortified and housed nearly one thousand soldiers, acquired from all the races of the Alliance. In total, the city garrisoned seven thousand, which rotated in and out more from the Rovelle State's Army and from the individual city states.

The Moon Dust Inn sat near the end of the main street, and he looked at the fortress near it and saw the flag of the States hanging from the battlements: a golden flag, with a six-pointed, white star in the middle. Inside each of the six points was the symbol of the six races of the alliance: the double-peaked mountain of the Aknon, a remembrance of their ancestors' home in the mountains of Hima; the crossed spear and sword of the Somdarei of Rovelle; the crescent moon over waves for the Bronlings; and a green spiny apple, or pineapple as some called it, for the Humans, who helped them survive when they began to colonize one of the other islands. The last two points were the two races he knew little about and had hardly ever seen.

As they entered the inn, he saw a member of one of the races he knew little about, as a guard at the front gate of the Septimar Citadel. As a female Malkienon, she stood in her plate armor with a spear in hand and the curved blade sword of her people, a katana, at her side. Her fur looked dark gray in the distance; white fur trimmed her face, and she had white, pointed ears. Her tail swung side to side, and just from a brief glance at her he could see there was a dangerous speed and quickness to her.

The Malkienons had started a small, singular colony, away from their home of Nyoko, on the island of Sizanda on the west side of Rovelle. In the star though, their symbol was one of their eyes, with two curved swords behind it.

Andross had seen a few Malkienon in the Rosenian port cities in the past, but he only ever saw females. Rumors said there were no males of their kind, but ship captains claimed otherwise. There were apparently fewer males, and they did not like to leave their homeland far to the west.

Inside the Moon Dust Inn, the innkeeper met them with a thin smile, and less than warm courtesies. "You must be the knight from Rosenia. Your room is up the stairs to the right, second door. Mind you I said second door. The first belongs to Master Edonde."

A group sat around a fire, and two soldiers sat at a table with mugs of ale. They stared at his sword. As he walked by, he nodded up in salute and they just kept staring. It was a nice change for him. Almost every soldier in both Rosenia and Paraduo recognized him or his sword.

As he moved up the wooden steps, creaking with each footfall, Baylan called out. "Sir Andross, Master Edonde would like for you to join us for dinner this evening. He said since you're a low-level

227

trainee in the Crimson Order, you're more than welcome to join us."

Athiny looked at him with a strange flick of his eyebrows, "You didn't mention you were a trainee. I could've helped train you on the voyage. You know, raised your skill with us."

"It's not something I mention often. Nor have I been given a lot of time to focus on it. You know the duties of a king's man. It's more of a request from his majesty to learn what I could of magic from a beginner's point of view." *As well to look at the fastest growing guild in Sancta*, he thought to himself. "And yes, I accept the invitation for dinner. Thank you, Baylan." He saw the young lad beam.

*****

Later that night, when Andross got some needed rest from his ordeal at sea, he went back down to the dining area. Many members of the Crimson Order were there arranging themselves around the tables. "Ah, good, Sir Andross, you're here."

"Good evening, Master Edonde." He lifted his head in respect. It was something he did so often it came naturally for him to do at most meetings as Grand Knight of Rosenia, but in this case with Master Edonde, one of the grand masters of the Crimson Order, and he a known trainee, he should have bent his head down in respect. Then again, should he? Who really trumped who? He was here as a liaison to the king, not as a trainee.

Edonde smiled. "Sir Andross, let me introduce you to someone. This is Master Urlita Neebka, of the Orbel, and one of the few who have decided to join a guild, let alone ours."

"It's an honor to meet you, Master Urlita Neebka. I'm Andross of the House Delaqeen." He put his hand out and shook the Orbel's.

"I know much about you," the Orbel said. "You're a high knight, favored by your king, a hero from the War of Men. I'm also a hero to my people."

"Then an even greater honor to you, Master Urlita Neebka," Andross said, wondering what triumph the small Orbel had done.

Edonde laughed at the respectful introductions and then the small Orbel joined in. "No need for so much formality, sir knight, you may call me Neebka." Andross watched as his small rabbit-like nose twitched. Neebka had red fur on his head and circling his eyes, and stood at about mid-thigh to himself, even smaller than the people of the Linga.

"Both of you sit near me, I insist," said Edonde. "With both your formalities, I'll end up chuckling myself to sleep tonight if I don't choke on laughter before that."

Andross smiled and sat down next to Edonde, whose long straight black hair sat on his shoulders; his sharp hairless chin reminded him of a spear point. The grandmaster wore a long, deep crimson robe with gold stitching of intricate designs on the collar and the shoulders. Neebka wore the same robe, but with black stitching in the same places. Looking down to the end of the table, where his friend Athiny sat, he noticed the same black stitched robe.

"Maybe I should know this as a trainee, but may I ask what the difference in your stitching is?" Andross said, pointing at the two shoulders.

Neebka spoke up first, adjusting himself on the cushion of his seat to give himself enough height to see over the table edge. "Well, the truth of the matter is I'm not a grand master yet. Nor is your

229

friend Athiny down there." Athiny must have heard his name, because he looked up and waved to him. "I'm truly only a master magelock."

Andross had heard the term before but was not completely sure of its meaning. Edonde must have seen it in his face; he spoke up next in his smooth voice: "Master Neebka is in all rights in the Order as Master Magelock Urlita Neebka, meaning he is a master of the arcane or magical but has not yet mastered combat. As you know, the Crimson Casters pride themselves on knowing both areas. In order to be truly called grandmaster, one must be an expert in both branches and have taken an apprentice at one point. Then your robe, if you want a robe, will have golden embroidery sewn on. Usually, those who focus on the arcane wear the robe, and those who focus on combat wear an armored hauberk of crimson or a doublet."

Neebka smiled, his cheeks pushing out, and said, "The truth is, Sir Andross, with you being a knight, you might easily pass the test for the combat side of the Order. In turn, you would be called warmagi and then take an apprentice as master warmagi. Well, when you get your magic side to a novice level, which is a step also."

Andross nodded at the thought of being a master warmagi in the Order. He would have to investigate that.

The chatter in the hall was loud with talk about the coming days, and how the opening ceremony would start later that night. The food came out, two large ducks for a main course, and red-striped tuna, roasted potatoes, platters of honey gravy, large loaves of peppered bread, and ale.

The night grew dark, but fires and lanterns lit the room. Andross, often a solitary man, found himself talking and eating and being jovial. He enjoyed it differently from a royal ball. It was a more liberating experience that let him be sociable with people, and at the same time be able to walk away untied to any sort of friendship. At that moment he wondered how Mahley fared. He seemed tied to her now, and he hoped she stayed safe in Nowann. Still, as much as he was enjoying this sort of get-together, he would never seek it out.

At one point, he got Neebka to explain the Orbel's symbol of some sort of flower on the States flag. "It isn't just any flower. It's a Forella Domi. Now, don't go eat it. For you, it's mostly poisonous. Only a few Humans have ever eaten it and survived. It's a healing flower for my people. When we eat it, it helps regenerate any wound we may have. It's a flower that has saved the lives of many an Orbel."

"So, it's poisonous for me?" Andross asked.

"Yes indeed. It still has healing properties, but it's so powerful, and helps mend your wounds so well, your Human bodies cannot take the stress and quickly shut down. Before long, you'll die. Though Humans and Darei have learned to make medicines and salves from it, which work very well, it's still dangerous in those forms."

The night wore on, and before long they walked the stone streets with a procession of mages from all sorts of guilds from around Sancta. A rainbow of long robes and cloaks dimmed in the darkness, moved like a serpent along the avenues of Septimar. They were headed for the massive assembly building on the middle island for the start of the Mages Congregate, and as always Andross felt very out of place.

Chapter 16

Lecture after lecture caused Andross' days to roll on, like the slow boiling of a pot while he watched. When the subject came to magic, which he held little interest in; his ability to focus was that of a child learning about banking.

He sat in the domed assembly hall, counting the hours until they broke for lunch. The hall rose elaborately, built with intricate, carved pillars, climbing high into the rafters. Decorated walls of burgundy were outlined in gold and pearl white, while soft, flowing carpets lined the floor, yet unworn by steps. The circular hall held thousands, towering above a bastion of beauty and art, the grandeur of a great building seldom used.

He sat toward the middle of the encompassing room, close enough to the stage to feel some of the effects of the magic on display. None dazzled him, and few held his attention very long. Irritated and uneasy, he became impatient.

During the opening night, fire tamers from Nyoko conjured fire from nothing, igniting it in their hands. They were able to play with it in amazing feats by throwing it back and forth or exploding it in waves of heat above the watchers. Unblinking, he watched while they turned the flame into whips and fought with them, coordinated and smooth. The thought of the fire dancers resonated with him, and he grew curious, but nothing displayed had held any value.

The same night, the Love Guild, comprised of attractive women revealed their new ability. In alluring white dresses, three stood on stage and began to bend the mind of a man with magic, controlling his more basic instincts. This held little relevance to Andross' actual purpose for being there. He and many of the others watching thought it was only a trick. Women already controlled men's minds, and they did not need magic to do it. Everything else at the assembly put him in a state of unrest, and the unrest soon led to discomfort.

Sitting, he tried to present himself as an important representative of the king. He watched the new uses of the arcane and elemental, along with rulemaking to add to the *Tome of Magicka*.

The book was the end-all, be-all of the mage's world, a tome holding spells, rules, and regulations, and even the history of magic. "I didn't pay attention much the last time I attended. Weren't there three *Tomes of Magicka*?" he asked.

"You may have seen three, but the truth is there are many more, hundreds of volumes housed in the library in Telaporawein. There's too much to be housed in just one book. See those scribes up there?" Athiny pointed.

Andross nodded, seeing three mages, a woman and two men in yellow robes.

"They're writing down everything that happens here. On their return to Telaporawein, they'll either add to the appropriate volume or create a new one. What you see them holding there is the only volume they copied and brought, where they knew information would need to be changed in regard to the rules. Like a ledger for keeping track of changes. The three will write in more detail and will add upon their return."

"I did not know there was that much concerning magic. Why not hold the gathering in Telaporawein? That seems simpler."

"Rovelle is a more centralized location," Athiny added in a hushed tone. "No one trusts being housed in that shady place. But some of it is repeated in the volumes, as many tomes came from different sources who may have found the same way to do something, or even the same result conjured two different ways. In a way, we're at the height of magic and lost in it as well."

"What do you mean?"

"The great wizard Tratton held great amounts of essential knowledge, and so did others before him. So much knowledge on magic that it's possible the tomes could be doubled." Athiny said, with great reverence. "Or so it's thought. We have spells and incantations today that they did not have in the past, but at the same time, much has been lost. The big thing now is the understanding that with enough work, most sentient and some non-sentient beings can harness some amount of magic."

Andross furrowed his brow. "What happened to Tratton and his knowledge?" he asked, now sitting on the edge of his seat.

"Several decades ago, his acolytes found him dead one day in his tower. They were so distraught that they went mad and burned the tower with his body in it, and his books, to the ground. Most of them let themselves burn with it." Athiny looked toward a group of mages sitting in the shadows. "Over there are a few of his remaining acolytes."

Andross looked and saw some shaded figures but could only make out that what they wore did not affiliate them with any of the guilds there.

The demonstrations went on, but none of them really seemed worth bringing back to King Coram. What good would it be for the king to know that a vote passed declaring that no mage, without permission from the Mages' Council, could delve into the study of necromancy, the waking of the dead? This was clearly important to some, but not necessary to the king. Zattu could deal with the laws and rules of magic.

He heard in past gatherings that mages came and conducted demonstrations and performances of unthinkable power. The elemental mages often displayed some new way to control the world around them, so when one did come forward to show his power, he leaned forward, his eyes wide with his attention.

The man wore brown, matching trousers, and a sleeveless shirt. Andross watched as the elemental mage began to pull earth through the floor, grain by grain, to fill a glass. It took hours, and while this impressed many of the mages, even the arcane users, it meant nothing to him, except that it wasted at least two and a half hours of his time. The value would be seen when they could pull something more substantial, like a person, through an object.

Through Athiny, he found that many rules were in place during the assembly. Sometimes the debate of the day would become heated. There were many different branches of magic. The arcane mages could conjure something from nothing and bend it to their will; they accounted for most mages gathered. They could call fire into their hands through their sorcery. Then there were the elementals; they could take the seven elements and bend those to their will.

Athiny explained that while the arcane mages could conjure fire, so could the elemental mages, but in two different avenues of magic. The elementals created fire in their hands by weaving the heat around them into a concentrated ball until the energy became so great that fire sprouted. Once there, they could control it at will. Andross knew there were many elemental forces: air, water, earth, light, dark, fire, and one he still did not know.

The arcane used their inner strength to conjure things like fire through spells. He understood the concepts of both, but to him it did not matter how you made the fire, so long as it was there when you needed it.

"There are other forms besides these. Mentalists alter the minds of living things to do their bidding, but so far only in the smallest of ways. Naturalists converse with nature and ask it to do things. This is something that many of the Darei, especially the Haldarei, are able to do."

Andross nodded, taking in as much as he could, while also trying to pay attention to the presentation on the stage.

"Some only consider this a natural-born skill for the Darei, but as this has not been disproven as magic, they're still invited to the Congregate, and often present. There are also summoners, necromancers, healers, destroyers, those who only focus on light magic, and those who work only with the dark."

Andross noticed the most heated debates were based around the rules of magic.

"This sort of thing has been happening since the early days of the Congregate. If one rule benefits a certain group of mages, but also hinders another, there will be an uproar."

"How are these things decided?" Andross asked, glancing toward the mage.

"Voting must occur. Those who propose it must abstain from the count. This gives the rulemaking a semblance of balance within the assembly. Each guild and type of mage is given a balanced number of votes, giving everyone their fair say. There has been tampering in the past," the mage said, shaking his head, the left side of his mouth upturned.

"You're being very helpful, Athiny," Andross said, shifting in his seat. "The last time I was here, I did not have anyone I trusted to speak to. You've explained a lot and almost made me more comfortable with the thought of magic. I'll say though, you haven't made the assembly itself any more enjoyable. Seems I'm now tasked with listening to old mages argue instead of fighting highwaymen or settling disputes of lords."

"Tell me the truth—you don't really want to settle noble disputes?"

The knight let out a laugh. "You do know me a bit. Even that's a huge bore. Just the highwaymen, and a scattered monster here or there."

*****

As the days moved by and the assembly came to its last day, Andross breathed a sigh of relief. Even with the constant conversation and learning with Athiny, and the dinners with Master Edonde and Neebka, the Congregate dug at his last nerve.

This seemed to be the case with many others as well. When a break for lunch finally came that day, he sat and enjoyed the fresh breeze on his skin in the city's beautiful gardens, something he felt Nowann could use more of.

Like in previous days, the shaded areas filled quickly. He watched some groups gathering around the pristine fountains splashing water, while he sat with a few of the Crimson Casters.

During these periods or in the afternoon, many of the different members of each guild would seek out other guilds for long and deep conversations. He rubbed his hand through his hair, thinking about his trip home soon.

Normally, he would converse with his friend, but today Athiny spoke with the Dream Guild. So, he sat outside of the assembly building and lost himself in its beauty. The assembly hall stood red and gray, bricks reaching what seemed ten stories high. Large windows with painted scenes circled the dome made of silver. The gardens were filled with verdant trees of oak and willow, surrounded with pink and red blooming flowers, and clean splashing fountains were scattered as central points along a maze of walking paths. Hedges lined corners of the gardens, and emerald grass sections littered the ground, giving ample room for the many visitors to sit and converse.

He took it in for some time before his relaxation was interrupted by a Shadow Mage who shoved Baylan over a bench and into a bush. "Now what was that for?" the talkative young man said, scrambling back up. The food he had retrieved for Master Edonde scattered all over.

The Shadow Mage laughed. "Fool. Your crimson robe disgusts me."

Andross watched four other Shadow Mages arrive laughing. One pushed the poor whelp back in the bush and he toppled out the other side. In his defense, a second Crimson Caster arrived. As she stepped forward to help Baylan, the group accosted her and she pulled her shortsword. Her face was stern and dotted in freckles, her hair curled short and red. She reminded him of Mahley, and he again wondered how she was faring.

"Get back," the young woman said.

"Oh, dear fellows," the antagonizing Shadow Mage said. "She's pulled her little sword. I guess she doesn't know how this works."

"Just leave us alone and be on your way," she said, waving her blade.

"We can't do that. You pulled a weapon on us. Didn't you know that by Congregate rules we can fight all we want without

238

punishment so long as we do not brandish any magic or weapons. We were hoping one of you red dogs would do something stupid."

She slid her sword back in its sheath as she helped Baylan up, having moved her attention to him. "We don't want any trouble. We want to be left alone."

Andross stood along a wall, near one of the fountains, watching. He could not decide whether he should step in or not. On one hand, it would be good for some young apprentices to get into a scuffle, but at the same time, he knew the Shadow Mages had the right to kill her. One of the many stupid rules Athiny had mentioned to him that the Congregate allowed for.

An orange flew and hit Baylan in the face. "I've had about enough of you Shadow Mages," the female apprentice said, standing her ground. "Your cruelty is unnecessary, and your focus on my guild is ridiculous." Her sword came out again in front of her, while the instigator stood looking at her, his face calm. "You're cowards. You wait until our masters are somewhere else, then come taunt us. You're too afraid to say anything or do anything in front of them?"

"It's funny you don't recognize us as apprentices as well," the Shadow Mage said. "We're your equals, but you're talking to me like we're more powerful than you. Is it because you feel our strength? Do you fear the abilities of our Order?"

Andross saw the eyes of the girl widen for a brief second and then relax again. He moved even closer; he did not want it to get out of hand, but having been in situations like this before, he knew it would.

"I am Forwin, an apprentice of the Shadow Guild," he said, in a smooth voice, "and I don't like your sword being pointed at me, child. I'm going to drown you in the fountain," he said, in a smooth tone. He pulled his gray hood away from his face. There were silver rings on one of his ears climbing from his earlobe halfway up. "See these rings. There's one for every Crimson Caster I've killed, and I can't believe the ease by which I did it. I even killed one by having a horse sit on him. What are they training you all?"

In a single movement, the unnamed girl charged him with her sword, stabbing at his chest. She almost ended him too, because his friends took too long to move out of his way. Once they moved though, the girl was no match for him. Baylan struggled to leave the bush, which grasped at his robes. Mages from the Sky Guild in their blue and white robes were trying to help him out.

She slashed at him again and he slid away. "Pull your sword and fight me, coward," she screamed. "I'll show you how easy we are."

Rubbing his forehead, Andross contemplated what to do next. He did not know where the other Crimson Casters were. Maybe if more came, the odds would be even, but the movement of the Shadow Mage made it apparent of his skill, and with the other four there, she had little chance.

"I don't understand. You're kind of a cute girl." Now the mage was purposely goading her. "Why stick up for this paper-thin halfwit? Do you like the pockmarked look?" Forwin taunted again, his companions laughing. "You should join us. I'll teach you a thing or two."

She swung, but anticipating his movement, slashed a second time and caught his robe, cutting a wide line near Forwin's hip, though she did not touch his flesh.

The arrogant Shadow Mage's eyes changed; they went from mockery to anger. He pulled his sword and lunged at the girl. She pushed aside the attack, the blade scratching the threads of her jerkin. Both blades rang in the open air of the garden.

At the same moment, pushing through the crowd, both Master Edonde and a gray-robed woman strode to the circle and yelled, "Stop!"

Immediately, the girl turned and began to walk away, but Forwin pressed forward.

In a flash, now close to the action, Andross drew his sword and redirected the Shadow Mage's lunge—so quickly that Forwin lost balance and fell to the grass.

Andross put his sword away even before Forwin landed. He watched him rise and turn toward him; anger and hate painted on his face. "How dare you interrupt?"

Forwin stabbed for him, and Andross sidestepped; the blade missed. The slash that followed also missed, and the knight wanted to laugh, but knew it was not chivalrous, no matter how much the young Shadow Mage deserved it.

He shook his head in disbelief. This young mage's swordsmanship was not anything of note. He had only been part of the Gray Foxes for a short time. Could it be too late to strengthen the kingdom?

Forwin lifted his sword for a huge arcing swing, and in an instant a dagger pressed to his throat, the point drawing a droplet of blood. His eyes grew big.

Standing with the weapon was the woman in the gray robe, a foot and a half shorter than the apprentice, her eyes lined with crow's feet, her blond hair turning white. "When I tell you to stop," she said, in a cool, malicious voice, "I mean stop. Now, do not make me draw any more of your blood and taint your robe *crimson*." She said crimson like it burned her mouth to mention it.

Forwin's face turned ashen white. "Yes, Mistress. I'm sorry, Mistress."

"Tell *them* you're sorry," she said next.

Everyone stood silently, watching the exchange.

Looking at the apprentice girl and Baylan, who had joined from the bushes, Forwin said, "I do humbly apologize for my actions." Then facing Master Edonde, he said, "Master of the Crimson Casters, please forgive my out-of-line behavior. Lastly, to you, sir," he said, now looking at Andross, "please forgive me for making you step into this fray."

The knight nodded as the dagger came away from Forwin's neck. The young man then walked away accompanied by the other apprentices. The lady in gray looked over at Edonde and gave him a slight bow. He bowed back in turn. Then she stepped towards Andross, the crowd parting.

She looked up in his face, her face stern, her voice still cool: "Do not presume to pull a sword on a member of the Shadow Order again or I'll have your hand."

He looked hard into her gray eyes and said, "I apologize, My Lady. It's my duty to keep the peace, and your apprentice broke it."

Mockingly she said, "What are you, some knight of Rosenia that you should put your nose in the business of others, with your sly comments and pompous attitude?"

"My business is others and all the people who encompass the word *others*. My friend, apprentice Baylan, is one of those others, as is the young lady. So yes, it is my business, as I am indeed a knight of Rosenia. My name is Andross Delaqeen, First Knight of the Dove. What might your name be, My Lady?" He smiled with his mouth, but anger showed in his eyes.

242

Her face changed in an instance; the tenseness calmed around her eyes. She looked at him hard for a moment and then said, "I know your name."

"To my great regret many do. I'm a Grand Knight of Rosenia, representative at this assembly for King Coram Lintrel," he said, unblinking.

"No, that's not how I know you," she said, still looking hard at him. "I can't speak here; there are too many ears and eyes. Meet me on the island of Levan at midnight. You may reach it by the small bridge to the south. Tell no one where you're going and bring no one. This is important. Probably more important than you know." She turned and walked away, disappearing into the crowds of mages adorned in all the different colors of the world.

*****

In the afternoon, as Andross waited, he found the bridge to the island so he would not get lost when time came to meet. Once the home of the Black Sun Necromancers, who tried to bring souls back from Parallin, the island itself was supposed to be a dangerous place where only brave souls went to mine for precious metals or bury their dead.

Not telling him why he asked, he had brought the island up to the tavern keeper earlier in the day: "For decades, an evil order performed experiments on loved ones only recently buried in the cemetery on the island. They were trying to raise an army of the undead through necromancy and dark magic, distorting bodies, even kidnapping live people for torture and testing. This went on until the Order of the Light Paladins and soldiers of the city found

243

out, marched to the island, stormed the stronghold, and killed or arrested every one of them."

He thought it was an interesting story but did not know how true it was. He stood near the top of one of the towers, looking over the water toward the small island. On the far bank, past some hills and the tombs of the buried, stood the black ruinous skeleton of a broken tower. However untrue or true the tale might be, some ominous group once took shelter there.

A hawker who tried to sell him a new sheath for his sword also told him the island was haunted and filled with all sorts of dangerous creatures, ghouls and ghosts, creatures who fed on the living. During some nights the screams and cries of the disturbed souls could be heard echoing across the waters.

He contemplated whether he should go. Just because some woman acted strangely and asked him to meet her there did not mean he needed to. His curiosity always did run high, even as a boy. Maybe it was a trap to lure him there and kill him, or a ploy to make him waste his night's sleep. He was departing home in the morning. If he did not sleep tonight, he would not be getting much sleep for the next week of rocky seas and constant vomiting and headaches.

Still, he must know. She said it was important. The moon hung high in the sky, but even in the broad expanse of the night, it floated a dark shadow. Its small light breaking through arches in the island tower. Lanterns and fire could only light so much. He breathed deeply, having traveled all over Rosenia and Paraduo alone except for Cleon. He would be fine.

He reached the bridge with midnight about to strike. Unsure of the rules, he hesitated about whether the guards would let him pass, so with quiet steps and the distraction of a passing lady of the night, he slipped behind them and down the long bridge.

Even as the lowest of the bridges, the bridge to Levan arched twenty feet above the water. It came out from a portion of a port district of the Malkienons' island and led out over the bay to an island further south.

When he arrived, there were more guards. As he drew closer, they did not hail him. When he reached their post, he saw they were not moving. He checked to see if they were alive and smiled to see they were. Somehow, they had been put to sleep. In Rosenia, it meant their death, if it could not be proven some outside source did not have a hand in it.

He walked by them and stepped out onto the sandy ground. A path led between two rock faces. He did not see the Shadow Mage, and even though the cliffs would be a good ambush spot, he walked along the path anyway.

He did not go far before he reached the cemetery of Septimar. It was unwalled, just an open expanse of the resting places of thousands on rolling hills. The moon held a much larger effect over the landscape than he expected. Shadows like giants from every tomb and gravestone stood motionless, seeming to face him. There were smaller tombs and then great monstrosities, and paths leading to all of them. Dark specters in the night, they stood quiet and still. He put his hand on his sword, and when he did a voice spoke.

"Don't worry, knight of Rosenia, no harm will come to you. At least not tonight."

Andross recognized the voice of the lady. "Why did you ask me to come here?" he said, still trying to find her in the dark.

She laughed. "That's a stupid question. Clearly, I wanted to tell you something under the secrecy of night and solitude," she said, her voice moving closer.

He made out her shadow now. "If you weren't a shadow before, you are now. You're like a fog on a snowy day."

She laughed again and moved close enough for him to see her. "My name is Kodren. I'm a master of the Shadow Guild. I wanted to know if the rumors are true. Are you still searching out the murderers of King Nurame?"

"Why? Do you have information I could use?" he blurted, thankful to have given this foray into the night a chance.

"Yes, I do," she said, dropping her hood. "I don't know how reliable it all is. I had to use my powers of persuasion to get it, but I have something you can use that I could not."

"First, why is this important to you? Why did you search out this information?" he said, trying to make out her face.

"Like you, I lost someone the night the king fell," she said, turning away and beginning to pace. "And like you, I'm not satisfied with the notion that by happenstance a group of bandits landed upon the king and his men and waylaid them. It's all too much to think of. Knights of the Thorn attacked on the road and killed… ridiculous."

"Who did you lose?" he said, watching her.

She sighed and turned to face him again. "My brother was a Knight of the Thorn. He rode with the king that night. My poor Laudrin."

"Well then, that makes you Lady Kodren, of the House of Ackart. I knew your brother well. He was a good man." Andross remembered Laudrin being selected by the king himself for sentinel duty, and only the best were selected for such a task.

The other truth was he had studied so much of the ambush and its every factor that he knew the name of every knight who accompanied the king. Ever since he had forgotten about the two boys, he had made it his business to know.

"I know he spoke highly of you as well," she said, her voice growing weak in the night air. "That's why I asked you here. I've searched for a long time, and I've tried to find clues for myself, even used my influence as a Shadow Mage and some of my abilities to do things to get answers out of people. I can't do it as often as I want, but maybe if you and I work together, we can solve the mystery of my brother's and of your king's murder."

"For your brother and the king, I will help you, but I've found little, except for a girl who claims she remembers that night, and swears visitors came to see her father. It may not be true, and if it is, she can't remember everything," he said, running his hand along the top of his head and filling his lungs with the cool night.

"Well, it's something. For my one piece of the puzzle, I throttled it out of a man in a village west of Faor. He claimed his son and himself might have been part of the killers there that night. I tortured him for three days before I believed it as truth. When I finally did believe, soldiers from the area showed up and I fled." She looked at the sky and closed her eyes. "His name was Vernor. You should find him. Maybe you can persuade him to talk about it. I couldn't."

"Why didn't you go back?" Andross said, excited for a new focus on the ever-taunting matter.

"I haven't had the chance." She looked down and over the shadowed graves. "Since then, I've been busy on business for the Shadow Guild, and haven't been within a hundred leagues of him. I'm bound to this guild by magic, otherwise I would."

He wanted to comfort the hard woman as she turned her back to him. Like him, she still mourned a great loss, but he only managed to say, "Then I'll see what I can find out, for your brother and my friend."

Chapter 17

Aija woke from a thin beam of light that found its way through the curtains and landed on her face. As she and Arnus were the master's supposed nephew and niece, they and Sani lived in quarters above the tailor's shop. In a nightgown, she went to the window and looked out into the busy street. She blinked as her eyes adjusted to the morning.

A man pushed a cart of carrots and cabbages, while a little boy, probably his son, sat on the back. An old woman in torn clothes begged for coin from a tall gentleman in fine olive-green clothing, and he ignored her outstretched hand. Two soldiers rode by, interrupting what might have been an illegal transaction. One of the two young men reminded her of Edwin. She had breathed a sigh having not been accosted by him. Her decision to sneak home had been rewarded.

Freshening up her face in the water basin, she saw a blue-eyed girl in the mirror with short black hair hanging just above her shoulders. She smiled at the fact that she still did not have a scar on her face from a mission; nor did she have blemishes, and her teeth were straighter than most. With her slim, toned body, she thought she might be considered attractive—at least the master said Arnus thought so.

Does he know any other girls his age?

Today, she would see what kind of attention she could draw from him, or anyone interested in that matter. She put on her newest dress; one she had requested from the master. She thought she would use it some other way. When she commissioned it, she had figured it would be a good dress to catch the eye of some lords at a ball. Today, it would be a trap for her blond-haired companion.

Now dressed, she realized that as thin as she appeared the dress clung to her body, emphasizing her trim physique. *A great tool to lure rats.* She smiled at the realization. The skirt hung midnight black, while the upper half was a dark red with black lace trim. It went well with her straight black hair.

"Morning, Sani," Aija said, coming down the stairs.

Sani looked at her hard for a moment and said, "Morning, child. As far as I know, you don't have a mission requiring such a dress and alluring look."

"True, but I need to try it on and break it in," she replied, her tone steady. Sani huffed out of her nose, but she had already skipped past, headed to the cellar to find something to eat.

When she came back to the shop level, Arnus stood waiting. His eyes grew large when he saw her, but then he turned and pretended like he did not notice.

Aija prodded him. "Do I look all right in my new dress, Arnus?"

He turned and looked again, this time with a straight face. "Of course you do. The master made it, didn't he?"

She scowled when he looked away. Stepping back in front of him, she said, "Yes, but does it look good on me?"

Arnus seemed to get the hint, and with a scowl said, "Yes, it does. You fill the dress well."

Aija smiled inside a little, but not enough to make her nerves calm. She had killed well over two dozen people, been in harm's way many of those times, and never felt as nervous or as odd as she did at this moment. "Are you doing anything important today?" she said, taking a bite out of a red apple from the cellar.

"No, I've been back from my mission for a while, and I don't think Sani has one for me. I've been learning the different poisons from Brother Iknon. I found a good one that I can put on my fingernails, so I don't get it on my own skin. I can dip it in someone's glass, and a few minutes after they drink it, they lose control of their bowels. If they aren't treated with honey and milk, they'll eventually die of the sickness," he said, with a wide smile.

Aija's heart hummed faster at his smile, but something about his eyes made her stomach feel empty. It was not the kind of conversation she wanted to have with him now either. "Well, since you aren't busy, would you like to come to the market with me? I have to pick something up."

He looked hesitant, his long hair framing his pensive face, and said, "Sure I'll come, just let me get ready," and ran up the stairs, every step quieter than a mouse.

*****

In the market, those who knew them from their uncle's shop greeted them as Lady Anya and Master Aramus. Pleasantries aside, her only concern was how to test the waters with him. She found it difficult with so many people around.

An old man with one eye sold crossbows and the bolts. She was a little wary about buying from him—not that she needed to. The Order made their own weapons, from superior supplies. Next to him, a hawker sold little trinkets, some made from wood, some from stone, also a small assortment of books. She liked books but did not want to look through them in front of Arnus.

Grocers sold food, and farmers sold piglets, kittens, chickens, and one even had a cow. Along with the many vendors were the many shoppers. Wealthy merchants' wives haggled over jewelry, and young men tried to buy flowers from a flower girl. Her comely looks were an asset to her, and Aija was not sure whether they were buying for their love interests or because they wanted to speak to the flower girl herself. She almost wished Arnus would buy her a flower, but then she remembered she did not care for flowers. Then again, she had never received any before.

She walked near the flower girl, but Arnus stared a few stalls down at a fat man trying to sell some custards. "These flowers are so pretty," she said, in a loud voice.

"Flowers, bah. Who wants flowers? They always die and never have much life in them. Flowers are a waste of good coin and of good life," he said.

A waste of good life? It seemed he cared about life, a strange concept coming from an assassin.

"Why waste life on something you can't get paid to kill, or better yet have a bit of fun with when you do," he said with a laugh.

That sounded more like an assassin to her. She gave a small, closed-mouth smile and moved on. They walked for a while, checking out different vendors. A few times Arnus did something funny, like putting on a wig made from a horse's tail, and they laughed, but she could not get him to open up. Not that she knew how to herself, with the life she grew up with.

At one point, she thought he might say something and turned to give him her full attention. "Have you ever thought about..." he said, in a subdued tone, "how we may have to kill one of these people? You know, someone who knows us as Anya or Aramus."

The question made her wince. Not just because she had expected something else, or because she hoped to hear about a subject other than murder, but because it horrified her to think she might have to kill someone she knew—someone she saw as more than a mark.

"No, I've never thought about it," she mumbled. She turned away and continued walking.

He went on talking about it, but she tuned him out, thinking about if one day she might have to kill a person she knew, as just the girl, not as the assassin. It never came up before, and so it never crossed her mind. Finding information about a random mark helped her rationalize their death. If she could categorize a mark in some area that made them unworthy of life, it helped her. If she could not, then they were just part of the job, a mark to erase.

Walking a little way from the market, they stopped on a bridge that looked over one of the rivers flowing from Lake Silvermane, or more commonly Lai Symerin, in the Dareian tongue. It shimmered between the north and south sides of Faor. Known for its silvery mirror-like look in the clear mornings, it was the reason for the city's founding.

The afternoon grew late. She and Arnus had been out all day shopping. Her excuse to go to the market had worked for spending time with the handsome man she had known for many years, but it had revealed little for her.

A pink sky reflected on the stream. She took a deep breath and stared out over it, but the relaxation was thrust aside when Arnus moved close to her. She could smell him and feel the heat from his arm almost touching hers. Her heart started to pound and her hands grew weak. She wanted to say something, she wanted *him* to say something, but nothing happened for a while as they stood.

The street faded around her. Her senses fell away as something inside her fluttered. A lightness came to her unlike anything she felt before. She could not explain it. Lost in a tangle of emotion, and the uneasiness of the situation, she no longer recognized the sound of the water below her or the breeze on her skin. She almost felt as if she would retch.

As a new sensation, it confused her. The world around her grew out of focus; her heart pounded harder in her chest. She did not know what to do, no guiding motherly figure. For her, growing up meant learning to kill, learning to be an assassin. Did someone explain this feeling to normal girls? Who could she talk to about it? The only female around was Sani. She could try, but the hard woman might not know anything about it either. Maybe she could talk to the master? He had noticed the situation first; he would have to know how to handle it. In his old age, he must have a fair amount of wisdom and knowledge on the matter.

Aija saw Arnus turn and look at her from the side. She turned and looked at him, his eyes digging into her soul, his smile luring her to him. "Arnus…" she said, in a whisper.

"Yes, Aija?"

"Do you find me acceptable?" She felt stupid for asking it, but she really did not know what else to say or how else to say it. "Do you like me?" The words almost stuck in her throat.

"Of course I like you. You're a part of Klor Dem. I like everyone in the Order—except Begla sometimes," he said, though he turned away laughing and nodding to himself.

"No, I mean do you like me as a woman, beyond me being an assassin?" she said, turning to look back at the stream, trying to hide her flushed cheeks. She shook her head at the thought of what she had just asked, but being straightforward was the only way she knew how to broach the subject. It was who she had become, who she was.

"Oh," Arnus said, "I... I'm not sure what you mean, because you're a great assassin. The master brags about your skill all the time, and..."

"And what?" she said, turning to him and standing straight.

"You are beautiful," he said, his face tilted down, but his eyes tilted up at her, piercing deep within her.

She looked at him, the stream still pink, reflecting the setting sun. A group of giggling girls went by, followed by an old crone barking commands at them. She leaned in close for a kiss and felt Arnus's lips touch hers. She realized when they pulled away, her eyes were closed, so she opened them. His lips were warm, and he tasted like tea leaves.

"I do like you," he said, his smile radiating, but his eyes were serious.

She smiled back, her heart still thumping like a wild boar in her chest. Her stomach rocked back and forth like a ship in heavy waves and her hands shook even more.

He is more awkward about this than me. He trained with me, and like me, he has no one to confide in.

Being trained to seduce or bed a person properly was not the same as expressing feelings for a person. She wanted to learn to overcome it and knew they both would need to.

"I do like you," he repeated, turning his whole muscular body towards her. "I did something for you," he said, his smile and eyes showing genuine happiness.

"What?" she said, perking up. No one had ever done anything for her before. The whole afternoon unfolded as a new experience. Someone liking her as more than an assassin, someone doing something for her... was this how normal people lived and felt?

255

"I removed your little nuisance," Arnus said, smiling wide and his eyes alight.

"What? What nuisance?" she asked, her forehead furrowing.

"I killed the boy for you. He won't be bothering you anymore." He puffed out his chest and reached for her hand.

Aija's brain scattered to the four winds trying to piece together all the words that had just come from Arnus's mouth. She tried to think of everyone he could mean and could not think of anyone she counted as a nuisance.

"The halfwit Edwin... I killed him for you. He won't be bothering you anymore." He smiled proudly, waiting for some sort of appreciation in return.

All of Aija's breath exited her body, and she fell to her knees. Arnus lowered to join her. She could hear him asking if she felt all right, but the voice seemed far away. Then her wits came back to her. "You killed Edwin?" She said it to herself at first, then repeated it louder. "You killed Edwin!"

"Yes, isn't it fantastic?" he said.

In a strained voice and with a tear welling in one eye, she said, "Why? Why did you kill him, Arnus?" Every tear she had ever held in, every tear she had fought to keep hidden, every tear of pain saved from bloodied hands and blistered feet from her training, had not moved her. She felt something distanced from her, something in her, dangling far away, a confusion that only the tips of her fingers ever grazed, and in this moment, it had stepped further away, and the tears came.

"Why are you crying? Aren't you happy?" he said, his face contorted in confusion. His eyes darted around at those who were now watching.

Aija did not know why she cried. She did not care for Edwin, but she did not dislike him either. He was not a nuisance, only a simple boy who showed her kindness. He had been genuinely nice to her.

"He was an innocent," she screamed out. Her voice carried across the water, and a young boy walking by looked and then ran off.

"Be quiet, Anya, you'll get us in trouble," Arnus said, looking around.

She grabbed him by his collar, the tears still coming. "Why did you kill him? He was just a nice boy, innocent. How could he be marked? A contract, for him?"

"Yes, a contract for him," he stated. "He was my last mark."

Her head rocked back in surprise, and she shoved him away, causing him to fall to the cobblestone bridge. "Why? Why would someone want him dead?"

"I don't know what's wrong with you, Aija," he whispered. "It was just some boy, an easy mark. Killing is what I do. It's my job in this Order. Just like it's your job to kill people who are marked. Doesn't matter who it is, or why they're marked." He stood, looking down on her as she sat crying on the bridge.

"Why him? I have to know why the contract?" She needed some reason, some place to put him in order to rationalize his death, to make it easier for herself. She did not know why it dug into her. She tried to push the emotion away like she had so many times before.

A moment of extraordinary happiness in her life, something she had long wished for, had turned to ash in her mouth. She wiped tears from her cheek. She knew she was making a scene. "Who marked him? Who paid?"

"No one paid," Arnus laughed without conviction. "The master marked him."

Her heart skipped a beat, and in that skip, she grabbed hold of herself, grabbing a hold of the part of herself that knew no emotion, that knew only the calm thrill.

"The night you left for your mission; the master gave me the contract. The boy brought us danger; he watched us too much. So, three days later, I slit his throat in an alley and threw him in the river. I made it look like a regular mugging."

"The master, but he said..."

"He said that to calm your nerves about it. He knew having the boy watch us could unmask the Order," Arnus said. He reached out for her again, but she pulled away.

"You slit his throat in an alley and threw him in the river like some worthless dog?" She stood up now, the tears gone, and felt a fire rising in her.

"He was a mark, Aija. What else do you want me to say?" he said, in a soft voice as an elderly couple walked by. "I did what I was told to do."

"You weren't told to throw him in the river like trash. You did it on purpose. You did it because you didn't like him." Her fists were clenched; she talked through her teeth.

"So, I don't like anyone I kill. It only seemed right that's where he ended up." Arnus's eyes were menacing now, but they did not faze her. She swung to slap him, but his hand shot up and stopped her. In a flash, she twisted out of his grip, grabbed his arm, and using her leverage flipped him over the bridge into the stream. Without a second longer, she started to run.

*****

The rose-colored sky disappeared, replaced by a gray, shrouded haze. She did not know where she had run, but when she gained her senses, she found herself on the street of the tailor's shop.

She ran hard in her heeled boots, and by the time she reached the doors of the shop, she saw the fires were burning, just like her feet. Sweat dripped down her face, and her heart pounded inside her. She barged through the door without knocking and Sani appeared in the store in a blink.

"How dare you not knock at this time of night?" Sani said, holding a dagger.

"Where's the master? I must see him."

"He's down in the secret chamber," the woman answered, confused at Aija's state.

Aija did not hear the rest of the woman's words, as she flew down the steps to the cellar. Her heart raced. She did not know what she intended to do, but she entered the open room and saw the master, old and small in his honored place, talking to Iknon. They both looked up.

She stopped at the edge of the table, tears welling in her eyes again. "How could you mark Edwin? He was an innocent!"

"Innocent, my child? He could've been our downfall," the master said in a calm voice, like a father to a raving daughter.

"You had no right. He was just a stupid boy, a simple, stupid boy." The tears poured again. She slammed her hand on the table.

Aija blinked a haze of instant flight, a blur. The old, wrinkled man in thick glasses, the man who was so meticulous and purposeful in his labored movements, threw his chair back, flew across the room, and hit her so hard she slammed her head against the floor.

Her world went black for a moment, but as she regained her sight, her head swimming in pain and confusion, she felt hard hands help her up. When she steadied herself and focused, she saw the small figure of the master standing in front of her, his eyes aflame, his face rigid.

"Do not ever presume to tell me what I do or do not have a right to do in my own guild," he said, with a finality of death. "I decided the boy's infatuation with you posed a danger. It's one thing for you to leave on occasion to visit your supposed parents, but if you're noticed leaving too often, then it brings questions."

Aija still reeled from the pain of the hit, dizzy from the fall, but she could understand his words.

"I will do what I must to preserve this place." He breathed deep. "I've given you and Arnus too much leeway. In my own folly, I began to believe the two of you are truly my nephew and niece. I won't make this mistake again. When he returns, he'll pack his things and be sent away. He'll take his orders from the outside now. You, child, will be here under my watch, until I see fit to send you on your next mission."

"Master," she whimpered, her knees wanting to give out.

"Hush, girl," the master hissed, "or would you like me to prick that finger of yours?"

"No, Master," she said, but her heart was gone now, broken in loss. She still could not understand why Edwin's murder hurt her so much, but things had changed. Three of the only people she had ever counted as showing her kindness were all different now. One lay dead, a meal for worms. The other two had betrayed some part of her she did not understand or even know existed.

Chapter 18

Andross contemplated how much time he had wasted over the past several months. No new answers from his search had been discovered, even after Lady Kodren. Like his search, the kingdom seemed to be floating like a cloud, heavy and gray, waiting to unleash its fury.

News after his return was more contentious than normal. Supplies from Robo had been trickling into the capital, causing disruption. Raids from the Norte tribes had pressured the houses on the northern border, and pirates had disappeared from the northern trade lanes and reappeared to attack the southern ones.

These were all things in his mind easily checked by the king and his lords, and it was not like things of the same nature had not occurred before, but so many at once seemed a strange coincidence to him.

He leaned over the stream and dipped his hand into the cold water. A snow runoff from the Pasanora range, it flowed from the east. The water flowed fresh, and the stars and silver moon reflected off it. The trickling over the pebbled bed calmed him.

Cleon in his gray splendor bent his head and drank from the stream, lapping up the water, and let out a loud sigh. Andross rose and rubbed at the great warhorse's neck. "That's what you needed."

Looking through some pine trees, he spied out the end of the forest line, leading out into an open field that stretched down into a valley, where Greenford Stump sat. He traveled east to visit the village and a friend who had written to him, saying she might have some information that would be useful to him, concerning Nurame.

He did not have any details on what it might be about, but on his way to Faor, it would not hurt to stop in and find out.

It had been a long time coming for him to make his way to the lands of the Greenfords, emerald grasslands, with roads that looped back and forth over rolling hills. Great forest expanses stretched out until they hit the mountains beyond.

With no new word or clue on the mystery of the king's assassination upon his return to Rosenia, he was annoyed that he could not immediately search for the man, Vernor. He had been commanded to travel north to deal with raids by one of the Norte tribes of the Roemenanora, the Rising Mountains. When he returned to finally search for Vernor, it took him longer than he suspected to find him.

Remounting Cleon, he turned the large horse back down the road with the twitch of his reins. He thought about how the man had gone into hiding. Lady Kodren's handling of the man edged on the verge of torture. He feared everyone, and every shadow. It seemed she had poisoned his mind, breaking it so the man could not function, then again it could have been the dream he kept mentioning.

Andross found him in a home for the confused and feeble-minded near the city of Faor. He was further disappointed the old, red-faced, fat man spent his days rambling on about nonsense. The only information he gathered from the man came in the cryptic phrase, "My son, who is not my son, how I miss him." This phrase, often repeated and accompanied phrases like "rambling water dogs, bushes with showered stars, and bloody rose petals." He also stated often, "In the rain the steel did sing," and he would laugh and then begin to cry.

He and Cleon trotted through the blue illuminated, grass field and down into the small valley to the village. Tired from the long ride, he rubbed the back of his neck. He could not wait for a pint and some sleep.

As the small village drew closer, the moon rose, and he thought about Mahley. She still lived with him in the capital. Their relationship in terms of friendship grew stronger, but their relationship beyond that flowed like the tide, a frothy mix of driftwood and seaweed. Some days their passions were like an engulfing flame; other days they could not stand the sight of each other. Either way, she had made it feel less lonely to come home.

Meeting the dirt road just outside the village, Cleon, in risen spirits at the sight of the lights in the distance, galloped faster. A wall of gray stone snaked along it. The night grew late, and most would be asleep except for the rabble who liked to frequent the small tavern at late hours. The same could be said for any village.

He perked up with the lights in many windows of the village's neat homes along the main street. He saw the sigil of Greenford: a green river with a gray bridge on it leading to a single purple peak. The people in the area grew good crops, protected from everything except small Horak and Mongrut mountain tribes who rarely came down from deep in the range. They grew beans and melons of all kinds, and made ornaments of threaded stalk, which they would paint and lacquer in beautiful designs.

In the middle of the village square stood a stump that long ago the Lord of the Greenford House tried to pull up because he wanted to grow grapevines. After three days of trying to dig it out and pull it up with great draft horses, but it being surrounded by large rocks, he gave up. The lord's mother said, "Maybe it's not supposed to be pulled up, but built around." At that, the lord started to build the village. Andross knew the story from some of the letters he had received from his friend.

When he rode up to the tavern, no stable boy came out to meet him, so he walked Cleon around and tied him up in the barn, undoing his saddle and gear but leaving it all by the stall. "Here, good friend, eat some oats. I'll handle the pay inside."

Walking to the tavern's door, he did not hear much commotion inside, as he might have thought. Cautious and with a steady motion, he pushed the door and stepped in. The light from the fire and lamps lit the tavern to a brightness most tried to stay away from. No one wanted to get drunk on ale and mead in the light of the morning sun. He blinked, letting his eyes adjust, and at that moment realized he had let his guard down. He felt movement to the right of him and saw the shine of a blade move to his throat.

In the blur of his survival instinct, his gauntleted hand came up to try and block it, but he was too slow. The blade moved too fast, faster than many he came across.

"It's all right, lads, it's a person. Oh, and not just any person, t'is my good friend Sir Andross of the Dove," said the echoing, harsh voice of a woman who emphasized the word *dove* in a mocking tone.

His eyes focused. He looked over as the knife came away from his throat. "Tez, it would be you to get a knife past my guard."

"Don't act surprised, I can always get past your guard," she said in a sensual way and reached up, wrapping her arms around his neck and giving him a wet kiss on the cheek.

He saw three men and a Goblin standing back away from the door and putting weapons down on the table. "What's going on here? This might be the strangest greeting I've ever had."

"Oh, well, praise be, there's no time to talk. It's our lucky day. Pay them no mind, the boys are just jumpy. We've been having some problems around here this past week."

As she moved away, he saw she was carrying a crossbow on her hip. He furrowed and looked again at the four. Youthful faces with fear around the eyes stared back.

She walked to the stairs and yelled up them, "It's all right, just a friend." She reached out to one of the lads and pulled him over. "Take this, my friend, get back on your steed. Jameston will show you the way. They'll need your help tonight." The busty tavern owner handed him a mug of ale. "Drink up. You'll really need it. Your arrival here may have just saved some lives. We'll talk when you come back—hopefully. *Come back*," she added.

Andross took a drink of the mug while contemplating his friend's cryptic words and the odd mood of the others. A freckled lad of twenty, thick-legged but scrawny in the chest, said, "Must I take him?"

"Yes, you," Tez said with a snap. "Tell him on the way what's going on. There's no time for me to tell him. I need to head back upstairs and let some of the ladies know it was just a false alarm. And don't worry, this is the Grand Knight of Rosenia," she said, in mockery.

He watched her braided strawberry hair swing back and forth with every step as she ascended. He took another swig, before slamming the mug down and following Jameston out.

"I'll come with you, sir, and point the way, but I've no mount," the young man said.

"It's all right. If haste is needed, you can ride behind me on my horse." He breathed in deeply and went to interrupt Cleon from his oats.

"Are you really the Grand Knight?" Jameston asked, holding the reins as Andross mounted. The horse gave a whinny and looked at Andross with a wide eye. He nodded back to the horse, before pulling the lad up to ride with him.

"Yes, I am, and which way are we headed?" he asked.

"Head north, sir. Last we heard, they cornered the creature in an old mine that caved in a few years back," Jameston said, holding too tightly for Andross' comfort.

"Creature, what is this creature?" Andross said, as they passed the last row of buildings on the north side of the village.

"I'm not sure, sir. Several weeks ago, folks' animals started disappearing at night, sheep, dogs, even horses. At first, we thought there might be a thief in the village, or some wolves. Then last week a girl went out to the privy and didn't come back. Poor Master Holmebrick's daughter. They searched for two days and found nothing. Then a little boy named Earl disappeared from a barn where he tends the sheep. Still no sign of him either. Last night we finally got a glimpse of the horrid thing. Some terrible creature, maybe a banshee. Me and the other lads from the tavern were out late, being a little reckless... you know how we do?"

Andross was not exactly sure what Jameston meant, as his own version of reckless meant hunting down criminals and fighting monsters alone, but he nodded anyway. He never went places he should not be, unless asked to be there. Then again, when he thought about it, there were many stories about him heading to places on command and getting involved in deeds far beyond his normal duties.

Is doing what you're told really reckless?

"Well, I threw a rock at the shadow, and the next thing I knew it turned and screamed a horrific bloodcurdling wail at us. My

266

friend fainted as it came toward us, but by then the scream woke people and they started looking out their windows. The banshee or whatever it is just turned and disappeared in the night."

"I'm not sure it's a banshee," Andross said. "I've heard that when a banshee screams, if you're as close as you lads say, then you should be dead." He heard Jameston gulp and clear his throat. "However, a banshee is something I still have not come across, so I don't really know."

"Well," the young man squeezed out. "Anyway, My Lord, we thought—and most of the village thought it would not be back two nights in a row, but apparently, it's hungry. Tez went patrolling with her crossbow, sneaking around the village like she were some great warrior and caught sight of the thing."

Andross laughed in his mind as to how little the boy knew of his local tavern lady. Little did they all know she had fought beside him many times, and how she had once gained great honor as a knight of Rosenia, a Knight of the Thorn.

"She spied the creature out, by my house," Jameston said, pointing back. "Anyway, she tried to shoot it with her crossbow and missed. The banshee or whatever turned, and before it could scream, Tez screamed. She says she ran at it, but it started to try and escape, but she screamed all the while. People came running out into the street, and the thing knocked Fred Olbeck through his door, breaking his shoulder."

"How much further?" Andross asked. The smell of pine filled his nose.

"Not far, just around the bend, through some trees and we'll be there. Tez tried to attack it, but it knocked her down too, and that's when the men grabbed torches and tried to light a fire. It doesn't seem to like fire or light. It kept shrinking away, until it escaped.

267

The men chased it up to the mine and have it in there, but every time they get close to the entrance, or someone goes in, great, horrible shrieks come out. Last I heard, they were forming a plan to all go in, while the women and children stay down in the village with the doors locked and all the fires going."

Andross did not want to mock the knowledge of the villagers, but most things hated fire and avoided the light. As they cleared the trees, he saw a large group of around thirty men, with torches, axes, and pitchforks, standing in front of the mine.

"Who's that?" one man called out.

"Hail, friends, fear not," Andross replied, holding his hands out.

"It's me, Jameston. Tez had me bring Lord Andross up here to help. He's the grand knight of Rosenia," he said, in wonder and excitement.

"Is the creature still in the cave?" Andross asked, helping Jameston down and then dismounting himself.

Several men answered at the same time, that there was no way out except through them. Then a man stomped forward. "Hello, My Lord, I'm Fred Olbeck." The man stood tall with a thick beard and thick arms, one in a sling. "The creature's still in there. We sent two men in. They haven't come back out. When I tried to go forward, the banshee screamed. I've heard the scream can kill you."

At least someone heard tales of the creatures. "I'll go then and see what I come across." Andross drew his sword; the blade looked like fire in the light of the torches. Murmurs echoed as Fred handed him his torch.

Making his way through the men toward the mine, he heard many say, "Thank you, My Lord" and "Blessing on you, sir knight." Often villagers were molested by creatures and monsters, evil doers, who meant them harm, though often motivated by greed. Most turned out to be less evil than people made them out to be.

Moving forward at the ready, he remembered a time having to explain to a village in the south that what they thought looked like an ape creature, devouring their chickens, was nothing more than a wandering vagabond whose hair grew out and had not cleaned himself in many years. Those sorts of tales were rampant across the kingdom. Though he knew better than most, Rosenia was a much safer place than the rest of Sancta, tamed by fighters like he and Tez for hundreds of years.

As he approached the mine, a scream struck out loud and sharp, and his ears hurt, but he did not waver. It did not have the power to make him faint or, even worse, die. Those who fainted must have from fear, though he would not bring it up. Still, as much as the villagers let their imaginations wander, he did not know what hid in the mine. Some horrible beast he believed, but what, he did not know. It was not a banshee, but it could be a hag or even a witch.

Inside, he almost coughed, his lungs felt heavy with every breath. The light of the lantern reflected off the walls and a small forming stalagmite. He moved slowly, trying not to make a noise, as he knew surprise would serve him well.

Glad he did not wear his chainmail, he smiled. It sat bundled on Cleon; all he wore were his thick leathers. His foot hit something, and he looked down. One of the men lay below him. The man breathed, only unconscious. About ten steps further into the mine, he found the second man; a large bump and gash marked his head. Looking up, Andross thought he could see light, so he put out the torch and tossed it away.

At first, he thought he made a mistake. Blackness swirled around him and he could not see, but when his eyes began to adjust, he could see something. With tender steps, his sword in front of him, he made his way to it. When he drew close, he could feel his heart pounding. He loved the feeling; the excitement of the situation overcame him. A challenge was his greatest foe. No matter what, he always felt he needed to take it on as a contributing factor in his rise as the Grand Knight of Rosenia. At the same time, he knew the danger in that type of mentality. One day he could face a challenge he could not escape. The idea had grown more potent in his mind now, after his run-in with the Gray Foxes. The idea had manifested during the kidnapping, when he thought he might not escape.

The light glowed around the corner, and he thought he could hear something, at first unclear, but moving closer he heard whimpering.

"Stop crying, little one," a squeaky voice said. "I told you I wouldn't eat you. Sell you, yes, but eat you, no. Now, for the boy over there, I may eat him…"

Confusion raked at Andross' mind. The question went from *what* creature lurked in the cave, to *who* lurked. It sounded like a person. Of what race, he could not tell, but it spoke the common tongue. As much as that calmed his thoughts, it did not alleviate the idea that danger sat around the corner.

"Ha ha," the voice echoed.

Andross stared into the light. He could see a shadow moving, a table, a bed, and a cage, inside which the children sat. A horrendous smell wafted through the tunnel, the odor of piled waste and excrement.

"Let me scream at the men one more time, and I think I'll eat the little boy."

He heard the girl whimper, but the boy lay prone in the cage and did not move. He saw the shadow put its hand to its mouth like it was going to yell, so he covered his ears as tightly as he could, holding his sword in a dangerous position between his legs, but he heard nothing. That was until he released his fingers from his ears and heard the echo of a scream coming from the direction of the mine opening.

Magic, he thought, the shadow could use magic, and that was how they screamed like a banshee. He heard the girl whimper again, and say, "Please sir, no, no, don't take him." He also heard the rattling of a key.

At that, he made his move and entered without a noise. Moving closer, he viewed the true form of the shadow. The village's malicious creature squatted near the cage, a wispy man with long black hair and the soft features of a woman. Before the man noticed him, he slammed the hilt of his sword on the back of the man's head and knocked him out.

The girl screamed and then began to beg to be let out. "One moment, child, let me tie this one up. He's going to pay for what he's done." Tearing several pieces of sackcloth into strips, he tied the man's hands several times and his feet. Then he opened the cage.

"Are you all right to walk?"

"Yes sir," the girl said, as she crawled out, brown-haired and filthy.

"Is the boy alive? What happened?" he said, in a whisper, looking toward the motionless child.

"He kept screaming when he heard the man say he'd been followed. He wouldn't stop, so the man hit him and knocked him out a little while ago," she said, reaching out to take Andross' hand.

271

He held her for a moment and then bent to look her in the eye. "All right now, the danger is over," he said, in a calm, soft voice. "I need you to be brave. I need you to take the torch and carry it out in front of us in the mine. I'm going to drag this vile man, but I have to carry the boy, so I'll need my hands free."

The girl's big green eyes dug into him; her dirt-covered face showed a blank stare, but then she slowly began to nod. He handed her the torch, which she held far out in front of her with both hands. Then he picked up the boy and put him on his shoulder. Reaching down, he grabbed the cloth that bound the man's feet and began to drag him.

Other than stepping over the two men who lay unconscious on the floor of the mine, the trip out was much less troublesome than the one in. As they got to the opening and the girl saw into the night, she yelled for joy and ran out, yelling, "Father, father!" She dropped the torch and Andross had half a mind to drag the man over it and let him catch fire.

The men started forward, and one man with a thick moustache whimpered aloud, "Earl, no, my boy."

"He's breathing," Andross said, handing him over, "He's just knocked out." Praises and many thanks began to flow again, until he threw his prisoner out in the middle of the men. Most of them jumped back. "There's your banshee," he said.

The men came over and crowded around the man lying on his side. "I know that man," one said, and then others began to agree. "That's the magician who came into the village for the festival a month back. Abecore is his name."

A man kicked him in the stomach, and a loud gasp came from the kidnapper, but a louder gasp and a jump came from the men when Abecore shot up into a sitting position. "Let me go," he said,

"This will end badly for you." His eyes were wide and red, with a crazed look, so startling that several men stepped back a pace. "Whether I handle it myself or let the dream take me," he sang, menace growing in his eyes, "you'll be sorry."

"Why are those men in the mine, and the boy still out cold?" Andross asked.

"Simple, stranger, I knocked them out with magic. They'll be out for a while," the bound man said. His squeaky voice made the hairs on Andross' neck stand. "You should let me go, warrior. You and I could kill these men and sell off the children. There's a tribe in the Thernat desert that's paying emeralds the size of raspberries for every child they're brought. The thought of it makes me want to cry in wondrous joy." Abecore then began to laugh hysterically, his voice echoing in the night.

"I've no need for emeralds," Andross mocked.

"Fine, then, I'll be leaving now," Abecore said, and began struggling with his hands.

"That won't be possible. We're going to take you back into the village and hold on to you until the Lord of Greenford comes down and deals with you," Fred Olbeck said, in a gruff voice.

The small man pulled his knees up to his chest and began to laugh. "I may have used up all my magic pretending to be a banshee, but I've one more trick hidden in my coin purse." And with that his eyes rolled back in his head so they could only see the whites, and his whole body began to jerk.

Andross was not sure what to do at first. The man began to shake and jerk all over the ground. He thought to untie him, to save him from self-harm, when the man began to let out a scream, just like the screams from before. It grew loud and echoed into the cave.

Its high pitch slowly started to deepen and turn into a low harsh tone.

"Get back," the knight yelled, stumbling back, unable to focus, "Get back!"

The village men looked confused at first, covering their ears, but then they saw the veins in the man's arms begin to bulge and the muscles in his neck tense. He had seen something like this before, but on a much smaller scale. He watched as the palms of the man grew thick and large; his teeth elongated. Hideous to behold, the muscles and bone distorted, cracking in the night. The men moved back a step with every step he made, still watching the man.

"Get your torches ready and circle him, do not let him through the circle or we'll never catch him." He finally knew what was happening. He stepped forward, prepared to do the only thing he knew to do to stop the man. He lifted his sword, about to bring it down on him, when the bindings around Abecore's legs ripped and his foot shot out and kicked Andross in the chest.

For an instant he felt weightless, then hit the ground. His vision flooded with darkness, and the pain in his chest felt like fire. Trying to suck in air, he looked up. He lay about fifteen feet from where he had stood just before. Jameston grabbed his arm, saying something and trying to help him up, but he could not hear him. His head swam, and even though his vision swayed back and forth, he tried to see what Abecore now did.

He saw a few men run off, back down toward the village. The rest closed around the roaring man, whom he began to hear again. He could see through a gap at leg level, as he pushed up, that Abecore now stood, his legs much thicker than they were. Andross picked up his sword and stumbled toward the circle. It began to break as more turned to run.

The clothed, vile man was no more. His growing body ripped through and he stood naked. Black fur began to sprout everywhere, starting on his ears and chest. One man grew brave and swung with his axe. The terrible beast broke the strips holding its hands and knocked the man away. Another roar let loose, and the nose began to push out and away from its now fur-covered face.

Andross nodded with the recollection. Abecore was not just a small-time mage, but also one of the Jhykan, a shape shifter—a cursed people who carried the ability to shape shift into a creature at times of emotional stress. Unfortunately, they could not always control the shift, and so were untrusted. Most were hunted when their secret came out. Of what little he knew, and what stories he heard on his travels, most turned to the form of a dog or wolf, but only one form was possible to any one Jhykan.

This man had a different form. He had found a way to distort his appearance as a banshee or ghost figure, most likely aided by his magical abilities. However, his form did not seem to be a dog or a wolf now, or even apparition. The creature contorted, and to the knight looked like a large bear. A moment ago, no bigger than a fifteen-year-old boy, the man now stood on hind legs as a bear whose size rivaled the cave bears of the Rising Mountains.

Andross saw the beast look toward an opening, and land back on all four legs. He knew the beast would try and make a run for it. It might be a massive bear, but some portion of Abecore still lingered. As a coward in Human form, it would still manifest in the animal.

He grabbed a pitchfork from a villager and threw it. Unlike a spear that could be thrown with accuracy at the beast's head, the pitchfork went off target, sailing down and stabbing it in the leg. It did not pierce very deep into its fur and thick hide.

The beast turned and looked at him. He could not let it get away. He grabbed Jameston's torch. The boy stood with his mouth agape; his eyes glazed over. Andross threw the torch at Abecore. It flew with better accuracy than the pitchfork, the fire sending sparks from the bear's head. It let out a roar and slapped the pitchfork from its leg.

Next, he grabbed another torch and moved toward the bear, his sword in one hand the torch in the other. He wanted more than anything to be wearing his finely crafted plate armor. Even his chainmail would have been nice. It would not have protected him from the impact of a bear swipe, but it would be some protection from the bear's claws. However, he had neither and only wore his leather jerkin and trousers. He poked at the bear's face, trying to keep the beast back. It swiped back every time, forcing him to keep a good distance as well.

Apparently, this made Abecore furious, because he charged Andross, missing him by inches. Others tried to attack, but the bear either knocked them away or chased them back, always keeping its eye on him. "Keep back, but stay around him," he yelled, trying to boost the spirits of the villagers.

When it rose up on its hind legs, the bear stood near twelve feet in height, twice his own size. Its paws were near the size of his chest. One direct hit now, while in full form, and he would never rise again.

He stabbed out and knew he had made a mistake. Seeing blackness again, and not being able to breathe, he was lucky he did not take a direct swipe. He took the opportunity to make his stab when an arrow from a villager stuck into the bear's flank. Thinking it would react, he stabbed in close, but the bear did not react. A prick near the shoulder of the arm that collided with him probably saved his life.

Turning over, he looked up, and through the blur could see the bear reared up on its hind legs. What men from the village were left, Fred Olbeck and even the lumpy Jameston were trying to get the bear's attention. Andross moved at a snail's pace as he tried to push up. The bear came back down, its massive head near his legs. Its teeth were as long as the blade in his boot. The roar reverberated in his ears; he felt his brain shaking in his head, and then the bear's head jerked. He was not sure what happened, but then he saw it jerk again. The massive head turned away and roared at Cleon, whose hind legs battered at the beast.

It was a saving distraction, as the bear swung at the horse, missing by only inches. Cleon reared back whinnying in the night, and then the bear stood on its back two legs. Andross looked around and found his sword had been lying underneath him the whole time. As the great bear landed back down on all fours, he scrambled to his knees and with all his might swung his blade, Ambra Nenoli, at the bear's foreleg.

At first, he thought he missed, feeling no resistance to the swing. The great head of the beast stared for a moment, then the bear screamed and rose back up, leaving the bottom half of its left leg on the ground.

He rolled back and tried to stand. He now saw the fear in the bear, the fear of Abecore. The bear dropped back down on three legs and started to turn, but without its other leg its movement slowed. Andross ran up to its flank and sliced again. Lost limb or not, the bear's head shot out at him and he dove away. Then some of the village men began to stab and poke with their pitchforks. One

277

man hit the bear on its great maw with a torch, and the bear roared a mighty blast.

Their pitchfork tines were too weak to penetrate very deep. He would have to do something. Stumbling behind the bear, he ran up and then leapt, his sword pointing down as he had barely leapt high enough to reach the great beast's back. He brought the sword down, plunging it in. The bear let out another roar, and like it had turned to stone, went rigid and began to fall. He felt it coming, and leaving his sword, he jumped away, not wanting to be crushed.

He expected when he looked up to see the villagers crowded around the beast, stabbing it to make sure it was dead, but he only saw them crowded around, staring down in the grass. The body of the great beast had disappeared. He rose and hobbled over. Looking down, he did not see the bear; he only saw a man, small, bleeding, burnt, missing his left arm. On his thin, dirty face were two growing red and purple marks. He looked so small now, he seemed like a child.

In the past, when Andross helped slay some wild beast or creature, there were celebrations and shouts of gratification, with feasts held. Looking down on the withered lifeless body of the man, no matter what his intentions or what ill he would have done still alive, it was hard for any of them to take any joy from his death, only pity.

*****

The next afternoon after Andross slept away most of the day, he woke from a bed given to him by Tez. His chest hurt and looking at it, he saw purple and yellow bruising in almost a circular pattern. His left shoulder felt sore as well when he stretched. When he rose half-dressed, he almost lost his footing, still weak and tired from the fight that almost killed him. He called for Tez, but she did not answer.

The top floor of the tavern seemed deserted, so he washed his dirty face in a bowl of water next to the bed. The water felt refreshing; the dirt and sweat turned the contents light gray. He used a towel to wipe his face and then dipping it in the bowl he wiped it over his upper body.

He dressed and put on his boots, then made his way down the steps. The tavern was full. Waiting at the bottom sat a crowd of villagers wanting to thank him for his deed. One man tried to give him chicken eggs, while a woman kissed his cheek and smiled. He looked at the wench behind the bar, and she knew what he was going to ask without him having to do it. Her cheeks were red, teeth were missing from her weak smile, and a lock of disheveled brown hair hung in front of her left eye like she was scarred. "She's in the stable with some of the men."

He pushed his way through the crowd, nodding and smiling, accepting the appreciation of many of the villagers. Past the crowd and outside, he breathed in deep, but the motion brought a stabbing pain to his chest. Drawing close to the stable doors, three men came out, all greeting him, and one put a hand to his shoulder, smiling and nodding in approval. He smiled back with a nod.

Tez waited inside. Her strawberry-blond hair pulled up in a bun. She wore a form-fitting dress, and when she looked at him, her eyes were red and puffy.

"You're sorry he's dead?" Andross asked, moving to Cleon's stall to look him over and rub his head. Tez did not answer right away, and he turned to Cleon. "Morning, old friend, you've gone and saved me again." The horse only bobbed his head up and down.

279

"I'm sorry," she said, in a small voice.

Looking back at Tez, he asked, "For what? I'm fine. You and I have been in worse scrapes, and I've taken worse injuries."

"No, Andross, you don't understand." She came to him and kissed his forehead, then kissed his lips; he could feel a salty tear drip down to where their lips met. She pulled back away and wiped her cheek. He winced in pain for a moment.

It was a strange turn. He and Tez were never loving before but were physical for a time and close friends for many years. They played a game that came and went with their attraction to each other. She had been a warrior with him on battlefields, fought and bled, but also a companion to share mugs and nights with, in times of peace.

"No, I'm sorry. I knew this man."

"You knew Abecore? Some of the men mentioned he visited the village recently for a festival," he answered, wiping some of the tear from his lips.

"Yes, I know, but that's not what I meant. This man Abecore," she hesitated, "he knows about Nurame's assassination—knew anyway," she said, with a pleading look on her face.

He moved toward the body lying on the table, that the village planned on burning at nightfall. "How do you know this?"

"When he visited before, for the festival, he came into the tavern. You know how people drink and can't keep their tongue. At first, he just sat boasting of things he had done, tricks he could do. Then I heard him telling a story, about him and a man named Vernor and Vernor's son. I didn't pay it much mind until I heard him mention dancing fire, then it jogged my mind. I thought I remembered the name from a letter you sent me, and when I found the name was the same, I looked for him, but he left. The men he spoke with only laughed about how he claimed to have killed a king," Tez said, her eyes still puffy.

Andross shook his head. It did not seem real to him, as if he was still lying in the bed dreaming. Vernor was the subject of conversation again. The information was now a sure thing, a recurrence among the clues. But because here he lay, lifeless, there would be no answers.

"I caught him before he left the village, and tried to ask him roundabout questions, but he closed up, like he discovered what I was after, and fled the next day. I meant to tell you about him when you arrived, knowing you were on the way. Here you are, and I had no idea that the thing molesting our village was him." She looked at the corpse, her eyes red and wide.

"You were never one for so much emotion, Tez." He tried to jest with her. He could not place fault on her. Who would have guessed Abecore and the banshee were the same? That the man returned to the village with evil plots in mind?

"I know how much it means to you; how much it still means to me too. Nurame was my friend as well, and my king. One of the best commanders I fought for," Tez said, looking at him. Her emotions gone, and her countenance showing the strong woman again.

"I need to find this son of Vernor's. There's nothing more I can get out of the old man. He's lost to us; his mind is broken. If anyone knows whether there's a connection, maybe it's the son. I have to track him down and find him," Andross said, gazing at the lifeless corpse. "He must know something."

Chapter 19

The birds were beginning to chirp as Neesa and Dreyandol prepared for practice. He looked over at her as she wiped down her curved blade. "What is your blade called?"

"A katana," she said, twisting it in her hand and feeling the weight.

"No, I know what kind of sword it is. What do you call it? Does it have a name?" He swung his longsword around, loosening his arm.

"No, it's a sword. That doesn't make any sense."

He rolled his eyes, as she laughed.

He enjoyed their practices, which were always early in the morning. She learned faster than he could teach, but it forced him to dig down into his training and recall drills and tactics that had become second nature to him.

"You almost ready over there? The dawn breaks and we've done nothing except clean," he said, with a smile.

"If you're looking to make a jab at me, you won't get any more chances," she said, her tail flicking behind her. "Today, victory is mine."

They were in a small valley between two hills. They had left tracks in the grass from their encampment at the top of the ridge. Others were rising, readying themselves for the day. The two of them moved far enough away to not wake any of those who chose to sleep longer. The escort held about forty in total, but there were people in the party who were important enough that they should not be prematurely woken.

Neesa splashed water on her face from a brook that flowed nearby. The cold water stirred their spirits. He watched as she rose slowly from her crouch and drew her sword. They smiled at each other and then bowed.

In a flash, she charged; he dodged her by a thumb's length. She was quick enough to keep him on his toes. He pulled his longsword, smiling all the while. She slashed at him and he parried it. The swords rang like thunder through the small valley, and though they had moved away to be quiet, their clash continued to ring out.

"First question, my apprentice," he said, his voice echoing through the thin crisp air. His breath misted in the cool morning. "What is the mission of the Crimson Order?"

He sidestepped a quick jab. The wide-eyed Malkienon smiled with a small nod, acknowledging the dodge. "Our mission is to serve, aid, and protect the land through the knowledge we acquire. Secondly, *our* mission," she said, juking toward him, "is to help escort this entourage of the king's ambassadors to Targon Vale, the high seat of the Belanov family. We are to aid in the building of a truce between the House of Belanov and the House of Skyfree. This dispute between the two great houses, who summoned their minor lords, has caused long tension over this land. Furthermore, *your* mission, to which my mission is tied to you, is to train two apprentices, one of which I am, and the other who we are currently searching for."

He parried another jab and sent his sword in a quick arc toward her, smiling all the while. "Could you be any more long-winded?" he said, rolling his eyes.

"I could…" she answered, breathing hard, her tail flicking as she jumped almost his height onto a large fallen tree trunk to give her the advantage, "explain the rules of the Order as part of our mission, and explain the specifics on how we're escorting this group with one other Crimson Caster, four knights, Azziza Zattu the king's ambassador, his six servants, and a retinue of guards, but then that might be too much…"

He chuckled. Another clang of swords shook the small valley and people gathered on the ridge to watch. She splashed some water from the brook up at him; he barely shielded his eyes with a small bit of magic, but she came on him in the distraction with a flurry of sword swipes. She had great agility, which was hard for one of the Darei to admit. Not only was she agile, she was fast for her race. Her attacks blurred, and he had a hard time defending them.

"What are some of the rules of our Order?" he yelled out in the attack.

"So, you're ignoring my question? Fine. The first is to always remember to love." She shook her head at this rule. It was the most obscure and the most unreasonable. He knew she still did not understand its necessity for the guild. Her intelligence astounded him, coupled with her caring nature, but in the end her logic overruled these attributes. It would do no good to try to explain, especially during her attack. He recognized a funny look in her eyes, and knew something was coming, but it happened before he could finish the thought.

Neesa, like lightning, reached into her belt and threw a knife, but not at him. It flew above him and sliced into a thin branch, not even big enough to hurt him, but the damage was done. His attention for a second went to it. At the same moment, she used an air spell to blow a gust of wind at his legs, just enough to put him off balance. He went to brace himself and in a heartbeat her sword touched his throat.

Claps rang out at the top of the ridge and Dreyandol smiled at her. He stood still for a moment, until she smiled back and lowered her sword. She bowed to the onlooking crowd.

"Enough of the questions. Very nice," he said, seeing her smile and sheath her sword.

She retrieved her knife, and they began to walk back to the top of the ridge. At the top, the king's ambassador, Azziza Zattu Nadal, stood in his great splendor and pompous attitude, his eyebrows raised. Robed in sky blue trimmed in gold, he rolled his eyes. Gold rings adorned his fingers, valuable enough to feed a small town of starving people. He held a smirk on his hawk-nosed face, his eyes squinted at them.

"It's always a bad sign when the apprentice is able to defeat the master," he said with disdain and a look of disgust in his dark eyes.

Dreyandol bowed low. "Your Lordship, as you can see, you're in great hands."

Azziza perked out his lips, sniffed loudly, and headed toward his tent.

"He's a very warm and kind man," Dreyandol said, rolling his eyes.

Neesa chuckled under her breath.

*****

Once they reached the boundaries of Targon Vale, where the Brolshivik people lived, they were escorted for a day and a half through mountain passes where the wind whipped so hard that it lashed their bones.

The Belanov soldiers who escorted them were large, gruff men. If Dreyandol did not know any better, and they were not so tall, he would have counted them of the Dwaling. They spoke with a harsh accent that made them difficult to understand. Across their backs were shields holding the crest of a one-eyed brown bear on its hind legs, wielding a bloody spear, all on a snow-white field. Their armor was hidden by fur; they wore no helms on their bald heads. They each grew a beard to a sharp point.

As they rode, Dreyandol looked toward the large man nearest him, astride a ram and said, "Can I ask why your horses are so small?"

The man he asked looked at him, but another man answered: "We breed them this way, and when we can't, we buy them stunted. They hold up better in the mountain passes. Not the best for long range marches, but they're better balanced on treacherous paths."

The Darei had assumed wrong, it seemed. The man on the ram was not the leader. He had been told only the leader of the escort would speak with them. "I'm Dreyandol of the Crimson Order. This is my apprentice, Neesa."

"I'm Potolski, escort for Lord Belanov. Welcome to our land," the large man said, while the other escorts laughed. From his chin hung a thick blond, curling beard. He sat taller than Dreyandol. He wore a round shield on his back and fur-lined armor.

"Why is he riding a goat?" Neesa said.

"That is *Skandaval*," Potolski answered, and then let out a loud laugh.

"His name is Skandaval?" Neesa said, looking at the thick but short, muscular man with a graying beard.

The Belanov escorts laughed again. "No, his name is Ligneia. He is known as Ligneia Skandavaly now. That's not a goat, it's a giant mountain ram, a Skandaval. They're incredibly agile, and able to climb steep cliffs. He is now a *Skandavaly*, honored by our people, because he captured the elusive beast and tamed it. Very few ever receive this honor, because only the very greatest of us can."

Dreyandol soon learned most men of the mountain houses tried their hand at capturing a Skandaval. It was so rare that Potolski said there were only three Skandaval riders in Targon Vale. He wanted nothing more than to hear the story of how to accomplish such a feat.

"I can see you want to know how, most do. It's against tradition to speak of. The trick isn't passed on from those who succeed, as the achievement is meant to recognize only the few great enough to do it," the escort leader said.

After the day and a half of frigid travel, the caravan moved through a gap into a valley of flowing green forest with bits of snowdrifts. Within the valley settled the city of Targon Vale, the high seat of the Belanov House. No walls surrounded the city, but Potolski explained that too. "Who needs walls when the mountains themselves are walls enough, greater than we can construct?"

Small groups of soldiers could hold the gaps against greater forces. He further explained that Targon Hall was not to be a fortress but a home. However, once they entered the city, Dreyandol did not believe him. The House of Belanov and its people were preparing for a battle that seemed to be drawing near. Tents were erected along the streets, in all the city squares, and around the valley in clusters. Soldiers in full battle regalia sharpened their blades and cleaned their armor; many slept on cots or under large fur blankets. He had seen this before, years earlier in his youth. Not to the same extent, but the mood felt the same.

His home of Ajencain, on several occasions, had prepared for an attack from the ever-growing Predan tribes. The faces of these men were stoic and hard, women in constant preparation, while the children old enough to understand emitted a cloud of unrest, just as he remembered.

"Sir Potolski, this feels like much more than a skirmish," he said.

"Oh, this is nothing. When we prepare, everyone prepares," Potolski said, glancing to his fellow escorts.

Dreyandol looked toward Neesa, who sat shaking her head back at him. "How many soldiers are housed in the home of your lord?" He emphasized *home*.

"Normally, Targon Vale houses five hundred guards."

"And today?" Dreyandol asked.

"Last I heard, there were near ten thousand encamped in the valley."

This preparation was more than a skirmish. Marching this many troops into the Skyfree lands meant taking control and never surrendering it. He looked at Neesa and raised his eyebrows.

She nodded back with widened eyes, then checked her saddlebag.

He knew the look into the bags was only a ruse to loosen her sword in her sheath. The air in the valley felt warmer than in the pass, but it would be no good to have a sword frozen in its sheath if things turned bad. Away from the eyes of the escort, he put his hand out flat, signaling her to relax.

Many of the soldiers raised spears to them as they rode by, but many more raised spears to Potolski and Ligneia. Dreyandol caught bits of a song that seemed to be praising the Skandavaly.

Their escort took them on a path toward a large black keep known as Targon Hall in the middle of the city. It did not loom very large, but with so many added residents and the tents stretching out into the farmland and forests of the surrounding valley, it seemed bigger.

He began to survey the beauty of the place. Gray and purple mountains towered above, higher than the peaks of the Rotsinora, and though they rode in a valley, they were already high above the flat lands of Rosenia. White snowcaps crowned them all, and though it was not snowing there, the crisp air reddened their cheeks.

The sky itself opened into a clear beautiful afternoon, but by his estimation it would turn dark soon. He could feel the thinness with every breath. The cold, frigid air brought an alertness and energy to him.

The people of the Belanov lands were proud, descendants of some of the old tribes of the Norte, most of them of the Brolshivik tribe. The Norte grew to be tall and wild in the Rising Mountains of the north. All the men, even the younger boys, shaved bald, though they grew what facial hair they could.

"There are many banners here," Dreyandol pointed out.

"Yes. You may notice that all the banners of the Belanov, hold some visage of a bear. Whether fishing in a stream or battering down gates on a field of blood, they're all there. Lord Venot, like his forefathers, believe this helps unite his people," Potolski added, with an air of pride.

"Do you believe it helps?" Dreyandol asked.

"We are all Belanov," was the answer Potolski and the escort gave in unison.

They made their way into the center courtyard of the keep, a fortress of the most ominous kind. No luxury showed on the outer walls, clearly constructed for defense. Murder holes and numerous portcullises were arranged at every angle, on every wall.

Surprisingly to him and Neesa, the inside overflowed in luxury. Through great black marble doors, they were led into a walkway where the floors and pillars were made of black marble as well. Dreyandol saw his apprentice's eyes grow large. Silver and white gold detail in the sculptures of bears and rams were everywhere. Large windows let in the light of the setting sun, stretching the shadows across the room.

The envoy continued to the great hall, where stuffed giant bears stood along the walls. Dreyandol looked closely at each. All were posed in a threatening posture. He smiled at the thought that there were no bears in Rovelle, though there were other creatures of the same ferocity.

A voice echoed through the hall: "My dear Darei, every vicious bear here has a name. With every death of a lord of Belanov, the descendants go out and hunt one of the great bears of the mountain. We stuff them, and through a ritual move the soul of our past leader into the body of the bear. We then put them up here in the hall so they may forever watch over us."

Having been addressed, he bowed low: "My Lord Venot."

Azziza pushed his way forward and bowed his head. "My Lord, we have much to discuss. Taking the time to indulge yourself in pleasantries with *my* retinue is kind but not necessary."

Dreyandol wanted nothing more than to laugh. The members of the Crimson Order were only there to help in the diplomatic situation as a courtesy.

Venot's face grew cross and with a fierce voice that echoed through the hall he said, "Zattu, remember, you're in my hall, and I'll speak to whom I wish. Now go sit over there and wait for me to acknowledge you."

Under his breath, Azziza said, "The king will hear of this insolence. I'm here as his voice. Lord Venot, you do more ill than good."

Only he, Neesa, and the third Crimson Caster, Jensing Fernand heard him, but all three looked at each other, ashamed to be associated with the advisor. Azziza moved back and stood with his men, scowling.

Jensing in his crimson jerkin, looked over at Dreyandol and whispered, "We're here as an aide." In his mid-thirties, with receding, light brown hair that topped his head, and a scar across his forehead, the third caster stood. He seemed like a serious fellow, who took to reading his tome of magic every day, and practiced bits of magic every night.

Lord Venot, on the other hand, stood tall, with a huge build, the size of a bear himself. Unlike all the other men of Targon Vale, long locks of black hair flowed down to his rear. One part hung braided with what looked like arrowheads or maybe spearheads. Unlike the other men, his face was clean shaven.

"Please, guests, excuse my rude outburst. King Coram's advisor forgets that in my land he doesn't carry the king's voice. He's only a messenger. He forgets his place. I'm overjoyed you've joined this envoy." Venot's voice flowed rough and harsh, and though his eyes seemed kind, they focused on each of them intently. "It would honor me greatly if you three would join me for some afternoon lunch. Your order is a curiosity to me."

Dreyandol and Neesa looked toward Jensing, who as the highest ranking of their three, led them. Jensing bowed low, smiling widely. "It would be our honor, My Lord."

Two tables of dark gray wood, polished to a shine, were brought out with many chairs. One table was placed in front of the lord, where he sat at the head.

Servants brought food to the lord first. After, meats, cheeses, and bread followed for the guests. The only type of vegetable offered was the frost carrot.

"For those who have never tried our frost carrot, it is served frozen, so beware of its hard nature. It grows white, in the small streams in these mountains, and is the only vegetable we can get with any frequency."

The meat on hand looked to be mountain trout, bear steak, and boar. However, the strangest of the food presented was a white cheese made from the milk of the Skandaval rams. When Dreyandol eventually tried it, he swore it tasted much like a mix of grass and mint but smelled like the salt used to wake the unconscious.

Handing a piece to Neesa, she shook her head and said, "Normally I would Master, but something about its smell makes my stomach want to lurch."

Only after everyone at the first table received their helpings of food and frost carrots and honey wine, did the second table, where Azziza Zattu sat, get served. His face oozed hatred, and though Dreyandol did not like to judge, he determined the advisor was far more unpleasant than he ever wanted to deal with.

The meal started with normal banter. Neither he nor Neesa enjoyed shallow conversation, though the realization that he could learn much came to mind, and it calmed his anxiety.

It soon became apparent that his host was a jolly man, quick to laugh, and like most rulers, quick to anger. He held power and a sly intelligence. The questions, even at the beginning of their meeting, were questions Dreyandol would ask someone if he were trying to understand them, almost interrogative. Things along the lines of, "So how do you like this area?" Or "Does Ambassador Azziza get on your nerves as much as he gets on mine?" All meant to gather information.

After a while, the lord started into the real reason he wanted to eat with the three Crimson Casters. "So, I know you've come to mediate the civil strife between Skyfree and my people. Yet I'm curious, how much are you willing to do? I ask because I know what I'm willing to do."

Jensing looked up from his plate of carrots and goat's meat. "I know what our mission here is and I know how far we're expected to assert ourselves and willing to assert ourselves."

Venot's eyes were confused, sitting on the verge of anger. "I'm not one much for cryptic games. In my halls, I play the games and everyone else does as I command, like puppets on a marionette. Now listen to me, Jensing. I know the plan of your Order. You're young in terms of guilds in Rosenia, and already you plant yourself in high places and like the ivy of the Paraduan jungles, you spread far and fast." Venot stood to his feet, glaring at Jensing. "Word has reached many an ear about your growth, the foothold you now have in the kingdom, how you've won your place in the heart of the king. You now help in the training of Rosenian soldiers and are asked to be envoys. I'll have you know there's a portion of the nobility leery about your rapid expansion."

Dreyandol thought about how fast they were growing. Things were slower in Rovelle, more focused and deliberate. It was in part due to the growth of magic as well. The concern puzzled him. Clearly, something tapped at Lord Venot's mind. Was the same concern spreading from other lords of the realm?

293

"My Lord, the Crimson Order is not in the business of ruling realms or starting problems. We're in the business of creating peace. If we must assert ourselves at the cause of starting trouble in order to avert a larger problem because we're commanded to, then we will." Jensing wiped his mouth with a napkin, his eyes as cold as a frozen lake in the high mountains of Hima. The deeper range that was just a week's travel north from where they sat now, through the same mountains.

A smile arose on Venot's face. "Good, as long as we're under the same roof of understanding."

His roof, Dreyandol thought.

The lord changed the subject to the niceties of the day. "What do you think of my city, Targon Vale?"

As Jensing answered, and Neesa moved unwanted food around her plate, Dreyandol thought about the size of the Order. The last estimation numbered nearly ten thousand strong. They headquartered in Rovelle, but reached west from there to Nyoko, and south to the Fang Islands, but here in Rosenia, they were growing fast, and the spread was reaching Paraduo. Were they something to truly be concerned about?

Chapter 20

Targon Hall bustled the next day. Venot invited many of his chief barons and landowners to council with Azziza Zattu and other Rosenian dignitaries. "There are fifteen lords of the Belanov here," Dreyandol said, leaning over close to Neesa.

"I heard a guard mention one lord guarded the pass leading to the Skyfree lands," she said. "Standing watch with soldiers on the western pass."

He did not often think of it as a great skill, but he often forgot about her ability to hear things she might not have been intended to. Since they made it their business to learn what they could, it was not a bad skill to have among them. "I recognize some of the Belanov lords' banners. Some from the other day and a few from when we were in the library in Crimson Cliffs. Plus, before we left, I took some time to read up on some of the histories between Belanov and Skyfree."

"I did that as well," she said, glancing toward Jensing and smiling as he joined their sitting area. She looked back toward him. "They've been feuding for a long time. Some of the great northern houses of Rosenia were once part of the Norte tribe, and that's when it all began."

Dreyandol watched as different lords of the Belanov took time to call for war. Each stamped their foot on the ground and chopped a mark into a trunk of wood they used for tallying the vote.

"The two clans where the feud began were the first two to break from the Norte tribes and seek to build settlements. One was the Brolshivik, who are now mostly made of the Belanov and

Malikova, and the other was Schifreizen, now known as the Skyfree."

Dreyandol kept listening to her quiet explanation while still watching the events unfolding in front of him. The vote so far was unanimous toward war.

"At first the two clans prospered, aiding each other in their survival, but as they grew and their borders began to infringe on each other, it caused strife. Chader Belanov first called for large-scale war against the Skyfree hundreds of years ago. The warring teetered evenly for a long time, while other Norte tribes settled portions of the Rising Mountains. The Belanov received a huge boost when one of their long-time allied clans aided in the war. With the promise of lands and aid, Malikova joined and turned the warring more vicious, as they fought for more."

He looked over to his companion, one eye cocked high. "You learned quite a bit, didn't you?"

"I enjoy history. These feuds and civil wars among houses are fascinating to me," she said, eagerness to her face.

"Fine, tell me more. You're like a giddy child sometimes," he said with a smile.

"Apparently until only the last decade or so, Belanov and Malikova prospered, growing in wealth and power. Things have slowed, but for Skyfree they're still good."

As the council went on, the story of the feud unraveled, and Dreyandol took this time to look over the lords. A great brute of a man stood with a graying beard, piercing dark gray eyes, and though a bit on the older side he had the muscles of a twenty-year-old. Many of the minor lords to the north did not care about showing their sigils, but this baron did. On a white field stood a purple mountain with a silver crescent moon, a black bear upon the peak. Called by many as Chief Deor Rapsich, the Stone Giant, his people were miners and stone carvers.

Chief Deor in his boisterous voice boomed through the hall: "I don't understand this meeting. We've met to discuss with these outsiders the terms of a peaceful agreement. The Schifreizen are spent. Lady Cymbol is not wed and will not take any man to wed. I know, I've tried," he said with a laugh, and others laughed with him. "Even our great Chief Venot tried. She has no heirs, and the closest relative who could take the seat is a nephew, who has been missing for three years. In the times of our grandfathers this would be over." He said this part with a great shout, and Dreyandol watched the chiefs of the hall all shake their heads. The only chief who did not shake his head was Venot. "I know we're not living the life of old, but she must take a husband or we'll take Skyfree."

Dreyandol and Neesa had discovered differences between the noble houses in this trek north. As descendants of the Norte, houses like Belanov, Malikova, Skyfree, Vulfreund, and several others like Conig, Egan, and Jayne, still held onto too much of their tribal traditions. It was the reason they called many of the lords or barons, chiefs. Belanov and Malikova held the old ways the strongest.

A great shout erupted, and Dreyandol noticed Venot looking at them with a blank stare. Azziza stepped forward to speak, with his olive skin, hooked nose, and beady eyes. His robes swept across the marble floor, as he seemed to float to the middle of the room. Grumbles went up as he did, and even Lord Belanov rolled his eyes.

Azziza raised his hand to stop the noise. "As you know, I represent the king of Rosenia, High Lord of the Houses, Guardian of the Rose, so on and so forth, King Coram."

Dreyandol thought it disrespectful to King Coram. In Rovelle, if any representative of the Dareian royal house were to skip or play with titles, some form of punishment would ensue.

Azziza continued: "The king will not support this tryst between the two houses. You'll bring your armies to the front and battle in the mountains, in a war that could last several years." The chiefs laughed mockingly. "You, as well as the House of Skyfree, have been charged with protection along the northern borders. With every day that passes while you feud, our enemies could be gathering to invade the realm."

The speech about the houses' duty went on and Dreyandol did not understand its purpose. The greater issue in his mind was the possibility of civil war breaking out through the kingdom, starting here with Belanov and Skyfree, then one by one other houses would take sides. The focus on duty and not unity by the advisor only made Dreyandol dislike him more. The last thing the pompous man spoke about was the liege lord and Marshal of Helsveg, Tyrone Ash of Avondale, but as soon as he brought him up, Venot rose and spit at his feet.

"Don't you bring him up in my hall!" His voice carried smoothly and low.

It unnerved him and he glanced toward Neesa, who sat tensely.

"I'll not have you bring up that no-horned goat who my father betrothed my sister Idalia to. Now she is dead!" Venot stamped his foot and the other lords followed suit.

"My Lord, she died in childbirth. What grudge could you hold against Lord Tyrone?" Azziza said.

Venot looked like he could pull a great axe from the wall and bury it in Azziza's head. Dreyandol and Neesa were ready for anything. Jensing did not stir.

"What grudge? What grudge you say? My sister the morning star of the Belanov House was to marry Lord Rodney Anderoy, Lord of Cliffwater, Marshal of the Gold Coast," Venot yelled, throwing his hands up in anger. "One of the richest houses in Rosenia, where our trade would be secured, and our house would rise to even greater heights. However, Idalia saw Tyrone win the tourney in Cliffwater and fell for him. My father saw this as a way to mend the rift between Belanov and Ash, so he allowed for the betrothal. My father, Kedrich, bless him, was a sentimental man. He and Lord Hundley Ash grew close, becoming great friends in fact, but now both our fathers are dead and Idalia my sweet sister died in childbirth. What do we of Targon Vale have to show for it now? Nothing."

Dreyandol watched as the great lord lost himself in his own rage.

"I've lost my sister and father. Tyrone has my nephew and niece, and I can't see them because of our long-standing hate for each other. Nor will he allow for a trade agreement. The Anderoys won't ship our goods or trade with us, for the slight we showed them. The flow of goods in and out of my lands are only held up by Malikova and Egan because Lady Cymbol won't help either. Your king sits in his great city and does nothing. I've sent him message after message, and nothing has come of it. Here you are, sent by him to tend to this skirmish. Well, I'll say this, tomorrow the chiefs of the Brolshivik, the House of Belanov, will ride through the pass and take the lands of Skyfree." His voice echoed through the hall.

The talks went from peace to war after the ill-spoken words of the king's advisor. Dreyandol sat amazed at how the man held his position. The lords were on their feet stomping. He looked at Neesa; her face looked sad. Azziza turned, his face grimacing, and headed to his fellow dignitaries. As the room erupted louder into war chants, Master Jensing only sat.

At that moment, while the hall screamed and hooted with cheers and cries of battle, the great door pushed open and a soldier rushed in. "My Lord..." he bowed, "Lord Tyrone and Lady Cymbol have entered the pass and are riding up the Targon Road. They come without weapons and with only a small escort. They wish to speak of peace."

Venot's eyes squinted and his forehead furled. "Speak of peace? Well, see them in. They can discuss their peace in front of my war council." Another cheer went up. He walked over to one of his advisors and lifted his arms from his side. A man with a scar across his cheek, and about the same age as the lord, reached into a chest near the wall and took out an ornate belt made of leather. Gold filigree lined it, while studded with black and purple gems. He put it around his lord, and then very ceremoniously handed him a war pick from the chest, who slid it into a loop on the belt. He turned to his chiefs and said with a great booming voice: "And now, I... am... ready!"

Cheers went up, and war chants. They sang songs of Ormond the Black Axe, and Tolstoy No Teeth. Food entered the hall brought by servants, while more speeches arose from the chiefs. Ledic Ramsfoot spoke of the richness of the Skyfree lands, while Chief Angolsky Brown Tear, who took his name from a scar under his left eye, set there by an arrow from a raiding Norte Tribe, danced a war jig.

Several hours passed before the entourage of Ash and Skyfree arrived. When the door was pushed open, they entered escorted by a host of Belanov soldiers, clad in thick furs and mail, carrying axes and long spears.

With them, a small group of soldiers, some dressed in orange and red, and a group so alike to the Belanov soldiers, except for a sky blue and white shield, Dreyandol glanced at them twice. However, they did not keep his eye long as the lord and lady entered.

Lord Tyrone Ash, Lord of Avondale and Marshal of Helsveg, stood a dark ebon-skinned man, short but muscular, with a round face and short black hair. On his breastplate of Galvorn shone the symbol of House Ash, a blazing flame of orange and red. Behind him came Lady Cymbol, who wore a beautifully embroidered dress of sky blue, and a breastplate emblazoned white. Her blond hair flowed, mixed with bits of white, showing a woman of mature age. She held her head high amidst the crowd of gruff men.

The hall grew silent while Lord Tyrone looked at the lord of the Belanov, their eyes digging deep into each other. Then Lord Tyrone bowed. "My Lord Venot, we've come to work out a settlement to stop this atrocity from occurring. We bring pledges to you, in order to alleviate your unhappiness and help you in the furtherance of your lands."

"What makes you think I want to treat with you, Tyrone? My men are ready. We've been slighted and looked over for too long. My father wanted peace and stronger friendships, and it's gotten my people nowhere." Venot stepped further down his dais with every accusation.

"I've come to correct that, My Lord. First, if you allow, I'll start with the friendship our fathers forged. I've done nothing to uphold it, which started among our families with my marriage to your sister Idalia." Tyrone's voice wavered. "I loved her dearly, and through my grief I wanted nothing to do with your house. I've failed in that."

301

Lady Cymbol spoke up, her sky-blue eyes piercing, her blond hair braided down her back. Now, widowed from a wandering knight she fell in love with, she held her land alone. "I've chosen to marry, but not you, my Lord Venot. This isn't a slight on you, but a protection for the preservation of my people. You would do the same if presented with my choices. To prove this isn't a slight, I offer open trade with you and your people and promise you this: should I have no son, and only daughters, the first-born will be betrothed to your son. Should I have no children, and my nephew not return, Skyfree and my people who are willing are yours, its land, yours. However, if I have a son or my nephew returns, then it should pass to them, as the rights of inheritance state."

"Nothing of your offer intrigues me. I dare say, Cymbol, if I were to march my men into Skyfree right now, I would have your lands, and it would be done." Venot raised his hands, looking at his chiefs, and nodded.

"As long distant brothers through the Norte, you know it would not be so easy," she stated, her voice cool and smooth.

Tyrone cut in: "I do not desire to see this happen and would have to step in as well."

Looking at Neesa, Dreyandol shrugged. It was exactly what his concern had been. One house stepping in to stop the fighting between others, which causes another house to step in and another. Civil war loomed in Rosenia.

Azziza Zattu shot up: "My Lord Ash, remember, in times of skirmish between houses, should one ally with another, the kingdom will see this as civil unrest and as an act of war, at which time the king's armies would have to step in."

Lord Tyrone looked angry but took another angle quickly. "You would lose my friendship, the friendship our fathers forged.

This would include trade with us and the House of Blake, who have already given me their word in forging trade agreements. My house and the Blakes would give your goods easy access into the capital."

Venot looked to the faces of his lords, who still looked crazed. "Not even that stirs me, Tyrone. With Skyfree at my disposal, I would have more land and more people under my rule, which not only includes people but their wealth. The only thing that has even slightly moved me to not attack is the promise of friendship my father and sister wanted. I care little for you, but they both wished this on their deathbeds. Yet you've done nothing, *nothing*, to appease this situation." The lord's voice grew harsher with every word.

Dreyandol saw Tyrone shake his head with disgust, unclear who it was meant for, but then the lord of Ash spoke.

"Children, come here and say hello to your uncle." Just then, some of the guards parted and two children walked forward—two small figures, standing among angered giants. The oldest of the two was a girl of about five, who did her best to walk straight and proud, with a little boy who waddled next to her.

"Hello, Uncle Venot," the girl said. She let go of the boy's hand and ran to him. "Uncle, Uncle…" He picked her up, and when he did his war pick fell from his belt and clattered on the marble floor, echoing through the silent hall.

He stared for a moment, his face blank. The entire hall sat watching as he examined her. She smiled at him and wrapped her arms around him. "My sweet child, you have the eyes of your mother." Venot smiled widely, his voice soft and the anger in his face gone.

"I'm Ida. Father says I'm named after my mother, your sister, Uncle," the small girl said.

303

Dreyandol could see tears forming in Venot's eyes. "That you are, my sweet." Looking down to the still waddling boy: "And what's your name lad?" The boy did not speak.

"His name is Kevin," the small girl said, her sharp voice cutting through the room. "He doesn't say much yet."

Tyrone then spoke up: "I'm sorry, Venot. I know you and Idalia were close. It was wrong for me to keep them away. I do speak of you often. I promise from this point forward I'll not keep them from you. You're their family, and they should know where they come from."

Venot twirled his niece in a circle as she giggled and said, "See that it doesn't, brother."

*****

Four days of talks passed within Targon Hall. Venot sent his chiefs home, many were not happy. The Brolshivik were people of war, and to get their bloodlust up and not let them battle was a dangerous thing. They obeyed, however. Treaties were signed among the Houses of Skyfree and Belanov; trade agreements with Ash as well, with many promises made.

Dreyandol and Neesa spent much of their time walking the valley as they were not needed in the planning of the treaty. Word from Targon Hall said the Belanov lord spent every afternoon with his nephew and niece and his two sons playing in the garden.

On the sixth day after their arrival, after things settled and the first snowstorm draped a white blanket across the valley, the envoy of the king, the same group who had traveled all the way from Nowann, departed with hopes of leaving the mountains before the snow blocked the gaps.

Dreyandol and Neesa rode next to Jensing out the gate of Targon Hall. The sun stretched above the peaks, and the people of Targon Vale came out for their daily duties and to see them off. All the chieftains had departed with their thousands of soldiers, and now the small city looked like a clean and beautiful place. Many of the people of the city waved from the streets and Venot, Cymbol, and Tyrone stood on the parapets.

Jensing looked over. "Well, I'm glad that's handled, and this mission is over. You know the masters never said you need return with us to Nowann. You could go your own way, maybe head southwest to Geowm. They may need some help there. I've heard it's a haven for hoodlums and criminals. Then again, you could come back with me and see if there's something else to be done."

"We'll at least travel out of the mountains with everyone. We'll probably discuss it for the next few days as we travel. Rosenia is much bigger than Rovelle. Both of us would love to explore its far reaches." Neesa nodded in silent agreement. "Can I ask you a question though, Master Jensing?"

"Go right ahead. I'm always willing to answer questions about Rosenia," the master said.

"This isn't about Rosenia. It's more about Lord Tyrone's excellent timing. I found it odd he arrived when he did, after not wanting to do anything for two years," Dreyandol said, looking over at the red robed man.

With a large smile on his face, his wispy moustache like an adolescent boy, Jensing answered, "All I'll say is this. Proper planning prevents poor performance. We of the Crimson Order must allow for all avenues of peace."

Neesa's hand shot out, thrusting her dagger in a blur in front of Jensing. Dreyandol heard the ping of two objects ricochet off it.

305

Jensing fell from his horse towards him, and he jumped from his mount to catch him before he hit the stone street. Protruding from Jensing's neck stuck a needle.

His eyes rolled back; a small trickle of blood ran down to hide itself on his robes. He felt limp. Dreyandol then heard Jensing's mount fall and saw a needle in its leg. Looking toward Neesa, she had disappeared. Soldiers from the caravan surrounded Azziza and him, and shouts echoed down the wide avenue.

He jumped to his feet, leaving the lifeless Jensing in the hands of a healer, who had joined them. He caught sight of his apprentice wall jumping up between two buildings, heading for the rooftops. He ran down the street in the direction the needles came from. People crowded the area to see what happened. He saw a ladder leading to a roof. With his Dareian agility, he practically ran up the ladder, where he saw Neesa running parallel to him across the street. He then saw a shadow-like figure running and leaping across the rooftops in front of her.

The figure seemed to disappear any time it entered a shadow, only to reappear in the sun. The assassin moved quickly, but not as quickly as Neesa. She was closing on them.

He leapt over a large gap between buildings, having to stumble and roll on the other side, but gained his footing in a flash. After, he used a bit of air magic to give him an extra thrust on jumps.

From rooftop to rooftop, they chased, until he ran out of roofs. He saw Neesa close on the attacker, her katana out. The assassin pulled two thin daggers. Rolling to the side, the assassin swiped at her, and she dodged by doing a side flip, her tail keeping her balanced.

He grabbed the side of the building and slid down to land in a cart of horse dung. Jumping out as if on fire, he ran down the street, catching a glimpse of Neesa sending a thrust of air at the assassin, who knocked it away with their own defensive magic. He ran into a building and up some stairs, now on their side of the street. Climbing out a window, he jumped to the roof.

Neesa was chasing the figure again, several buildings away. Moving to join the hunt, he saw the assassin trip after a jump. Neesa moved on them again, as he ran. She went to leap over the gap. But as she landed the assassin turned on the ground, flew up to their feet, and lunged at the leaping Malkienon, to slide a dagger deep into her chest.

For a moment, he saw Neesa looking straight in the eyes of the assassin. Her tail flicked and then fell limp. His heart skipped a beat, and he stopped breathing as he watched the assassin, in all black, let go of his apprentice and friend. He watched her like a leaf fall to the street with a thud and heard a deafening scream.

Chapter 21

Aija used the tips of her fingers to put ointment on a gash across her shoulder. It smelled like mint leaves and liquor and stung a bit. The pain in her left arm went deep, like a pulled muscle in her shoulder mixed with the burning pain of fire on the outside. Every twitch or movement sent flames reeling up into her head. She had limited range of movement.

That stupid cat. In their exchange, she had leapt out and bit with her curved blade. The caster was fast. Faster than most she usually dealt with. She should have known by the way the cat caught up in the chase. She should have been more wary fighting not only a member of the Crimson Order, but also one of the Malkienon race. They were known to move like the wind, so the stories were true. She had never fought one before in the many battles she found herself in.

Tying a bandage around her arm, she winced at the pain. Blood was trickling down her arm and side during her flight out of the city. She heard guards in the streets, gates being closed, bells ringing and horns blowing. The warnings of her presence echoed across the cold-stoned Targon Vale. Most of all, she heard his scream, the painful cry of the other Crimson Caster, the Darei, the Elven master. She heard it echoing in her mind as a scream of great loss. She had slain someone close to him, a friend, someone he loved, and in that moment of his loss, she heard him break. In her mind it was like shattered glass, the crash of thousands of pieces.

Was it the same for her? Had she broken, in the same way when she heard of poor Edwin's murder? She did not really know him except for being a boy infatuated with her, only wanting to talk with her, occasionally meeting her with flowers and a boyish smile. Could it have been the reason for her hysterics and attack on Arnus?

She felt weak and lay back. It would take a bit of time to recover from the trauma of the gash. The ointment would help heal it and return some energy, but right now she was losing strength. She sat, tired; her eyes kept closing. It affected the rest of her body too, making her movements slow and cumbersome.

She thought more of the scream. If she had broken with the news of Edwin like she did, how broken was this Darei? Was he and the Malkienon friends? Were they lovers? They must have been closer than she and Edwin. Could that cause someone to lose themselves, to fall into some dark recess of their mind?

She felt herself falling into the black. In a last moment, she nodded, thankful she stumbled upon a small, abandoned shack outside the city. She did not know how long she could hide here. They would send out searchers once they realized she had left the city. If she could just get a little rest, she would be on her way and then they would never find her. No one ever did. At that, she slipped into the void.

When she woke, the night sat dark outside, and the cold air of the mountains nipped at her cheeks. She lay covered though, in a thick bearskin blanket she did not remember putting on. She realized someone was there with her, sitting in the shadows.

She pulled her dagger with her good hand. "Who's there?"

"Don't be scared, Aija. It's only me," said a voice from a dark corner.

"Arnus? What are you doing here?" she said, trying to find him.

"The master sent word to keep an eye on you during your first mission since the incident," he said, exiting the shadow. "He wanted to make sure you were up to the task."

She looked around. "You found me here. Has anyone else come this way?"

"I actually found you two days ago. I watched your little fight yesterday. Good ploy to lure the stupid cat in with a fake fall," he said, then chuckled.

"She was fast, maybe faster than me. I was too concerned with getting away than fighting her. Has anyone else come this way?" she asked again.

"No, not since I killed two soldiers about to break down the door. I hid them in some brush and snow. More may come when they realize those two haven't returned," he said, moving closer to the door and looking out.

She could see him better now in the light. He wore his leathers and a thick coat, his movement smooth and effortless. She readjusted herself on the floor. Her arm was stiff, and pain shot through her when she tried to move it.

"It'll be a few days for the ointment to close the wound. It's not too bad. I checked it out and re-bandaged it. We'll need to be on the way soon though. You should eat something. You'll need some strength." Arnus stood up and pulled something out of a pack. He handed her some cold cheese and dried, hard bread. Not what she desired, as meals went, but she shoveled it down.

"I took the two horses from the soldiers here. I wanted one of their famous rams though, I've never ridden one. We can use them to find a new hiding place," he said, peeking out the door again.

"Why a new hiding place? Shouldn't we head south?" she asked, standing up on her weak legs. Arnus took her good arm and steadied her.

"No, we can't leave yet. Remember the master sent me to make sure you handled your mission," he said, helping her onto an old wooden chair. It felt cold beneath her.

"I don't understand, I'm finished with my mission," she said, taking in a deep breath. She coughed from the cold.

"No, you're not. Your mark isn't dead yet. You failed the kill."

"I didn't fail. That isn't possible. I shot the Crimson Caster Jensing with a needle. I watched him fall," she said, strain in her voice.

"And I watched him get back up when the other two went after you. You sent three needles. Two were blocked, one ricocheted into a horse, and killed it, but the one that hit him didn't seem to do anything. He lay there motionless, not seeming to breathe, but then I saw his eyes move and he sat up. We must go back and finish the mission. You need to kill him if you don't want to have the wrath of the master on you." Arnus sounded concerned, but it made her feel sick.

"I appreciate you finding me and taking care of me. Especially dealing with the soldiers who were about to discover me here, but no." She felt sick, unsure whether the idea of finishing her contract or Arnus made her want to vomit. Was it both?

Every word out of his silken tongue, every smile on his thin, sharp-chinned face, made her want to tear her hair out. She mistrusted him, but was it all because of Edwin, or was there more to it? Something turned her stomach.

"No," she said again but with disdain.

"What do you mean, no? You must, you must finish the mission. You know what will happen. He'll be killed eventually anyway, but if you don't do it, you'll have failed. Don't you remember the woman from when we were young? She failed a

311

mission and the master killed her. You're worthless if you can't finish your job." His voice began to plead toward the end.

"No, I… I can't do this anymore," she heard herself saying. She shook her head, looking at the rotting floor of the shack. Not sure why, but in her mind, she believed it. She started to understand.

"Don't say such stupid things, Aija. You don't have a choice. We're part of Klor Dem," he proclaimed, his voice growing louder and frustrated. "Our duties to the Order and our duties to the master are final. We kill. This is what we've been trained for, this is what we do."

"It's not what I do anymore," she said, still looking at the floor.

"And what are you going to do? Go to the master and ask him to let you go?"

"I don't know," she said, looking up at him. "But I know I don't want to go back and kill the mark." She could not face the Darei, the Elf whose friend she murdered. Something about that thought caused her to shiver, as tears welled up. "And I don't want to do this anymore." The Darei's scream kept echoing in her head. Or was it her crying at Edwin's death?

In the darkness, she was not quick enough to see the slap that connected with her cheek, almost knocking her out of the chair. "Snap out of it, Aija. Do you know what you're saying? You're asking for death. To fail a mission is death."

She rubbed her throbbing cheek with her good arm and with defiance in her voice: "I don't care."

That was when they heard snow crunching in the distance.

"Someone's coming. We have to leave or they'll find us," Arnus said, grabbing a pack on a table and reaching over to help her up.

"I'm not going with you," she said, pulling away from him and standing on her own. The pain almost brought her back down.

"What're you going to do? March out there and turn yourself in? Or do you think you can run? You know you can't run from the Order. The master will put a mark on you and anyone who finds you will be rewarded." The sounds were getting closer, and he looked in their direction though he could not see through the shack's walls.

"I don't know, but I'm not going back," she said, walking toward the door. Arnus pushed it open and followed her out. "I'll hide as long as I can if I must. I'm not going back and I'm not going with you."

He yelled in fury and pushed her. She fell face first in the cold snow, her arm bursting with pain that made her clench her teeth; her head whirled in fog. "You're ruining everything. Someday we were going to lead the Order, the king and queen of the greatest assassin's guild. Our children would be born into it. They would be the greatest assassins in history. Rulers would cower before the name of Klor Dem. Peasants would tell our stories to scare their children." He laughed, and Aija could hear him pacing in the snow. "You're destroying everything! Why are you ruining this?"

She winced, turning to look at him. "What are you saying?"

His voice grew calm: "If you won't finish the mission, and you won't come back with me, then I might as well deliver the punishment myself. There's no need to waste time when I'm already here."

She rolled over more in the snow when she saw the fury in his eyes. He held his dagger and he moved to pounce. Then she heard shouts echoing across the cold ground. Charging out of the white blanketed pine trees, she saw two Belanov soldiers on horses. One carried a crossbow. "Halt," he yelled.

Arnus turned and dodged a bolt. She heard him laugh and watched as he retaliated, throwing knives at the crossbowman. She heard them clang off his armor. The soldier charged. One wielded a spear, and the other dropped his crossbow to pull a one-handed axe.

In a flash, Arnus dodged them and sliced at the horse's legs with his daggers. They buckled, and the soldier went tumbling into the snow. The other lunged with his spear, but Arnus was too quick. He slid into close range, where the spear was unwieldy, and plunged his dagger into a weak spot at the back of the knee. The soldier screamed and grabbed at his leg, falling from the mount.

The other soldier, back up on his feet, swung his axe. Arnus dodged a few swings, the shouts and screams of the large northern soldiers echoing like some great beast.

Arnus continued to laugh at his fun.

Another attack came from the hulking man. He had a long red beard with a scar on his face. He was rough and ugly, much like his axe wielding form. Arnus blocked the clumsy attack and kicked out, pushing the soldier back, then in a quick tumble he went under the next swing and up came the dagger into the underside of the bearded chin. The soldier screamed in pain and surprise, arm still swinging weakly, blood pouring from the bottom of his head, leaking down into the pure white snow. He went limp and fell.

The other attacker stood weaponless, having dropped his spear. She watched what fear could do to a man. He wore a sword at his hip and would not move to pull it. He hobbled, trying to get away, his hands up in front of him, his palms out trying to show no threat. "Please no, don't kill me. I won't say nothing. I never saw you or her even. I can say a bear attacked us, and I'll even fix up his body to look like it did." The soldier pleaded, but the young assassin looked unmoved, except to cock his head.

His dagger sliced the fingers from one of the extended hands. The soldier screamed, grabbing at the bleeding stumps. More blood in the snow. Arnus smiled, a look of menace and power on his face.

The man's fear gave him pleasure, she saw. She heard her protector laugh, just a small chuckle, barely audible. Then a moment later, a slice of reflecting metal arced across the air, and the soldier was then falling, holding his neck with his good hand. It seemed slow, like hours went by, until he hit the snow, never to rise again.

Arnus stood over the bleeding man, who lay gurgling in death, and she watched him dive down with his dagger and stab several more times with it. All the while he laughed louder, his face full of elation.

When he turned toward her again, he still smiled, his face wild with pleasure. He focused on her, murder in his eyes, drops of blood in his long straight hair that framed his beautiful face. He was no longer looking at her as someone he knew, but as his next mark. He hunched as shadowed death, come to take her, but she was not ready to go.

A small, blue-feathered needle poked out of his neck. His eyes flicked wide. "You little b—" was all he could utter before he fell to the snow with a crunch, next to the soldier he had repeatedly stabbed.

Aija took the blowpipe from her mouth and with the same hand brushed a lock of her black hair from her cheek.

She sat for a moment in the snow, gaining control of herself and assessing the situation. She stood with some difficulty, cold and shaking, weak and worn, and trudged over to the immobile Arnus. The stars, her stars, her only friends it seemed, shone in the night sky, bright and blazing. The steam from her breath disappeared with every inhale in the freezing cold of the mountain air. She stood over him. His eyes stared back at her.

"It was only a blue feather. I don't want to kill you, but if the weather does or other soldiers come and find you here, then so be it. I'll even give you a blanket, but I'm not moving you. You'll be mobile soon enough—sooner than most," she said, scanning the area.

She took a coat of ram fur, thick and heavy, from one of the soldiers, and covered him in it. It would help some, though he lay in the snow.

"Please don't follow me. This life isn't for me anymore. I've seen and felt what it means to kill and steal the life from those who care. Maybe my understanding is weak, because like you, I've never had a real family and never had someone to care for me. I feel the pain… at least some small portion of it."

His eyes stared back unblinking.

"Please, let this go. I beg you. Tell the master you don't know where I went. Don't come for me. I'm taking the three horses that can still travel. I should be able to get far enough from you to negate your tracking. You'll be wasting your time. Disappearing is what we shadows are made for."

She kissed him on the cheek. "That was for being like a brother to me those years in training, through all the hardship and pain." Then she slapped him hard. "That was for killing Edwin, just a poor boy who favored me. Cared for me in a way you'll probably never understand, and maybe I'll never understand. Whether you did it by the master's plans or by your own willingness to kill, it was wrong. I hope you see that one day."

She stood up over him in the darkness of the night, blood in the snow around her. The only noise was their breathing and the deep whimpering of the wounded horse. In the cold of the northern mountains, with tall green trees standing like sentinels, Aija turned and rode toward the coming dawn.

Chapter 22

A jostle from Cleon brought Andross back to focus as they came out of the Embracing Mountains and down through the Denita Gap. Tired and uncomfortable, he looked over the dust-covered city of sorcery, Telaporawein. It stood as the last city to the south before the harshness of the Thernat Desert.

Far from the prying eyes of the capital and hidden deep in the lands of the House of Nadal, it settled. Flags of a red sun with three violet eyes lined the road. Though situated in the Caihn region, the lords Hadire and Nadal held little command over the city. That power resided with the council of the Oreon, the rulers who only by necessity paid their taxes to their lord.

Riding Cleon down the road, past a group of weary travelers, Andross nodded and smiled. He got little response in return. Though it was a part of Rosenia, the crown held little power here as well. He brushed his hand through his short hair and breathed in the arid air, already making its presence known, though he had not reached the desert yet.

He needed to be cautious and not draw attention to himself. All grievances, all lawmaking, and all first rights fell to the Oreon. They were a strange group, all males, known by their violet and black swirling eyes, magic users who focused on summoning the souls of those who had died, whether creature or person. There were no greater summoners in all the lands.

Bard songs littered the kingdom. Songs and tales about their harsh punishments, hanging the living from the walls by their arms and letting them die in the heat, or taking them deep into the desert and leaving them there to die of thirst or hunger. Stories of their cruelty were heard far and wide. Tales of their cruelty were as prevalent as grains of wheat in a mill.

Andross also knew they could easily be bribed. No crime was too wrong for them to accept payment, except any committed against them. Their only other rule was if one of their kind saw a crime and took displeasure in it, the criminal could be punished immediately and without trial.

So, if none of their violet swirling eyes saw or you carried enough gold, anyone could get away with almost anything. This attracted many scoundrels to the city, even more than Geowm in the north.

A small garrison of Nadalian troops and an even smaller garrison of Rosenian soldiers could do nothing to really stop the crime. Neither did they add to the protection of the city because it was unnecessary. No raiding tribe from the desert or savage clan of Horaks would dare attack a city with thousands of mages.

When Andross reached the gate, he laughed and saw four different guards. A soldier of the House of Nadal stood in a red jerkin with a violet eye on his chest, his skin almost the light red color of the city's clay walls. His upper lip housed a black moustache. A soldier of Rosenia saluted him with a head nod, and a soldier of the Shadow Mages in a dark gray robe only stared. Their guild was very prevalent in the city, and other than the Oreon held the most strength. The last guard was an Oreon acolyte in a black robe, trimmed violet, with a violet rope tied around his waist.

He stared at Andross with his swirling eyes. The few times he had been close enough to see them, he felt drawn in, lost in some hazy world, and then suddenly back to the exact place he was supposed to be at.

The acolyte's hood lay down; his light purple hair shaved everywhere except for a long strip that reached from his forehead to the back of his neck. Andross heard it referred to as a scalp hawk. The longer it grew, the higher status the Oreon held with his people. The other hair commonly styled by the Oreon was complete baldness, except for violet and black tattoos, intricately designed into swirling circular patterns. He did not know their significance.

The streets bustled with robed figures. Almost every magic guild housed a station there. The surrounding mountains almost wrapped completely around the city and were supposed to be enchanted. Without many laws, mages were able to experiment any way they could conjure. Many of those ways broke the rules of the Congregate and the *Tome of Magicka*, so were done in secret. At least those were the rumors passed on to him.

Trotting deeper into the dusty city, he noticed there were not many actual homes, as there were not many families. Most of the women were found in taverns or brothels if they were not part of a mages' guild. It made Andross sick to think of the children born there. Many were orphaned and many disappeared, rumored to be the experiments of dark sorcerers. They ran through the streets dirty, begging at his boots, and skulking in alleys.

With no female Oreon, the males took Human women. Most males born from the coupling were Oreon, born with purple eyes. All females were Human, many of whom disappeared, orphaned in the streets, or worse, taken to be used for more disreputable situations, sold into slavery with the desert tribes.

Andross focused on four great towers made of red clay, their points the shape of tear drops, and each embedded with a mixture of opal and amethysts. One tower stood as the large fortress of the Oreon, where it was said several thousand of these men lived. Their keep stood as the original settlement. Two of the other towers were for the academies of magic, Sorca and Rebladi, where great masters attempted to learn new magic and create new spells while teaching their disciples.

The final tower was called Selda Faw, or Shadow House in Dareian. The Shadow Mages built it as their headquarters, and over half of their people were housed in it.

The air hung dry this far south. He discarded his cloak halfway down the mountain, then he looked across the great sand sea of Thernat that ranged for thousands of leagues.

Andross once heard a blind man say he had lost his eyesight when he looked across the dunes at sunrise. He dismissed it but did not intend on testing the idea either.

His hand rested on his sword as he rode deeper into the city. He wanted to be ready for anything. He traveled here to search for a Goblin named Gnik.

He had returned to Faor to see Vernor, and with the help of a local mage, he pried information from the insane man.

Vernor rambled on for hours about fire dancers, shields that sounded like drums, and sharp feathered birds. Many times, he repeated the phrase about his son, and many times Andross asked for his name. The other phrase came up as well, about steel singing in the rain, but it never made sense.

He was about to leave when the man began to seize on the floor, his body flailing and then vomiting out his lunch of cheese and bread, while the healer tried to calm him with magic. That was when his eyes focused on him, and he said, "Find Gnik. He's sorry, I know it. And so am I. The dream haunts us… always haunting us." Then the old man passed out, and the healers took him away.

321

Andross had no idea how to find Gnik, until one of the healers said that someone visited weeks earlier. He told him the visitor was a Goblin, and when they spoke, the Goblin claimed to be heading south to Telaporawein. He would not give him his name but did hear Vernor call him Gnik.

So here he traveled, looking for Gnik, and some clue to his friend's assassination.

The first day he rode to the Rosenian garrison and spoke to a Knight of the Wolf named Arjen Longbary, a stocky, red-haired youth just sent there for his first post, one of the lesser sons of Lord Longbary.

"Sorry, my Lord Andross. I've asked around," the man said, upon returning from a walk around the garrison, "neither myself nor any of the men recognize the name Gnik. Of course, there are a lot of Goblins in the city. Most hang around the Oreon district. One popular tavern to start at is called Yellow Eyes. Be wary though, because if you can't tell by the name, most people aren't welcome there."

"Thank you, Arjen, I'll check there," Andross said. He hated feeling disappointed after having only asked one group, but the search wore on him. The trip alone to the far south was difficult, and he had little sleep.

"Of course, you should ask some of the guilds. The Shadow Mages are in their tower of Selda Faw, that's the gray one to the west, and the Crimson Order works out of the Sorca Tower on the eastern side of the city. Everyone knows they're only here to keep tabs on the Shadow Mages. Those two groups are always getting into tussles."

*****

The afternoon sun had set when he entered the Yellow Eyes Tavern. It had very few patrons, and all who were there, including the tavern owner, were of the Goblin race. The tavernkeeper's dark yellow eyes stared at him, so he walked straight to the bar. Two of the Goblin men shifted in their seats to keep an eye on him, and one of the women with her light-yellow eyes, like a daisy, came from the kitchen, saw him, and turned right back around.

"Clearly, you're not here to drink," the owner said, rubbing his hand under his large, hooked nose and squinting, "so why don't you skip ordering one and just ask what you want, so we can tell you we don't know anything, and you can leave."

Andross nodded. He was not the first person to come into this bar unwanted and out of place. "Fine." He threw a gold lief on the bar and watched the owner's eyes bulge. "I'm looking for a Goblin named Gnik. I was told by his father he'd be in Telaporawein."

The tavernkeeper picked the gold lief off the bar and threw it at the tavern door. Andross noticed he did not want to throw it back. "We don't know any Gnik, so take your gold and be gone."

"Are you sure? I'm not after him for any specific reasons. I just want to ask him some questions, and his father said to look here," Andross repeated.

The tavernkeeper spit on his own bar and snarled, "Get out."

As he turned to walk out, one drunk Goblin stumbled from a bench and added, "Liar, Gnik ain't got no father," and then fell face first to the sticky floor.

Now he knew where to start. He left the tavern and put Cleon up in a stable just down the dry, busy road. He threatened the stable boy that if Cleon was not there when he returned, there would be no stable boy at the judging of the Oreon. Of course, he did not

323

mean it, but he would have said anything to make sure the boy did not sell off his horse.

Night fell, and the tavern drew in more customers. He waited outside, watching as mostly Goblins went in, sometimes the occasional Human, and even a Dwaling with vomit on his beard and a missing ear. He waited for hours, spying from the shadows across the dirt road for the Goblin who passed out to exit. Even at night it was still hot; sweat dripped down to his waist, under his leather jerkin, his armpits damp with every movement.

He watched as a troop of Rosenian soldiers went by, two of them stumbling with drunkenness and the other not fully geared. This city bred a pit of disgust, and the soldiers almost made him angry enough to confront them about their lack of respect and attire, but he only shook his head.

When the moon sat about two hours past midnight, he saw the Goblin stumble out of the tavern and begin to walk down the road. He took about three steps to the left and stopped and then turned the other way. There were still a lot of people out: drunks, prostitutes, mages in their robes, so Andross did not feel the need to hide in the shadows; he followed just far enough back to not give himself away.

He trailed the Goblin until he saw him enter a dark, leaning building that looked deserted. He did not enter right away, but tried to look through a window. He saw nothing until a spark of tinder lit a stick, used to light a single candle. The Goblin then said something to a mirror on a table and fell to his bed.

Andross circled the building and entered through a broken window. He made his way with light steps to the room the Goblin lay in. The rest of the building was dust filled and empty. Old broken furniture and discarded items littered each room.

The Goblin lay sprawled on the bed, except for one leg that had not made it on in his collapse, and drool leaked from his mouth. He wore dirty, thin silk that seemed to have been luxurious at some point. He looked at the mirror on the table. It leaned cracked and smudged. Next to it were some silver petals, and next to them an exquisite black dagger. The blade and hilt were made of Galvorn, intricately designed and sharp enough to slice firewood like bread.

He wondered at first if this Goblin was part of the Dark Paladin's, because their symbol of two crossed scythes was etched on the hilt, but second guessed himself when he saw there were no other pieces of their armor in the room or anything depicting their presence.

So, this Goblin is a thief. He flipped the blade in his hand. After examining the rest of the room, he sat in an old wooden chair and waited.

It was well past noon in the heat of the day. The Goblin had screamed out several times but never woke up until now when he stirred a last time. Andross' backside throbbed from waiting and he felt relieved as the screams had been sudden and haunting, but he would not want to take a chance of losing this man. "Are you awake?" he said smoothly.

The Goblin jumped up and pulled a dagger from his boot, all the while rubbing the sleep from his eyes. "Who are you and what do you want?"

Andross sat with Ambra Nenoli across his lap, the sword hidden in the shadow. "There's no need for the dagger. I just have questions. I'll even pay you if you want." He hated to offer payment so early, but he wanted to see if this Goblin would have the same reaction as the tavernkeeper on taking gold.

"Show it to me," the Goblin said, stepping back against the wall, his dagger still in hand.

Andross pulled his money pouch out and threw it on the table, knocking over the few silver petals that were stacked. He saw the Goblin lick his lips and stare at the pouch. "Where can I find a Goblin named Gnik?"

"I don't know anyone by that name," came a quick response.

"Please don't lie to me. I've traveled for weeks, and my patience is running thin," Andross said, lifting his sword and bringing it back down to rest on his lap. "In the tavern you said Gnik has no father. That means you must know him. You're wrong in your statement, but you must know him to make it in the first place."

"I don't know what you're talking about. Take your money and leave," the Goblin said, his voice raised, the knife still out in front of him.

"I can't, I must know. If you can just tell me where to find him, then I won't bother you anymore. His father's ill, and I need to pass along a message and ask him some questions."

True or false, he would say anything to reel the Goblin into answering. He only hoped this would calm the other's nerves.

The Goblin stood for a moment, quiet. "So, he's not well?"

"Who? The father?" Andross said.

"Of course. Who else?"

"Why do you know him?" Andross said, rubbing his chin.

It was silent for a moment and then the Goblin lowered his blade and said, "He's my father. I'm Gnik. How bad is he? What did he say?"

Andross was taken aback, not expecting the reply. "How do I know he's your father and that you're truly Gnik?"

The Goblin's voice rose again, "Because his name is Vernor, and I only saw him a few months ago, maybe weeks ago, I don't know. I saw him in the healer's house for the dimwitted and insane in Faor."

Andross stood from the chair, bringing his sword to his side. "He said that he was sorry, and knew you were as well."

Gnik's face grew pale, and then in rage he knocked an already cracked vase against the wall, shattering it. He slumped on the bed. "Father. Poor Father, I know his pain, and he knows mine."

"What? I don't understand?" the knight said, looking at the withered man.

"We should never have been a part of it."

"What?" Andross said. "Been a part of what? What pain?"

Gnik went on holding his face in his hands. "Vernor isn't truly my father…"

Andross only nodded, focusing on the sharp teeth and yellow eyes. Gnik was full-blooded Goblin, not a mix.

"He took care of me as best he could. Found me in the streets and showed me how to survive. Just thieving and stuff, nothing that hurt anyone," Gnik said, looking up, his eyes pleading. "We lived our lives doing small jobs together… never hurt anyone…"

Andross looked at him, rubbing his fingers on his hilt.

"Not until the day my father's friend Abecore came."

The knight perked up, a connection from the Goblin's own mouth.

"He said they needed two more hands for a high paying job. We weren't told the details until we traveled to meet the others, but Abecore kept swearing it would be worth our while. Payment was in gold, with the promise of never needing it again. We didn't know it was for a murder." Gnik looked at him again, his eyes watering.

327

"Go on," Andross said, his heart thumping, hanging on every word.

"Once we found out what they wanted, we were going to leave, but there were mages there who swore if anyone left, they would be killed. So, we stayed and were given crossbows. Other than the three of us, we didn't know anyone else except for the mage who told Abecore about it. I never got his name, but I remember him always playing with fire and making it dance in his hands."

Fire dancer, Andross thought.

"I remember that night, waiting, hidden in the tall grass, the storm coming in and the rain beginning to fall. There hadn't been a cloud until right before and then there was a torrent. We heard the riders coming. There were nearly four hundred of us lying in wait. All of us who weren't mages were given crossbows, with many bolts. Someone said they were crossbows made in Kiamel Po, made for piercing armor with a fast reload. My father told me that if things got bad, to get back down in the grass, but soon after we heard the horses."

"Was it the Kiamel Posians who gave you the crossbows?" Andross asked, his mind trying to take in everything. His brain tried piecing everything together, but in that short amount of time, so many questions were being authenticated and answered that he was having a hard time forming words.

"No, I don't think so. A wagon met us, and dark robed figures gave us the crossbows, but they weren't from Kiamel Po. I can never see their faces, only blurs now. I remember them saying the weapons were a gift from their lord." Gnik rubbed his face and wiped some of the tears from his eyes.

"Who's the lord?" He needed nothing more than to hear the name of the lord who called for the king's death. No king reigned without enemies, but Nurame was becoming the greatest king to rule Rosenia. He needed to know who the traitor was.

"They gave no name. That same wagon and several more returned when the deed ended. They collected the bodies of those in the group who died. More than I thought too. By the end, the king and his knights slew nearly three hundred, even with our ambush. The dark robed figures carted them off, but I don't know what they did with them." Gnik shrugged.

"Those of us still alive were told to walk single file to the north and meet at a river where boats would be waiting with our payment, but my father didn't like it. He thought it strange; how nonchalant they were about the number dead. So, he took me and coerced Abecore to stay at the back and then split away before we got to the river. Of course, we didn't get paid, but we heard screams and then watched from afar as they were slaughtered. We had made the right choice or so we thought."

Gnik stood up, wiping his eyes. "I didn't know we would be killing the king. We were never told, even in the fight. I tried to get down in the grass to hide, but some force wouldn't let me. I had no control. We were told to just keep shooting. Fear consumed me. I don't think I hit anyone until a knight with two bolts in the back of his leg focused on me, and I shot him in the eye."

"And you can describe nothing of the other men or the men in the dark robes?" Andross asked, his fist clenched. He tried making sense of it all. Dark figures, all hired by a lord?

"Only one more thing. The one who made the fire dance, he and several mages wore the same dark robes as the wagon drivers, but I did not recognize them. I thought to see some here, in the city of sorcery, but I haven't," Gnik said, his eyes lit up like an excited child.

329

Andross could see it now. He could see the fight and his friend fall. He could see faceless robed figures like ghosts, causing death with their spells. *Who were they?* There were a hundred magic guilds with dark robes and just as many assassins' guilds with magic users. He was thankful though, and more content than he thought he would be. A piece of his puzzle had been filled in. It had not been random bandits on the road, nor was there a party of Kiamel Posians. Some great lord called for and organized the death of his king. A traitor hid among the great houses.

"I cannot forgive myself. My father can't either. We're scoundrels, thieves, but until that day we never took a life. Now I'm a shell of who I once was. I've killed, murdered, and tortured. I can't look at myself in the face anymore." Gnik glanced at the table, the excited child gone.

Andross saw the cracked mirror. He was not sure what to do. Bringing Gnik in for judgment and execution would only paint him a target for whatever lord caused the situation, and yet the poor Goblin might still know more. As much as he wanted to see him beheaded, he also believed the Goblin's remorse and believed he did not want to be there. Andross wanted payment for his friend's death, but he would not find it in the man weeping before him. Only through the justice of the one who had called for it would he find even a small bit of peace.

Gnik spoke through the tears: "Kill me, sir knight. Release me from them, always in my head, they're always there."

Andross wrinkled his brow.

"Please kill me. I'm a wretch, a king slayer, I've committed regicide and homicide. The lowest of the low. I don't deserve to live." The Goblin looked at his knife, until Andross reached out and took it from him.

"No, I may need your help finding this lord you speak of," he answered, knife in hand.

"There's nothing else I can tell you. Don't make me wake up another day and look in the broken face of a man who has committed an evil beyond forgiveness. Don't let me go on when soon my only friend, my father will be completely ripped from Sancta. This thing has broken his mind, and I don't want it to take me. Kill me and be done with it, I need this out of my head, I need them gone," Gnik pleaded. "I can't keep living. I can't move to Kiamel Po with my people."

For a brief moment, the knight lost focus. Was that just a confession about the Goblin exodus? Were they truly leaving? He would ask when given the chance. "I can't do it," he said, trying to tread with caution. "You're the only one who can tell me more of this. You're the only one who can point out the robed figures. Your father's mind is gone, and Abecore is lost."

"Abecore is dead? What happened?"

He breathed deep. "I had to kill him," Andross answered.

"Did he ask for death too?" came a whisper. "It was eating at him as well. He never did forgive my father for making us leave. Even though he knew the others were dead."

"In a way, he asked for death," Andross said, cryptically.

"And you granted it, but now you won't grant me my own request." Gnik's voice grew harsh and his face went red. "Who are you to grant life or death?" Now the Goblin was in a rage. "I want forgiveness. I want to be released from this curse, this incessant nightmare that haunts my existence."

"I can't release you," said the knight. "You're too important. I don't know how to get that point across, but you could redeem yourself some by helping me."

331

"You released Abecore, and there is no redemption for me," Gnik snapped, tearing at his matted hair.

"No, I defended myself from him."

Gnik lunged for the black dagger on the table, his eyes wide. "I stole this off the dead corpse of a Dark Paladin who I slew in his sleep, days after I saved his life. If you won't kill me, then I'll kill myself." He lifted the blade. "Get out of my head," he yelled, his eyes crazed and darting around the room, as if searching for something or someone.

Andross jumped forward and grabbed his hands, halting Gnik's thrust into his own stomach. He tried to wrest the dagger away.

"Stop this! There's still time to redeem what you've done."

"It cannot be done!" the Goblin screamed. "There's no deliverance from this spiraling destruction except for death." Andross saw his eyes change focus. "If you won't let me kill myself, then I'll force you to kill me, as did Abecore."

Gnik turned the blade toward him.

He saw the craze in Gnik's eyes. The Goblin would kill him if he did not stop him. So, he kicked the Goblin in the chest and sent him across the room. He lifted his sword with Gnik still holding the black blade.

The Goblin lunged again, and he parried the attack, punching him in the face and sending him back again. Gnik wiped blood from his mouth and charged, yelling, "I'll kill you for that." The remorseful Goblin disappeared, and a killer took his place. Gnik's mind, like his father's, and Abecore's, was slipping away. Andross was not sure if it had to do with killing the king or if there was something else involved, but the Goblin wanted nothing more than to end his life.

Gnik threw a small stool, forcing him to bat it away. With the distraction the Goblin was on him. He barely shoved the attack away, the blade cutting through the thin leather at his shoulder but not touching skin. Gnik jumped back and started to move the dagger back and forth in figure eights. All the while he laughed, blood coming from his mouth, his crazed yellow eyes not blinking. He attacked again, and Andross easily stopped the slashes, and cut Gnik on his thigh, with only slight recognition from the Goblin he had been injured.

Andross circled around the room, but Gnik attacked again and caught him in a bad position. He tried to sidestep but slipped on part of the broken stool and stumbled.

In order to catch himself and still stay in a position to see his attacker, he had to drop his sword. Gnik came on him in a flash, and Andross stopped his thrust again by grabbing his arms. They were wrestling for control on the ground, and he was having a harder time on the bottom. The weight of the smaller Goblin created enough fatigue to wear him down, especially since he had not slept all night, waiting for the Goblin to rise. This time, the black blade came down on his shoulder, piercing it.

He watched the blade, like slow motion and without resistance, slip slowly into his flesh. Pain tore through him and he yelled. All the while the hot breath of the Goblin hit his face. Gnik, his eyes bulging, screamed in fury. The pain stung like fire, so Andross did what he could and headbutted the Goblin in the nose. As his only recourse, it worked but cost him as well. The blade slid deeper in, causing him to almost lose consciousness. His warm blood spilled on the floor, but the Goblin stumbled back, leaving the dagger in his shoulder.

Andross touched two hilts at one time. He pushed his sword out of reach of the Goblin with the tips of his fingers as he dove for it, his eyes in a haze, and yanked the blade from his shoulder. With the Goblin missing his sword and falling next to him, Andross used the butt of the knife to hit Gnik in the face several times, knocking him from his frenzy. Dizzy and in pain he dragged his attacker up and to the bed. He held the knife to his neck. "Stop this, I've won."

"I'll never stop," said Gnik with blood pouring from his nose and a gash above his eye. "I'll never stop, because they never stop."

"What the dream? It never stops. Who are they? If you can even answer a few more questions, I'll end your life," Andross said, lying.

Gnik looked at him, blood circling one eye. "If you promise to kill me the moment I'm done answering, I'll try."

"Who are they? Are you referring to someone specific? Is there some sort of symbol that differentiates these dark robed figures from the hundreds of other dark robed figures?"

"I don't know who they are, but there was a symbol. I caught a glimpse of it, not on the robe, but on the arm of the figure who we met."

Andross was looking straight in his eyes, his heart pumping in anticipation.

"It was a tattoo, like an orange fl…," Gnik said, but then his face contorted.

Andross watched, not knowing what the hesitation was for, but then Gnik began to scream out, louder and louder it grew. Andross did not know what was happening, but went to strike the Goblin, whose eyes were now bulging from his face. Just as he connected another hit with the dagger butt, a spray broke across his own face. Wet, warm blood covered him and dripped from his cheeks and chin. He could taste iron from what had flown into his open mouth. He stumbled back trying to wipe the red from his eyes. When he finally did, he looked up to see Gnik lay prostrate on the bed. His eye sockets were bloody and now empty holes, blood was splattered across the bed, from what seemed his ears.

Andross first stepped back from surprise, but then pain seared in his shoulder. He breathed deep, angered and confused at what had just transpired, when he heard a creak. "Is someone there?" There was no answer, but then he noticed a shadow out of the corner of his eye at the window. He did not look toward it right away but feigned stumbling and then reached for his sword. As he gripped it, he shot a look at the window. There was someone there, a shadow, in that moment a flame of pain stabbed into his wound again. He almost collapsed but then pushed it away and looked back at the window.

Was the pain from the watcher? Did they do something to Gnik? His pain felt unnatural, more like magic. He grabbed the dagger also and moved out of the building to the street.

It was midday, but what few people were there stopped and stared at him, blood clearly visible in the light still dripping off him. He looked around, hoping to see the shadowed figure. Face after face met his, staring in wonder, until he turned and saw someone walking away, not looking at him. It was someone cloaked and hiding their face.

"Halt there," he yelled out, moving toward them. They looked up and began to run. He gave chase, moving past some onlookers and down a street.

He turned into an alley and standing there facing him was the shadowed figure. Again, a searing pain pushed into his wound. He

335

looked toward it expecting to see something there, but it was only the tear in his leather jerkin and blood.

The figure began to move toward him, and he noticed them reach into their cloak. The pain in his shoulder was almost paralyzing, almost enough to make him fall to his knees.

For a moment, he found in his mind enough strength to push the pain away. It subsided, his mind cleared for a moment, and he threw the black Galvorn blade from his wounded arm.

It did not connect, it was not meant for throwing, but it was enough to startle his assailant and, in a flash, Andross lunged with his sword and sliced. The blade connected just as the pain came on full blast again and felt his mind go into a black haze.

Chapter 23

Andross did not know what hour it was when he heard his cell door open and felt himself yanked off the floor.

Rock-like arms pulled him to his feet and pushed him out. "Move," a harsh voice said.

"What? Where am I going?" Andross asked, stumbling out into the dark hall.

"Does it matter? Would you like to stay?" said another voice from the darkness, this one smooth and sinister.

Another push moved Andross with it. His shoulder hurt from the yank. It had begun to heal to some degree, with the pain relieved, but it was aflame now.

Andross was barely able to see in front of him as they walked down the corridor. Dim purple flames lit small bits of the path, and once he caught a glance out of a window and saw the moon. He estimated the time around two at night.

Heading down some steps, the door at the bottom opened before them, and orange and purple light flooded in. Stepping out, he was in a guard room, with a red brazier and Oreon guards standing around it. Purple swirling eyes stared, as a shove forced him in.

For a moment, he caught the smell of the stew on the table and his mouth watered as he passed. Several men sat eating and watching as he shuffled by, and one opened a great oak door at the other end.

He stepped into the night, taking a deep breath, but it was cut short as he jerked forward from another shove. Across a stone bridge he marched, to his right he could see the Embracing Mountains, and the moon hanging above. To his left, his face was hit by a dry breeze, hot but welcome compared to the stagnant, filth-filled air of his jail.

A wall of purple clouds could be seen flashing with lightning. "Hurry up. Storm's coming and I want to be back at my post before it rains. If it rains."

"If?" Andross said.

"Doesn't rain much this close to the Thernat," one captor said. "Storms themselves are rare enough, but every so often one comes from the west and brings a torrent that floods the city for a day."

Andross stared at the looming clouds as he continued across the causeway. "Where am I going?"

"Questions again? Didn't my first answer help you?" one guard said.

Andross turned toward one in the dark, standing just a few inches taller than him. He had stopped dead in his tracks. It caught them off guard and both of them took two more steps before they halted.

"All we know is you've been summoned. Now come on, I don't want to have to clobber you and drag you the rest of the way."

Andross began to walk again, his shoulder hurting. He rubbed it and said, "Who summoned me?"

"There's only ever one group who can summon you in the dead of night," the other guard said, and then laughed. "That's the high council, and they didn't seem so happy either. This might be the end of you."

"Yeah," said the other, "usually by this point you've asked for a different punishment, or you've given up the ghost. You're a bit lucky since you were given leave to take a visitor. Apparently, they kept sneaking you bits of food and water."

Andross looked back at the guard who had said it, just as they reached another great oak door.

"Yes, we knew he was doing it. We let him think he was sneaking you contraband, but truthfully, we were told to let him. Word was to be a bit nicer to you than we usually are to our customers."

They entered the door and headed down another long flight of steps. It was dark most of the way and Andross had to watch his footing.

At the bottom, they pulled him through an opening in the left wall, and one took a torch burning purple flame from the wall and led the way. "Gets pretty dark in this walkway. Best stay close."

As they started, a strong breeze ripped down the steps and through the darkness, howling past them. Each breath Andross took through his mouth felt dry and left a bitter taste in his mouth, so he began breathing through his nose. It was not any better.

Near the end of the long corridor, they took a right and went through two locked doors. It was not until they passed through the last door that he saw another person.

A single Oreon robed in black and tied off in violet, stood alone at the edge of a black pool. The water sat mirror-like in a large expanse across the long room. Purple flames rose from braziers on its far side, and orange from the side they were walking on. Ornate windows of purple glass, depicting a violet eye, showed the moonlit night. The singular figure stood motionless, looking down into the dark water.

As Andross marched by, his feet echoing on the marble floor, he tried to look into the waters where the man stared. There was nothing there that he could see, until he saw the faint blue image of his face and it looked strange, ghostly even, almost unfamiliar. It

339

stirred an empty feeling in the pit of his stomach. Then he was shoved again and off to the other side of the room.

Down several more passages and through a large corridor, they came to two double doors, and the guards pushed in. A crowd of Oreon stood in a high-ceilinged hall, lit by torches, their faces shadowed. A thunder crash shook the large room.

Andross faced them, his guards on either side. A thin voice rose: "Sir Andross, prisoner of the Oreon, found at the slaying of two people, in our fair city of Telaporawein…"

Andross rolled his eyes. The city was a hive of hoodlums and mages who wanted to live on the edge of the king's reach.

"Your fate," the thin voice continued, "has come forth and been presented to us."

After three months in their prison, and in the middle of the night, Andross had not been expecting this. What had they decided would be his fate? They had given him no chance to speak or for any sort of justice. They were known for their harsh penalties if one could not pay, and he had not been given the chance to do so.

A torrent of rain began to pour down on the roof above; the roar of it filled the room as thunder boomed nearby.

Looking at the group in front of him, he was weak from lack of provisions and the awful conditions but did not want to show it. He stood as straight as he could, awaiting their verdict. They did not move, and stared back, faces hidden.

A soft touch came to his shoulder. Not from a guard, as they had not moved, but he had not heard anyone approach; with the storm descending outside.

"Andross, come," a soft but powerful voice said.

He turned, and the light of the torches lit the face of Queen Sehra, her blue eyes blazing. Her hood was down, and a circlet of gold shone in the fire. Her face was stern, but her eyes seemed compassionate. He wanted to fall to his knees in relief but knew he could not.

Just over her shoulder, he saw another familiar face, her brother decked in full armor, shining silver, his face stern as well but looking hard toward the Oreon now behind him.

"Remember, Andross, to pass along how well we treated you, when you reach your king," the thin voice said behind him.

Andross went to reply but was cut off by a small whisper only he could hear. "Come, Andross, pay them no mind." Queen Sehra turned and headed toward a pair of large doors. Standing at them, Andross noticed the only friendly face he had seen over the last three months, Arjen Longbary of the local garrison. With him, a Knight of the Thorn pushed the door open, into the torrent. It was so strong that a wave of mist and droplets came in from the night.

"Queen Sehra, you are welcome to stay here through the night to wait out the storm," the Oreon said.

She turned back toward them, pulling her hood up. "I am grateful for your offer, but I have a prior engagement I am committed to and must be on my way. Thank you ever so much." She nodded at the summoners and stepped right out into the rain.

Andross followed her, and neither her brother, Prince Owen, nor the knight moved until she was outside. Andross went to help her even with his limited strength, as the wind tore at them and the rain crashed but noticed that she was already being taken care of.

Several knights helped her into a beautiful carriage. Around the carriage was a retinue of what seemed like another two hundred knights on horseback in the courtyard of the Oreon's tower. He looked around for where he was supposed to go but was then summoned to follow her majesty into the carriage.

341

A bolt of lightning cracked across the sky; the boom caused several horses to rear up. He stepped into the carriage where Queen Sehra now sat with someone else. Following him in came Prince Owen, and the carriage door was closed. Within a moment it was moving with the hoofbeats of the knights outside and the thrashing of the rain all around.

Queen Sehra lowered her hood and looked at the person sitting next to Andross. "Check him please and give him something to eat. I don't doubt he is famished."

Andross did not recognize the face but did recognize the feeling. A wave of magic rushed over him and through his muscles like a cool breeze. Immediately he felt relief all over. The fatigue dissipated and the smaller pains subsided.

The mage was a female in a long red coat with gold lining. She had raven-black hair and a beautiful but stern face. "Arjen told the queen you sustained a wound to your shoulder?"

"Yes, I was stabbed there. When I woke in the prison, it had been seared closed with fire and wrapped in a bandage. It opened back up in the first couple days."

The woman closed her eyes and put her hand on Andross' shoulder. More intense magic rushed through his shoulder. She stayed there for a few moments; sweat began to build on her forehead. When she pulled back, she said, "I've done what I can. It wasn't well taken care of, but it is useable. It may be stiff on certain mornings and need loosening, and some days it may have a twinge of pain, but full range of motion can be acquired with work."

She handed Andross a bag. "Here, eat this."

Looking inside, it was filled with fruit. He took out an orange from Rovelle and tore the skin away. A sweet fragrance filled the carriage, and he became self-conscious.

"Your majesty, my apologies. I must smell and look like death," he said, looking up at Queen Sehra, who was smiling at him.

"Come now, Andross." She laughed. "No need to worry about that. I've smelled worse." She then reached up and knocked on the side of the carriage. Through the storm, a shout rang out and the carriage stopped. The door opened and a strong wind broke in.

"I'll be right outside, Your Majesty," the Crimson Caster said, and exited.

Andross tried to look at her more closely as she did, trying his hardest to see out into the night. There was a horse waiting for her and she mounted it, but the whole while he never could tell what she looked like.

"Don't strain yourself, Andross," Prince Owen said. "She has a way about her. She doesn't like to be noticed."

"Who is she?"

"She is a master in the Crimson Order. That's all you need know for now," Owen said with a smile from ear to ear.

"I have the faintest feeling that she is a beauty, and yet I can't tell."

"Maybe you're right and maybe you aren't," Owen said. The carriage door shut and began to move again.

"Come now, boys, there are more pressing matters," said Queen Sehra.

"My apologies again, My Queen. I didn't mean to offend."

"I know, Andross, it's a strange spell she weaves to hide herself. Some would say it's better not to be truly noticed than be invisible. Gives someone an air of mystery. Now, what is the news?"

"Pardon?"

"What happened here? Why did the Oreon imprison you?"

343

"I'm not exactly sure. They didn't tell me much of anything once I found myself in their custody. The first couple of days no one spoke to me at all. I got little to eat or drink. Finally, Arjen came to me and told me that they were holding me for two murders. I of course told them they weren't murders at all. It was self-defense. One of which I don't even think I committed."

"Who were they?" Owen said, looking at him and then to his sister.

At that, Andross froze, only his eyes darting back and forth between the pair. What could he say that would not give too much away?

Both seemed to understand his silence. "Andross, my brother knows I've sent you out to find what happened to my late husband."

"And my sister knows what connection you have with the Gray Foxes. She herself is a major contributor to our growth."

Andross was not surprised that Owen knew what she had asked him to do but was surprised that she was aware of the Gray Foxes.

"The first was a Goblin named Gnik. I tried to stop him, but I couldn't. He forced me to fight him. Some power had taken hold of him, just like his father, and another of the same curse, that I found—a dream that was eating away at their minds, haunting their days and nights. I wanted to help him. He had answers I needed…"

"Help him how? What answers?" Sehra said.

"I told him I could help him with his dream, find some way to stop it from reoccurring over and over, stop it from eating away at him. Also, to help him right the wrong that he had committed."

"I don't understand," Sehra said as the carriage took a small bump. "Where did this curse come from? What was its purpose?"

"I'm sorry, I'm starting in the wrong place, getting ahead of myself," Andross said, running his hand through his longer-than-normal hair. "The purpose of the curse was to drive these three men mad. To tear at their sanity until they could no longer function, no longer live with themselves. This is why Gnik wanted me to kill him."

Both siblings looked puzzled at him.

"I'm still not making sense. I'll start from the very beginning. Vernor, whom I found in an asylum near Faor, was the adopted father of the Goblin Gnik, and friend of the man named Abecore that I was forced to kill in Greenford. All three men were afflicted with some sort of curse, because all three men were the only surviving men from the assassination of King Nurame."

At that, the countenance on both the siblings' faces changed, and both leaned in closer.

"One thing I had plenty of in the prison was time. That time allowed me to do a lot of thinking and puzzle together some of the clues I've gathered. These three men were part of the group that attacked and killed the king on the road. They were hired to do this job."

"Who hired them?" Owen said.

"That's the question, isn't it? That's what I've been trying to piece together. Someone hired several hundred hoodlums, with the promise of great wealth, to attack the king. It had to have been great, because Gnik swore that his father and he were not killers. He almost made it sound like they didn't even know why they were there, but once there they could not escape it."

"You believe him?"

"I'm inclined to," Andross said, as the sky boomed outside. "He and his father were sick with what they had taken part in, and not only that, did not trust who had hired them. They convinced their third friend to escape with them before they were paid. That was why they were still alive. The rest were not rewarded but slain to keep the secret."

"All of them slain?"

"Gnik said they watched from afar as the others were attacked and killed, waiting for payment. Still, even escaping did not clear them from danger. Whoever hired them had powerful magic, some magic we have yet to see. They were cursed with the dream. They kept reliving the event. At first it started light, but more and more the nightmare kept haunting them, making it hard to sleep, eating away at their minds. For Abecore, who did not feel as guilty, I think it was just on the edge of making him mad. Vernor was completely mad, and Gnik was losing it right in front of me."

Sehra's face was filled with anger and hate, and even a small bit of compassion. "I want to say it serves them right, but it also sounds like they got caught up in something far beyond them."

"I think they did. I didn't want to hurt Gnik. There was remorse in him, and I knew he could help me find answers. He almost killed me, so I had to subdue him."

"So, he was one of the two, but who was the second the Oreon was holding you for?" Owen asked, reaching for a wine bottle and offering it to Andross.

Andross shook his head. "When I was speaking to Gnik, and he was trying to tell me answers, it was like the curse wouldn't let him. He sounded like he didn't have full control. Only too late, I realized someone else was there. Someone used magic, I think, to kill him from inside his own head. I chased them into the street and down an alley. They tried to curse me or conjure some magic on me. They attacked me with it. I remember swinging my sword… and then I awoke in the prison."

"Arjen was able to gather small bits of information for you," Sehra said. "He was the one who sent word to the king that you had been taken. He tried to force their hand to let you go. Even a message was sent from the king to do so. Did you notice my annoyance with them?"

"Yes, but I assumed it was because it was late."

"No, not only did they message back and tell the king that only through an envoy would they release you to the king's custody, but they wanted payment for your release."

"What payment?" Andross said, furrowing his brow.

"They asked for consideration in becoming their own noble house. They claim that they come from the same bloodline, so they are technically family."

"What did King Coram say?"

Sehra smiled. "He diplomatically said he would consider it. Little do they know that he's tripling the Rosenian garrison in the city, with the order to start taking more control of the streets."

Prince Owen continued, "So, my sister, leaving my new nephew at home took up the call and we rode down here to get you."

Andross looked at the Queen, realizing his mistake. "Your majesty, the baby, I forgot. I apologize."

"Don't fret, Andross. There are many other things happening here," she said.

"Are you well? Is the baby well?" Andross's mind was only just catching up to the idea that his being imprisoned for three months meant the queen was now a mother.

"He's well. He's in Garian's Den with my family, servants, and wet nurses. He has an army to take care of him and his name is Bastian."

Owen looked at Andross, "It was important we come down here and get you."

"I hate that you were forced to come all this way," Andross said with a clenched jaw. "No wonder you were annoyed with them."

"It wasn't just that," Owen continued, "we were there waiting for almost twelve hours before they brought you to us. We almost ordered the knights to storm the tower and find you. Tempers were high."

"Thank you both. I was never sure what was going to happen to me. Arjen was my only communication. He kept sneaking me bits of food and telling me that help was soon coming."

"You're welcome, but please, back to what you were saying. Who was this other figure?"

"I don't completely know, and on this I'm only piecing together clues. Some great magic users were involved in Nurame's assassination. The evidence is there. The witnesses describe them as hooded in black, with no specific markings. They had the power to kill all those villains, the power to curse these men to madness, and the power to hide themselves. I believe the man I killed was there for Gnik and was causing his madness to get worse. He attacked me as well, knowing I had knowledge. They're a part of this, but there are also clues in the mix that they're getting help from one of the major houses. Gnik said there seemed to be a lot of wealth involved in it."

"How can you be sure of this?"

"I'm not. The truth is still too far off. I need to search more, but if I'm right, then Rosenia is being attacked from the inside and from the shadows, and it won't be long before the cracks begin to show and its true enemies reveal themselves."

Both the siblings looked at each other, and then back to him. "Andross, there's a reason we took so long to come here to retrieve you. In the past three months, four different houses almost went to war. There's contention among them, and the king is having to do everything he can to stop war from breaking out. We suspect that someone is sowing discord across the land. If what you say is true, it matches what's happening. It hasn't gotten bad yet, but too many small things seem to be going wrong all at once. A gray cloud seems to float over the kingdom."

Chapter 24 - Epilogue

A shift in his weight caused a twig to break, echoing through the night. Tramping footsteps pounded through the darkness, matching his thumping heart as they came bounding toward him from a short distance away. He darted out of his hiding thicket, breaking branches that would wake the late hour. *Or is it early now*? How far was the sun?

There was no time for pondering, nor muted steps; he ran at full speed, though his legs wanted to give out. His horse had given out, and he had left it at the edge of the dense forest.

A voice cut through the air, sharp and commanding: "Teslin, stop running, you fool. Where are you going?"

He had ridden hard for several hours south through the tall grasses of the Sea of Winds. The hilly plain had seemed to rise for a while. Under the open sky, he had pushed his horse until he caught the glimpse of the forest he now trekked through.

He ran harder, trying to drop more of the weight he carried by tossing his sword. It thudded off a tree and he caught a glimpse as the impact caused the blade to slide from the sheath and reflected a small bit of the moon.

It flashed in his mind, and he wanted no more of it. Something else about the blade made him sick to his stomach as he pounded on. The idea that they were only meant to hurt and maim.

He put it out of his head and ran on. If Razelind caught him, she would bring him back and they would put him back to his duties. Sliding down a short slope, he caught himself on a tree root and charged on again.

With every step his feet caught dead leaves, kicking them up. He heard Razelind yell again in the night: "You're making this so much more difficult than it needs to be. Stop running!"

He could not be a part of that world any longer. He would not endure it. Every day they would make him do his steward duties for the Knights of the Thorn. He sat in their archive, with the brave stories of so many written around him, knowing he was not one of them. He did not die for his cousin and king.

They would make him practice his skills to keep them honed and in hopes that it would pull his strength back out of him. He knew it would not. It would be fruitless, and in its fruitlessness he would waste away.

He did not care so much for wasting away, except that maybe he would find his time better spent distracted.

He dodged around a tree and stopped to listen. The cracking of twigs and padding of steps on earth echoed in his ears and he tried to calm his breathing. His pursuer slowed just above a slope and moved a little away. He began to tiptoe the opposite way, sticking to the shadows. He needed to create more distance again.

Razelind was formidable, known for her athletic abilities and fighting prowess. Given enough time, she would chase him down and catch him. He was weak now; already his breathing was labored, and his feet hurt.

In his current mental state, he did not eat often, opting for bare minimum sustenance and water. He thought about more ale, but few would give him the satisfaction, always stopping him from drinking any. They would not let him drown his pain.

Brushing a lock of thin hair out of his face, he bent down and crawled through a small gap in a line of sharp-thorned thickets. On the other side lay a path that seemed much like a worn animal track. He followed it downhill.

Using small trees and limbs, he slid down another long slope, dirt and leaves thrown up around him, at one point losing his grip and rolling several times until he reached the bottom and sank into the wet, harsh, stinking mud at the edge of a stream.

He drank some handfuls of water, trying to catch his breath, his heart never relenting from its heavy pounding. The taste of dirt and something like sick, made him gag for a moment, before downing another handful and moving on.

He trudged for another hour, sometimes having to walk in the stream and along jutting cliff walls, his feet numb in the cold. He shivered, wet and covered in mud, the cliffside causing small breezes to whip around him.

At one point, Teslin wished he had not left all his gear on his horse, and a moment later wondered why it mattered. He deserved the torment the world now doled out on him. It should be worse. He was a disgrace and unworthy of kindness. If he escaped the forest and Razelind, he meant to live his life as a punishment for his own faults.

The small stream reached a larger one, where the water was a little less babbling, but of course it was deeper. The moon shone down on it, and he stood staring down into it until he saw his own face and reeled. Looking around to see if it was clear, he waded across. The water reached his waist, cold but still smelling pungent and unclean.

It became clear to him; this stream was no mountain runoff with fresh snow melted waters. It was the overflow of some stagnant swamp where rainwater gathered from all around and moved down through the sloping forest.

He did not have a good bearing for where he was, other than to know he was south of the grasslands. Then again, maybe he was still in the Helsveg region in some forest pocket that sprouted up along some higher hills.

Whatever the case, he needed to get farther away. Razelind would not be so easily lost. Nor would it take her long to realize she had traveled the wrong way; she would backtrack to find him.

Teslin did not fare well in the skill of tracking, but it was known that Razelind, having trained with Andross and other great Knights of the Hawk, was often called upon to hunt down enemies of the kingdom.

He began to move fast again, still following the stream, but on the forest side versus the short cliff side. He had lost too much time traversing that path to stay hidden.

Sometimes he lost sight of the stream due to the forest growth and then made a point to cut back toward it. Sometimes he tripped on fallen trunks, or roots. The night was still dark, even with bits of the moon. Soon the sun would rise, and he would be able to traverse faster as it would become brighter out. Though it no doubt would become hotter as well. Who knew what annoying bugs would come forth to feast on him in the light of the day?

Coming back toward the stream, he bent and scooped some of it up to run through his hair. He breathed in deep; his legs quivered and his back hurt. Even looking at his dirty hands as he tried to rinse them, they shook. Standing and stretching, he looked downstream. The almost disappearing moon lowered itself through a small gap in the forest and lit up the last section of the water. He followed the reflection, knowing the sun would rise soon.

That's when his eyes caught an image shadowed down the way. There stood Razelind splashing water on her face, and almost as if the world called out to her, screaming his name, she looked up at him before he could slink away into the shadows. Her voice pierced his heart.

"I've got you now, little rabbit. I'll skin you alive," her voice echoed, ringing in his ears.

Just like a rabbit, he was off, running into the dense trees again, his heart in his throat. He ran and ran, bounding over bushes and squeezing through thick brush, with her screams echoing behind him.

"I can't believe the trouble you've caused. When I'm done with you, you'll be begging for death. Oh, the satisfaction I'll have. Traipsing around in the forest after you. You don't think I want to go home? I should have left you here, but no, I promised I'd take care of you."

He kept running, but he knew she would catch him. If he could hear her screams, she was right behind him, too close for him to lose her with a trick, and she was being more wary now. He was not sure what to do, how to get away.

Somehow, he found his way back to a stream. It was larger now, probably not the same one. The first one he followed most likely ran into this one and cut back toward him. He might even have to cut across this one eventually. He could hear a rumbling nearby.

As he ran, the trees became denser, and pushing through some he came out atop a cliff. Hearing footsteps behind him, he moved to the side as Razelind barreled through and passed him.

She did not react fast enough. In her anger, she lost her sensibility, came through the brush and flew toward the edge of the cliff. She tried to stop, but her feet slipped out from under her, and she slid over.

Without thinking, Teslin's hand reached out and grabbed her arm, her weight dragging him to his knees. It happened in a blink, but there he was holding her arm as she dangled off the cliff. It was not a high precipice, and with the last bits of the moonlight he could see water down below her.

Only now when they had both stopped moving and her screaming quieted, could they hear the rumbling of a waterfall not far from them more clearly. The lake below shone in the moon, and Razelind's face was shadowed in the night.

"Don't let go," she said, her tone soft like silk.

Using both hands, he held her arm. His fatigued muscles strained to just keep her there. The tension in his neck from the weight caused his shoulders to feel like knives stabbing him.

"I'll try to find some footing, and then I can help get myself back up," she said. One of her feet found a rock.

Teslin felt a small bit of relief as she removed some of the strain on him. He breathed deep, but then he was yanked down again as her foot slipped. His fingers almost lost her, and he almost lost himself. His eyes were closed as he tried to steady himself.

"That's it. Good job. I'll try again when you're ready."

He opened his eyes to nod, but he saw a glint at her side. The moon reflected on something. He looked closer and saw the blade in her other hand, and it flashed in his mind, and he felt sick again.

Why did she have a blade out? He looked back at her.

"No, don't focus on that. There, look, I dropped it," she said, as it fell to the lake below. "Teslin, stop, don't make that face."

"You said you were going to skin me. You said you'd kill me."

"That's not what I meant, and you know it. Calm down please, you know that's not what I meant. Don't do anything rash."

355

Teslin's eyes flared; his face was flush. "I knew someone would come for me. Someone would want to kill me for my disgrace. Better to run off in the night and live away from people. Too bad, Raze."

"No, Teslin, please don't. Please, you must calm down." Her voice was still calm, if not a higher pitch. "Don't, Teslin, please."

"I'll never be rid of this or people like you," he said, then his fingers loosened.

Acknowledgements

I want to thank the LORD. He gave me a few talents. I can recognize faces really well, and I have a love of storytelling, that doesn't always make sense. Without Him, I have and am nothing.

Second, to my parents, you tried to get me to read for so long, and I always fought it. My bad! Don't worry, I like it now.

To my proofreaders, the first people who read my book. It's not easy doing that and calling to the surface what doesn't work. That kind of bravery is hard to come by.

To my third-grade teacher, who gave me my first real assignment to write a story, I blame you and thank you.

To my eleventh-grade English teacher, for giving me the best compliment I ever received. Saying, "You were allowed to write whatever you want in the weekly journal, I'll let it go this time, but please stop copying from books."

To everyone else who has played a role in the cultivation of my life, for good or bad. There is a part of you that has become a part of me. Thank you for that, I pray when you look at the role you played, you are proud of what you've contributed.

Remember This

God loves you.

John 3:16
For God so loved the world, that he gave his only begotten Son, that whosoever believeth in him should not perish, but have everlasting life.

Give all glory to God

1 Corinthians 10:31
Whether therefore ye eat, or drink, or whatsoever ye do, do all to the glory of God.

Now Released!
in the World of Sancta

"Dark Anvil Rising" book 2 of the Gray Horizon series.

Epic Fantasy - In "Dark Anvil Rising", follow our heroes, as they face a new threat on the horizon. Prepare to journey beyond the borders of "In Between Storms". What do their futures hold, in this epic adventure?

Join the newsletter, and one person will win a signed copy of "Dark Anvil Rising".

www.michaeldarin.com

About the Author

Michael Darin is a christian, a father, and a lover of story. All have played a significant part in his life.

As an author and world-builder, his desire is to create a fantasy world, you can disappear into, only to come back to the real world and impress your friends with, all the interesting things you discovered from your adventures. LOL!

He graduated from Florida State University, and greatly appreciates his time there, but the greatest lessons he found are from living.

Glossary

Aija (AY-ja) - female POV character (Human)

Ajencain (a-JEN-kayn) - city ruled by Dareian king in Rovelle Islands

Andross (AN- dross) - male POV character (Human)

Coram (KOR-ehm) - new king of Rosenia (Human)

Darei (DAH-rye) - one of the many races of Sancta

Dareian (DAH-rye-an) - the people of the Darei

Diversi (DEE-ver-sigh) - one of the original races of Sancta

Dreyandol (DRAY-an-dol) - male POV character (Dareian)

Drogan (DROH-gan) - one of the many races of Sancta

Faor (FAY-or) - city in the southeast of Rosenia

Fissionari (FISH-uh-NAH-ree) - one of the many races of Sancta

Gnik (geh-NIK) - male POV character (Goblin)

Hima (HIGH-muh) - region to the north of Rosenia

Kageria (KAY-JEE-ree-uh) - capital of Paraduo

Kiamel Po (KAI-uh-mel PO) - region to the northeast of Rosenia

Linga (LING-guh) - one of the original races of Sancta

Malkienon (MAL-kee-nen) - one of the original races of Sancta

Nowann (noh-WAN) - capital city of Rosenia

Nurame (NOO-raym) - past king of Rosenia (Human)

Nyoko (NYOH-koh) - city on the opposite side of the Crescent Sea

Paraduo (PAIR-eh-DOO-oh) - kingdom to the east of Rosenia

Roemenanora (ROH-meh-nuh-NOR-uh) - the Rising Mountains that mark the northern border of Rosenia

Rosenia (roh-ZEH-nee-uh) - the featured kingdom in this story

Rotsinora (ROT-sih-NOR-uh) - The Roost Mountains in the Rovelle Islands

Rovelle (roh-VELL) - islands in the middle of the Crescent Sea, also an alliance of peoples

Sancta (SANK-tuh) - the world this all takes place in

Septimar (Sep-tih-mar) - capital of the Rovelle Alliance

Thernat (THAIR-nat) - a desert to the south of Rosenia